Praise for *Lady Anne's Dangerous Man*

"A seductive pleasure—indulge yourself! Stories like this don't come along often. Jeane Westin weaves sharply observed historical detail into the tale of a seductive battle between a rascal and a bluntly spoken young lady: It's a true pleasure to read!"
—*New York Times* bestselling author Eloisa James

"Westin's debut is a sparkling gem complete with wild adventures; actual historical personages, events, and colorful tidbits; and authentic dialogue. The era, the people, and the story are brilliantly brought to life by a shining new star on the romance horizon." —*Romantic Times BOOKclub* (Top Pick)

"Jeane Westin brings Restoration England to life in a sweeping tale of passion and adventure."
—Lauren Royal, author of *Lost in Temptation*

"A spirited lady, a dashing highwayman, and a rich cast of characters make for a delightful swashbuckling romance."
—*New York Times* bestselling author Jo Beverley

"An old-fashioned swashbuckling romance with smart, sexy overtones." —Suzanne Enoch, author of *An Invitation to Sin*

Other titles in Jeane Westin's
Restoration Series
from Signet Eclipse

Lady Anne's Dangerous Man

Lady Katherne's Wild Ride

Jeane Westin

A SIGNET ECLIPSE BOOK

SIGNET ECLIPSE
Published by New American Library, a division of
Penguin Group (USA) Inc., 375 Hudson Street,
New York, New York 10014, USA
Penguin Group (Canada), 90 Eglinton Avenue East, Suite 700, Toronto,
Ontario M4P 2Y3, Canada (a division of Pearson Penguin Canada Inc.)
Penguin Books Ltd., 80 Strand, London WC2R 0RL, England
Penguin Ireland, 25 St. Stephen's Green, Dublin 2,
Ireland (a division of Penguin Books Ltd.)
Penguin Group (Australia), 250 Camberwell Road, Camberwell, Victoria 3124,
Australia (a division of Pearson Australia Group Pty. Ltd.)
Penguin Books India Pvt. Ltd., 11 Community Centre, Panchsheel Park,
New Delhi - 110 017, India
Penguin Group (NZ), cnr Airborne and Rosedale Roads, Albany,
Auckland 1310, New Zealand (a division of Pearson New Zealand Ltd.)
Penguin Books (South Africa) (Pty.) Ltd., 24 Sturdee Avenue,
Rosebank, Johannesburg 2196, South Africa

Penguin Books Ltd., Registered Offices:
80 Strand, London WC2R 0RL, England

First published by Signet Eclipse, an imprint of New American Library,
a division of Penguin Group (USA) Inc.

First Printing, August 2006
10 9 8 7 6 5 4 3 2 1

Printed in the United States of America

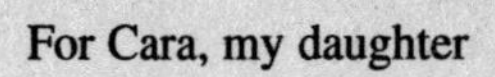

For Cara, my daughter

Chapter One

Escape from Bournely Hall

Katherne Lindsay woke with a start. It wasn't the first misty light of an Essex summer morning coming through her thick top-floor windowpanes that forced her eyes wide open, but the sound of her door latch slowly lifting and scraping, iron against iron. She called out, "Martha, is that you?"

The kitchen maid who shared the small room, her cousin Lady Joan's way of reminding Katherne of her lowly place in the household of Sir William Pursevant, often came late to her corner pallet after a dinner party.

"Martha?" she called again louder, then heard someone breathing heavily, and sat up, tightening her hold on the rough linen sheeting that covered her. Had one of Sir William's amorous guests, perhaps the one in the uncombed French periwig who was unable to keep his hands in their rightful place, come looking for agreeable company? She would soon send him on his way with a hot rebuke he would remember long after his cod cooled.

A shadow loomed over her bed, and the gamy odor of

venison pie, stale wine and a rosewater-and-nutmeg scent filled her nostrils. A rasping voice confirmed a worse fear. One, she realized, she'd half expected ere now. "Hush, cousin, or you will wake the house."

Gathering her wits, she asked, "Sir William, has my cousin Joan's time come?"

He was moving closer, sending his scent before him. "No, her belly still holds the babe. You know full well why I am come. Do not play the innocent with me, Mistress Lindsay."

"I am no player at innocence, Sir William, as well you know, but an innocent in truth. It is you who are in the wrong here. You must leave," she said. She willed her voice not to shake, but could not keep out all anger at this monstrous deceit and added, "At once!"

He laughed softly, wafting more stale wine her way. "I'm lord here, my sweet Kit, and best you not forget again. Have I not protected your honor, fed and clothed you for these many years and turned away the poor squires seeking your hand and dowry?"

Did he think to jolly her? "Not without recompense from my father's estates," she said sharply, now grown to full anger at William's ill intent. He thought to make her a whore, the low cocksman.

"Your father's estates no more. Rosevere is mine now. The Stuart king has confirmed me in it." He bent closer. "And you, my sweet, are most unkind when I would demand so small a favor well within your power to grant." His fingers stroked her arm, which she snatched from him. "Come," he said sharply, "you need but show me due affection. Any village harlot will give me that for twopence."

"My honor is not for sale to any man at any price, sir. I

am Lady Katherne Lindsay, daughter of Sir Robert, a knight dead in the king's service." She inched away, wishing for something to hit him with, and seeing only a small chapbook of Waller's poems, not heavy enough to teach him the least manners, at hand on her clothes chest.

Katherne had received but escaped William's unwelcome attentions during every one of her cousin Joan's frequent pregnancies, but of late he had become more persistent, trapping her in halls, brushing against her when there was no need. Now she could feel the close heat from his overfed body, and pulled the rough linen sheet tighter to her chest. She must find some reason in the man. "Your lady wife would not understand your night wanderings, William," she said, forcing her hand not to slap the grin from his face. Though she could not see it clear, she knew it was there. "Leave before Martha comes to her bed."

He laughed again, an edge of malice in it, as well as a gamesman's delight. "Your kitchen maid is unfortunately detained, Kit. I had cook put her to breadmaking for the morrow's hunt, and knowing the wench, she is probably devouring the last crumbs of spice cake."

It was like him to plan so carefully to gain advantage. He had been a staunch Parliamentarian during the Lord Protector Cromwell's time, only to go over to King Charles II when he saw the protector's son had not the command of his father. Her own father, Sir Robert Lindsay, ever loyal to his sovereign, had lost all during the late troubles—sons, estate and finally his own life—leaving Katherne to fall to such low degree of dowerless waiting woman to her cousin Lady Joan Pursevant, not quite servant but not quite equal.

Not quite anything at all, she thought, struggling to remain upright against the hands pushing her to her pillow.

"Stop!" she said sharply, and this time could not control the tremor in the word or in her body. "Stop, or I *will* call out and accuse you for a rat bastard blackguard before all."

He laughed again right heartily. "Tut, my well-born lady. Don't you know such words do but strengthen my cod?"

She was chilled by his humor. "You deserve foul words of a plenty, sir."

He pretended a lover's lingering sigh. "Cry out if you will. Most of my guests are so deep in their cups, they would ne'er hear a cannon fire under their beds. And if they heard, who would believe you, Kit, if I said you did send for me as a trick? Surely not your cousin Joan, my lady wife, who already thinks you will replace her if she dies in childbirth, as indeed you might if you please me much, although I have your dowry these many years, and once I have your maidenhead . . ." He lowered himself onto Katherne and licked her ear, leaving his spittle behind in his haste to fumble at her breast. He wrapped the fingers of his other hand through her hair as it spread upon the pillow. "Quite lovely," he breathed the words, "though yellow hair is so unfashionable in these days of a Portuguese queen. Yet you did use it to flaunt yourself and torture me, singing and playacting in the great hall until I was sore with want."

"Never! You are a monster." Katherne gasped from the weight of him.

His voice had lost the last of its fake humor. "Monster or no, I have a monstrous need. Come, you owe me this sport and I will have it!"

Her panic choked her. She could not draw breath from bearing his weight. She groaned and wrenched one hand free to rake his cheek with her nails, feeling skin come away. She could see his face clearly now that the light had brightened through the casement, and saw his bright red blood start and drop onto her shift.

A fist slammed into her head.

"Cunt, you will pay well for that. Submit or no, I will take you as it please me. You owe me a debt for the great care I have given you, and my debtors always pay."

His breathing was harsh and fast, and she wondered that he did not faint away, though her head was ringing so she had scarce wits to wonder.

"After I have finished with you, I will marry you to the meanest cottager on my estates. Hah, no, on your father's former estate. Someone who dunged your garden beds, someone who collected your night soil. You are mere female chattel, and I can do as I like. Time you knew that, my fine lady."

She struggled to twist herself from his hated hands, to speak, to bring sane thought to this awful discourse. "And you are drunk, William. If you leave now—"

But she was not able to offer him her desperate bargain of silence, because his hand hard on her mouth shut off her words. She pushed against his great weight, more than twice hers, arching and pulling at his hand, which was cutting off her breath.

"I knew you wanted a hard prick," he said, to her astonishment, misreading her struggle. "If you give me what I want, I could surprise you with a secret that you would very like to hear."

For answer, she bit down as hard as she could on his palm and he jerked back, cursing her, leaping from the bed and dragging her roughly to her feet.

"I am your master, and it pleases me to make you a whore!"

"Stop!" She gasped out the word again, but he was beyond hearing, his blood enraged.

He ripped at her shift, and its knotted ribbons showered the floor until she stood naked, his one hand around her throat, his other forcing her hand to stroke his fully aroused cod. His breath came in great grunts now, and she knew that he no longer had even his usual modest control. She used the last of her strength to kick out, though her bare foot caused him no seeming pain and hurt her toes mightily.

His florid, enraged face close to hers, his teeth bared like an attacking hound, he lifted her and tossed her across the room and into the wall. She fell in a heap of limbs that no longer worked. For a moment, she was stunned, beyond speech, beyond helping herself, and in that moment he was on her, yanking her legs apart and mounting her, his breeches around his ankles.

"How do you like this cock, you ungrateful slattern?" His voice rasped against her ear as he began his thrust. She saw him above her as through waves of swift-flowing water, a face still but blurred. And then his body slipped slowly away, falling heavily to one side.

"Are ye hurt, Lady Katherne?"

It was Martha's voice, and Martha's hands with the smell of yeasty bread on them lifting her shoulders.

"What happened?" she asked, her head clearing though all else ached.

"I murthered him, my lady, and I will hang for it and worse. It be petty treason against the order of things to kill a master."

Katherne twisted to look at William crumpled to the floor, silent, his chest not rising or falling and his face a deathly white. His proud prick, now a shriveled thing, lay against his leg. "He's dead?" she asked, almost unable to comprehend such a calamity, but feeling no sorrow.

Martha was tossing her best wool gown, a clean shift, and her small clothes into a basket with a rope handle. "I don't rue it, my lady. He has taken more than one kitchen maid's bridehead."

Her mind buzzing with too many questions, Katherne asked, "Yours?"

"When I be but a girl of twelve years, my lady," she said, her pocky, round face set in grim lines. "I bled for a day and cried for a fortnight. I was that innocent girl again as I saw him ravishing ye, and I grabbed the iron candlestick by the door and hit him hard. Now I must away before the hue and cry, or I will pay the awful price."

Katherne knew the price was hanging and the drawing out of Martha's entrails while she was yet alive, then cutting her body into four pieces to hang on the gate of Sir William Pursevant's manor of Bournely as a lesson to all who would defy a master's rule.

"Wait, Martha," she said, struggling dizzily to her feet, her mind beginning to clear and race ahead. "How will I explain this? My cousin, Lady Joan, will blame me, perhaps even accuse me. She has never liked the family duty that brought me here." Katherne shivered at the thought of Joan's revenge and at the irony of escaping the husband to be condemned by the wife. Still, the words that followed came reluctantly. "I fear I must leave with you."

"It be not possible, my lady," Martha said, alarm on her face. "The high road be not for a well-born lady such as ye. It be hard and dangerous, full of terrors and worse."

"Worse than rape? Worse than the loss of family and home and all that belongs to me? Then, good Martha, I have no place in all the world, because Bournely cannot be my home, and I do not rue it." Her own words surprised her, but as she spoke them, her voice grew stronger with the surety of her new thinking.

Martha stared at her, then shrugged, picking up her basket. "Quickly, then, gather what ye can carry. It be soon the early full light of summer, and the house astir."

Katherne slipped into an everyday green wool dress with a buttoned stomacher and her lace cap, and covered all with a matching cape and hood. She left a good red satin gown on its peg, wrapped another wool gown and shift, the miniature of her father and the bag of gold guineas her father had left with her when he went to join the king's army—everything she had in the world—in a large shawl, and without a final glance at the room she'd lived in for seven years since a girl of fourteen, she was ready.

Martha stepped to Sir William's body and without hesitation kicked his white upturned arse. "If they hang me, I be remembering this on the gibbet." She stepped to the casement and opened it.

"Martha, there is no safe way over the roof," Katherne said, assuming her right of command, and so they crept down the gloomy stairs, hiding in a dark niche to avoid a maid carrying coals for the fires laid the night before against the morning chill. Katherne could not help but think that Sir William was already in a far warmer place, then tried to regret the blasphemy, but managed less remorse than she knew she should.

They stopped twice more for grooms going to the stables to ready horses for the planned hunt that Katherne realized now would have quite a different quarry than the wild boar Sir William had released in his parkland. The Sheriff of

Essex County and the eager young gentlemen invited for boar would ride harder to run down two women who had murdered their host and spoiled their amusements.

For one second, Katherne stopped in the soaring galleried Hall at the dais where she had enacted plays and masques with the children. She touched the polished wood of the virginal on which she played and sang at every opportunity. The latest ballet music from the court in France lay unopened on the chair. Would she ever play it? Her hand reached to take the pages and thrust them into her bundle. It was theft surely, but how many times could they hang her?

"Hurry, my lady!" Martha whispered. "We can go through the kitchens, since cook be always a friend to me and there be spice cake uneaten."

Katherne shook her head. "We dare not chance it. The spit boy will be sleeping there, too, and cook will not understand why I am with you. Questions will waste much precious time. Let us out through the banquet hall, since it is closest to the woods. Quickly now, before Sir William is missed."

The pale sun was just showing over the horizon, while thick wisps of fog swirled across the parkland as they ran. Katherne's satin shoes were soon sodden with dew, making them slippery and heavy. She ached in so many bruised parts that she limped the last steps, throwing quick glances behind her to see if they were espied.

Martha, despite her ample kitchen maid's flesh, reached the woods first, plunged inside, and turned as Katherne caught up, her face angry. "My lady, ye must keep my pace. I will not hang for your dainty feet."

Katherne was shaken. No servant had ever spoken to her thus. "You forget yourself, Martha."

"Nay, my lady, it be ye who forget," Martha said, plunging deeper into the woods, with Katherne running to stay abreast. "We be both fugitives here. Your slender neck will break as sure as mine. And now ye will be my lady to me no more. Whether my life be minutes or years, I have no master now." It was clear by her face that her own gasped-out words had shocked her. "No master," she repeated, running her tongue over and around the words as if they were the sweetest marzipan.

She ceased the flow of words in what Katherne thought must be the longest speech of her life. "Are you a Puritan that you wish to be masterless?"

Martha didn't slow her pace. "I'm no dissenter . . . Mistress Katherne . . ." she said, finding an address that pleased her, "but I do like the idea that a freeborn maid needs no master, although when we get to London the parish beadles may think the other way."

"Last summer there was terrible plague in London, with a quarter of the populace dying, and it may be so this summer."

"There be the hangman here certain," Martha said, putting a hand to her throat. "And I do hear the rope takes *all* to their grave."

Katherne slowed to a fast walk to catch her breath, intrigued by this new person in the rough wool and wooden shoes of a servant who made good sense when need be. "Agreed. Now we must fly to the south, although I doubt me we can go as far as London town."

They were half running again, several furlongs from Bournely and already winded, when they heard horses crashing through the woods behind them. Katherne made a sudden decision. Danger had concentrated her mind wonderfully. "We must go to ground like the fox, Martha, and travel at night until we are beyond the sheriff's reach." She made for a deer copse, carefully obliterating their footprints by sweeping her cloak to and fro as she'd seen her father's gamekeeper do to scatter scent. They burrowed deep inside, scratching their arms and rending their dresses. "My brothers and I used to hide like this from our Latin teacher." Her whisper caught on a sob at the memory of the carefree times of her childhood, and the all too real possibility that the rest of her life could be soon over.

Martha took hold of her hand awkwardly as they settled to the ground, both hardly breathing as the thunderous noise of men and horses crashing through the woods and brush broke into the clearing.

Chapter Two

Two Masterless Women

Katherne and Martha sank deeper into the nest of wet, moldy leaves that a doe had built for her newborn fawn, Katherne stifling a sneeze with a shaking hand as the sounds of horses and men rung around them.

"Two women can't have come this far," a man shouted.

A second loud voice agreed, although a sword probed into the copse, scarce missing Katherne's leg. "Weak women can't travel fast afoot and in discomfort. Let's away east to Witham. I'll wager ten shillings we'll find them snug in an inn by the fire, with lardy cake and mulled sack. What say you?"

Someone grumbled, "Aye, cake and ale would sit as well on my stomach."

With much thrashing about, the men wheeled and rode away toward the east.

Exhausted, Martha curled into the leaves and lay with eyes wide. Katherne hugged her knees against her chest, still sore from Sir William's heavy body, and stifled angry sobs.

"No master." Martha's words tumbled through her mind,

and she found the idea more intriguing than she could have imagined just hours earlier. She tried to pray, but could not. God had abandoned her and allowed his first creation, man, to bring her to this ruin. Cromwell had taken her father's estates and hanged him after the Battle of Winchester for his loyalty to the beheaded king. That king's son, Charles II, once restored to his realm, had awarded her dower rights to Sir William for changing his coat. And now, William, her male next of kin charged by the laws of man and God to care for and protect her, had forced foul rape upon her. All had violated her woman's rights . . . what few a woman possessed in this world made for men, who made law to please themselves.

God's nails! She would have no more of their protection. Whatever her fate, she would make her own. The thought thrilled her blood, and she could sense the strength it bestowed on her. But this decision, though calming her mind, left one question remaining.

"Am I no longer virgin?" she asked Martha, her voice trembling.

"I don't know, mistress. Don't you remember?"

"Nay, nothing till you—" She stopped, unable to speak the act that had sent them fleeing for their lives.

Eventually, huddled for warmth under Katherne's cloak, they slept until hunger woke them as the sun slanted low, casting shafts of light through the tree branches.

Inch by inch Katherne crept from the copse, listening hard for the sounds of pursuers. Bees were busy at a hive nearby, and birds were singing their final birdsongs of the day, but no human sounds intruded. She called softly back to Martha, "Hurry, for we must make for the southwest road before it is too dark to find our way. By full night, we will pass near my home at Rosevere and find food if I have friends remaining."

Martha bent to pick up some old chestnuts, burst open with age and showing mold, stuffing them in the pocket hanging under her skirt. "I ate these as a young one when I could keep them from the pigs. They be better pan roasted on the hearth fire, but . . ." She held one out to Katherne, who shook her head, and with a shrug, Martha popped it into her mouth, muttering, "I be giving anything for some barley beer."

Katherne walked quickly through the woods, feeling her legs grow stronger with every step, until at dusk she came to a familiar road. A mile or more to the south she saw the gray stone towers of Rosevere silhouetted against the sky. "We must not talk," she warned Martha, "but ever listen for riders."

They encountered no one, all good husbandmen having left the fields for their homes, with their long scythes over their shoulders after early July haying, and all honest travelers now buying a place in an inn bed, hopefully with few bedmates and fewer lice. A half-moon gave them enough light to trudge the deeply rutted road.

With Rosevere before them, Katherne knocked at the door of the cottager who guarded the gate in front of the long avenue of spreading yews, leading to the manor house.

"If ye be the devil," said a shaky voice, "I have me fowling piece to hand."

Katherine smiled reassurance at Martha. "No devil knocks, good Thomas, but an old friend who more than once gave you cider from the first pressing."

The door opened and a wrinkled man with thin white hair and a sunken, toothless mouth lisped, "My lady, I would know the woman from sweet memory of the child. It be ye for certain, or be I dreaming." He bowed her in.

"No dream, Thomas, and this is Martha, my . . . friend."

"She be welcome, too, my lady," he said.

"We be hungry," Martha announced, sniffing the air.

A fire burned in the fireplace and a bubbling pot hung on the hook, filling the cottage with the smell of rabbit stew and wild onion, strongly reminding Katherne that she'd had nothing to eat for all the day.

Thomas bowed them to backless stools around a plank table, a bed and thick mattress sack and chest being the only other furnishings in the single room. He got out two wooden bowls and ladled them full, reaching to the dried thyme hanging from his ceiling and adding a pinch. Thick slices of dark bread and a tankard of strong ale finished the meal.

Katherne saw a hundred questions in his eyes, but he squatted on his haunches before her and asked nothing until they had finished the first bowl and started on the second.

"What troubles have ye, my lady? I would give ye a place to rest and hide for yer sake and for love of the old master, your father, God rest his soul. I cannot take ye to the manor, for I be forbidden that house by Sir William on pain of death."

"Why, good Thomas?"

"The new master does not abide questions, but cottagers be shot at who wander close."

Katherne stood. "We must be gone from this place, Thomas. I can only tell you that I did no wrong but was sorely wronged against, as much as any woman can be. Now we must away quickly this night before the sheriff comes this way. I have no wish to put you at risk for your head."

"The sheriff's men were here at an early hour, Mistress

Kit. I opened the gate and they be searching the manor grounds, trampling Sir Robert's knot garden with much merriment." He took an old apple sack and began to fill it with fruit and the remaining bread. "This be all I have, but ye be welcome to it." He reached atop his mantel and brought down a small stoppered vial of green glass. "This be an herbal for those bruises, my lady."

Katherne felt tears starting their slide down her cheeks. "Remember, you have not seen us, Thomas."

He opened the door, and she threw her arms around him, placing a kiss on his weathered cheek, as she had from a small child though she was now a full head taller than he. "I won't forget your kindness."

"Wait," he said, quickly going back into the cottage and opening a chest at the foot of his bed. "This be my wife's, God rest her soul," he said, holding out a yellowed cloth day cap. "That lace cap ye wear will not pass for a servant's."

He called one last time as they walked beyond the gate. "God bless ye, my lady, and take ye in his care. There be gypsies about and worse, strolling players."

She was too choked with gratitude to say or do more, in fear of breaking her heart, and so without a backward look, Katherne and Martha started south, following the road in the half-moon light. She had not been this near to Rosevere for many years, but she could not bring herself to stand and study its long shadows. There was too much pain behind its ancient battlements. Memories of the day news had come that both her older brothers had died at the battle of Worcester, their bodies thrown into a common grave, and horror upon horror, the word that her father had been given up to Cromwell and hanged. Finally came the day she lost even her home, when Sir William's allegiance to Cromwell had earned him Rosevere and Katherne's wardship and dowry.

They walked on quietly for hours in the pale moonlight and enough sparkling stars to light a thousand candelabra, drenched by a sudden shower, meeting no one except for a straying cow, which Martha knelt beside and milked, drinking from the tit.

When Katherne was offered a tit, she laughed softly. "We are running for our very lives, but you find food everywhere."

Martha wiped her mouth on the back of her sleeve. "We be doing for ourselves and best be eating when we can. That be part of this freedom from masters, Mistress Kit, as ye be now called by me."

Katherne smiled. "I was so named by my brothers, being not so tall in those days. Come, we must travel more miles before daybreak if we would keep from the sheriff's men."

They walked on, Martha's sturdy legs never seeming to tire, although Katherne's slippers were now past repairing, the dainty soles flopping with every step, her feet bruised and beginning to bleed.

"We must get ye new shoes," Martha announced, "or I be riding you on my back before we get to Chelmsford."

Katherne sat down by the side of the road and looked at the hopeless ruin of satin slippers. "I will be no burden to you, but will go in my bare feet, if I must," she announced, "or crawl on all fours like a babe."

Incredulous, Martha put her hands on her ample hips. "When hens make holy water!" But there was a new admiration in her voice.

Kit laughed and Martha joined in until Kit shushed, and they walked on, Kit without shoes, near dancing over the pebbles and hard ruts that tortured her narrow, tender-skinned feet. They passed some sorry cottages with sagging thatch, tossing some of their precious bread to quiet a dog tied to one.

"Wait here," Martha said, turning back toward the cottages after going a few paces beyond.

"No. We stay together," Kit said to Martha's back disappearing behind one of the cots. Against the shed used for a closet of ease in the back . . . the odor proclaimed it . . . hung several fishing poles.

"I hoped so," Martha whispered, picking up a pole.

"We cannot stop to fish," Kit said with exasperation.

Martha stifled amusement, although her ample bosom shook with it. "I be angling for something better, although a nice, tender sturgeon would not go amiss." And she crept toward the cottage before Kit could say more, although she refused to stay behind.

They advanced toward an open window, shutters ajar, stepping carefully around the barnyard clutter of abandoned tools and some nesting boxes empty of ducks since the spring. The only noise she heard was the swoop and rustle of bats in the thatch overhead. Martha looked inside, then stuck the pole and hook in and with great care inched her catch out the window and into Kit's hands.

A monstrous loud snore that seemed to rattle on forever shattered the night's peace and caused Kit to stifle a hapless laugh.

Waiting quietly for some time, Martha then stuck the pole in again and slowly drew out a second item, a worn leathern shoe to match the first. Kit could hear the uninterrupted snores from inside, but afraid to breathe herself, stayed Martha's hand when she raised the pole to fish again.

"Sausages!" Martha mouthed.

Kit shook her head and drew a gold guinea from her handkercher, leaving it on the window's sill in extravagant payment. The cottager would surely think the fairies had come in the night. She guided the unwilling Martha, still mourning sausages, toward the privy house, replacing the fishing pole.

Back on the road, a light showing in a cot sent them scrambling some distance to a log where Kit could put on her new shoes, much too large for her. They were hard pressed against her sore feet.

"Here," said Martha, reaching into her basket, "take these thick wool hosen. Those silk ones be for fine ladies and their dancing slippers, not for the likes of us."

"Thank you, Martha," Kit said, realizing that she had learned much from a kitchen maid, a woman she had never thought to converse with at any length. "Where did you learn to—"

"Be an angler? From my brother Jacob, who was a right good thief until they caught and branded him on his thumb and forehead, then transported him to the Jamaica plantations. That be when my indenture was sold to Sir William," she said, and walked on, carrying what Kit thought must be a sad story of a starving family forced to sell their daughter's youth to service.

"Sorry about the sausages," Kit said quietly to her back, vowing never again to tease Martha about her appetite, since the only hunger she had ever known had been nothing to compare.

Before first light, they began looking for a barn or shed to hide in, and found an abandoned cottage, its thatch having collapsed onto its dirt floor, leaving a skeleton of rafters exposed to the sky. A hollowed-out log trough outside the byre at the back of the cot was filled with fresh rainwater, where they drank their fill, then washed their hot feet to cool them. Kit bent over the clear water and saw a face she hardly recognized as her own, dirty, bruised, yellow hair escaped from her cap to swirl wildly about her face, a knot above her dark-circled blue eyes, and her lower lip split and still swollen.

She found the herbal balm Thomas had given her and spread it on her face and feet. She must heal before they appeared in a town, or the constable would mark her as a vagrant or thief, both of which she realized she now was or soon would be.

They ate the last of the bread and each an apple. Kit spread her torn and dirty cloak upon the hard-packed ground where once a family had lived and worked their small holding, wondering what had happened to them. So many had been carried off by plague or driven off by lords enclosing land for sheep runs. But exhaustion soon conquered curiosity, and Katherne lay down next to Martha to sleep under the ridge pole where enough thatch still clung to give them shade.

The sun was high overhead when she opened her eyes, her back stiff from the hard ground, no softer on this second day than on the first. She tried to sleep again, but her mind went racing down the road ahead of her. What would happen to her if she escaped the perils of travel and finally came to London town? There were only two ways for an unwed woman to make her way in that world: as servant or as prostitute. Perhaps with her gold pieces it might be possible to set up a dame's school, though she would have to be careful not to attract the attention of parish constables or curious competitors. She took a long, trembling breath and let it go slowly. This solution gave her little sense that she would be her own master.

She stood up and stretched her aching muscles, walking out to the ancient wooden trough. The sun sparkled upon the clear rainwater, and she felt a great desire to bathe her bruised and violated body. . . . To wash away the last memory of William's perfidy, the man scent of him she had carried in her nostrils these many hours.

Overwhelmed by the need to be clean and fully rid of him, she stripped off her bodice, gown and shift, then stepped into water warmed by the sun, slowly sinking into its shallow depths with a groan of pleasure though the wood scraped her skin. She wished for some good lye soap, but settled for scrubbing herself and her hair between her hands until it was as clean as it could be. It was the first time in her life that she had bathed without a bathing gown, and thought never to wear one again.

Martha called softly from the cottage floor, risen on her elbow, "Ye will catch yer death, Mistress Kit. It be only July and not a bathing month."

"Then I will die with a clean skin, if not a conscience," Kit said, laughing, and dipped her head into the water, coming up with her dripping hair blinding her. Tossing it back, she opened her eyes and turned toward Martha, covering her breasts with both hands, and swallowing a scream.

Martha was not alone at the cot door. A tall man, wearing a fancy French rapier in a gold-embossed baldric, held a cocked pistol to her head. His eyes were in shadow, but Kit saw smile creases in both cheeks and an arrogant tilt to his mouth as he bowed slightly in her direction.

"I would agree, mistress, that skin such as yours should

never be unclean. As for your conscience, I would beg you never to allow it to hinder pleasure . . . as you find it."

The bastard mocked her!

Although he did not move the pistol from Martha's temple, the ruffian bowed again, and she saw corded muscle ripple along his neck to disappear inside his open shirt. Kit gathered herself to leap. She had not come so far to lose all now.

"Do not think it, mistress," he said, aiming the pistol at her head now, "since you cannot outrun my powder and ball."

Still, she could not see his face in the shadow formed by his wide-brimmed hat. What she did see were two long, well-muscled legs covered in fine silk hosen the color of bluebells and high black Spanish boots turned down. Some dandy out for a lark? Perhaps she could cozen him. . . .

"You must come up and out of the trough," he said in a tone of voice that did not seem easily fooled. "It does not suit you, though I must admit to never seeing a finer young filly."

She spat the words. "Sir, I have need of my clothes."

"So you do," he said, walking Martha to them with a sidestep as deft as any French dancing masters'.

Kit didn't move to come out of the water. Whoever he was, a sheriff's man or no, she would not stand naked as a babe before him, though she was shivering now. "Sir, allow me to cover myself," she said, trying to keep a note of pleading from her voice, which she now knew inflamed men.

He prodded Martha, who was staring wide-eyed and openmouthed into his face. "Help your mistress to maintain her . . . modesty."

Stung by the laughter beneath his words, Kit flung a challenge. "A gentleman would turn his back."

He laughed openly as she struggled to exit the horse trough, her hands slipping on the wet wood. "Nay, mistress, you cannot think me so slow-witted, nor could I turn my back on such exquisite loveliness," he said in a musical baritone that made a confection of every word.

With Martha shielding her, Kit left the trough quickly and dressed faster still, watching him as the pistol never wavered. She had barely returned the old cap to her head when he walked forward and studied her for a very long minute in which she found herself holding her breath. Before she could chastise his impudence, he introduced himself.

"Jeremy Hughes, Jemmy to those fortunate ladies who love me, a peddler of poetry, of words to charm, to persuade or to command." He bowed again even more gracefully and continued, his resonant voice stroking the words, while Kit tried not to stare at the wide, full mouth saying them. "I am, sweet lady, a strolling player to neither of their Majesties as yet, but that is their loss and soon to be remedied," he added, crowning his pretty speech with another bow, sweeping his fashionable wide-brimmed black hat adorned with red ostrich feathers before her to the ground. "And dam'me, Lady Katherne Lindsay, if I would give up that lovely neck of yours to the sheriff's hangman for the ten guineas on offer . . . though I think me I can bargain for more."

Chapter Three

Oh, Beauty, till Now I Never Knew Thee

Don't bother to deny it, lady," Jeremy Hughes said. "Your features and speech tell the tale." She had been going to say him nay, that was plain in her face, though that face was anything but plain. Dam'me, he thought, but she had a rare beauty even her thunderous scowl could not hide.

"Now, bring your bundle and don't try to run away if you would live yet another day. The sheriff's thieving men are before and behind us. I would give you over to the magistrate in Chelmsford to assure your better care and my full reward."

Pure loathing was upon her face now, eyes as hard and glittering as sapphires. "You poor Judas. You need sell us for so little silver!" Her voice trembled with rage.

He pointed his pistol in a well-practiced way. "I do not regret doing the duty charged of every one of His Majesty's loyal subjects. Now walk, Lady Lindsay!" He moved around behind her and slapped his hand across her rump, but the wench only stiffened her back. He prodded her sharply and rested the pistol barrel on her shoulder, but if truth be told, he was losing his stomach for this game. Both women marched slowly ahead of him, down the path through a stand of trees toward the road, while he busily damned himself for a fool that she had so reached his pride.

No matter what the right of the law, he did truly shrink from it. He'd blessed his good fortune when he'd left the road to search the old cot for straw to feed his horse and seen her sleeping. Recognizing who she must be and what she was worth from having overheard talk by the sheriff's men at his performance last night, he'd waited to determine if she was unarmed. But his intention to better his purse had almost fled when he'd seen the sun glinting golden off the curves of her young shoulders, water sluicing from her full, rounded breasts and rosy, hard nipples, a sight to make his hands and lips ache with their own wanting.

Sensing that his body could betray his purse, he pushed both women to speed their steps. Though he could not now see the face of this murderess before him, the picture of her must have burned into his eyes because she was everywhere in them, cascading masses of blond ringlets, eyebrows of darker hue to frame wide violet eyes as deep as a stormy summer sky, and skin turned to cream by the golden sun, to put the best India ivory to shame. *"Oh, beauty, till now I never knew thee!"* He murmured the line from old Will's *Henry VIII,* and wondered if speaking it at last night's performance in Witham's inn yard had been a witchy foretelling.

With every step toward the road he knew he'd repent this day often and probably soon, but empty pockets and remembrance of the king's favorite courtier young Lord

Rochester's final words, "Bring me a profitable summer season in the provinces and you will win a high place in my theater by it," had overshadowed his sympathy for a most beautiful face. This first memory must dictate his course.

"Player, I have a right to know where you do take us," Kit called over her shoulder in a voice as cold as a North Sea ice floe.

He nudged her neck again with his pistol to remind her that his weapon was master to her sharp tongue. "You speak of rights like a Dissenter," he jibed, then relented and spoke true. "To my scenery wagon waiting just off the road, and thence to Chelmsford, lady. I must meet my troupe, who have gone ahead and are even now hiring a hall and obtaining a license for our performances. The town is full for the racing meet and in want of entertainment. . . . And I doubt not the ladies await me, too. . . . And as usual, impatiently." He laughed and saw her arms go rigid against her body, as if to declare she was not such a one. "Move smartly, now! I do see your legs are long enough."

They reached the road, where a wagon piled with boxes and painted cloth rolled on poles waited, its horse dozing, head down, eyes half closed. Jeremy pointed the pistol and cocked it, handing Kit a rope. "Tie your servant's hands."

"I won't! Go ahead and shoot me and bring down the sheriff's men who will take it mighty ill that you cheated them."

"Mistress Kit," Martha pleaded, "I would live a few days more, so do as he says."

Kit thought of flinging the rope in his eyes, but she could not bring Martha into danger from this low player. When Martha was tied, she scrambled awkwardly up inside the cart.

"Now, you, Mistress Kit, as you are called, hold out your hands, and no tricks. I would mislike to harm so beautiful a murderess."

"I did not murder Sir William," she said slowly, holding out hands that were clenched into fists, wondering why she cared what this rogue thought.

"The sheriff's men do say you did." He could not allow such a belief to creep between him and the reward that waited. The sheriff had cheated him last night by declaring the performance a benefit for the poor of Witham, and put all gate monies in his own purse. It was right that he collect a reward for this felon from that very sheriff.

"I like not this necessity," he said as he tied her hands before her, "and you can believe me or not. I must have money, or my players will starve till the London season begins in the fall and with the plague still on us, it will surely be very late."

Did he think to win her obedience with such an argument? "Then I will hang happy to think I die for your good and not the sheriff's." Her voice was harsh, for she had nothing more to lose after her life.

But she gave him such a proud look, her chin high, her eyes flashing fire, that it sent a surge of lightning through his cod. He pulled her bindings tighter, keeping his face scornful enough to cover his mounting regret. He had a dozen times in as many minutes wished he'd never started on this course, and damned if he trusted the way his body was aching. "As you will, mistress, though you will be ducked for a shrew long ere you hang."

"Better a shrew, sir, than a rogue who makes his coin from innocent women's lives!" She knew she worsened her case with each word, but she could not govern her tongue with this man. Reckoning that she had pricked his pride and caring not if she had, she stared at him, angry still, but no longer blinded by despair, seeing him in full for the first time.

In all her life, Kit had given few thoughts to the male body. She had seen little enough at Bournely to inspire her. All changed in that instant. Before she could close her eyes against Jeremy Hughes, they collected every part of him and stored them in her memory. The waving black hair that lightly touched his broad shoulders, the darkly magnificent eyes and sharp-angled features that bespoke a Welsh forebear to go with his name. The full lips that seemed to ever hide a breaking smile, and shining white teeth that showed unusual diligence with rubbing salt or even the use of one of the new brushes for the teeth lately come from France. His shoulders, in a shirt of fine lawn under an unbuttoned doublet edged in silver lace, tapered to a waist that topped narrow hips and long, finely muscled legs. She doubted the tight blue knit hosen showed them to best advantage. And she could not help but notice . . . well, she had eyes . . . that he had been endowed with a manly part that gallants in the last century would have paraded in a giant codpiece! He was a man to take away a woman's breath and keep it. . . . Though never hers, she'd vow to that. Still, something stirred to a shiver deep inside her body, much against her will, and she went to the greatest effort to suppress it, lest he see and take some vain male pleasure, which he already had in obvious plenty.

"And now, Mistress Kit, if you have looked your fill, into the wagon with you."

Embarrassed, Kit's answer was as sharp as she intended. "Gladly, if I am spared further discourse with you." She would master this strange feeling that made her heart pound in her ears and pained her in the very nether regions of her stomach. She denied in her own head that this Jeremy Hughes was the cause. It was hunger that a good pottage and fine white bread would easily remedy.

He shoved her none too gently into the cart and covered both women with a painted scenery cloth of a darkling plain with a brooding castle in the distance. "Too bad you are not a player, mistress," he said, not resisting one last jibe. "One of the witches in *Macbeth*, I think, would be a right role for you."

He climbed upon the cart seat and slapped the reins against his horse's back, but not before he heard her declaim, "Fair is foul, and foul is fair, player."

So she knew *Macbeth*! If he was not careful, this woman would turn his head and cheat him of his reward yet, though he must admit on his honor that she intrigued him mightily. . . . And knew just as well that he must hide it.

Some minutes on, she spoke again, her voice muffled by the scenery cloth. "Player, I will equal the sheriff's reward if you will free us, and more if you take us to London."

"And earn me a dance at the end of a rope when they find you with me. Ha! You must think me a great fool."

"Aye, fool and coward, player!"

Her muffled words stung him, and he determined to say no more to her. Every minute with the woman increased the tightness of his chest. Happily, she said no other word to him all that afternoon, although he could hear the two of them whispering together. Let them plot. They could do nothing against him. He brought a leathern wine bottle to their lips once when he checked their bindings and watered his horse, but said no more. There was no more to say, and he feared a clever trap. God, keep me from a women of beauty and daring wit, he prayed, as no doubt many a man had prayed. He drove on into the dusk, eager to deliver his troubling cargo.

He reached Chelmsford as the waxing moon rose over the ancient church spire, the sun already set over the western horizon but shining its last rays against the underside of the clouds, turning them into a rosy canopy, surely a sign of heaven's favor. He asked the way to the constable's house, and the constable, in a doublet stained with soup and wine, the gold buttons barely restraining his belly, answered his knock.

"What do you want at this hour?" he said, wearing his badge of office and holding a candle high to light Jeremy's face.

"Jeremy Hughes, strolling player," he said, bowing. "To the contrary, sir, I believe that I have what *you* want."

"And what might that be?" the constable said impatiently, as a woman called to him from another room.

Jeremy hesitated. This was going to be as difficult as he'd thought.

"Come, man, I have little time for vagabond japes."

"No jape, Constable," he said, and with a final hesitation that he conquered, he added, "Come with me." He walked to the rear of his wagon and before he could change his mind, quickly threw back the scenery cloth. Kit was looking at him with scorn writ huge in her eyes. Damn if he would ever forget it except deep in his cups, which he would be this very night as soon as may be. "Constable, these are the two runaway women from Bournely Hall, wanted for murder."

The constable's eyes widened. "How come you by . . . never you mind. Bring them into the house at once. I will lock them up until the sheriff arrives to claim them."

Jeremy helped both women stand. Kit held herself stiff and even shuddered under his hand, though she stumbled going up the steps. Inside the constable's parlor, wall sconces flared, but Jeremy avoided her hard eyes and said what he had to say. "There is a reward."

"Yes, yes, ten guineas."

"It has cost me a night's performance to bring them here, sir. They are worth fifteen guineas to me."

"A pox on *your* worth! I will make it a week in the stocks if you try to bargain with me. Ten guineas is generous, since Sir William is not dead. . . . Near death from a broken head, but living still."

Kit could not believe what she'd heard. "Did you say that Sir William lives?"

"No thanks to you and your servant girl. And, mistress, do not think that saves ye from the rope," the constable said sternly, his chins wagging.

She tried to feel some happiness that William lived, but she did not. She felt nothing.

Martha shoved in front of Kit. "Mistress Kit did not harm Sir William. I murthered him when I saw he be forcing himself on her just as he done on me."

The constable waved away her words, his face reddened. "You impugn your betters at your peril. One more word, my girl, and you will rue it for the rest of your very short life."

Jeremy stood still, his mind racing. Could Kit be innocent? Sorely wronged against? It would not matter to the law, since she was found fleeing with an admitted murderess. If he could, he would retrace his steps, but it was too late and he could not.

"Here, player," the constable said, digging into his purse. "Two guineas is all I have. Take them and be gone." He pushed the coins along the polished hall table toward Jeremy. "I set your troupe on the road at an earlier hour. I need no more rogues and vagrants in Chelmsford. Be gone, I say!" He raised a hand menacingly, but lowered it when Jeremy's hand strayed to his rapier.

"What will you do with them?" Jeremy asked, almost choking on the words and the answer he knew full well.

The constable opened the door. "That is no affair of yours, player. Leave now or sit in the stocks until Lord's Day, praise be his blessed name."

Jeremy's mind working furiously, he was out the door on the constable's stoop before he realized that he was without his two guineas, and glad of it, although damning himself for a fool at the same time. He had sent two women to their deaths for naught.

He drove his wagon down the street and tried to continue moving ahead, but his hands were listless on the reins and his horse stopped to munch grass by the roadside. Curse it! A strolling player's path was not one for fine feelings. Any such weakness would jeopardize his chance to play the major roles in Lord Rochester's new theater, roles he was born for, and indeed, the future of all in his troupe. Curse the girl doubly.

Why risk his livelihood and the distinct possibility of putting his own neck in the noose? He searched his head but found the answers in his heart. Aye, once seen, she would be hard to forget. What mortal man could? Amidst all the women he'd known, and there had been many, she stood as out of place as a vibrant red rose in a stable dung heap. That she had proved to have spirit and wit enhanced her beauty, though he'd tried to deny it.

That look of freshly lost innocence on her face had called

to the deepest, most hidden part of his heart and brought him back to the morn when Cromwell's troops had raided his small England-Wales border town, killing his father at his workbench. He had yelled for his sister to run, but she had disobeyed, staying by him. One by one the soldiers raped her while he, a struggling schoolboy, was roughly held down by laughing troopers. Kit had the same haunted look that his sister wore till the pox took her, and she glad of it.

Since that day and hour, he had been set on a course from which he'd never strayed. He was not totally aware that in the dark recesses of his mind he had eschewed love as too risky and too apt to be lost to a willful woman. He had been saved from a dour demeanor by his excellent humor and his natural abilities as a player that caused all those around him to happily follow where he led. This mastership had kept him near to others without the danger of becoming too close or of losing his heart.

And so, against his will and swearing heartily that he was playing worse than a fool's role for the first time in his man's life, he doubled back behind the constable's house and garden, which marched in neat vegetable and herb rows down to a stream. Quietly he crept to an apple tree heavy with unripe fruit and scanned the house with its overhanging second story built in the old queen's time. He saw a candle lighted in a lower back room, and Kit and Martha being led in, still wearing his ropes tied to their wrists. The constable's man fastened their feet to the bed frame and the constable, brandishing a large key, left them. Minutes later another man came out to the stable, retrieved a horse and galloped away to the north. It would be midmorning before the sheriff could arrive, unless he was close by, and then only hours. Jeremy damned himself for every kind of fool again to risk all for the haughty maiden whose scorn had pricked his pride, but his disobedient legs carried him closer.

Kit fought against tears, although Martha had given in to hers. She tried to feel the courage her father would have shown, to be her father in female guise. He had not cringed from the rope, nor would she, although she would die damning Sir William and Jeremy Hughes with her last breath. Thinking of her last breath, she inhaled deeply and held on to it.

She tested the bindings about her wrists once more and realized that the more she struggled, the tighter they became. She lay back-to-back with Martha and inched close. "Can you reach my ropes?" she whispered as softly as she could, as she was certain the door with its huge lock was guarded.

Martha answered in a faint voice, gulping sobs. "Aye, mistress, but my fingers be numb. I cannot move them."

Kit stretched her fingers toward Martha's and began to rub them, but soon gave it up because her own were growing useless. "Martha, we must get us away."

"How, mistress? There be a guard sure, and we be tied like hogs for the fall butchering."

"Damn him for a rogue," Kit said, and she did not speak of the guard. "I hope his two guineas bring him hellish misfortune."

"But, mistress, did ye not see that he left the coins where they lay?"

Kit did not answer. Jeremy Hughes was without doubt a stupid as well as a greedy Judas, and if by some happenstance he had changed his heart . . . well, what good would that do her on the scaffold . . . or him in hell?

"Listen, mistress," Martha said, bumping her slightly.

The sound of a window slowly being opened filled the room. Kit expected the guard to crash through the door at any moment, but he did not. If this was some further mischief upon two bound women, she would call out and raise the entire town.

It was mischief aright, but when one long blue-hosed leg came over the sill and reached the floor, she held her ready scream and her breath. The rest of Jeremy Hughes came soon after his leg, with a finger to his smiling lips. Without meaning to, Kit's heart quickened as the candlelight flickered across the angles of his dark face.

He went swiftly to the guttering beeswax candle and snuffed it, leaving them in the dark. A moment later, she felt his hand far down her back. "You are a damned bastard rakehell to take such liberty!" she said angrily before his hand clamped upon her mouth.

"Language, language, my lady!" he said close to her ear, and his breath was hot on her neck. "I am trying to find the rope and cut it with my rapier, but you are tall e'en in bed and I cannot find the end of you. I will continue to search most diligently. Ah, I think I've found—"

She wriggled. "Sir, you take advantage."

"Quiet, if you would not have my blade slip." He sawed upon the bindings, hands and feet, until she was free, then sat her up and rubbed her hands and arms quickly to life, the rubbing just short of rank impertinence.

"Enough, sir," she whispered, and could sense his wide grin in the dark.

After loosing Martha, he said, "Follow me."

They were at the window when a key turned in the lock and the door opened. A candle was thrust inside, held by a man blinking in the light, as startled as they were. At the first sound, Jeremy stepped quickly into the shadows behind the door. Kit had seen no tall man move with such speed and silence.

"What do ye there?" the guard said, squinting into the candle as he entered.

The butt of a pistol came down on his head and he slumped into Jeremy's arms without a sound, the candle rolling on the floor, its light going out. "Don't stand there gawping," Jeremy said, dragging the guard inside, and they dropped their bundles out the window and scrambled ahead of him.

He leaped like a lithe cat to the ground and motioned them to stay close, running toward the bottom of the garden. On the way, Martha bent, without breaking her stride, to pull up a turnip plant.

"Under the scenery cloth, quickly," he said, pushing them into the wagon.

"We know the way, sir," Kit answered, her head high again but near crazed with puzzlement.

"Hold your sour words, mistress."

"I suppose you wish a reward now, player," she said, crawling under the canvas next to Martha. "You will find you have made a poor bargain, because the constable took the coins my father left me. I have nothing to give you. If you want my thanks for saving me from the endangerment you placed me in, then you have them."

He bowed, exasperated, as her head disappeared. "I have decided, mistress, to dispense with your gratitude as a poor thing, and put you to another service."

Before more could be said, he vaulted to the wagon seat and drove at a slow pace out of Chelmsford, equally fearful of drawing attention by speed and allowing time for the guard to come to his senses and raise the hue and cry behind them.

They were well on the road to Basildon before he told them that they could sit up and breathe the rain-washed night air full of country smells, of cow byres, dewy green grass and smoke from cottage chimneys. "It is a monstrous fair night, after all," he said, and lifting his face to the sky, laughed so heartily that Kit almost allowed a smile to play upon her own lips. . . . Till he began to sing, shouting the words into the night.

> *"I am a lusty, lively lad, arrived at one and twenty,*
> *I'll court and kiss—what hurt's in this?*
> *The ladies shall adore me.*

"Tell me, beauteous Kit, can you sing a bawdy song?" he asked, and she could sense his insolent grin in the dark.

"I have been gentle raised and know none."

"Can you read?" he said, clicking his tongue to speed the horse.

"Of course, and in Latin and French." Did he think her unlettered?

He shrugged. "These are the provinces, not London, my fine lady. We give the redheaded country lads a bit of bloody Shakespeare and some farce, jigs and music between acts."

"What of me?" Martha asked.

"There's a good lass," he said over his shoulder. "You could be our lewd Harlequin."

"With a costume and all?"

"Aye, and all."

Kit glared at his back. "You would turn us into strolling

players, harlots of the road? No, not e'en to save our necks will I—"

He twisted in the seat, glaring back at her, and the moon lit his anger. "It means naught to me if you would rather meet Master Hangman, but I put it to you that you will be safer in my troupe than on the road for any highway rogue to find and work his will. And I doubt your tongue would help you there, though it is a sharp weapon, I grant you."

Kit sought to speak, but he overspoke her. "Make up your mind. All must pay their way, mistress. We have only one woman, so that men must play the woman parts, and that is no longer the fashion since good King Charles did decree that women must play women on the stage. If you can read and learn lines quickly, then I will help you make your way to London, where you can do as it please you and welcome."

The night air or her restored freedom had finally cooled her anger at his perfidy. "I have acted in private masques and such and can play the virginal. Some do say that I have a fair voice and true."

"Good, it is rare that beauty has talent, but I would put nothing past you." Before she could find fault with his answer, he called to Martha. "Lass, look in that chest in front of you and hand Kit the black wig." He looked behind him. "No, that one is for a man. The other one. Now fit it to her. We won't go far with that yellow hair to give us away."

Kit adjusted the wig, noticing his glance of approval.

"Your own mother would not know you."

"My mother never knew me. She died in her childbed." It was a useless thing to say and she did not know why she had the need to speak so. It had never been her way to engage the sympathy of others, especially so unsympathetic a rogue. But all things had changed, so maybe she had, too.

"Martha, come up by me," Jeremy called. "I long for pleasant womanly company."

Martha looked at Kit, who shrugged her uncaring, and Martha clambered up and over the seat.

Jeremy smiled and winked at Martha, who blushed a deep crimson. "Don't worry, lass, I'll teach you to be a proper Harlequin."

"But won't we be risking discovery, Master Hughes? All those people be looking at us. Best we hide somewhere."

He shook his head. "That is what the sheriff expects you will do, lass, and he will search every foxhole in Essex. He will not think to look for you in so public a place." He laughed because it was so simple and true.

"Won't he search for you, Master Player?" Katherne asked.

"Why? I gave you over and was seen leaving town alone on the Billericay Road, turning toward Basildon when none observed."

Martha swallowed mightily. "I be thanking ye, Master Hughes, but I be asking ye—" She gulped again.

"Yes?"

"I be asking why ye take such risk of your life for ours?"

He glanced back at Kit, a wry smile lifting one corner of his mouth. "I've been asking myself that same question."

"And what did yourself answer?" Kit said, staring back, her defiance rising again to sweep all kind thoughts of him away, which turned her face hot. Damn his roguish ways!

He slapped the reins against the horse's back, and clicked his tongue. "I like that I can make a fool of a thieving sheriff who deserves no better. And for the good company of Martha here." He laughed. "And to see, Mistress Kit, if your feet really fit those giant's shoes you wear."

Kit repressed a grin, but only just. She hated it when he was charming. It gave her less to dislike.

They rode on in silence for some time until they came upon the troupe's second costume cart pulled into the inn yard of the Two Angels, more than halfway to Basildon. Jeremy climbed down and stretched his stiff limbs, only to have a woman rush from the inn door with a shrill of laughter and throw herself upon him.

"Jemmy! Jemmy, where have you been? I've been crazed with worry since we left you in Witham. I thought the sheriff had you sure." Standing on tiptoes, she kissed him right heartily and pressed herself into his arms.

Obliging, he danced her about and kissed her back. "Lucy, never and a day will the sheriff lock me in gaol. He's chasing his tail right now."

Kit saw her in the yellow light of the inn's lantern kept lit at night for late travelers. She had the dark hair and white skin that was all the mode, with reddened lips, kohl-darkened eyes, and two beauty marks in the shape of tiny roses near her mouth. Did actresses sleep in their paint? Though barely average height, this Lucy's carriage made her seem taller, but beyond her makeup, Kit sensed more years than first appeared.

"What new baggage do you carry, Jemmy? Have you seduced two tavern maids to join us?"

Her words seemed humorous, but Kit heard more than curiosity behind her questions. If she had made an enemy without opening her mouth, then she was about to make a bigger one. Kit slipped over the tail of the wagon. "No tavern maid, madame, I assure you. As for seduction, I am the last woman in this land to be drawn to Master Hughes's too-obvious charms."

"If that is truth, mistress, then why do you protest it so?" Lucy said, her mouth in a tense smile, stepping closer to Kit for a better look.

Jeremy appeared pleased as any man who provokes a quarrel between two handsome women, and bowed slightly, thrusting out a leg. "May I introduce Mistress Kit and Martha," he said. "Both would be apprenticed to us as players. And this is"—he made a grand gesture, sweeping his feathered hat before him—"Mrs. Lucy Wylie, late of the Cockpit Theater in London."

Martha dropped a deep curtsy, but Kit merely bent a knee and held her ground.

Lucy's carefully drawn eyebrows rose and remained high as she walked around Kit. "By my soul, Jemmy, she seems a stiff wench without guile, and her face is ill used. How could she make the shillings flow, let alone hold the rowdies on the hard benches in the pit?"

Jeremy glanced at Kit and was pleased to see that she was angry, which he much preferred to the disdain she had formerly shown him. Anger, at least, revealed some passion in the woman, passion he had sensed from the first. "Lucy, her face will heal and we will instruct her in stagecraft, for I think she has more skill than a sharp tongue."

"Ah, a man's eyes see what I do not?" Lucy seemed unconvinced until he drew her into his arms and kissed her soundly again, delighted to see Kit turn away. Lucy sighed reluctantly. "You are a mighty scoundrel, Jemmy, but she may indeed do for small parts. . . . Very small."

He laughed. "Madame, I tire of you playing a witch and Lady Macbeth together in one night, when Mistress Kit here could handily play all three witches at once." He threw back his head, laughing heartily, his teeth shining in the lantern light, then walked with Lucy clutching his arm into the inn, both very merry, leaving a strangely furious Kit to follow in Lucy's perfumed wake.

Martha fell in beside Kit. "Oh, mistress, he be so wonderful!" she said, barely able to catch her breath.

Chapter Four

The Play's the Thing

Inside the Two Angels, giant smoke-stained oak rafters crisscrossed the hall, and the remains of the evening's fire glowed in the huge stone fireplace. Jeremy Hughes stood at the head of a trestle table around which sat five men eating from a large platter of pigeons. The smell of the roasted meat made Kit weak in the knees. Jeremy, with Lucy clinging to him, waved them over.

"Gentlemen, I offer you Mistress Kit, performer of masques, singer and mistress of the virginal, and Martha, buxom Harlequin, who would 'prentice to us as far as London. They are mostly untutored, but very willing. We are in need of players, so let us take them on."

There was a general muttering around the table and more than several curious glances thrown Kit's way, until one young man of no more than twenty years, medium height, slight build and delicately handsome features, stood and put one foot on his bench. "And what will I play if this lady takes the women's roles and she a-wearing my wig, monsieur?" he asked with a French accent and a noticeable pout.

"You will needs keep your breeches on more, Alain," shouted a player at the table's end, to general merriment.

"Laugh at your peril, monsieur," Alain said, his hand going to the intricate hilt of the sword at his side.

"Hold!" Jeremy shouted, instantly getting all their attention. "There is no time for such japes. I would away from here at first light so that we arrive in Basildon to rehearse and open my rewritten version of *Macbeth* by five of the clock tomorrow."

"The Scottish play again," a player muttered unhappily.

"Aye, you know the village lads do love to see the stage strewn with bloody bodies," Jeremy answered, "and since we have no proper stage, trapdoors or machines, we must amuse them for their shillings with our bedlam."

"Jemmy, what of her?" Lucy said, impatiently pointing to Kit. "We have not decided whether she is fit to join us. I say let her perform for us now. What say you all to a jig from the lady?" she asked, smiling slyly at the men.

The troupe began to pound their tankards on the table in agreement, and Kit backed away. She would not dance, and she could not sing without her virginal and music, nor for such rowdies.

Jeremy saw her shrink and knew Lucy would pounce on her like a barn cat on a timorous field mouse. He loosed himself from Lucy's clinging hands and reached Kit in three steps, forcing her to look at him. "You must give them something or you are lost. If you get a share, they have a right to know you will well earn it."

"But I cannot—"

"You can. Do you know 'She Loves and She Confesses, Too'?"

"I have often heard it, but it has a double meaning and is not the kind of—"

He would not leave off, his eyes flashing a warning. "Follow me, Kit, for I have not troubled so much that I would see you set on the road to the gallows now, or find a rope around mine own neck."

He held her with the dark warning in his eyes though she tried to turn away, and began to sing slowly in an intensely rich baritone that filled the hall and turned all heads toward them:

"She loves and she confesses, too,
There's then at last no more to do. . . ."

Hesitant but determined not to be overmatched by a strolling player, since she knew in her soul that she could not be vulnerable for even a moment before this man, Kit opened her mouth and sang, the familiar words returning quickly to her mind:

"The happy work's entirely done,
Enter the town which thou hast won."

At first her voice was small and trembled some, but her clear, resonant contralto found its way past her fear, growing stronger and more sure as he looked at her, holding her troubled gaze with his mocking one. She matched him note for note, until more of wonder and delight were present in their eyes than either intended. The song became a soaring duel, and as it soared, he reached for her hand. His strong, warm fingers sent their vibrations around and through her as the harmony grew to an unexpected and wondrous pleasure.

She clasped his hand tightly, knowing full certain that she would fall if he let go.

It is a rarity when two voices that have no experience of each other are so suited from the first note that they find a sound all their own. Kit knew it, and Jeremy's eyes told her that he knew it well, as they sang the final words:

> *"But I shall find out counter charms,*
> *Thy airy devilship to remove*
> *From this circle here of love."*

As the last long-held note died away, Kit wondered how and when they had moved so close together, his mouth just inches from her own. A sudden unison shout from the table and a vigorous pounding of tankards brought her to her lost senses, and she took back her warm, moist hand and stepped away, feeling an instant loss that was almost a blow to her heart.

"The girl has a pleasing, if small, voice," announced Lucy, the straight line of her mouth saying something far different. "She will do for entr'actes on the road." With a dramatic swish of skirts, she moved abruptly to the wide oaken stairs that led to a gallery. "Coming, Jeremy?"

"I have much to do before early light, Lucy. I'll sleep here tonight, if I sleep at all," he said, stepping back but without taking his eyes from Kit.

Kit pretended she had not heard, though she still trembled. So Lucy and Jeremy were lovers. It meant nothing to her, less than nothing. A man did as he pleased in this man's world, and a woman could not let it rule her head or her heart.

"Alain Morel, mademoiselle," the young French actor

said, bowing over her hand as Jeremy turned away. "I ask your forgiveness for my poor welcome."

"*Merci, monsieur, je vous pardonez.*"

"You speak French," he said, pleased. "But we must speak English, since your countrymen hate the sound of my beautiful language no matter how many treaties we sign together against the Hollanders or how often you steal our food and our fashion." He giggled. "*Et maintenant,* speaking of fashion, why do you wear a wig that is so wrong with your bright skin color?"

"Jeremy wished it," she said, thinking to put an end to his questions.

He viewed her with a cocked eyebrow that she realized had been darkened from its natural light brown and shaped with kohl. "You sing much better than Lucy, and she takes it very ill, *ma belle*. I fear you have made of her a double enemy, for you have also quite taken the eye of Jeremy Hughes."

"You are mistaken, sir. Master Hughes and I have little liking, but are come together by happenstance and will soon part and both of us be glad of it." Her glance kept going to the table, and her stomach growled at the aroma of meat growing cold.

"Come, Keet," Alain said, taking her hand as if she were a child, though he was not quite so tall as she, "you have hunger plain to see." He led her to the table and made a place next to Martha, who had nothing but white bones on her plate, an empty tankard and a satisfied smile. A pewter platter with a pigeon breast and a piece of bread was passed through several hands to Kit, while Martha refilled her mug and pushed it toward her.

"Mistress, I heard ye sing many times in the great hall, but it be never like tonight."

"There was no difference," Kit replied, nearly choking on a bit of bread hastily swallowed.

Each player in turn introduced himself while taking the occasion to get a closer look at her.

"In farce I play the ranting friend to Jemmy's lustful rake," said one, and Kit stood and curtsied as all bowed to her with individual flourishes. Then, wrapped in their cloaks, they found places to sleep by the dying fire, on the settles and on the floor.

Kit was aware that Jeremy was lodged at the head of the table, busily writing out parts on the backs of old pages. Her stomach full, her head became so heavy that she laid it on her arms on the rough plank table and fell immediately to sleep. Twice she awoke before first light and heard the scrape of boots on boards and knew that the player was sleepless and circling behind her. But each time, still full in her stomach and sleepy-eyed, she could not dwell on his strange behavior, or indeed her own, although she knew that she would take up such matters again on waking.

What she did dwell on before sleep overtook her once again was how all her life had been changed by the animal lust of one man, Sir William. She was used to a quiet daily round of duties, of being ignored or ruled by her cousin Joan, of caring for small children, but most times left to read, play and sing her music and dream fantastical dreams of having her father and brothers alive, of laughing and having a hope of being loved again. She was amazed to feel no real longing for her former life of some comfort at Bournley Hall, for she would never again be prisoner of a man who could betray her, and that included Jeremy Hughes. Most especially, it included Jeremy Hughes.

When she awoke as light crept around the entry door and through the bottle-glass windows, a stout pair of lady's shoes sat before her on the table. "Thank you," she said, approaching Jeremy, genuinely touched by his thoughtfulness.

"You were disgracing the company," he said, not looking up from his writing.

For a moment, her temper flared, but then as suddenly she did not believe him. She found that his inability to admit a kindness worked some strange charm on her.

After an early wash of rain damped the dusty road, Kit and Martha jounced along in the second scenery wagon over the gently rolling Essex countryside or took their turn walking to the hill overlooking Basildon. There they stopped and the players dressed in costumes to charm the townspeople, including Martha in a white, red and black Harlequin suit, a ruff at her throat and a flopping red hat on her head.

"What do I now, Master Jeremy?" Martha asked, smoothing the diamond-patterned sleeves with a great smile, hopping a little on one foot.

"You go before and beat the drum and play the fool, girl, to gather a crowd. Then you pass out these playbills, and if you see some likely lads, a few kisses," he said, handing her a sheaf of pages, which he turned right side up for her when he saw she could not read. "I'll go to the magistrate to get a license to perform in the inn yard." He gave the reins over to one of the men and dropped back beside Kit in the road.

"Did you sleep well?" he asked, although that was not the question on his mind. He was about to tell her she would sing with him that night between acts, when her sharp tongue intervened.

"I slept well enough, sir, considering someone was pacing the boards behind me."

"After a long wagon ride, I have need to stretch my legs," he said, sensing a coming joust.

Before she could stop herself, Kit looked to see that his long, muscled legs remained as they had been.

"Ah, you still approve of my legs," he said, an uncommonly satisfied grin playing on his lips.

Kit's reply held an edge of embarrassment. "I will approve, if they carry you down that road and away from me."

He bowed to hide the sting of those words. "I am all eager for such approval, mistress."

Without a backward glance, he set a fast pace down the narrow road ahead of them toward the town, leaving Kit to wonder why she had spoken so, there being no need for sharp words. She stared at the curve of his buttocks as his rapier swung beside him, and almost called to him, but stopped herself in time. Jeremy Hughes was too eager to prove his mastery over women, and that she could not accept. Still, she had never had a harsh tongue and did not like it that she had acquired one. But her former softness belonged to another world, not this one. Whatever this world held, she could never be off her guard, especially with a man like the player.

Kit saw everyone in costume and pulled from the open chest a scarlet gown with a very low bodice.

"That is my gown," Lucy announced, already in the fearsome makeup of the scheming Lady Macbeth. "If you value a place with us, then remember your place, which is nothing. You cannot work your pretty wiles with me. I am not a man to be ruled by my prick."

Kit was furious. "Nor are you a lady to be ruled by the least of good manners, Mrs. Wylie."

With a cry of rage, Lucy snatched at the gown with one hand and slapped Kit's bruised face with the other. The gown tore as Kit stumbled backward, and she would have fallen into the dirt except for Alain's catching her. "You will pay me for the mending of that gown from your share," Lucy screamed, and stalked past the other actors, who gave her wide room.

"Keep an eye out for madame, *ma chere amie,*" Alain said as they walked on, "for she will do you an ill if she can. . . . And she can. She is even jealous of me. But then, I am much prettier." He shrugged to show that his words were a tease, but they were true nonetheless, for he was a very pretty man.

Kit reached into her bundle and removed the only other dress she now owned, a deep red wool with slashed and gathered sleeves and a bodice that showed the swell of her breasts but not beyond modesty. She stopped behind a hedgerow and dressed with sheep looking on. At least she would not shame herself or the troupe by wearing tatters.

Alain was waiting when she emerged. "No, no, Keet," he said in a fussy voice. He quickly pulled and patted and lifted until the gown fit her better than it ever had. "Even that gown does not deal fairly with your eyes." He bowed and kissed her hand.

She curtsied. "You are most gentle kind, Alain."

Lucy called from the cart, "Don't waste your pretty poses, sir. Save them for the audience."

Alain muttered under his breath, "The she-devil Lady Macbeth is a role made for madame's black-bile humor."

Since she had been the cause of this exchange, Kit took his arm, and with lively discourse, ignoring Lucy to that woman's chagrin, they walked on in the rain-freshened morning, talking of silly things. Alain made Kit laugh as she had thought never to laugh again. With lowered voice, he also told her that she misjudged Jeremy. "I do not know what ill lies between you, but he has proven to be hard but fair for a master player, for they do usually cheat strolling players of their last penny. . . . Their first one, too," he added, his bright hazel eyes twinkling.

They reached the town as shops began to open, and wives and maids came out to bid good morrow and give over their chamber pots to the night soil cart. Martha danced ahead, cavorting as Kit had never seen her and banging on her drum with right goodwill, making a racket to raise any still asleep. Lucy flirted with the men, commenting on their brawn, while the male players bowed to each side and in pretty couplets praised the beauty and virtue of the town's women, collecting a crowd before the troupe reached the common and rested under an ancient horse chestnut tree. Alain declaimed some poetry to openmouthed village folk, while Kit watched all, not knowing what part she could play in this. "Smile, Mistress Kit," an older player called to her, and she did until her face hurt.

Jeremy returned, waving a signed magistrate's warrant. "I've taken the town," he said to the troupe's cheers. "We play here for three days in the inn yard, maybe more, and we'll all sleep abed tonight.

"Good people," he said, addressing the crowd, bowing and sweeping his hat before him in the courtly move that Kit admired more each time she witnessed its grace, "at the Bull and Ram, tonight and for three nights running, will be acted a tragedy called *Macbeth*—with all witches, songs and dances as they were recently performed at the Cockpit Theater in London. Beginning at five of the clock," he added, sweeping another bow toward a group of goggling townswomen. "Only one shilling for the pit, and sixpence for the upper gallery. Long live King Charles in this the sixth year of his restored reign and of our Lord, 1666."

Jeremy and the men maneuvered the wagons into the yard of the ancient cruck-timbered inn called the Bull and Ram, past a bowing innkeeper eager for all the business the players and their audience would bring him in exchange for the use of his yard, stabling for the horses and two rooms. All the men were to have a room and all the women another.

"Jemmy, do not jest. I need my own room," Lucy said, wearing an extremely unhappy face.

"Lucy, when the doorkeep has brought us the first money, you may do what you will with your share, but for now—" But she had already marched away, her back as rigid as a grenadier's.

Kit watched Lucy's pique and felt some satisfaction that she would not have her way in all things; then realized that Jeremy was beckoning her as the men, with Martha's help, finished unloading the costume chests and scenery rolls. "Come here, mistress, there is no time to stand about idle if you would act with my company this night."

She bristled at his order. "No lord commands me, sir, and certainly no low player." She walked languidly toward him, pretending an afternoon stroll, her defiant gaze locked on his face, which was wiped clear of emotion.

Chapter Five

Toil and Trouble

Jeremy held tight to his tongue, and every other part, as well, as he watched the minx obviously thwart his will. Then he abruptly turned his back on her and strode toward the stable. He would give her display of bad temper no audience.

Kit stood warily before Jeremy where he sat on the rude bench against the stable wall. He motioned for her to join him. Would the brute hit her? When he made no move, indeed did not so much as look her way, her anger collapsed. She had been unpardonably rude. For a long moment, she stared hard at him, struggling for words of apology called for by the least knowledge of good manners.

"Have you lost your tongue, or is that a vain hope?" he asked, his mouth suppressing a superior smile.

She felt her anger rise again, all thought of apology flying away. God's nails! He did that to her with such ease, pulling her mind first this way then that.

Jeremy held out the pages she had seen him writing at the Two Angels. "Here is your part for tonight. You will play the three weird sisters as one role."

"As you threatened . . ."

"Aye, as I promised. You will forget that you are the soft sex. . . . If indeed you ever remember, and alter your voice to a wicked crone's."

She looked in his face, certain that he mocked her, but could determine nothing beyond what she had seen from the first moment ever she had spied Jeremy Hughes. The handsome rogue yet had a tender mouth behind the mocking words. She must be wary that she did not read more into that mouth than was there, or if there, believe it was meant for her good and not his own. All men would be her master, and that she would never have again.

"Now let me hear you read the lines," he said, handing her the new-written part, his hand brushing hers deliberately until she snatched the sheets away.

"Remember now," he added, a slight smile lifting one side of his mouth, "*all* the apparitions, if you think you can speak old Will's lines as he intended."

Kit concentrated her gaze on the pages, her eyes adjusting to the lower light under the stable eaves, the smell of warm horseflesh and leather mingling with the manly aroma of open air and sunshine that she'd noted whenever Jeremy Hughes came near. She angled the pages to the light, cleared her throat and began to read:

> *"Round about the cauldron go;*
> *In the poison'd entrails throw. . . ."*

"No, no, mistress, do not read as poetry for a ladies gathering. *Be* the witch, with all the passions in your voice and body. You do have passions?"

"When I have need," she said, wishing for more time to frame a clever answer to his provocation.

"Prove so," he said, that maddening smile playing upon his lips, until he began to repeat her lines and quickly became a stooped old woman before her eyes, bending to stir the cauldron, his voice crackling evilly on every syllable. "Now try again."

She did, thinking all the while that she would make a better witch than Lucy if it did kill her to do it.

"That's better, in fact, more than better, but do not screech so. It is as menacing to speak low and let the voice rise and fall. And put your hands into it as if the cauldron was truly full of foul and ugly things, but you, being a witch, do adore them."

She stood and bent over, stirring furiously, trying hard to follow his direction.

"No, no, that's not—" He broke off, stood and, stepping behind her, moved her body as he willed, muscled length against hers, swaying and bending until she was faint from holding her breath and having his hair brush against her cheek. She began to struggle, but his grip was like steel on butter and she could not deny Jeremy Hughes's body its own way. She felt him in every part of her, as if they had been melted together by the hottest sun of Araby. An enthusiatic applause greeted them from across the yard, where the men were watching in high good humor.

She pulled away from him, frightened by his intensity and stunned by his touch, even more by the way she understood it. When she spoke, her words were husky and slurred. "I am witch enough for now, Jeremy Hughes. Please . . . leave be."

"As you will, mistress," he said softly, his eyes like bottomless dark seas flecked with sunglow, "but be ready to speak those lines by five of the clock, and to be prompter, candle snuffer and gatekeep to earn your share."

She opened her mouth to ask if he didn't want her to sweep the courtyard and muck the stable, too, but he put a finger to stop her lips, and shook his head. "Kit, all players have more than one duty to perform. You must learn that well."

He left her, with the taste of his finger on her lips and the scent of him on her burning face, buried in the pages of her role, knowing more than he had before she'd read aloud to him. Not about her—she remained a mystery—but about himself. Aye, she was beautiful, but she was more. There was something separate in her that he could not reach, that he longed to touch and yet feared, knowing that it could most surely make him a captive, when as a man he must be free and master.

In all his thirty years, he had loved many women, had dallied and made love to them and, when he'd turned jilt, left them with many merry memories. Not a one had kept him sleepless, regreting, yearning and wishing he could begin anew as a different man in her eyes. Not a one until two days gone. His hand dropped to his side and he gripped his rapier hilt. He must beware. He had worked too long for the place Lord Rochester had promised him in his new London theater venture to risk all now. And for a woman who despised him more each day.

Kit watched him walk away, imagined the play of muscles under his doublet and saw them along his calves, the smell of him still enveloping her, the sound of his voice echoing in her head. She grasped the pages of her part as if to keep from falling, and as soon as he was out of sight, ran to her room to rest herself from a kind of exhaustion that made breathing rapid and difficult.

Alain came later and insisted on helping Kit to kohl her eyes and redden her lips with cochineal dye. He drew a hag's wrinkles on her skin, praising its silken texture, and seemed to be merrier doing so than she had thus far seen him. "I'm playing Duncan, Banquo and his ghost, but I will be nearby if you need me." He placed his hands on her shoulders and looked close. "Cry mercy, Keet. You are still a most beautiful witch! You will cast a spell on all the men in the village."

She laughed and impulsively kissed his cheek. Alain seemed to make her laugh without jest or jape, just by being himself. "I will this night be three witches such as Beelzebub himself would applaud."

"And Jeremy admire?" Alain said, with his Frenchman's shrug. His laughter rang all the way down the inn stairs as he went to rehearse.

Shutting out all distractions, Kit practiced in front of a small mirror for the rest of the afternoon, changing her expression with the words she read until she was satisfied that she would not disgrace herself in front of Jeremy Hughes. When she arrived in the inn yard, scenery cloths had been draped to form wings on both stairs running up to the outside gallery. A line of candles in reflecting holders had been set across the yard to separate the forestage from the benches in the pit. Jeremy was everywhere, showing her the promptbook to use as a prompter stationed under the stairs, where to stand as doorkeep to collect the crowd's shillings, and staring at her face without commenting on Alain's work.

The next two hours were the busiest Kit had ever spent. Not even cousin Joan could issue as many orders in so short a time as Jeremy Hughes. After turning her hand to several tasks, she stood at the inn yard's coach entrance and called out in a loud voice that would have brought a reprimand from her childhood nurse, "One shilling, the pit; sixpence, the gallery!" And yet half the people asked again, "What cost?" digging under their doublets and withdrawing their coins from pockets tied about their waists. The town constable and his lady wife, or so he announced loudly, demanded free admittance, and Jeremy, passing nearby, already wearing his crown and robe as Macbeth, bowed them in.

Kit whispered, "I thought you did say all must pay."

"Aye, but it is good to seat the town law, as his presence keeps the ruffians and sharpers from hectoring the players overmuch. In London that is a greater sport than the cockfight."

"It seems a poor profession to me, this playacting," she said, handing him the bag of coins she'd collected.

"If you do think so after tonight, then it will not do for you." He was away in a swirl of robes before she could answer that she had no desire to think one way or another.

Alain came to fetch her while Jeremy was speaking the prologue to a crowded pit. "Don't worry, Keet, you will be wonderful and frighten the poor villagers to pray harder for their souls this Sabbath."

Kit was amazed at the quaking in her knees as she entered the stage alone, her cloak pulled about her head, wisps of black wig going in every direction. The scenery cloth to her back showed a distant castle on a darkling plain, the same that she had hidden beneath in the wagon as Jeremy's captive. A large pot from the inn kitchen stood before her, a wooden paddle across the top. She dared not look at the audience for fear she would take fright and run as far as her weak legs would carry her. Surely, the constable was watching and would soon wonder who this poor player was. Anon, the thought of the gibbet steadied her.

Alain beat with his hands upon a large barrel over which was stretched a cow's skin, making a passable sound of thunder, although the sun still shown, as she began to speak.

> *"When shall we three meet again*
> *In thunder, lighting, or in rain?"*

She did not need to make her voice to croak. It did so without any urging from her. And as she stirred the pot, she swayed over it, her stomach roiling. Nor did she remember later how she exited.

Jeremy stood just behind the wing, waiting to make his entrance, and he made move to come to her, but she turned away as if she didn't see him. She could not bare his scrutiny now, for she would, she must, be a better witch for the next scene. She quickly read over her lines, praying she would remember them.

At the sound of thunder, Kit took a deep breath and started to step forward, only to feel hands on her back give her a mighty shove, which sent her reeling toward the candlelights, where she sprawled flat against the ground. People on the front benches in the pit leaned back as one, and for a moment Kit could not think what to do. She glanced to where she'd stood and saw Lucy smirking. A townsman before her began to laugh, and soon others took it up.

Anger flooded through her, and a determination to take all satisfaction from Lucy gave her legs new strength. She staggered to her feet, croaking and swaying stage left and right, throwing curses about, and the laughter turned to silence as she spoke her witch's charm. She began to feel a kind of strange truth in those lines. She had been pretending for the sake of others since she'd been a young girl of fourteen parted from all she'd ever known or loved. Now she would pretend for herself! Her cape clutched about her, she exited at stage right, and Jeremy and Alain came on. Lucy was not in sight.

Martha cavorted between acts, crudely taunting the other actors who sang or declaimed, becoming more riotous with each entrance, obviously much removed from the kitchen maid she'd so recently been. Jeremy sang with Lucy between the second and third acts, and Kit felt a pang of envy that he'd not asked her again, but she quickly thrust it from her mind. She settled 'neath the staircase with the promptbook and cued the actors, watching them, even Lucy, noting what moves and gestures they made and what changes of voice they assumed to indicate certain emotions. By the time she entered the stage for the last time in act IV, she was surprised at how eager she was to say her words with Jeremy as Macbeth. He gave her direction with his eyes, seeming to pull the right lines from her, and she found that his and hers wove together in an intricate dance of words.

When she came forward with the others to bow before Jeremy's announcement of the next evening's performance, the rude shouts and applause directed at her gave her more pleasure than anything she could remember. A hand took hers, and Jeremy led her to the front and bowed with her curtsy. "You did well, Kit," he said in her ear. "You did not stop the play because you fell."

"I did not fall," Kit said through her teeth as she continued to curtsy.

He caught her as the audience began to leave through the

inn's gate or enter the inn for refreshment at the innkeeper's urging. "I know you did not fall, but that is not important."

She stared at him openmouthed. "It is to me, sir."

"No, it is not. What is important is that you continued in character no matter what happened. The play was the chiefest thing to you, and that tells me you are an actress born."

She did not answer him because he had set up enormous confusion in her mind. The daughter of Sir Robert Lindsay of Rosevere, an actress, no better in most men's minds than a whore, displaying herself on the stage . . . no, it could not be! She did not dare to desire such disgrace. And yet she did.

With the troupe, Kit and Martha shared a light supper of hot pottage, cold mutton pie and a thick custard. It was a merry table now that all had food in their bellies and money in their pockets. Martha and Kit received five shillings each, which they hid in their bundles before going to bed. Kit wondered when Lucy would join them, and prepared what she would say if the actress taunted her, but Lucy was heard first in the gallery outside their room.

"You cannot mean it, Jemmy!"

"I do mean it, Lucy. She will need training, but I want to try her in a comedy role to match her wit. Didn't you hear the music we made in that act four scene? I think maybe *A Mad Couple Well Matched* or some such with quarreling lovers."

"Jemmy, I will not be so humiliated!"

"Lucy, there is none intended. You are a great actress of tragedy. Content yourself with that. There will be roles to spare when we return to London and the theaters reopen, if the plague is indeed at last gone."

Their voices faded with their footsteps, though Kit lay

awake for some time, hoping to hear more or for Lucy to come to bed. One idea filled her: Jeremy thought she had done well, and she believed him. Finally, she slept from exhaustion and exhilaration, repeating the play in her dreams, only it was her voice playing all the roles to thunderous applause.

Kit woke to bed curtains thrown open on the other side to a bright July morning. She knew she had slept late. If Lucy had been to the bed, she had come late and left early, or she and Jeremy had ceased to quarrel and . . . Kit shook herself and did not go further with that thought. Nor did she allow herself to examine why she did not. What Jeremy did or did not do with his woman was nothing to her, and if it was, she refused to allow it. She refused to allow it until her brain hurt. Martha was already up and gone to break her fast, leaving a fresh water pitcher and bowl for Kit to wash. She did so, and sponged the dust from her red wool dress before donning it.

As Kit descended the stairs from the gallery, all the troupe greeted her with upturned faces but no smiles of greeting. Martha's face, still bearing the evidences of white Harlequin paint, was tear-streaked. "What ails you, Martha?" she called.

"Come down, thief!" Lucy yelled in a voice that carried to all the inn's patrons, who put down their tankards to enjoy the scene.

Jeremy pointed to Lucy. "Leave be, madame. I am master here."

Kit reached the table and put her arm around Martha. Martha didn't look at her. "I am no thief," Kit said to Jeremy. "Lucy has shoved me once; I will not allow her to do it twice."

"Then explain this!" Lucy said, her voice triumphant. She threw Martha's pocket to the table and it clinked heavily, spilling at least two dozen coins.

"I can't explain it. I know nothing of this money."

"You stole it as doorkeep and meant to get away today. She stole it from us all," Lucy said, looking at the grim-faced men watching her.

A fury seized Kit and she wanted to do a hurt to the lying woman. "I am no thief, I say. I do not know how the money came to be in Martha's pocket. We had five shillings each. Perhaps you should ask the woman who found it."

Lucy drew herself up to medium height and said in her Lady Macbeth voice: "The clever minx now accuses me. She may be witch in truth."

An older actor, his lined tragedian's face somber, coughed. "I do not know the right of this, Jeremy, but we cannot have a player we do not trust with our earnings."

"Lucy has been with us all the summer, and knows all the women's roles," said another.

"Wait!" Alain leaped to his feet. "Monsieur Jeremy, you must stop this. You cannot—"

Jeremy held up his hand for silence, his eyes most troubled. "Mistress Kit, has there been some mistake? Did you mean to give me the money and forget?"

"No."

Lucy pounced. "Ah, she admits to thievery."

Kit looked at Jeremy, her mouth a thin, straight line. "I tell you that I never had the money! I gave all to you last night and had but my five shillings when I went to sleep." She would tell no more than the truth and would never plead for Jeremy Hughes's help.

Lucy sneered. "There is no truth in the hoyden, Jemmy. Call the town constable."

"Quiet, Lucy. There will be no constable called. Mistress Kit has talents she has shown us and—"

Lucy did not stop for breath. "Thieves *must* go at once, Jemmy," Lucy said, triumph writ on her face.

"So say you all?" Jeremy asked, his face showing nothing.

There was no hesitation. All heads nodded their agreement.

Chapter Six

To London Town

Martha was still sniffing back tears when they reached the Harwich-London road an hour's hard walk out of Basildon. Kit had tried to quiet, then ignore Martha, but could no longer. "Stay your tears," she said gently. "We are better out of that woman's way. She did wish me great harm and would have taken you down, as well."

"But I be not a Harlequin now. I have no place of my own."

Kit squeezed Martha's arm. "You have five shillings, ten between us, and we will eat until we reach London town."

Martha brightened at the thought. "Aye, we be the better for our playacting, at least in our pocket. They be not taking what we rightly earned. Master Jeremy would not allow that." She sighed. "He be a most generous man, but he has only kindness for me, mistress. It be you he wants." And she sighed again.

"Don't jest, Martha. I met the man scarce two days gone and we have said not two civil words."

"It be not words I saw, but what be between man and

woman," Martha said, her voice showing some pique. "I be a kitchen maid, and a mean cottager afore, but I am a woman with eyes and know to use them."

Kit tightened her grip on Martha's arm and set her own gaze on the road, trying to block from her mind all thoughts of Jeremy Hughes and any other man who would be her master. The sun was now high overhead, a wafting breeze ruffling her long hair, free of its wig and seeming to dance on the air for joy. But that was all the joy she felt, for she had once again taken the measure of the man, who it seemed would sacrifice her again and again for a few coins. For a too-brief moment she had allowed herself to remember the scent of him as he'd held her in the inn yard, his hard body against hers, the magnificent planes of his face becoming Macbeth in truth before her eyes. . . . But, oh, not so, dear Lord of blessed name. She must deny that she had ever thought thus or had the least womanly interest in that rogue player and his tempting tongue. She was well away from him.

Kit reluctantly pulled the cowl of her cloak over her hair to hide its bright color. Best she remember that the sheriff and his men might still be on the roads, and now she was where they would expect her to be.

She stepped along faster. If Sir William yet lived, he would never find her in London town, for it was said to house near half a million souls, some fewer after the plague of last summer, but still a great number she could scarcely imagine in one place. London would hide her well, or nowhere would.

Minutes later, Kit heard shouting and a galloping horse behind them, and they quickly ran from the road to hide behind a grove of black poplar trees as a rider breasted the rise.

It was Alain, calling Kit's name, and they walked out to meet him.

He was breathing heavily. "Thank *le bon Dieu*!" he said, crossing himself, the reins flopping in his hand. He jumped down from his horse, gave Martha a loud buss, and kissed Kit soundly on both cheeks, not once, but twice.

"Alain, you are crushing me!" she said, hardly knowing what to think. "What do you here?"

"I am but a post rider and have two letters for you," he said, handing her two white folded sheets withdrawn somewhat crumpled from his beribboned wine velvet doublet, slashed to show a wondrous soft shirt. The first letter with a red wax seal was addressed to Master George Jolly. The other was addressed simply: *To Mistress Kit*. Recognizing Jeremy's hand from the lines she'd studied, she almost destroyed it, but the look on Alain's face stopped her.

With a deep sigh, wondering if she would ever be free of this player who had seemingly become part of her life whether she wished it or no, she opened her letter, and seeing there was no greeting, read silently:

I do believe and know that you were in the right of it, and are no thief, but I must hold these players together for the good of the many, including yourself, and you were too spirited of both body and mind to escape my regard, or the enmity of Mrs. Wylie, and therefore the disruption of this company.

In the accompanying letter, I have applied to my friend and teacher George Jolly to add you to the company in training for my lord Rochester's new theater in London, for which he hopes to gain a warrant from the king. Alain has further instructions and monies for your safekeeping, and has fewer faults than

Your obedient, etc.
Jeremy Hughes

She folded the letter and thrust it warm into her bodice, her hands trembling, her mind in turmoil, many of her sureties gone, except one. . . . She would meet Jeremy Hughes again and she would needs prepare for what such a meeting could hold. But she refused to think on it now, and with a deep sigh looked a question at Alain.

"I'm coming with you, Keet. My sword is at *votre service*," he said, his hand sliding to his sword hilt as he made an exaggerated stage bow that would have done the king's court an honor and was near a match of Jeremy Hughes's.

"No, Alain. I cannot accept kindness at such cost to you. You do not know how great my troubles are."

"Mam'selle, you have no choice. I am here, and here I stay beside you. Have you so many friends that you do not need one more? I do not see them." And here he pretended to look under a giggling Martha's skirt and behind the horse. Then he smiled and raised an eyebrow, as only a Frenchman could. "And I have missed the coffeehouses in London, and my tailors," he said, straightening the lace at his throat, "and would see what new fashions have come from my homeland." He grinned broadly at her. "To be badly worn by Englishmen."

He handed first Kit and then Martha up onto the horse and began walking briskly down the road, holding the reins. "Alain," Kit said, watching his slender form striding ahead, "is this your idea or Jeremy Hughes's?" She had to know.

"I do think we came to it together," Alain answered, not breaking stride or looking back, "for we are both quite in love with you, Keet, only I submit to my love and Jeremy denies his. But these are the only two ways a man can love. All or none, *n'est-ce pas?*"

Involuntarily, Kit shook her head. Loving a man meant submission, dominance and the loss of her will. It was the last thing she wanted. Yet she was not threatened by Alain's love, nor angry, perhaps because she sensed his love demanded only friendship from her, while Jeremy's would demand and take all. Friendship she could easily give the sweet Frenchman, while love she could not, would not give to . . . Kit deliberately routed the name that was on her lips, whispering to Martha, "It is only fair that we tell Alain what danger he may be submitting to." Martha nodded.

"Alain, Martha and I are wanted by the sheriff of Essex County for a hanging crime. You have a right to know before you are taken as accomplice."

Alain didn't break stride. "I knew that Jeremy was hiding you, but I thought you'd run away from a husband who beat you. Surely, that is no crime for the gibbet unless it be for the bastard wife beater."

Kit smiled because Alain used English curses instead of profaning his beloved French, and for the next mile or two, she told him her story. How Sir William Pursevant had secured her father's estate from Cromwell's Committee of Sequestration, had the estate confirmed by the restored king, appropriated her dowry, treated her as a servant, and finally violated her in her own bed. Martha took up the story and told how she'd come upon her master raping Kit and broke his head, after which both had run away, leaving him for dead, and only later learning he still lived.

Alain stopped the horse and looked up at Kit, frowning. "How did Jeremy find you?"

Kit recited the story of being captured near the wooded stream surrendered to the constable at Chelmsford and then rescued again and spirited away. . . . All by the same man.

They left the road to allow an overloaded hay wain to pass.

"So if you wish to return to—" Kit began, but Alain dismissed her words with a wave of his hand, gilt lace like yellow froth at his wrists. "Nonsense, Keet, I will write a play of this tale one day." His face was alive with the possibilities. "And I have my two principal actors already in my mind. Come, we have far to travel today before we stop for a night's lodging. Then I do wish to come into London town tomorrow before the dark."

And so they did, passing the hamlet of Mile End and the gardens stretching on either side of the Harwich road at dusk, then on through Whitechapel and Spittalfields, the low rumble of city noises, smell of smoke and the rankness of the Thames River at low tide reaching out to greet them. The Tower loomed to their left; St. Paul's single spire ahead. On into the narrow, crowded alleys off Cheapside they rode, shops and houses with two or three jettied stories leaning against and toward each other, whole streets in like embrace.

Exhausted, Kit was relieved when Alain stopped at the Lion's Head on Milk Lane for supper and a room. Behind her, the Bow bells rang for vespers and the end of the work day. "'Allo, innkeeper," Alain called to the frowning owner in the crowded common room.

"Frenchman, you owe me six shillings these five months, so I will wait for the sound of your coin before you hear the sound of my greeting."

Alain laughed and poured coins onto the table. "Two of your best rooms, innkeep, and a supper for these ladies, and none of your English mutton, but a good beef pie with cheese and tea."

"And ale," Martha added. "I be fair dry to the bone. And a black pudding?" she added hopefully.

Alain nodded, and soon they were eating for the first time since bread and ale broke their morning's fast.

Kit looked at the repast and was troubled. "I am in your debt, Alain, for any monies you spend. I will repay you every farthing when I am able."

"You repay me with your presence, *ma belle*," he said, smiling, and Kit could see no deceit behind his natural charm. But she still determined he would not suffer in his purse for her, nor would Jeremy Hughes. A moment of fear and exasperation caught at her. She had scarce made her vow to have no male master, and here she was, beholden to two men. She must earn her own way in the future or be slave to any man who could pay, and that she would never be.

"This is my first China drink," Kit said, sipping the hot, slightly bittersweet brew from its bowl. "It is most calming and, I do hear, good for the digestion." She leaned her head against the high-backed settle, the events of the last few days almost overwhelming her mind.

Alain bowed in his chair. "I will remember that, Keet. You may have need of both curatives in the coming weeks while you are in training with Master George Jolly, who keeps a 'nursery' for young players. That gentleman is a most exacting teacher, since he did once play the woman's role himself as a youth, even Will Shakespeare's Cleopatra. Tomorrow we will present ourselves at Master Jolly's with your letter of introduction."

"Alain, do you truly believe I can . . ." She could not finish the thought that had been never far from her mind since she first played the witch, lest he tell her something she could not bear to hear.

"*Oui*," he said, grinning. "I do think you can play the woman *almost* as well as I, myself, and Jeremy is sure you are an actress born. You have never learned to hide your emotions from your face, as do most people, and that is the beginning."

"Jeremy is sure." She tucked that information away to think on later. "But what if I am discovered by a constable?"

"In costume? With face whitened, your cheeks red and a towering wig? *Non*, mam'selle, I think not. And when you go abroad, you must go masked and cloaked as half the ladies in London do in the streets. As well, the town is full of thieves and rogues of every kind, enough to keep all the parish constables as busy as they want to be."

That night just before Kit fell into the deepest sleep of many restless nights, Martha, at her side, whispered in her ear. "There be no place for me in this new life, Mistress Kit."

"We will find a place for you," Kit said sleepily, as moonlight flooded through the large oriel window overhanging Milk Street. But when Kit awoke, Martha and her basket were gone, although Kit's five shillings were in a neat pile on the chest next to the candleholder.

Alain was waiting for her as she raced down the stairs. Before Kit could speak, he nodded, "*Oui*, she's gone to find work in a scullery."

"But she loved being a Harlequin."

"Keet, she could play the rude role in the provinces, but the theater in London is about witty comedy and drama. Even the farce is well acted. She cannot read, and she does not have beauty, good skin and good teeth." He looked saddened. "I did tell her the truth when she asked. Lying to give false hope, *ma chere*, is too cruel."

Kit started for the door. "Yet she has much of courage and friendship, which I value above all else. I will go after her."

Alain took her arm firmly in his. "She said she will find you when she has a place. I think she has her own pride. You, mam'selle, of all women, should understand such pride."

He was right, of course, and that was another strange thing about Alain. Silly and vain he was, but he also had an ability to see beyond apparent things. She was surprised to realize that Jeremy Hughes had some of that second sight, as well, seeming to know what was in her mind before she herself did. Perhaps it was an actor's skill, and she would discover it, too. It would do her no harm to know what was behind Jeremy's handsome face when they met again. No harm at all.

And so out into the cool morning air Alain and Kit went, as the city came fully alive. They walked west through ranks of 'prentice boys sent on their master's errands, along dirty, narrow streets where everything was for sale, shops had goods heaped on shutters made into tables, jostling milkmaids were yoked to pails, a flock of geese foraged in the gutter, and a woman cried her ripe cherries at four pence a pound. Thence they walked on to Ludgate Hill and into the Strand, passing palace after palace on the Thames side, and on toward Covent Garden and Master Jolly's house in Bedford Street. They also passed an early-morning cart collecting the bodies of plague dead.

"The black death is still with us," Alain said, crossing

himself and drawing an angry hiss of "Papist!" from a severely dressed passerby.

Kit shivered at the red-painted cross marked on a sealed door. "But the king and his court returned months ago."

"*Oui*, because not as many die as last summer, which was the greatest plague year ever anyone remembers, but still the carts go every day to the common graves outside the city."

He bought a penny bunch of violets from a flower seller. "Here," he said, handing her half the bunch, "hold this to your nose so that you won't breathe in the foul vapors which carry plague."

In that more pleasant way, they came to Master Jolly's house, and knocking on the door, presented the steward with the letter from Jeremy introducing Kit.

They were shown into a large paneled withdrawing room under a fine coffered ceiling with manuscript pages piled about on every flat surface. A fire burned in a brazier, which was being fed Jeremy's letter by a slender, small-boned, older man who thirty years gone could have looked very much like Alain.

Chapter Seven

She Could and She Did

Allo, Monsieur Jolly," Alain said, and the two bowed in greeting. "I hope you did not burn the letter before you read it."

"Nay, I respect Jeremy Hughes's judgment next to my lord Rochester's when it comes to feminine beauty. Tell me, madame," he said, taking in the whole of Kit in one quick glance, while she wished mightily for the satin gown she'd left behind on a peg at Bournely, "what do you upon the stage?"

"I am unmarried and not madame, sir."

"In the theater," he said in a decisive tone not to be questioned, "all women are advertised as married."

"Why?" Kit asked. If this man was to be her teacher, she must be able to ask for reasons behind such pronouncements.

"It is our custom, and that is all you need to know." Since her face showed him no acceptance, he shrugged and continued, "I imagine for their safety and reputations, women must be seen to have a master, although it does them precious little good with the gentlemen of the pit. But . . . er, mistress, you are here to answer *my* questions."

She was taller than he and took advantage by standing even taller. "I will, sir, as long as you answer mine, since you are the teacher."

He stared up at her, but there was more interest than disapproval on his face. "Again, mistress, what roles have you played?" he asked, and settled himself into a large baronial upholstered chair, waving Alain to a stool, while Kit remained standing before him like a supplicant, for which she had no liking.

"I have played in masques that I wrote myself, and the witches in *Macbeth* . . . all three at once," Kit replied, not entirely comfortable with Master Jolly's sharp-eyed scrutiny, although she rather liked his blunt speech because she was not left to guess at his meaning.

"That is all. . . . Just the one Shakespeare role?"

"Yes, Master Jolly. I was with the strolling players for a single performance only."

At that, Jolly's eyebrows arched high and remained so. "My dear, you did, indeed, make a great impression on Jeremy Hughes." He looked to Alain for more information, but receiving none, handed Kit some close-written pages.

"Read these lines for me."

Kit saw that the pages were a scene from Mr. Dryden's *The Wild Gallant*, a comic marriage bargain, which she had read in chapbook. She cleared her throat and began to read both male and female parts, changing her voice and tone, trying to remember everything that Jeremy had told her and that she had observed.

Master Jolly stopped her in midscene. "Do you understand what you are saying?"

"Yes, they forsee the pitfalls of marriage and the loss of freedom. I understand the scene right well, and I agree with it, sir."

"Indeed! Then why do you take such an unpleasant tone when I do perceive you to have a musical ear. You must seize the passion behind every word and translate that into the manner of the characters. Try it again."

After she had read the scene thrice over, Jolly correcting her incessantly, she asked in exasperation, "How many times would you have me do this?"

"If you are to learn enough for the London stage, then ten times ten, if needs be." His face softened, seeing she needed, yet again, more explanation than he was used to giving. "I am determining, Mistress Kit, whether you can be taught, and when taught, can learn."

Her voice suddenly quivered with stored tension. "And what have you determined, Master Jolly?"

"That you read well and Jeremy Hughes was right to send you to me. You are quite ravishing. Not even Nell Gwyn has your beauty of face and form. With training you may do for minor roles as soon as the theaters open in September, and with experience perhaps make a living, if you find a protector."

"A protector!" Kit said, her voice rising well beyond the polite supplicant's. "You do mistake me, sir. I have had protectors, yea, who used me for their own ends. Now I will have no other protector in this life." Her voice quivered and angry tears filled her eyes, overflowing them. She swiped them away as if affronted by them and stepped toward Master Jolly, who drew back with what looked like alarm on his face. "Do not be fearful, sir. I use no force, as your sex does." She bent down, her voice lower and heavy with a profoundly weary disappointment. "I have read Shakespeare, Dryden and Molière, and thought such words and tender emotion made truth flow from the stage." Realizing she was too close, she straightened and stepped back. "Thank you, sir, for setting me aright. This is no school for actors of truth, but a school for whores and liars, and I will have none of it."

Kit turned abruptly and stalked for the door, her hand reaching blindly for the latch, when she heard Master Jolly speak.

"Huzzah, mistress!" he said quietly, and applauded from where he sat. "Jeremy Hughes was true in his judgment. If you perform that scene at the Theater Royal, you will have all London prostrate at your feet."

Alain, who had been rooted where he sat, jumped up and reached her, smiling. "I was sure of it, Keet," he said, kissing her hand and squeezing it companionably.

"There is another question, Master Jolly," Kit announced.

He cocked one eyebrow. "I am not at all surprised, mistress."

"How will I pay you for your teaching me?"

Both eyebrows rose again in his expressive face. "Jeremy has made those arrangements. . . . But I do suspect you wish to change them now."

She raised her chin even higher, her hair falling in curling masses across her shoulders, the light from the brazier setting off sparks of gold. "If you are indeed as good teacher as I am told, then you will wait upon my successful employment, when I will gladly pay your price with good interest."

Jolly tied a blue ribbon around the pages Kit had read and gave them back to her. "There are three lengths of forty-two lines each that you must learn tonight. You will need to learn long parts in two or three days if you are to be an actress, so best to begin."

"Then I am accepted."

"It would be safe to assume so, mistress," he said, while ushering Kit and Alain out the door with no further ceremony. "Tomorrow you will be at my door by eight of the morning clock."

"Yes, Master Jolly," she said, somewhat meekly, as the door closed behind her.

On the stoop, Alain turned his sweet face to Kit, shrugging his elegant shoulders. "You do constantly amaze. Is there any better reason to love you?"

"Aye, Alain," Kit said softly. "In hope of love's return."

"*Non,* Keet. You mistake me. I love what is most beautiful for no return . . . usually," he said, chuckling, although there was some different pain behind his laugh.

They walked back the way they'd come an hour earlier, arm in arm, Alain continuing to shake his head and sigh. "That was a great performance, lady."

"Thank you," she said, a small smile playing upon her lips. "It was the only way I could convince him."

Alain stopped so suddenly, he nearly tripped on a cobble, amazement growing on his face, his mouth opening and closing without his usual ability to find the right words in either of his languages. So not finding them, he laughed aloud, throwing his head back, and doing a small pirouette, so infectious that half the people in the street began to laugh with him, including Kit.

Jeremy Hughes climbed wearily to the gallery of the Bull and Ram, wondering in his mind, as he had done all the day. Had Kit, Martha and Alain reached London town? Had all gone well with them? All had not gone well with his players. Lucy had kept them riled, and shillings from their performances had kept them drunk so that he feared their days as strolling players were near done for this season. One more performance in Basildon, perhaps one more town after, and then away to London earlier than planned with all the theaters still closed, until the weather cooled and the plague subsided. He tried to convince himself that he was abandoning the road from necessity, but a nagging voice in his head said otherwise. "Kit," he admitted aloud, for she had not left his thoughts for any two minutes together.

"She has indeed bewitched you, Jemmy," Lucy said, stepping from a gallery shadow, her still-pretty face now twisted with jealousy.

"Lucy, you drove her away. Be satisfied with your victory," he said, reaching the landing to face her although he had rather be alone.

"Never, until we are as we were before that woman so distracted you." She walked into him, her body pressed against his length, and entwined her arms around his neck, then slipped one hand inside his loosened shirt to play against his nipple, tilting her head back for his kiss. "Jemmy, my love, let me give you what you long for. . . . You know you want it." She pushed her female parts even closer, and her breathing was deep and rapid.

He couldn't disagree with her. He did indeed long to kiss a lovely lass in his bed, to mount her, holding her wide gaze with his until the scorn slowly turned to hot, pleading passion, to dote on her, to feel . . . Ah, he could not think further on it without starting a delicious pain in his cod, and so he must not think about it at all. He would do anything to get the woman out of his head, to be once again as he had been, a man of . . . well, a man who took a woman, gave her pleasure, then moved on, still master of himself.

Jeremy firmly grasped Lucy's frantic arms and pulled them away from him, holding them firmly to her side while she struggled. "I'm sorry, Lucy. I never promised you more than a summer's pleasure."

"There was more; there had to be more."

"No, Lucy, I never lied to you." He took a deep breath and tried to smile. "Perhaps I am bewitched, but you do not have the physic against it. I doubt any doctor in the kingdom does."

With a wrench, Lucy freed herself, shaking with rage, her face flushed, her red lips pulled into the most fearsome grimace. "You will pay mightily for this affront, and so will your paramour. I do swear it as I live!" She left him, flinging herself into her room. Later he heard the crash of objects being thrown against the walls, and she continued to make a terrible racket for some time.

Jeremy worked in his room until the next afternoon, when he did need to prepare for the final performance of *Macbeth* in Basildon, which had grown to be a hectic thing with Alain and Kit gone. He had cut and patched the play to give actors time to come offstage to answer their next cues as different characters. They were tripping over their own selves coming and going.

Lucy, who could play Lady Macbeth in her sleep, had trouble with her lines from the first scene. Jeremy saw each time she looked at him that she lost her words in high anger. They struggled through to act II and then to scene two, after Macbeth had murdered Duncan. Lucy gripped a dagger and spoke, and he would not have been surprised if fire and smoke had issued from her mouth:

"Why did you bring these daggers from the place?
They must lie there: go carry them, and smear . . ."

Jeremy saw she had lost her way and seemed almost blinded, so he picked up her part and his, as well, giving her a warning look:

"You want me to smear the sleeping grooms with blood.
I'll go no more:
I am afraid. . . ."

Lucy rushed at him, and he felt the white-hot thrust of the knife in his shoulder. He cried out as she pulled the dagger out, then grabbed her wrist, struggling with her before she could deliver another blow. The audience applauded this unexpected violence, thinking it some new trick in the old play. "Heed me, Lucy," Jeremy said between clenched teeth. "Finish the play, then ever leave me be, or I will see you shamed before all London as a jilted woman and poor player."

Staunching the blood with his handkercher, he played out the last scenes even to the end.

One of the troupe helped Jeremy to his bed and applied a hot compress of red cloth to his throbbing shoulder. "It will draw out the black humors," the actor said, not knowing what else to do. "I can inquire if there is a doctor in the town."

"No!" Jeremy struggled to his feet, weaving a bit, and bundled his clothes using one hand. "The troupe is yours. I can do no more. You can divide my share for tonight's performance and the scenery cloths, and I will take one of the horses in payment. But I do warn you to keep watch on Lucy, for I think her gone completely crazed."

Lucy was nowhere to be seen when Jeremy descended the Bull and Ram's stairs and went into the stable yard to meet the innkeeper, who was accepting a letter from the London post rider. "It's for you, sir," the innkeep said, holding out the sealed and folded sheet.

Jeremy quickly read the message, noting the inn where Alain, Martha and Kit were staying, and with a final, "God keep you," mounted and made for the London road, his horse happily stretching out its legs after days in the stall. With one last backward glance, he thought he saw Lucy standing in the inn yard gate, her fist raised high, but he could not be certain because a chill caught him even in the summer sunlight, and he reached to pull his cloak tighter.

Within a few hours, a fever was upon him, but he rode on through the night, stopping only to water and feed the horse, berating himself along the miles that he had given Lucy so much cause to hate him. In truth, he had never loved her, but that had not made so much difference to him ere now. How could this woman, this hunted woman, this Kit, with her airs and scorn, make him turn from the woman in his bed, who desired him, to one who despised him? He continued in this way, mile upon mile, and the confusion in his mind kept him going when any ordinary man would have fallen from his horse to lie in a swale by the side of the road. Jeremy reached the Lion's Head in Milk Lane early the next morning to find Alain and Kit merrily breaking their fast with dishes of tea and honey-dipped bread.

"Greetings, Alain, Mistress Kit. No, don't let me disturb you," he said, staggering to their table, sweeping his hat before him and collapsing on the floor after it, blood starting afresh from his wound. "Now, mistress, you must admit," he said, looking up into her astonished face with a smile that contained much of its old bravado, "I am not wanting for a most dramatic entrance." And then he could speak no more.

Chapter Eight

The Beau Attraction

Jeremy was carried to Alain's upstairs room in a faint, waking to curse once when roughly handled, but at last he was in the bed under the eaves with a sloping ceiling so low, Kit, following closely, bent over to save her head. She could not take her eyes from his white face and dark hair, in stark contrast to the red blood on his shirt, the stain still spreading.

Alain cut away Jeremy's shirt, as tenderly as a mother, and ripping one of his own fine lace-point shirts, pressed it against the wound. "Keet, I must go for a doctor," he said, his voice shaking. "You'll stay?"

"Yes," she said, not taking her eyes from Jeremy Hughes. Once again he had come into her life and changed it. Master Jolly was expecting her, and if she did not arrive at the agreed hour, he would not be happy with her excuses.

Then let him be unhappy! She used the rest of the shirt, dipping it in a bowl of Alain's scented shaving water, to wipe Jeremy's face, which was so hot it frightened her, his dark stubble of beard catching at the linen threads. She could not forsake the player, no matter how ill he had used her. Indeed, she realized with a start, she could not remember what had once angered her so.

As Alain clambered noisily down the stairs, Jeremy groaned and Kit took his hand to comfort him. His long fingers curled around hers, strong even without consciousness. "Kit," he murmured in his deep sleep, or she thought he did, and her heart beat faster, near to leaping from her breast.

"I'm here, Jeremy." He had reached her soul with that one word. She held on to his hand for some time, murmuring words of comfort, singing softly the song they'd sung together in what seemed long ago. The sounds came from some deep, untouched place in her heart, while she watched the pain pass across his face, studying his features more closely than she had ever allowed herself to do. He was even more handsome in every part than she had realized, and she had realized much. His wide shoulders sloped to a narrow waist, and when he turned slightly in his fever she could see the beginning curve of his tightly muscled buttocks. In all, he gave much appearance of strength without anything of the brute. God's nails! She had been in the wrong about that. His face could have been chiseled by an ancient Greek sculptor, so perfect in proportion was it. His mouth now in repose, the waking grin that so often pulled it wide and so infuriated her, was replaced by something more at ease, at once more fully sensual and deeply gentle. She bent to him, drawn by a sudden, helpless urge to kiss that mouth, when his head rolled from side to side in agitation, and from deep in his chest a hoarse, broken cry erupted: "Lu-cy!"

Kit dropped his hand and jumped away from the bed, as if the name were a sharp blow intended to kill or at least maim. While she cared for him to her detriment, he wanted only that false accuser. On her honor, she would make no more mistakes with him if she lived forever!

Alain opened the door, narrowly missing Kit in the small room. A very short man in an enormous three-tailed wig came after him, wearing a doctor's dark gown with signs of the zodiac embroidered on it. He went to the bed and laid out his instrument roll, inspecting the wound, announcing as he went, "Doctor Josiah Wyndham, member of the Royal Society and graduate of the University of Padua, specializing in all manner of puncture wounds. These young gallants will have their duels." He looked at Kit. "Are you his wife, madame?"

"No, physician, I am not," she answered, perhaps a bit too haughtily.

The doctor noted the hauteur, and his round face beamed. "You will see blood, mistress, so if you are the fainting kind, depart now."

This time Alain answered for her. "She is not the fainting kind, Monsieur *le Docteur.*"

"Then I will bleed him to bring down his fever by drawing down the heated blood to cool the residue in his vessels, and to bring his four humors to a proper balance. Do you know if he was born under Sagittarius? Oh, surely not Aquarius. The water bearer is a bad sign for bleeding."

Alain shook his head at every question, and the doctor harrumphed, "If I knew his astrologic nativity, I could better treat him."

Without the planets and stars, Kit watched as the doctor

cut a vein in Jeremy's arm and let blood flow into the water bowl, turning it instantly scarlet. She knew bleeding or leeching was a cure for fevers of all kinds, but she could not help but wonder at such a cure for a man who had lost much blood already. Next the doctor mixed a simple of mostly brandy, herbs and spices, and with Alain's help they sat Jeremy partway up and got some of it down his throat, although much of it ran down and into the wound, raising a great howl from the patient, and bringing him back to full, angry consciousness.

"Damn you, leech! Are you killing me?" Jeremy shouted.

"Brandy is known in many countries for preventing decay in a wound, sir, and for a gentle purge to cleanse your bowels of impurities, lest they find their way into your blood."

He also provided a bandage soaked in balsam for the wound, telling his patient to stay abed until the wound closed and the fever abated, taking nothing by mouth but meat broth and perhaps a little buttered ale.

Dr. Josiah Wyndham presented his fee, but before he took his leave he looked closely at Kit's face, although he stood on his toes to do so. "You have great beauty, mistress, and I would wish to help heal you of those faint bruises." He reopened his medical case and withdrew a small stoppered crockery jar, which he handed her with a bow. "Wyndham's Infallible Miracle Salve, mistress, used by the Countess Castlemaine and Lady Anne Gilbert, formerly of the queen's bedchamber and now mistress of Burwell Hall, celebrated beauties both, and guaranteed to give you skin fresh as country morning dew . . . with my compliments to your beauty."

Kit smiled at the little doctor, unable to decide if he was

a charlatan or no, but sensing a gentle soul under the bravado. "My thanks to you . . . most kind," she said, giving him her hand, which he kissed. "You will soon beggar yourself if you give away your medicines."

"Mistress," he said, bowing again, "the world would be beggared without your beauty."

Jeremy was still propped up in the bed as the doctor's footsteps receded. He stared at Kit with fevered eyes and she stared back, not allowing herself, in pride, to show anything on her face. "I thank you for your help, mistress. Alain will take care of my further wants. Where are my clothes? I must be on my feet ere . . ."

Although the words were halting, they were not to be misunderstood. Her head came up, and she held herself tall and straight. There was no grace to the man. He wanted only Lucy, and she was in the way. She dropped him a curtsy that bordered on discourtesy and was gone before he could read her face, and whatever it was showing of the hurt she felt but did not understand. Then she was out the door and away running into Cheapside's narrow alleys toward Master Jolly's, dodging gutters running with the morning's showers mixed with kitchen leavings or worse, thrown from windows on either side, wending through a flock of ducks awaiting a butcher's pleasure. She refused to acknowledge the tears that gathered in her eyes, preferring to think the smoke from a thousand chimneys to blame. Later, she was without any memory of leaving the Lion's Head.

In the small room under the eaves, Alain brought a bowl of broth, holding the bowl to Jeremy's mouth while he sipped. "You should sleep now," he said.

"I can hear in your voice that you think I . . . you think me a fool."

"*Mon ami,* I think you both mad enough for Bedlam withal."

Jeremy shifted on the rope bed overlain with a horsehair mattress, wincing as it scratched his back. "You may be in the right of it, but did you take her to Jolly's? Did he—"

"*Oui, oui,* Jeremy." And he repeated all that had happened, and the way that Kit had cleverly used her spirit to gain admittance.

Jeremy smiled at that, his eyes shining with more than fever before they closed. "You understand now why I cannot allow her to see me helpless like this."

Alain laughed. "I understand much more than that, monsieur," he said, still laughing, although his laughter would have seemed bitter, sad, to any person not nursing a fevered stab wound.

Kit retraced yesterday's steps at a run, dodging hackney coaches, wheeled barrows, trundles and all manner of Londoners going about their business. She arrived at Master Jolly's in Bedford Street next to Covent Garden an hour late, determined to push Jeremy Hughes from her mind and heart, flushed and breathing hard from her efforts. She was ushered by the steward into the withdrawing room, where Master Jolly was writing furiously at a large oaken table. He did not look up, and since Kit doubted a forthcoming invitation, she sat down in the baronial chair to regain her breath.

At that he did look up, and she understood that he waited for an explanation.

"A sudden illness I had to tend," she began, sensing this would not be an explanation Master Jolly would accept without question.

"Your poor grandmother?" His eyebrow was cocked again.

"No, Jeremy Hughes collapsed of a stab wound."

"Mistress, I expect nothing but the best from you, and now you have given me the best excuse I have yet to hear all the week."

" 'Tis no fraud."

"I do not doubt it. You are much too clever to play me false. Did you learn the lines I gave you?"

"Yes." And at a wave of his hand, she began to recite.

Several prompts and twenty minutes later, she stopped and waited.

He sighed deeply, as if he had been holding his breath. "And now I know you can learn a part quickly. You continue to intrigue, mistress. Follow me," he said, standing, and she followed him up the polished wood staircase to a second-floor ballroom with floor-to-ceiling windows, alight with soft morning sun, and a lovely painted Italian harpsichord in one corner. Several young men and women were circling about, dancing a French garamand pattern, called by a dancing master with a long white rod beating out the rhythm. Another group to one side played a scene with much laughter from manuscript pages.

Master Jolly clapped his hands for silence and got it. "This is Mistress Kit, our new apprentice. She has just returned from the provinces, where she performed as a strolling player . . . for somewhat less than a season, and as you can see, needs help with her wardrobe, lest she disgrace us. Elizabeth, I will leave that in your hands."

A pretty young woman with a graceful neck, curling brown hair and a mincing step left the dancers and dropped Kit a brief curtsy, who returned it.

"As for the rest of you, I will set Mistress Kit to watch you for the next few days, so be at your best lest she fall into your bad habits." There were giggles and nudges, which Master Jolly ignored, following Kit and the young Elizabeth to the wardrobe room. "She'll need two decent gowns, and I wish you to try her in breeches. She is tall enough for breeches roles."

"I will pay for the gowns, Master Jolly, when—"

"Yes, yes, Mistress Kit. You may be sure I am keeping a tally to provide for my old age." Although the words were hard, his face wasn't, and he didn't offend. She rather liked his amused irony, since it was rare.

Elizabeth proved to be a talented mistress of the wardrobe, but before they could choose Kit's new gowns, Elizabeth asked Kit to don a whalebone bodice, which brought the remembered discomfort Kit had been glad to shed during her race from Bournely Hall. "Master Jolly insists on keeping the body straight and the breasts raised," Elizabeth said.

After much trying on and taking off, together they chose two gowns of the current mode, one a lovely gold-and-red satin brocade with a leaf design, another blue and silver with delicate lace framing the low-cut bodice to great effect, or so the long mirror told Kit.

"Only one of your coloring could wear silver so well," Elizabeth said admiringly. "I would do anything to have your fair skin."

Kit showed her the doctor's salve and allowed her to use it, and they both marveled at how freshened they felt.

"I must find this doctor and purchase some for myself," Elizabeth said, opening a chest of gloves and high-colored hose to match the gowns, and another of fans, large and small, made of ostrich feathers. Embroidered slippers came next, with a warning not to wear them in the streets without the galashios lined up near the front door for use in the filthy byways. "Now, you must allow me to do your hair. It wants control."

Kit agreed, and Elizabeth expertly combed and brushed her hair into the latest style, with side curls falling below the ears, and one long twisted curl, which she called a lovelock, to hang upon her right shoulder. "As the Duchess of Portsmouth has so lately made all the rage," Elizabeth assured her. Because Kit's hair was naturally curling, she would not need to put it up in sugar water and curl papers every night, and for that Elizabeth looked on her with additional envy.

Next Kit tried on a pair of clinging satin breeches, a fancy lace-point shirt and silver buckled shoes. "Well, do I look the gallant?" she asked, not entirely displeased with this amazing new image of herself. With a laugh, and with pretend rapier extended, she struck a pose she could imagine of Jeremy or Alain. "I do find it passing strange," she said in puzzlement, "that a stage which so recently held men dressed as women now wants women dressed as men."

Elizabeth laughed. "Don't you know why?" she asked, and proceeded to tell. "The gentlemen of the audience like to look at an actress's legs, which they cannot do in our gowns. And Lord Rochester is the worst of the gallants. He would have us play breeding queens in breeches!" She giggled.

"You know him?" Kit asked, still preening in the mirror.

"He is often here when he is not with the fleet fighting the Dutch. He is a very pretty young man, but a fearful libertine, exceeding even Jeremy Hughes, so I am told, in the most outrageous japes." She lowered her voice. "My lord Rochester last year did try to kidnap a woman for marriage against her will, and the king put him in the Tower, although His Majesty did quickly forgive him, as he ever does, for Rochester is a high favorite at court."

"You mentioned Jeremy Hughes," Kit said without much apparent interest, and silently damned herself for showing any.

"Do you know him?" Elizabeth asked.

"A passing acquaintance," Kit replied, which was true, and not true, as most things about her knowledge of Jeremy Hughes were.

"Beware, mistress." Elizabeth tittered behind her hand. "He is named the Prince of Cuckholdom for good reason."

"Then I am safe, since I have no husband to cuckhold, nor a desire to have one for any reason."

Elizabeth stared, uncomprehending, at her, then returned to gossip that she did understand. "They do also say"—Elizabeth bent toward Kit's ear—"that Jeremy's friend Lord Rochester has set up an office near that same Tower where he was jailed, and pretends to be a physician, one Doctor Alexander Bendo, who cures infertile women . . . and that he has had some *success*."

A peal of laughter followed, which Kit took the meaning of, determined to be on her guard against this lord when they met. She was not at all surprised that Jeremy Hughes would find a mentor in such a man. They were two of a kind. But almost immediately she thought better of her too-hasty opinion. No, that was not wholly true. If there were such a thing, Jeremy was an honorable rake and would never take a woman under pretense of being other than the man he was. He did not deserve much merit, but he did deserve that. She was secretly pleased with her forbearance in this one conclusion, because it made all her other conclusions more reasonable.

The first day of her training passed as well as any in her memory. She watched a rehearsal of *The Comical Revenge*, listening carefully to Master Jolly's directions. She played the harpsichord for dancing and singing, her own and others, finding the instrument marvelous beyond any virginal she had played upon, the delicate sound like angels plucking upon harps. Whenever her thoughts began to return to the small room under the eaves at the Lion's Head and the vivid face of the man lying in its bed, she was able to distract herself with some new and wonderful discovery in this strange theater world she had entered. She was dreading her return to the inn because she would need to know how Jeremy fared and that would expose her to his . . . his . . . she could not think what to call it. He had made no roguish move toward her, offered her no personal effrontery. Yet when she was near him she felt on guard, tense, ensnared. And equally protected. God's nails! Such confusion made her head ache.

She worked hard in Jolly's last class, repeating womanly gestures for surprise escalating to alarm. As she was securing her galashios, steeling herself to return to Milk Street, Elizabeth invited her to come with the other apprentices to a chocolate house near the Royal Exchange.

They were a merry band of three young men and Elizabeth with Kit when they entered the common room of the

Moon and Tides near the 'Change, full of men of business and an occasional women shopkeeper or wife. If there were whores, who were said to ply their trade in such places, they were not in sight. The group ordered chocolate, which was delivered to the table in a small block. One of the young men took mortar and pestle and ground the chocolate into a fine powder, put it into a pot of hot water, and added milk, egg and sugar, informing them all that this was the Spanish way, which had been kept a secret from the world for more than a century. Kit put one of her precious shillings onto the table to pay her share, looking up as the scullery maid delivered the bowls for chocolate drinking.

Kit opened her mouth in surprise as she recognized the tavern maid. Her former companion, Martha, shook her head in warning, and tipped it toward a table in the far corner, where a lone man held the staff and bell of a beadle who worked with the parish constable. He raised his head, noticed Kit staring, and smiled, showing a partial set of terrible teeth. Kit adjusted her mask, which she always wore in public, and tried not to look obviously in his direction again. Minutes later the man rose and departed.

Relieved, she accepted her dish of hot brewed chocolate, smelling the tantalizing new aroma and tentatively tasting it. The strange, heavy sweetness washed through her so quickly that she drank down the rest without stopping. She wanted another dish almost immediately, but took a warning from the others to fast a time, because too much chocolate could cause a griping in the gut, although it was said to cure one, as well.

Elizabeth laughed at her. "Mistress Kit has been seduced with the rest of us by Master Chocolate." There was much laughter until the pot was empty. Kit looked for Martha, and not seeing her, knew that she would have to talk with her before she could return to the Lion's Head in Milk Lane. Parting from the actors, Kit made her way outside and almost ran into the beadle.

"Hold, mistress, lest you run me down in the street and I have to take you to the Fleet gaol."

Chapter Nine

Seduced by Chocolate

Kit shivered, imagining the hangman's rope already tightening about her neck. She stepped back quickly. "My pardon, sir."

The beadle bowed, smirking through gaps in his teeth. " 'Tis a jest, mistress," he said, obviously thinking himself a merry-Andrew.

Kit tried to laugh, but it sounded more like a screech in her ears.

He stepped closer, blocking her way. "I would take a bowl of chocolate with ye, lass, say, tomorrow at this hour?"

"I doubt my husband would approve," Kit said, and blindly sidestepped to run off through an alley to the rear of the Moon and Tides, calling Martha from the scullery.

"Hold, Mistress Kit, ye look like ye seen a ghost! Be ye well?"

"I'm well," Kit said, embracing her friend quickly, then holding her away to see her the better. "Are you happy here?"

"Happy? I be eating, Mistress Kit," she said, patting her belly, "and I have a pallet in the attic. That be all I ever had."

"What was the beadle doing here? He frightened me," Kit said, telling Martha of her encounter.

"He thinks all women be whores for his use," Martha said. "But there be worse," she added, and for further answer pulled a folded paper from her plain gray gown. She handed it to Kit, leading her to a rough bench against the half-timber and-brick wall in the yard running with chickens and, judging from the pungent smell, piglets. "Sir William or the sheriff be hunting us for certain, Mistress Kit, to take their revenge," she said, low-voiced. "Please be reading it to me."

Kit saw a crude drawing of herself and Martha, and read of a reward of ten pounds by Sir William Pursevant of Bournely Hall in Essex County for the return of a runaway servant, Martha, followed by a description that could apply to half the women in London, and his ward, Mistress Katherne Lindsay, tall for a maid, with pretty high color and yellow hair, having suffered a criminal attack on his person by these ungrateful women almost to his death. Finally, Kit added, "Martha, no one would recognize either of us from this poor drawing."

"The beadles be posting them outside every inn and coffeehouse in London," she said, downcast. "There be those who sell their children for less."

Kit tried to keep her hands still and her voice calm. "If you are too wary, you only draw attention. Go about your business as you would, but be watchful. I must away quickly to the Lion's Head to see how it goes with Jeremy Hughes." She told Martha of Jeremy's wound, and in the doing brought back the image of the player bloodied and calling for Lucy. She allowed none of that hurt to reach her face.

"I be going to see him when I can, mistress. He be always kind to me. Who would try to kill him?"

"He has not named his assailant. Perhaps he was set upon as he journeyed to London. The highways are a danger for all."

Martha concentrated, then shook her head. "Nay, I did hear Alain say he be master of his sword. There be only one who put him off his guard, who hated him. . . . For your sake."

"Lucy?"

"Aye, she did, and she be quick to temper."

This put Kit's mind into a spin, not helped by the chocolate still affecting her with a kind of wondrous sweet lassitude. Maybe Jeremy had named his attacker after all, and she had completely misread his words, unfairly blaming him.

After placing the constable's notice in the bundle containing her second wardrobe gown, Kit parted from Martha with instructions to send for her if needs be, and took a different way through the streets to Cheapside, her head in a whirl about the beadle and Sir William and his intent. But over all she tried to contain her wondering about Jeremy Hughes, and her scarce acknowledged need for him to be whole again and once more able to joust with her, as they had from the first moment, as equals. Even when tied by him in his cart under the scenery cloth, she had not been afraid of him, and even experienced a strange kind of enjoyment in their contentious discord. Though she acknowledged it, she admitted to no understanding of it, and therefore, tried to sweep it from her mind.

At the Lion's Head, she quickly climbed the stairs, stopping in her room to leave her bundle, slipping the constable's notice into her bodice, then walked to Alain's room. He was waiting for her in the narrow hall.

"I heard you return, Keet. Let us sup."

"Gladly, later. How is he?" she asked, taking Alain's hand, trying unsuccessfully to keep pleading from her tone.

"*Mon Dieu*, he is *imposible*! He will not stay abed, and swears mightily if I try to help him. *Le petit docteur* did seem to work a magic."

Kit dipped her head to hide the relief on her face.

"And wonder of all," Alain added, his eyebrows arching, "it was Lucy herself who stabbed him right in the middle of *Macbeth*, act two. *Mon Dieu*, can you believe such a crazed thing?"

"I thank you for telling me."

"I like the silver and lace gown," Alain said appraisingly.

"Oh, Alain, I have another and most beautiful satin gown in my room."

"Yet I do not like that tight-boned bodice. It makes all women have the same shape, which is most boring, *n'est-ce pas*? And, *ma chere*," he added, studying her face, "do not allow Elizabeth to talk you into mouse-skin eyebrows. They are completely last year's mode."

Before Kit could answer, a resonant voice came from inside the room. "A plague on all your chatter." The familiar voice was followed by a cascade of feminine giggles.

Alain looked a question at Kit, and she nodded. "Mistress Kit has returned," Alain said and opened the door.

"If she would risk the sight of a naked male chest," said a familiar mocking voice, "then I would have her wait upon me."

Kit made a wry face, but had to admit that her former anger at his calling Lucy's name was not totally in the right.

Indeed, quite wrong. "I am happy that you are recovering your light heart, Master Hughes," she said, stepping inside the door and allowing her eyes to adjust to the little light afforded by the window under the eaves and by a single bedside candle.

Jeremy was standing by the bed, pale but not flushed. His dark eyes swept over her new gown, his mouth smiling an approval. And on either side, acting as pretty crutches, were two serving maids from the common room, their faces turned up to him and rosy with pleasure. "Ah," he said, "even Jolly's wardrobe can scarce do your beauty justice, mistress." He performed a credible bow, though it must have pained him.

She curtsied formally so that she could hide the mixed chagrin and amazement on her face.

Before she could find words of response, the innkeep appeared. "Sir, release the lasses! There's no work being done in my inn because all the ale maids are now nursemaids!"

Jeremy bussed them both on their cheeks and slapped their arses gently as they ran from the room, leaving a trail of sighs and blushes.

Kit glared at him. It would have been easy to blame him for such behavior, and she tried. How could a man brought so low just hours earlier now be on his feet and challenging her as a man does a woman? Since the first moment, he had been good at that. And still was. "I thought to find you . . ."

"Weak as a babe, so you could work your will with me." The old audacity was there, and despite her annoyance, relief swept through her.

"Do as I will, sir? That is a tempting offer," she said, smiling guardedly, and before she thought to stop herself, she stepped to him like any woman and put out her hand to check his forehead for fever. Indeed, his skin, while still warm, was damp, as if his fever were breaking. Before she could snatch back her hand, he captured it in his own, kissing it gallantly. Her stomach quickened in its lower parts, and she feared the chocolate might be causing the grip.

"Sit with me," he said, settling on the bed and smoothing a place for her on the rough linen sheeting, "and tell me how it goes at Master Jolly's. I long for news of the theaters."

She sat, careful to leave an ample space between them, though the heat from his body easily bridged the gap. "All do hope both the Theater Royal and the Duke's Theater will open in September, and auditions are set for earlier."

His eyes were admiring her face. She could read the depth of their approval. "I see Elizabeth has painted you, and a mighty high lady you are."

"Elizabeth is known to you?" Kit knew she was, but she was asking quite another question.

"Not in the biblical way . . . if that is your inquiry." She could see laughter in his gaze. Did he always see beyond her words to their real meaning?

The idea of Elizabeth and Jeremy lying together had been torturing her, but Kit shrugged and quickly changed the subject to recounting her day at Master Jolly's. "I have many lines to learn again tonight," she said with a sigh.

"I will give you some instruction, if it please you."

When she didn't answer, he, like any man, took that as agreement instead of contemplation. "Of course," he began, sounding much like her old Latin master, "you must repeat the words over and over, but first I try to decide what emotions are present by separating the scenes into smaller moments. . . . That helps me to remember. When you have more time I can demonstrate. . . . Emotional moments, that is."

She edged away slightly. Even wounded, this man was a danger to women. "I take your meaning without demonstration, sir." She was surprised that this was true. His instruction did seem immediately helpful, but she said nothing to that effect. He was not a man who needed encouragement in his own opinion, as, indeed, what man did?

"And recite the lines just before sleep; somehow that stays best in the mind," he added, then slumped a little, his eyelids heavy, though he quickly straightened his shoulders.

"You are weary. I'll go now," she offered.

He could not bear for her to leave, since he had waited the entire day for the sight of her. He rolled his eyes and clasped his wounded shoulder with a hearty groan.

"You must rest," she said, assisting him to lie back upon the pillows. "Shall I call Alain to—"

"No, stay but a little time," he said, using a smaller voice. "A woman's sweet laughter is so restorative." He laid his limp hand into hers.

Her heart softened further, though she was almost sure he was acting. But with Jeremy Hughes, nothing was sure. "You do not hear much of laughter from me."

"No woman is all cynic. Thus laughter is always a possibility with a woman of your wit and daring."

"Daring?"

"Yes, you have courage. I saw that at once." His eyes closed, and she wondered if he was imagining her naked in the horse trough as he had first seen her, but he didn't move for several minutes. Again her stomach quickened, and she was almost certain this time that it was the chocolate. But not entirely certain.

When his dark eyes opened again, she was looking at him, and he smiled with obvious delight, his gaze storing away every change in her lovely face. He no longer cared if she saw his growing regard, though he was not above a bit of role-play. At first, he had pretended to sleep and then slept in truth. Why had she stayed beside him, his hand still in hers? "It is passing strange," he said hoarsely, "that we can talk so easily about being players together, and yet not about being . . . friends together."

"I vow to no certainty that in the future we will be . . . either," she said, her voice catching on the words. At his look of first anger and then concern, she gave over the constable's notice from her bodice and told him about her meeting with Martha and of her encounter with the beadle, and his seeming interest in her.

He read, let the notice rest against his good shoulder, then held it to the window's fading light and read it again. "Promise me," he said, his voice strong once more, "that you will not venture upon the streets without a mask, and that you will go no more to chocolate houses." He silently cursed his wound. It would be days before he could regain his good sword arm and provide her with a man's protection. . . . If she would set aside her prideful fear and accept it.

"I cannot live my life in hiding. And what of my being a player when the theaters open in September?"

Jeremy mused aloud, "I will approach my lord Rochester when he returns from the fleet. He has the ear of the king. We can hope for a royal pardon, since your guardian is a blackguard."

"But Lord Rochester is also a scapegrace. I am told everywhere that His Majesty joins in his japes. The court is a scandal."

"Aye, all you say is true, but not all the truth. Rochester has the heart and mind of a poet. . . . At least betimes. He may help you for the right of it. . . . And the king, though oft silly and a devoted libertine—indeed, they say he does exercise his cod above twice a day—yet does he have a certain honor and sweet nature." His eyes closed; his voice hardened. "It is a chance worth taking . . . unless you wish to emigrate to Jamaica or the mainland colonies, as so many are doing these days. Indeed, they say many maids in London will never marry with so many lads leaving, although that will not be your concern, mistress."

"I have no thought to marry, sir, but . . ." There was more she could say, but attraction and caution pulled her in two directions, and for once attraction seemed to win just by a small amount.

Jeremy watched as Kit made her way out, sweeping her shimmering gown aside, the door closing quietly behind her. He whispered to no one except himself, "Aye, Rochester has the heart of a poet, I'll vow, but the cod of a whoremonger."

Was Jeremy Hughes a better man? He dared hope that now he was. "Dam'me," he swore at himself. The woman would ruin his reputation yet.

Chapter Ten

Sweet Combat

The next morning Kit awoke to find that her monthly flow had come, and a sense of relief overwhelmed her. Sir William had not planted his seed, thank the good Lord of blessed name, although she did not know if William had made her unchaste and whore, because she would trust herself to no future man and thus would never know. She had a growing sense of the difficulty Jeremy Hughes made of her choice. Still, she was determined to resist the accomplished rogue by taking a firm grip on her thoughts. . . . And staying away from chocolate.

The sun bounced off the white-plastered walls in her bare room, and drew her from the bed to open the diamond-paned oriel window looking down upon Milk Lane. Hoping for a waft of early-morning mist to chill her too-warm thoughts, and finding none, she lingered to hear the bells of St. Paul's and the Bow Bells in the old Norman church nearby, followed by bells in a half-dozen other churches, vying for London's ear.

Hot, dry August pressed upon the town, the hottest in

memory, so that all who could exit the city for the cooler, cleaner country breezes did so. The plague continued, with the dead carts still rumbling through the streets but abating somewhat.

The theaters were scheduled to open as soon as there were fewer than fifty plague deaths reported in the Diseases and Casualties list of the week. That prospect set all the young actors at Master Jolly's to working harder, not the least of them Kit, who longed for the ability to earn her living beholden to no man, a freedom few women could hope for or seemed to desire.

Kit eagerly sought to take more major parts in rehearsal and to bear her teacher's almost incessant corrections with good grace. Indeed, he seemed to single her out.

"Watch your body movements," he shouted time and again. "You are not a drayman, but a fine lady. Your legs must dance as they move." And again, "Hold! The Lady Trickery has just spent a debauched night creeping under beds. She would not be lively in her movements in the morn. And so begin again, Mistress Kit, and let me see your aching head." Scenes were rehearsed until she was still acting them in her sleep at night. But she no longer resented Master Jolly's direction, because she could see that each time she repeated a scene, she had the better of it, and Jolly's tongue was less sharp, and occasionally he even let fall the slightest word of faint approval: "Faith, mistress, I am surprised I liked that scene as much as I did."

As for her fellow actors, she turned down the young men's overtures one by one, until they ceased to importune her. Elizabeth was less discerning, making them each in turn her beau, though she happily worked with Kit each day to perfect Kit's use of face paint for the rehearsals.

"Master Jolly does not want us to use ceruse and egg white because it dries and cracks long ere the play is done," Elizabeth explained, telling of the actress Mary Davis, who smiled until her cheeks peeled away.

Instead, Elizabeth applied a starchy paste over an oil base to whiten the golden glow of Kit's skin. She demonstrated the use of Spanish paper, impregnated with cochineal, for the rosiest cheeks, and a blue wax crayon for the upper eyelid and the tantalizing tracery of veins on her bosom, and a red wax crayon for the lips, all the while exclaiming over the dewiness of Kit's skin.

Kit again shared her Wyndham's Infallible Miracle Salve, which she had been using night and morning.

Elizabeth applied some and exclaimed with the same delight as before. "I will beg Master Jolly to call this doctor to demonstrate. If his salve gives me your complexion, he will be much sought after by our rivals at the Duke's Theater, so we must have him."

After several sessions, the two moved on to vanities or beauty patches of moons, stars, birds and animals of all sort. Elizabeth giggled. "I do hear that the king's chief mistress, the Countess Castlemaine, does have patches of six horses and a coach racing across her cheek!"

Kit laughed. "I think one or two patches quite enough. I would not turn my face into a hostelry!"

Elizabeth laughed. "You will have the Molly Boys outdo you, then."

"Molly Boys?"

"You know, the buggers who dress up in women's gowns and hold notorious parties in their Molly houses. Even members of the court attend, though buggery's a hanging crime."

"No, I didn't know," Kit said softly, her mind whirling with questions, all with one name attached: Alain. She thought back and remembered the tender care he had taken of Jeremy, and her heart broke a little. Did Jeremy know? Of course he did. Jeremy knew everything, but she would wager that the knowledge remained unspoken between them, as it would with her forever.

Speaking of Jeremy, which she tried not to do, he continued his quick recovery, accepting no well-intended effort to slow him down. He made his way down the narrow stairs to take his supper in the common room and listen to the town news; then much too soon he was out upon the town.

When he was at the inn, Kit avoided being alone with him, lest the conversation take a turn she couldn't control. A wounded Jeremy Hughes was dangerous, a recovering Jeremy Hughes more so, she discovered one night when she heard a noise in the passageway and literally ran into his arms as she exited her room.

"I assumed it was you lurking about," she said.

"You have such faith in me."

The scoundrel was smiling as he held her tight against him. She feared opening his wound if she pulled away too quickly. That was not all she feared, but she would not allow herself to examine those feelings, though they raced through her body, demanding examination. He brushed her hair away from her forehead and she shrank, trembling, from his hand, too warm, too gentle for a scoundrel's. "You take a liberty, Jeremy Hughes," she said proudly, lest he think her unsettled by his touch.

"There are ladies who . . ."

"I do not doubt it, sir, but as you well know, I am not one of them." At least, not yet, you double rogue.

"My pardon, mistress, I did mistake you"—he stepped back to allow her to pass—"for a woman."

He bowed, but not before Kit saw the beginnings of that maddening smile. God's nails! It was certain that he'd been born with it, for a smile that practiced would take two lifetimes to acquire. She flounced away without looking back, down the stairs and into the common room. There she ate a quick meal, while she engaged the innkeep in meaningless conversation, completely ignoring Jeremy across the room, flirting with the ale wife. Kit was so determined not to look in Jeremy's direction that she started a spasm in her neck that left a sore reminder into the next day.

Kit also saw less of Alain, who seemed always away about the town, especially at night. She missed him, though she knew where he must be, since he sometimes borrowed her gold-and-red satin dress.

During the final days of August, as all her fellows waited for a September casting call from either the King's, the Duke's or the new Earl of Rochester's theaters, Master Jolly seemed to always have his eyes on Kit. At last she approached him with a demanding question. "Tell me, sir, how am I not pleasing you?"

"Mistress, how can I tell what I do not know? But I soon will. I have written a short entertainment called *The Love Arts* or *Lord Lovemore and the Lady,* and I wish you to play it tomorrow for some special guests who could do you much good. Prepare your part tonight," he said, handing her a sheaf of manuscript pages, turning away before she could ask him any of a dozen questions that were on her lips. Foremost: Why no rehearsal?

Kit rushed home to the Lion's Head, hoping to read with Jeremy. This would be her first public appearance in London, and she would risk being close to him for his help. But she found his door closed to her knock, so she took a supper of meat pie and a bowl of tea to her room.

She opened the door, expecting to see the familiar plain furnishings and bare walls, but her room had been transformed. A lovely inlaid face-paint box, complete with all she needed, stood open on a small table before a wall mirror. A large caned chair sat by the window with a candle table beside it. A round turkey-work carpet lay bright against the dark plank floor. Fresh violets were strewn across her bed, filling the room with their country morning scent.

Alain! This sweet scene was surely the result of Alain's deep feeling. Yet her red-and-gold dress did not hang on its peg. She refused to believe what her mind told her must be true. No, and no again. This could not be the act of that accomplished cocksman Jeremy Hughes. Banning the name from her head, she sat in her new chair and forced herself to begin to learn her lines.

Late that night she thought she heard his footsteps in the hall outside her door, even a hand faintly rattle the latch. She quickly blew out her candle, held her breath, and tiptoed to stand before the door. If he knocked, would she dare open to him? If he had done this sweet kindness for her, did he expect payment? The rakehell! Then she heard heavy footsteps walk away, and sighed, whether in relief or distress, she refused to examine. Well, why should today be any different?

It was another hour before she slept, listening to the

muffled nonsense of roisterers in the street below and wondering that she was so restless.

She arrived at Master Jolly's near Covent Garden the next morning, her head swimming with ideas of how to play the satirical little comedy, to find the rehearsal hall set with chairs as in a theater pit, and the small stage a bower of flowers surrounding a bench under an arch, the backdrop and side wings of pastoral scenery. Elizabeth spirited her away to the costume room and helped her dress as a shepherdess and don her face paint.

"Your color is so high you need very little Spanish paper today, Kit. You must have heard that my lord Rochester will favor us today. He is the handsomest of men," she added, sighing for emphasis.

"No, I had not heard, and I wish that he wasn't coming, for the thought does make me shake in my slippers. I fear I will disappoint. And who is to play Lord Lovemore?"

"Master Jolly will not say. He is testing you, Kit, to see what you can do without instruction and to keep his comedy fresh. Now calm yourself. Breathe slowly and deeply or you will surely swoon."

Kit let herself into the rehearsal hall through a small side door that opened behind a large wall hanging, and made her way to the bower with only one quick glance at the richly dressed gathering of four or five gentlemen seated before the small stage, the rest of the school's actors seated behind them.

Master Jolly introduced his small play and begged the audience's indulgence for a work in progress. "And so your attention, sirs, to this, my caution for lovers," he said, as Jeremy Hughes stepped from behind the scenery cloth and swept a low bow before Kit, carefully keeping his head up to better manage his towering peruke, the absolute twin of the one worn by the little doctor who'd cared for him. Jeremy withdrew an ivory comb and began to arrange his curls, the perfect court fop, though his strong features and well-built body made him scarce believable.

"Lady, my compliments," he declaimed in the languid, high voice of the courtier; then knelt and grasped her by her skirts, pulling her roughly to him so that she felt the muscle working beneath the extravagant costume.

She was not acting her surprise and fright, for her heart was pounding in her ears. "Why didn't you tell me that you were up to this?" she said, a bit strangled but not so loud that the audience could hear.

"Oh, did I not, mistress?" he whispered. "And if I had, would you be here? You seem afraid of me."

"I am not afraid. . . . Just sensible of your reputation."

The rake was grinning!

"Then act your part sensibly so that Rochester will want you for our company. . . . And not to forever play the witch. Show me that you can imitate the coquette, for I do not see that you are a natural one."

"There is much you will never see, sir," she replied, hoping to wipe the grin from his face, and failing. Kit took a deep breath. She would play the damned part with all her newfound skill, maybe enough to surprise even Jeremy Hughes. She would show him and show him well, she would. . . . Swallowing hard, she spoke now for the audience, her voice rising in maidenly fear. "Sir, keep your distance! What are you, my lord, a gentleman or a devil?"

"What am I?" Jeremy asked, turned aside to the audience, his eyebrows raised in comic question.

"A devil!" they shouted as one.

He looked as satisfied as any man who'd been complimented. "Nay, madame, I deny it, for I am no devil, only a gallant who thinks he ought always to show eager ardor for your sex. Is that not the right of it? Do you not want a love joust? I think you do. Tell me true."

Though these were the right lines, she knew he meant them for Kit the woman and not Kit the actress. Vexed, she leaned away. He was too close, and she felt an overwhelming heat from him. It was a wonder his sword didn't melt. The warmth made her voice high and querulous. "This is not the bear pit, sir, that you paw me. You don't know the gentle art of loving a lady."

At that, Lord Lovemore pulled her even closer, and Kit was all too aware that it was Jeremy's face behind the exaggerated painted features of the courtier, and Jeremy's strong arms thrown around her. For a man recently wounded, he had uncommon strength.

"I may be a bear in truth, but a bear at your feet, lady. You must tame me with your charms." His hands outlined the curves of her body.

The audience howled as the lady stepped away in obvious fright, her hands fluttering everywhere. "My lord," she said in a rising voice that trembled just the right amount without breaking, which took all her control. "You do most seriously need schooling in the arts of gentle love for which your sex is so often lacking."

"Then school me," he replied, rising with his arms spread wide and a broad wink for the gathering, who applauded.

Kit heard Elizabeth's loud, excited giggle. Did Jeremy command the entire audience?

Without his hands on her, she was determined to concentrate on the humor of the lines and to use her changing voice and pauses, her arch glances to add to the scene, and bring some of these courtiers to her side and maybe teach them a woman's way.

She sat herself primly on the bower bench, spreading her skirts, and raised her hand like a schoolmaster or a church divine with forefinger pointing skyward. "First, my lord, you must gain my complete attention."

"I can do that, lady," Lord Lovemore announced, swaggering to and fro in front of her, making dramatic bows and ridiculous thrusting poses, all strut and cock-o'-the-walk. He drew his sword and shouted, "*En garde*, thrust, parry!" accompanying himself with the proper movements.

She thought he overacted, especially those thrusting poses. If the man had any subtlety, she didn't see it. "No, no, my lord," Kit said, making her contralto voice sing the lines, and showing shrewd amusement at the coxcomb before her. "A woman wants no jack-a-dandy. You must walk with arms behind your back, head down, murmuring sadly as if from some great loss, sighing deeply. . . . Deeply so that I will be drawn to you with a woman's sympathy. Now, let me see your great melancholy."

Jeremy stopped gracefully, his long leg extended as if he practiced an Italian courante. He withdrew a snuffbox, tapped the lid, pinching and snuffing, then flicked the dust from his sleeve, wrist cocked just so, and suppressed a sneeze that rocked his head. Every movement was a finely orchestrated comic imitation of the young blades in the audience, who burst into applause. Jeremy wiped at the corner of his tearing eye with an excessively large handkercher.

Kit was astonished by his skill. This man held the audience

with a turn of his head or a dangled wrist and a raised eyebrow. One day she prayed that she would acquire half his skill. Jeremy cleared his throat, and Kit realized she had to leave her amazement and continue her part. "My lord," she said, her voice shrill as a jade's, "the aim is for me to notice you in your sadness, not in the curve of your leg."

"Ah, but you did notice the curve of my leg, lady?" he said, turning his leg from side to side in front of her to exaggerate what was indeed a very fine, powerful leg, not the first time Kit had noticed.

She stared at his leg despite every effort to turn her eyes away. As a result, she pounced a bit too hard on the following lines.

"Come, come, now, my naughty lord, you stray from the lesson. Next you must break my heart with your gloom and claim my tears, so that when you kneel before me, I will know no other man has the heart to love me as you do."

Jeremy looked at her, his mouth too knowing. "Dam'me, lady, but I will have you know it 'fore the hour is out."

The line had not been in her manuscript, and while she searched for an answer to that scoundrel sentiment, Jeremy picked up the dialogue. "If you would have me take your love instructions to heart, you must improve upon your own arts, which are not as fine as you imagine. Would you heed my advice, lady?" he asked.

"That depends, my lord," she answered, but she showed the audience by simpering with arched glance beside her fan that she doubted this lord had aught to teach her.

Now Jeremy took the pose of an instructor, all too easily she did guess, remembering how he'd shown her with his own body the witch's part in the stable yard of the Bull and Ram, indeed remembering that body's demands much too well.

"Do not succumb," he said pompously, "so quickly to my sadness, but show me indifference. Don't you know a woman too easily won by a man loses all her charm?"

"What is your remedy for fickle man, sir?"

"Greet my arrival as if surprised."

Kit unfolded her fan with a snap, trying to read his eyes because she feared he would take her off her guard again. "I think I understand, my lord. I should play with my fan, like thus," she said, fluttering it excessively in an arc about her head, not part of her acting, but from necessity. His warmth had surrounded her from their first exchange and overheated her blood.

He winked, and she thought the rogue was reading her every thought again.

"Or you could pretend you were just leaving to visit a sick friend," he offered.

"Or have many household things to tend," she said, turning a puzzled face to the audience. "But tell me, my lord, I thought men accused women of being false in love. How now are you counseling a lie between us?"

"Only a little lie, lady, because truth is too often the end of love for a man."

The men in the audience applauded.

Kit turned to them, smiling. "I do know that a man oft finds a woman's truth difficult." Ha! Now she had injected a new line, for which Jeremy had no answer.

"Touché," he whispered, as if he welcomed her retaliation.

She raised her voice. "So, my lord, it would seem that only a very little distraction is needed for a man."

Lord Lovemore chuckled. "Aye, my lady, you could say that, but listen well. The best aphrodisiac for a lazy cod, I vow, is a woman's indifference."

She looked all amazed. "Say you so?" Not for the first time, she wondered if he'd had a hand in this dialogue. The words suited his rogue's nature, and she would wager that he'd meant "a woman's indifference" for her and not her character. She took control of those thoughts lest anger put her at a further disadvantage.

"And the best indifference," Lord Lovemore continued, "is to talk of ladies' fashion." Jeremy used his hands wonderfully to paint the words in the air. " 'Tis satin, 'tis silk, 'tis lace, 'tis heaven knows what, or you could remove to some distant place so that I would be forced to yearn . . . to swell . . ." At these last words he thrust his private part rapidly in a gesture well-known, delighting all.

"I could move away, as you say, or I could do more," Kit said, seeming to fall in with his teaching suggestions. "I could be merry, then angry and thoughtful, or a hundred ways crazed. Tell me, Lord Lovemore, doth such variety please a man in a wife?"

The audience hooted, ever more raucous than before. More than raucous, Kit realized. They were aroused.

"Nay, variety does not please in a wife, if you would be one, my lady. Wives must never change so that a man is sure of what he will find in his home, or why leave his whore?"

The agreeable audience stamped their feet, shaking the floor beneath her.

Angrily, Kit stamped her feet. "How, then, will man and woman find their true way together, my lord?"

"I think we talk overmuch most times." It was a line in

the script, but Jeremy meant it, and he could see that Kit knew he was not speaking as Lord Lovemore. "Lady, your eyes must beg me, and you must clutch your bosom as if in a faint, so that I, as your lord protector, will kneel once more and press mine own body to your body, like this!"

Chapter Eleven

A Play and No Play

Jeremy, as Lord Lovemore, knelt before Kit, his lady, and lay his cheek against her bosom. Kit tried not to breathe, but she could not sustain it and when she did breathe, it was too deeply and rapidly. His head bounced to rest between her breasts, hidden in her flounces, ruffs and furbelows, his lips seeking the warm flesh beneath. "This is not in the play," she whispered fiercely.

"It was sadly omitted," he whispered back, his warm breath setting her to trembling and forcing her to go on with the scene with his face lodged deep in her cleavage, and her body washed through with aching.

Taking a deep breath, she tried to remember her next line. "Then I will play with your hair, like this," the lady announced, making a moue to the audience. "Cupid could be hiding behind every curl."

Her heart pounded. The rogue was licking the swell of her breasts. She pinched his ear hard.

"Ouch!" he grunted in response to the pain, then recovered. "Ah, then I will plant soft kisses like this," Lord Lovemore said, returning to her bosom.

And did. And did.

She felt his lips slide naturally to the place where her whalebone bodice thrust her breasts to a height that nature had never intended, then his lips moved to her neck and finally he chased her escaping mouth and bent her back until they o'erturned the bench and both tumbled behind the bower to applause that neither heard.

He whispered, his heated breath coming fast, "Have you lost your tongue? Never mind, I'll find it."

"You take me at a disadvantage," she said, the words escaping through gasps. "I cannot fight you, lest your wound be opened anew."

"You are ever a most loving nurse."

"Was it you?" she asked, her mind searching desperately for a way out of this trouble, and her body helping not at all. "The paint box, the chair . . ." she murmured, the words melting against his lips, which were searching hers.

"Possessions you needed."

"The violets?"

"Especially the violets."

And then she lost all sense as Jeremy departed entire from the manuscript, inserting his hand into her bosom and pressing his body to hers, whispering scorching words that described his need in most graphic terms that no lady should hear even as playact, let alone respond to as she was.

Master Jolly called them for their bow, twice, before they heard. Jolly finally righted the bower to free them.

"I think you have entertained the audience enough," he said, as a dazed Kit and Jeremy reluctantly emerged.

Jeremy removed rose petals from Kit's hair, while she,

recovering herself in part, swiped away his hand a bit too frantically. She caught her breath and raised her chin, trying to deny the kisses Jeremy had pressed on her, his tongue teasing hers, teasing that she had returned without thought of aught else except to hold that tongue. . . . So completely must she have been in her role. She could not decipher more of her jumbled thinking, or look at his face for fear of what she would read there, or guess, or worse, understand.

"Bravo, brava." Lord Rochester stood before them, clapping his hands together, tall and slender, so handsome as to be near beautiful, young but with an old man's hooded eyes. . . . And very drunk. "Madame Kit, how completely charming you are, and with a rich talent, as well. Perhaps you will teach me the arts of loving as you taught my dear friend Jeremy here?" He kissed her hand, rather too long, sliding his fingers under her lace-point sleeve. His laugh was genuinely delighted.

"My lord overpraises," she said.

Jeremy bowed, coming closer and removing her hand from Rochester's. "My lord, I doubt any woman dare to tutor you in what you have already mastered."

"Jeremy, that is a riposte fit for the king's ears. Come now, I would hear of your summer's triumphs in the company of this particular lady." He winked at Kit. "And then we'll lay our plans for the Earl's Theater, for that is what I mean to call it."

"Has His Majesty agreed to give you a patent?"

"He has not said me no, and he listens to my plans with right good humor." Rochester reclaimed Kit's hand and placed it on his sleeve, covered it heavily with his own kid-gloved one, and began to move toward the door, entourage in his wake.

"Your lordship," she said, trying to disentangle her hand from his firm grasp, "I cannot leave, but must finish my day's training. I have much to learn."

"Then I will teach you what you need to be an actress of the first rank," he said in a tone that allowed no disagreement. "Is that not so, Master Jolly?"

Master Jolly bowed with a helpless shrug. "No man of sense would refute your knowledge of theater, my lord." Unspoken but obvious, George Jolly could not block an earl, peer of the realm, close friend of the king and one of the court's band of merry wits that made the king laugh and lightened his burden of governing. Such a lord could do as he willed, when he willed.

"Come then, no more delay," said Rochester to all. "I am parched in this desert, and need wine."

Kit looked at Jeremy with alarm. She did not want to go with the young Lord Rochester, probably the greatest rake in the country, but Jeremy had already moved close and taken her other arm.

"Beg pardon, my lord. I look forward to talking with you about strolling the provinces, and about your new theater, but this lady and I have unfinished business of our own." His meaning was obvious, even to Rochester deep in his cups.

"Is that the way of it?" Rochester said with a decided pout, showing briefly how very young he was and how often he had his way with women. "Although you speak like quality," he said, addressing Kit, "if you be of the theater, you may not be able to save yourself for one lover, even if he be the renowned Jeremy Hughes."

Kit was furious and did not care that she showed it. "I save myself, my lord Rochester, for myself. I am my own master and determined to remain so."

Rochester, not an unaccomplished actor himself, made as if he was extremely startled. "A masterless, chaste actress? But, mistress, such is unheard of in this modern age. A woman of your beauty will find that a very dull tune to dance to." He laughed, and his companions echoed him.

"Then I shall not dance at all, my lord. You may count on it," she said, and realized at once that she had gone too far, been too haughty, changing the tone from raillery to pique. . . . For now the thwarted boy in Lord Rochester won out, and he lost his humor. For want of something to lessen the tension, she dropped him a low curtsy. "I am most sorry to disappoint, my lord."

Rochester frowned. "Indeed, mistress, you are delightful in comedy, but I like you not in drama. On our next meeting, I will endeavor to cure your impudence. I have found no chaste woman honest, and if they are, it is not from principle, but from a most unwomanly vanity." His cohorts applauded politely, delighted with his wit, and Kit knew that it would soon be repeated at court, and ultimately on the street, with her name attached to it.

The earl turned suddenly, staggering a bit, and grabbed for Elizabeth, who allowed herself to be drawn away with only feigned reluctance. His fellows, bowing quickly, hurried after them.

Kit sagged against Jeremy's arm, needing support and finding it.

"He means exactly what he says, our sad young lord," Master Jolly said, obviously relieved that his guests had departed. A look of compassion settled upon his face. "But I think that he secretly loves your principles, Mistress Kit, as only a confirmed rakehell can."

Kit's chin came up. "I doubt my lord Rochester will

allow my principles to disarm his temper. I cannot hope for a place in the Earl's Theater when it comes to pass."

Jeremy's arm held her, his face close to hers. "You were wonderful in performance," he said. "And wonderful after," he whispered against her cheek, setting her to shivering in places where she had not often been so shaken before today. "You inspired me to be nearly at my best."

"That was not your best?"

"Remember," he said, softly but in his Lord Lovemore voice, "never give all to a lady in the first bower bed. I will do better next time."

Without thinking, she had stayed in the comfort of his embrace, and suddenly aware of too much closeness, stepped away quickly, in all confusion.

Jeremy removed his wig, handed it to Master Jolly, donned his broad-brimmed hat and bowed, adjusting his cuffs. "I must go after Rochester and soothe his injured manhood, since you seem unwilling to take on the work, Mistress Kit." His crooked smile showed he jested, before she could flare at him. "My lord must be made to see that he will need a 'mad couple' for his new theater, and we are a mad couple, I vow. Is that not so, Jolly?"

"As mad as ever I have seen," Master Jolly said, smiling. "When I have finished correcting Madame Kit's performance, it will be perfection."

"Master Jolly, I never dispute you, but I did have a most perfect actress in my arms this day."

A few nights later on September first, Kit, exhausted from long hours of rehearsal at Master Jolly's, fell into her bed, happy that the next day was Lord's Day and would be one of rest. The innkeep brought her a note from Alain saying he would be occupied for a few days and not to worry. She had hoped to have his bright company, for she was heart-sick.

She had not seen Jeremy since the day he'd gone to seek Lord Rochester, but word everywhere was that Rochester's merry gang was roistering in the stews of Whetstone Park in a serial debauch, so notorious it was published in a news sheet and sold for a penny on the street, and talked about everywhere. She spent hours putting conjured scenes out of her mind, swearing that she had never trusted Jeremy Hughes, didn't now, and never would. The fact that she had to repeatedly swear told her how weak the oath really was.

A strong, hot east wind was blowing oppressively, the dry, dusty air forcing her to keep her window closed, as she lay sweltering in her shift, wondering if Jeremy was at this moment . . . well, she'd not think on glistening naked bodies entwined, or the stories about Madame Creswell's famous bawdy house, where pictures were religious scenes until turned upside down and then they were . . . well, she could scarce imagine what lust they depicted, or, at least, she tried not to, ultimately failing even that.

Of late her heart had been full of some tangled mystery that caused her to burn and ache in every part, and she felt sick from the effort to deny and push it away. And there was the seductive memory of the bower. . . . Always the bower.

At Jolly's, she often attempted gaiety as she heard the stories of Jeremy and Rochester repeated, but only to hide anger. Jeremy was hers. The thought startled her at first, but the more she pushed it away, the faster it returned. If she would not allow his ownership, how could she own him?

The hour was late before she stopped tossing from side to side in her bed and fell into troubled sleep, swearing she would not think more on what Jeremy Hughes was doing, and yet the fevered love scenes that came and went almost at will in and out of her mind were a searing agony.

What waked her in her dark room, she never remembered. Perhaps the smell of smoke seeping between cracks in the ancient inn, perhaps the cries in the street below barely touching her exhausted consciousness. But wake she did with some alarm and rushed to the window to throw it open and call below. No one heard her in the din of shrieking people rushing by in their nightclothes or pushing carts piled high with household goods. And everywhere around her she could see the glow of fire against the dark night sky, leaping high, ringing the inn. Indeed, the whole of the old city burned.

Chapter Twelve

Old London Ablaze

Jeremy felt a terrific pounding in his head, which was sore from having spent a full four nights and days in Rochester's company. All the while he'd attempted to slow the earl's frantic search for pleasure and to lay serious plans for the Earl's Theater. Every hour he'd longed to see Kit. He opened his eyes now, and the pounding continued, this time on the outer door.

"Open the damned door!" he yelled at the innkeeper of the Southwark tavern, sleeping near his tapped kegs. Taking only one tankard of wine to Rochester's two or three had not helped Jeremy avoid a sick head, nor had it helped him learn if the young lord would accept Kit as a player. He had endured many jibes about his "chaste mistress," and happily would have endured more to ensure a place for Kit. She deserved her chance, and every peer of the realm could be damned before he'd see her lose it. Rochester was not used to his company or his bed being refused, and took it as a fault of Kit's, even though Rochester was still courting the Lady Elizabeth Mallet, the same woman he'd tried to kidnap the year before. Jeremy had never seen his lordship so wild, and he feared his youth would not save him from the worst results of folly, or an early death.

The innkeeper shuffled to the door and opened it as a beadle stepped over the threshold, his face smudged with gray ash. "There's a great fire burning in the city," the man shouted in a high, excited voice. "Above three hundred houses are gone and Fish Street by London Bridge is all afire, so you cannot return that way. If you must, go by water."

Jeremy reached the beadle in three steps. "Milk Lane, man, what of Milk Lane?"

"Gone or near to. The stones of churches be exploding, and the lead from roofs be melted and running in the streets," the man said, prying Jeremy's hands from his doublet. "And mayhap the fire be coming to Southwark if it makes way across the bridge." He was away in that instant, before more could be asked.

Jeremy rushed to Rochester, sprawled over two chairs, and shook him mightily. "Awake, my lord, London is afire."

"What?" Rochester struggled up, squinting his reddened, puffy eyes away from the lantern being lit by the innkeeper. Jeremy repeated what the beadle had said.

His lordship stood, steadying himself against Jeremy and reaching for the remains of a wine bowl to steady himself further. "We must to Whitehall. The king will need us."

"No, my lord, I must find Kit. I fear she is in more danger than His Majesty." And without waiting for an answer to his true but slightly treasonous response, he grabbed his sword and buckled it on as he rushed out, leaving the rapidly sobering Rochester to rouse the sodden company.

When Jeremy reached the first river stairs, he saw the

waterfront across the Thames in flames, with cinders leaping and whirling in the wind to light upon another thatched roof or warehouse. The steeple of St. Magnus was turned into a flaming candle in the night, and his heart was so near to breaking that his chest hurt. "Oh, God, of most blessed name," he prayed over and over for the first time in many years. He took the water stairs two at a time. "If you let her live, I will . . ." The bargain he made with God was drowned in the shouting of watermen eager to make way to the other shore, where customers removing their worldly goods would make them rich men this day.

Jeremy jumped aboard the lighter already moving away from the steps, tossing his coin to the man at the tiller. The wind was blowing fiercely, and the closer they came to the other shore, the more heated the air became. All along the bank, warehouses were burning, their contents of oil, hemp, tallow and brandy exploding in sudden fiery bursts. People were waving frantically from the bank for a boat, any boat, some tossing their goods into the water, some jumping in themselves.

Jeremy grabbed the end of an oar and pulled hard to reach the shore faster since the tide was running out. When he leaped upon the first water stairs, he asked a man standing with a cart of furniture, "What caused this? I saw no lightning."

"They do say the fire started in the king's bakery at Pudding Lane," the man replied bitterly. "The king will get no bread this morning, nor will half of London."

The heat was intense, and Jeremy raced back down the stairs, dipping his cloak into the river and wrapping it about his head and shoulders before running on, dodging from street to street, trying to circle back around the fire toward

Milk Lane. Lines of men and women were fighting the flames with wooden buckets, but most were old and rotten and gave way with little use. He crossed the Fleet and raced up Ludgate Hill toward Cheapside, moving against the people crowding toward him with possessions and shrieking children, and often families struggling to carry beds with the old and sick still in them.

He yelled to the people crowding past, "What of Milk Lane?" But they couldn't hear, or couldn't care in their panic.

He came upon a gang of men with long hooks, trying to pull down houses upon the Lord Mayor Bludworth's orders, but the fire overtook them and caught their roofs before the work was complete. Even where they succeeded, the piled rubble only burned the faster.

Everywhere he saw doves from dovecotes dropping into the streets, their wings singed from the heat and blowing cinders. It seemed the whole world was turned into a hellish inferno. His cloak was dry again and there was no water to wet it, and he could feel cinders sizzling against his exposed skin, but he was now so filled with horror at the thought of what could be happening to Kit at that very moment that he scarcely felt their sting.

As he raced up Cheapside, he searched the face of every woman. Finally, he began shouting at everyone he could stop, "Have you seen a tall, pretty lass with yellow hair, and . . ." People shook their heads and rushed on. Who could remember one lone woman in the thronging, shrieking humanity?

Jeremy's sleepless nights with Rochester, the intense heat and dry wind constantly blowing, were taking their toll, and by the time he neared Milk Lane he used the last of his strength to fight the towering flames that threatened to sweep over him. Finding another way in, he was beaten back again until a constable and some soldiers readying gunpowder to blow up houses to form a firebreak ordered him to safety in the king's name.

Gulping hot air that seared his throat, Jeremy raced back the way he'd come, searching for yet another route until, pounding his fists against a shop wall whose thatch roof was beginning to smolder, he railed at God like a madman, cursing as he hadn't since he'd seen Cromwell's soldiers ravage his sister time and again. He had never meant to fall in love with Kit. The woman had entered his heart by stealth, against his will. He had been ever ready for dalliance. . . . He would not deny it. . . . But not for this . . . this raging, hopeless torment at the thought of losing her forever.

He drew deep breaths, turning toward the maelstrom once more. He'd find her, if he had to descend into hell!

He did not see the brick and timber wall opposite him in the narrow street begin to tilt his way.

As Kit watched Milk Lane below her, firebrands began to fall, sending people screaming in every direction. One woman, already mad with fear, stood in her night shift, holding a Bible before her, and warned all who would listen, "Sinners! God has sent this against us for our king's wickedness!" Kit watched in horror as a driverless carriage ran her down and left her frail body broken and lifeless in the street, the pages of her Bible blowing in the flame-driven wind.

Kit could understand the poor woman's madness, because the scene before her was surely a kind of inferno that even the old Florentine Dante could not have imagined. She quickly gathered her few belongings into a bundle, including the lovely little mirrored box that held her face paint, and hurried into Alain's room, which was lit by fire through the window. Finding neither Alain nor Jeremy there, she added their clothing, hanging on pegs, to her own bundle and started for the stairs to the common room, only to be met by smoke billowing up the stairwell toward her.

Coughing deeply, she backed into Alain's room, grabbed the hilt of his sword hanging from the bed and broke out the window, thrusting her bundle through and following it out upon the next rooftop. The wind was hurling bolts of flame into street after street as if propelled by the angry God of the dead woman's prophecy. Kit dared not linger to survey the destruction that seemed to surround her, but kept her eyes steady upon the rafters. She carefully placed her feet one after the other, crossing two roofs, then a third one, then another until she had reached an intersecting street and could go no farther.

She called below and waved frantically to the crowd. "Help me!" But few heard her as the high wind caught and blew her words away. Those who looked up were dazed and stumbling. One man, pulling his pregnant wife and children in a cart, stopped for a moment before hurrying on: "I have me no rope. I will send a constable."

But no constable came, and the fire raced closer, fingers of flame reaching out for her along the rooftops. Quickly, she began to tie the clothes in her bundle together, making a bulging rope of shifts, shirts and breeches that reached partway to the cobbles below. Praying that her makeshift rope would hold, she clutched her mirrored paint box and began to clamber down, grabbing rafters and projecting windows and jumping near breathless the last few feet to the street below. She spent precious minutes trying to pull the rope after her, but the advancing heat convinced her to abandon the clothes and save herself.

She ran down Cheapside, and behind her heard explosions like huge guns. "What is happening?" she asked three men hooking smoldering thatch from rooftops. "Are the Dutch come?"

"Nay, the king be giving orders to use gunpowder," said one, "and best you be away, because they be coming this way in all speed."

She needed no prodding, but ran on in the red light of a hellish new day until a collapsed wall blocked her way. She was telling herself she did not need a badly turned ankle when she saw a doublet-covered arm and then a long leg emerge from the rubble. She glanced about her for help, but the streets had emptied rapidly of the people fleeing toward safety to the west and north.

Climbing carefully over the bricks, dislodging them and nearly choking on the dust she raised, she reached the man just as he slid from under a huge beam fallen against the wall.

"Stay back," he commanded, looking up at her. "This beam is unsteady."

Red brick dust covered his face and blood tricked down from a scalp wound, but there was no mistaking that face, those piercing dark eyes, or his crooked grin. He gingerly touched his scalp. "Kit! Dam'me, a man could lose his head following you." Then he remembered his bargain with God. *Lord, let me find her whole, and I'll never lie with another!* He'd lost more than his head. He'd lost his freedom. Jeremy Hughes groaned.

She could scarce believe that voice, choking with dust

and smoke. "Jemmy! Where do you hurt?" She touched his face, wiping it as best she could with her sleeve.

He stood then, straight and tall. There was steel in him no matter how many bricks fell on his head.

Reaching for her, he clasped her to him, his chest heaving with the effort to breathe the smoky air. "Kit, is it truly you? I am not in heaven?"

She stopped herself from reminding him how unlikely it was that he would ever find himself with the angels. Instead tears started in her eyes, her words having to make their way past an enormous lump in her throat as she gently pulled away. "Jemmy, are your bones broken?"

"I don't know," he said, so relieved by the sight of her that he swallowed to cover his emotion, "but I would give a bone or two to have you call me Jemmy again."

Quickly, she began to run her fingers over him. He squirmed with a little groan.

"Quiet yourself, Jemmy," she said, moving to his head. She had not been aware of using that tender name, but it felt right and she could not recall it, or find the will to want to. "Can you walk?" She tried to sound brusque.

His hand slid about her waist and he drew her close again, his teeth shining amidst a face made devilish red with plaster and brick dust. "Aye, and more than walk."

"Hell and furies!" she snapped. "I thought you were injured."

He grinned. "That was my thought, but your tender, probing fingers proved me wrong. Er, a part of me does seem to always rise at your touch."

Abruptly, Kit threw back her head and laughed for the first time in days. There was no mistaking the mischief in him, and of a sudden it was very dear to her. She tried to make her voice severe. It was indeed dangerous if she had come to loving this man's faults. "God's nails, Jeremy Hughes, you have proved a giant fraud once and again," she said, but her voice trembled with some deep emotion, although whether from frustration at herself or at him she was not entirely certain.

He wiped his face on a handkercher pulled from his dusty doublet, retaining only shreds of its former fine texture. "Not quite a total fraud, although I will admit to more broken heart than broken bones when I thought you dead in the fire. But, lady," he said now in his Lord Lovemore voice, "if that be not enough of manly pain for your compassion, then I beg you to go, save yourself, and leave me here to suffer for my folly."

She suppressed her desire to smile at the role he acted long enough to wonder why he was not roistering with his noble friends. "What brought you here when there are yet whores at play?" she asked warily.

"Don't you know?"

Instead of the hasty riposte that had been on her tongue, she asked what now seemed obvious to her. "Were you coming for me?"

"That was the folly I spoke earlier." He gave her his hands and she grasped them. "We must help each other, Kit."

And despite his many charades, she looked in his eyes and believed him, feeling the fool for it, although she realized that the part of fool and lover were ever mixed in almost every play she'd studied at Master Jolly's, be it ancient or modern.

Her heart was beating hard against her breast, and she thought to pull away, but could not. He clasped her closer still. "Our stars are on the same path, Kit. I was meant to find you in that horse trough, and now we are meant to live and to—"

"Those are the words of a practiced lover." She willed her heart to stop its pounding.

"I'll not deny my past nor my present feelings."

"And I do?" She knew it was no longer a querulous question. "And I do," she repeated, but they were words of surrender. Placing her hands upon his face, she drew his lips toward hers.

Several men with blackened clothes rounded the corner. "This be no place to tryst," the leader yelled. "I have orders to blow up the street. Set the gunpowder, lads!"

Kit plucked her mirrored box from the rubble and quickly checked its contents to see that nothing was broken or spilled.

Jeremy laughed. "Now I know you are an actress born when you save your paint at risk to your life."

They moved off quickly toward Ludgate Hill, Jeremy's arm around Kit's shoulders, her free arm around his waist, her dress torn and hanging loose. "All we own is gone," Kit said, telling Jeremy how she had been unable to save his clothes or Alain's.

"All we own at the Lion's Head is gone," Jeremy agreed, the corners of his mouth softening, "but not all we had there."

She looked at him and remembered the scent of violets. "You are a philosopher."

"No, a philosopher has rules, and I've broken my first one."

"And that was . . ."

"To ne'er lose my head and heart."

She dared not ask for an explanation. They had already come to a fork in their conversation. She could either ask his meaning or . . . She chose the cautious way for now, until she had time to examine these trembling feelings of wanting to be . . . well, very close to Jeremy Hughes, feelings that she realized were not new. She changed the subject. "I fear for Alain and Martha."

He grinned, reading her mind again. "We will talk again of this later, sweet Kit. As for our friends, don't worry. Alain will come to Master Jolly's and find us there while Martha is well out of harm's way in her chocolate house." He stopped to allow Kit to rest against a pillar. "She did come to me at the Lion's Head."

"Martha is a good soul. I sent a message by Elizabeth to her, but am most heartily ashamed that I have been so busy with my own affairs I sent only the one greeting in the past fortnight." Kit made a silent vow to remedy that neglect, and soon.

They walked on slowly, tightly entwined, leaving the fire behind them, coming at last to an open square. Families and men of business were flocking past them, shouting that citizens were assembling in the open fields of Islington and even far Highgate. Children ran and laughed to be free of chores and schoolmasters, as if on some frightful holiday. Animals scampered between legs and under carts piled with all the rescued family goods. Kit knew that pillagers would move in behind them to easily take what was left, knowing the constables were busy elsewhere.

"London as we knew it is gone, Kit," Jeremy said, stopping to look back at the growing fire from a small rise. "And with it our hopes of the theaters opening this season. There is too much of chaos, and too many have lost all."

"They will open," Kit said, sure of that if nothing else. "People will need to laugh and to forget their troubles." They must open, she thought, not willing to admit a doubt before Jeremy, nor to herself.

Jeremy smiled into her eyes. "Ah, wise as well as beautiful. You are much changed, Kit. You are not the angry young goddess I found bathing in the horse trough."

"No, Jeremy, I'm not," Kit said, returning his smile, her teeth bright against her smoke-smudged face, her hair a wild yellow halo. "I'm very much dirtier."

They reached Master Jolly's after several detours around clogged roads. The steward opened the door, took Jeremy's dirty and torn cloak with some disgust and escorted them to the withdrawing room.

George Jolly greeted them with considerable relief. "I feared for your safety, my friends. Sit you down yonder," he said, noting their grimy condition, "though not on my brocade chair." He pointed to a bench by his writing table, then stepped to the door and called for ale, bread and cheese and a basin for washing. While they were eating, he pulled a note from a pile on his writing table. "Elizabeth brought this message back for you from the chocolate house yesterday, Mistress Kit." He excused himself. "My training continues as if the theaters will open," he said, not sounding hopeful. "On the morrow, we will rehearse again as is our custom. Be ready."

Kit received and opened the grimy note, unsigned and written in an unpracticed hand. *Martha be taken in shackles to the Fleet Prison.*

Chapter 13

A Desperate Scheme

Jeremy took the note from Kit's trembling hands and read it with more alarm than he wanted to show. The Fleet on Faringdon Street was more notorious than Bridewell or Newgate. Prisoners had to pay for food, were loaded with irons and then charged to have their shackles removed, sent to dungeons and extorted in every way that could be imagined. In order to survive, they begged for pennies through a grill opening on the street. Even worse, the women sold themselves for a crust. If charged with a capital crime, they asked nothing in hopes of getting with a babe to escape the rope, or the fire if they'd killed their husbands, which was a treasonous crime against the natural order.

"I must help her," Kit said, her voice choked with anguish. "This is a fault of mine. I cannot let her die for saving me from ravishment." She stood abruptly and took a step toward the door.

Jeremy rose in his turn. "Hold, Kit! You cannot assault the Fleet in your petticoats. You will only be arrested yourself and handed to that bastard Pursevant. We must be shrewd and enlist help." A plan was forming in his mind, but he could not relate it to Kit because it was a faint chance and probably doomed to disappoint.

"Who would help us?"

"Lord Rochester, mayhap, if we approach him with care and the right idea. He has a taste for unlawful adventure, as do several in the court. My lord Buckingham fancies himself a highwayman in the odd moment."

"But I would have to offer him . . . myself."

Jeremy took one head-clearing draft of ale. "That is why I want you to stay here and wait for me to return. Promise me." He clasped her shoulders and shook her in his great concern.

"Wait and do nothing like a ninny!" The idea obviously did not appeal. "Don't order me. Martha is in prison because of me, and I would be a part of her rescue."

"Be sensible. It is obvious to me that you need ordering, for there is a warrant for you, as well. How would it help, if you are shackled with her to die on the gibbet?"

"What would it be to you?" she said, too loud and with too little forethought. Immediately, she tried to withdraw the sting of those lashing words. "Jeremy, I am most heartily sorry. Forgive me."

"Of a certainty," he said, but she could see that the hurt had not entirely left his eyes.

Still, a stubbornness took hold of her. "Master Jolly wanted me to continue my training, and so I will. . . . I'll train for a breeches part, a young fop who comes to the Fleet for entertainment."

"While London burns? You are mad!"

"Most probably, but if I am to live, I must be worthy, and I wouldn't be if I didn't do something, everything to save her from—" She could not go on. To do so brought the gruesome fate Martha faced into too real a picture in her mind.

Jeremy could see in her face all the determination in the world and knew any forbidding of his would be useless. She had as much courage as any of the bravos in London, perhaps more. Better to watch over her than to let her go her own way into certain capture. "Then come to the costume room and we will dress ourselves, and devise a plan to entice Rochester into our adventure."

An hour later, two well-dressed and groomed young men exited Master Jolly's house, one very young, of delicate features, in a full wig, with a silver-headed cane, his sword tied with a large red ribbon; the other gallant, broad-shouldered, with handsome, manly carriage, in a blue silk suit and scarlet cloak . . . beaux to gather the glances of every woman in the street, fire or no, and some few did flirt most shamelessly with the older man, one even raising her mask as a tease to the younger.

"You may not want to hear this, but you do not capture all the ladies' glances," Kit said, pretending amusement.

"Sad."

"Very sad." She could see he was unused to sharing female attention.

They walked rapidly toward Whitehall, Jeremy instructing her, "If you would pass for a blade of the town, give a rakish toss of your head with an impudent air. Stride a little longer and firmer with a bold step, my lad. You have no corset stays to bite you."

"I am taking great pleasure in that, believe me, sir," she answered in her natural contralto voice, and in truth, she was feeling freer in her body than ever she had out of her bath.

"Indeed, if all women could dress in breeches just once, I think they would rebel against whalebone and petticoats."

He laughed, eyeing her critically. "But I would keep my cloak tight about me, lad, because you are displaying hips that no man ever sported." He walked on, laughing still, because Kit sputtered, but for once could find no suitable riposte.

She hurried after him, the blade at her side troublesome. "How do you control your sword, Jeremy? Mine seems to want to throw me to the cobbles."

"No time for lessons now. Keep a grip, especially when you're on stairs or sitting down." He smiled at her and winked. "You are doing well enough for a lad so recently come to manhood and not yet acquainted with a razor."

Ash fell in the street, although the wind seemed to have abated some, but the red glow to the east had grown closer since they'd made their way back to Bedford Street and Covent Garden square.

"Where will the fire stop?" Kit asked, not hiding her fear.

"At the water."

"You mean at the river Fleet? But the prison is on the *east* bank before the river! Will the prisoners—" The question was too horrible for her to continue.

"Hurry, we must find Rochester. If he is in humor—" He left the alternative unsaid.

They reached Whitehall to find a crowd of petitioners in the anterooms. Jeremy asked the clerk for paper, ink and quill and hastily wrote a note. "Give this to my lord Rochester."

They waited an hour, and then another and another, until they lost count before Rochester appeared, worried, haggard, looking years older than he had a few days earlier in the rehearsal hall. They both bowed, Kit just catching herself before dropping into a curtsy.

"My lord," Jeremy said. "May we have your private ear."

"I don't know this young gentleman," Rochester said, looking closely at Kit, a knowing smile growing on his face. "Although I think me that he is the prettiest boy I've ever seen at court."

She had not fooled him, and bowed again. "I thank you, my lord. I hope I wear my breeches with half the gallantry of your lordship." She had tried to sound sincere, but her worry for Martha had made her less an actress.

"Mistress, you are even more alluring in your scorn as I remember," Rochester said, seemingly unaffected. "How can you stand it, Jeremy?"

"I scarcely can, my lord."

Kit refused to join in what seemed a man's game in a man's code, ignoring the warning thump on her back from Jeremy. "Amusing dialogue, my lord Rochester," she said, "but this is not a play for an audience, but a play for a life."

Rochester bowed. "As I said, more alluring in your scorn." He drew them both to a corner of the antechamber. "Your note mentioned an adventure. Now, what is this about?" he asked, and listened intently as Jeremy outlined a plan to rescue a servant girl from gaol.

His lordship's eyes widened. "And this serving maid is a lord's love child. . . . A beauty?"

"Nay," Jeremy admitted, "I cannot vouch for any sire but a cottager, or any beauty except of a great good nature."

"I am all amaze, Hughes. What would I want me with an ugly country maid when I have better serving me now? This would make us a laughingstock or land us in the Tower, and I do not relish either."

He began to walk away, and Kit called softly after him. "My lord, before you return to your pleasures, get me a pass into the Fleet, and I will go alone."

Rochester turned slowly, his handsome face unreadable. "As I said, more alluring in your scorn. You do challenge my courage?"

"No, my lord, I challenge your heart to do a justice for which you will have no reward on this earth."

"Do not prate of heaven to me."

Kit bowed to him. "I most heartily agree, my lord Rochester. I have exhausted all reasoning for this world, or for heaven. By your leave," she said, her voice trembling with anger and high emotion. She turned and strode away with a bold step, a rakish toss of her head and an impudent air.

Jeremy caught her at the door. "Dam'me, Kit, why did you speak to him so? He needs to be jollied and brought along slowly."

Kit's face was grim. "No, Jeremy, he needs a good birching. I'll not jolly about while Martha lies shackled or worse in the Fleet."

"You have let your temper get ahead of your sense," he said, genuinely angry with her and not willing to hide it.

They were outside Whitehall, walking back toward Covent Garden, arguing spiritedly, when a carriage with two footmen stopped and the door opened.

Rochester's drawling voice issued from the dark interior, along with the scent of a fine Madeira wine. "Well, if we are to do this noble thing, my fine gentlemen, then let us to it."

Chapter Fourteen

An Unexpected Coupling

It was full dark when they reached the foreboding stone walls of the Fleet prison, although the night sky was an angry red not far to the east, the great fire devouring centuries-old houses, churches and shops, creeping ever closer.

A footman announced them to the guards. "Make way there for his lordship, Earl of Rochester."

Kit felt clammy under her cloak and was grateful for Jeremy's reassuring hand on her shoulder. Events began to move swiftly, too swiftly for her to have time for shrinking from what she must do. A short prayer was in order, and she silently sent it on its way.

They were instantly passed inside the prison, escorted down long, stinking corridors resounding to distant shrieks and groans over the sound of their footsteps, until they reached a large room with a trestle table and benches. They were announced to a small man who sat eating roast fowl, his hands and chin slippery with grease, his too-large, unbuttoned doublet showing even older stains. His wig rested on the table before him, the sparse hair on his head and the growth on his face wanting a barber.

"You are warden here?" Rochester asked in a tone that demanded immediate attention.

"Who asks?" He wiped his mouth on his sleeve.

"John Wilmot, Earl of Rochester!"

The man was on his feet immediately, donning a wig that had never visited a nitpicker, bowing deeply. "I am warden of His Majesty's prison of the Fleet, my lord, Nathaniel Burden by name, and I give you welcome." He broke off and bowed again, "And welcome to the other gentlemen. Will you sit?"

Rochester, ignoring the courtesy, reached inside his doublet past overflowing lace and satin and pulled out an official-looking parchment. "His Majesty has some concern for the safety of these his prisoners, and wishes some transferred to the Gatehouse prison in Westminster in case the fire does reach this far."

The warden accepted the paper and read it. "Most unusual, your lordship," he said. "Just the prisoners taken in the last twenty-four hours."

Rochester withdrew his snuffbox, executing the ritual with such supreme courtly elegance that the warden's fascinated eyes never strayed from the performance. Kit could imagine him attempting the same later to impress his betters. "There could be more prisoners moved"—Rochester delicately suppressed a sneeze—"later if the fire approaches."

"This document is not signed, my lord," the warden said, looking on it with confusion and a dawning suspicion.

Rochester put his hand on the hilt of his sword. "Come, man, you rake me," he shouted in lordly dudgeon. "Do you think the king has time for every attention while the capital of this his realm burns down about him? I am a Gentleman of the Bedchamber, sir, and I suggest you have a care. If I return and tell His Majesty that you refuse his order, you may as well ready a cell for yourself. . . . A lower cell, I vow!"

"My lord," Kit said, bowing, her voice unnaturally gruff, "shall I return to Whitehall and bring His Majesty's guard?"

Rochester raised an eyebrow in her direction as if to say *Don't overplay*, but he was well entertained by her role. She could see that as well as she could see that Jeremy was not.

Jeremy moved idly toward the warden, his eyes never leaving the man, which move Nathaniel Burden seemed to find most menacing.

The warden scurried from where he stood on the other side of the table, dropping into another deep bow before Rochester. If his fright grew any greater, it would slide off his face. "Your pardon, my gracious lord. Of course I will have them brought up immediately. . . . Except for one scullery maid. She was taken by a beadle for attempting to kill her master, Sir William Pursevant. I'm waiting now for him to arrive from Essex by coach for the trial not two days hence. She'll surely burn or hang, if the judge is merciful, though her master survived."

Rochester was cold with fury, and Kit saw it was no act this time. He was genuinely affronted by the warden's denying him his entire will, probably thinking it a remnant of Cromwell's times when the commons, not content with regicide, thought themselves the equal of nobility. She trembled inside to think of the two times she had defied that same will.

"I will take all," said Rochester, "or you will answer to His Majesty that you followed the order of a country knight rather than that of your king. I vow, you will bear the results of your perfidy before this night is done," he added in a low, soft voice that would have brought a chill to a much braver man than Nathaniel Burden.

The warden's body seemed to collapse inside; he noticeably shriveled in stature. "Your most gracious pardon, my lord. As you say, my lord. All of them and at *once,* my lord." He stepped to the open door and spoke to the guard, his voice atremble. "Bring up the three prisoners in yesterday's holding cell . . . and quickly, man. My lord Rochester," he said, turning back, "may I offer you and the other gentlemen some refreshment?"

Rochester turned a sweet and generous smile on the warden. "I thank you most heartily for it, sir. I am parched and starved from a long day of duties for the king." He walked to the pewter plate that held the warden's dinner, broke off the bigger leg and ate its meat in a few bites, wiping his hands on a handkercher of Flemish lace points, which he tucked into a sleeve.

The warden watched him with no protest, then produced three bowls and a bottle of good wine with a speed that said to Kit that he wished to be rid of his guests with all haste.

Kit had to remind herself to breathe normally, especially when the clanking of chains came closer. She moved away from the lantern on the table, lest Martha recognize her and cry out.

A terrified young man, lank brown hair hanging, eyes darting from face to face, was brutally prodded into the room by a guard with a club and an air of knowing its use. "I be innocent, good sirs. I am no cutpurse," he babbled, trying to fall on his knees but prevented by the short leg irons. Behind him shuffled Martha, her face battered, one eye swollen near shut, one hand holding a bundle of belongings, the other a starved, ragged boy no more than eight, who clung to her and hid his face against her side.

Kit reached out to hold tight to a chair back, biting her tongue to keep from calling out Martha's name. She might not have contained herself had not Rochester spoken in a curious voice that sent a shudder of fear through her.

"Is this the maid, Jeremy?" Rochester asked, a half smile on his lips as he licked the last morsel of his stolen meal from them, eyeing Martha up and down.

"Aye, my lord," Jeremy said, obviously startled by the question, and looking a warning to Martha, who had raised her head and opened her one good eye wide at sight of him, a glint of hope leaping forth where none could had been before.

The warden stepped forward, puzzlement writ on his face. "A moment, if it please you, my lord. You know this prisoner?"

"I do not," Rochester answered, "but she is the betrothed of my friend Jeremy, here."

Jeremy jerked a quick step forward. "My lord Rochester, if this is a jape, I think it overdone."

Rochester smiled sweetly, something of the angel in a devilish face. "All japes are overdone or they be not japes, and this one, my dear fellow, is called *payment due*. I will have it for my work this night. I think you will not deny me." There was a wealth of warning in those simple words.

The warden looked from Martha to Jeremy, his eyes narrowed in unbelief. "My lord, are you saying that your well-favored friend here has a passion for this lumpy baggage?"

"Do not be so unbelieving. Passion, dear warden, is indiscriminate, like lightning . . . like lightning, sir. Betimes, I myself form an instant passion for beautiful young actresses, e'en one who denies me. Can you countenance it, sir?"

In that moment, Kit began to hate Rochester's fastidious manner, his excessive diction and repetition of phrase. It was no longer elegant and courtly, but evil when used to manipulate lives. And that was his game, she had no doubt.

Rochester continued smiling on the warden. "Sir, everyone knows of a clandestine Fleet marriage. . . . Not banns nor license are required, and any clergyman may do the deed. Have you a clergyman?" He produced a gold guinea and pressed it into the warden's hand with a wink and a close whisper in his ear.

"Aye, my lord, imprisoned for debt."

"Bring him to me."

The warden was slow to respond, trying to decipher this turn of events.

"At once!" Rochester said, and there was true menace in his tone. Kit saw that he was tiring of the game and that would make him all the more dangerous.

The warden spoke in low tones to the guard, who left immediately.

Rochester clapped the man as a comrade on his shoulder. "Since the wench is to die, why deny the lovers these last fond moments?"

Kit was rooted to the stone floor in a gathering fury that did not allow her to think with a clear head. She pulled Jeremy aside and saw that he was struggling for the right course. She examined his glorious face, every inch of it, as if she'd never truly seen it before. Perhaps she hadn't, because now she saw more of courage and compassion than she had ever known. "Oh, Jemmy, I never meant this for you." She tried to find the words to say that she had never thought her stubborn insistence on rescuing Martha would cost Jeremy such a price. "Can we not reason with Rochester?"

"In his eyes, he is all reasonable, asking only for just payment. He is telling us that he will not be used for a fool, or denied his will."

"That is again a fault of mine. You cannot—" she began, but did not know where to take her words without dooming Martha to death.

"Do you want her life?" There was resignation on his face.

Kit swallowed hard. "I will give myself to him this night."

"Then I would have to die fighting him. Answer me. Do you want her life?"

"Jemmy, please do not make this decision mine."

He expelled a deep breath that touched her cheek, and she thought herself more than crazed to smell violets. "I made it my decision when I took two women from the back room of the constable's house in Chelmsford."

Rochester stopped their low-spoken words, swallowing the last of Jeremy's bowl of wine as well as his own. "Come lads, be sporting," he said, quite pleased withal. "If you would be a mad couple, what is madder than this?"

"You are right, my lord, as always." At least, Jeremy thought, I will remove some of his smug pleasure. He walked over to Martha and kissed her hand. "Say nothing but what you should, Harlequin," he said softly.

The divine entered, blinking in the light. "Ah, Master Burden, you wish me to join young lovers in holy matrimony?"

Jeremy stepped forward. The guard pushed Martha to Jeremy's side, the boy still clinging to her skirt.

The minister cleared his throat, eyed the wine bottle, and when none was offered, he began. "Dearly beloved, we are gathered together here in the sight of God, and of this company. . . ."

Kit watched, though she could not hear the words for the blood pounding in her ears. She allowed no emotion to escape her breaking heart and show on her face, lest she show less courage than Jemmy. But she knew that nothing this man ever did would surprise her again.

Chapter Fifteen

A Wedding Night

Rochester had truly tired of his jest by the time they reached Westminster, and unceremoniously left them on the cobbles before the Gatehouse prison to do with the prisoners as they would. "Take your bride and make merry your wedding night, Jeremy. I wish you joy of her."

They could hear him laughing above the sound of horses' hooves as he drove toward Whitehall looming ahead.

"Good sir," choked the man shackled to Martha, trembling so violently his chains rattled while he stood unmoving. "I be innocent. Free me, and I swear by almighty God that I will take me from London forever."

"Hush, man, you are more fortunate than you deserve." But Jeremy's voice softened when he spoke to Martha. "You cannot stay in the city, Harlequin. There will be a hue and cry as soon as Sir William arrives and finds you not locked in the Gatehouse, ready for trial."

Martha stared at him. "The lad here be due to hang for stealing food," she said, looking down at the cowering boy. "I must take him with me."

"Don't worry, Martha," Kit said, and watched recognition dawn in her eyes, which had been fixed on Jeremy since the moment they were wed.

"Oh, mistress—"

Kit surrendered her shoulder to Martha's tears. "Mistress Kit, be it truly you in those breeches?" Martha began laughing and choking, struggling to speak. "I be not able to say a thank you—"

"Hush, Martha, there is no fault due to you. All this has come upon you because you saved me from Sir William. I will not have you suffer more for it."

Jeremy thought quickly, keeping an eye on the prison gates. He pulled all back to the shadows. "We must get your chains off, but how? No smith would—"

"With this, good sir," the self-described innocent cutpurse said, producing a key from his ragged sleeve. "I took it from the careless guard, but I swear it be the first time I had me hand in another's doublet."

Jeremy laughed. "Then you have an uncommon natural talent. Unlock the fetters," he said, but the man was already doing so.

"Martha," said a sober Jeremy, "are you willing to emigrate to the Virginia Plantations? It is the only way you will ever be safe. Even as my wife, you would not—"

"Master Jeremy, I be planning to go all this time, and saving my wages." She thrust her hand inside her dress to her pocket and jingled coins. "I be near five pounds rich. I thought to give it to the hangman to make it quick for me and the lad."

"How did you earn so much?" Kit asked, and then wondered if she should have. There was only one sure way for a woman to earn that much money, and she did not want to believe that Martha had been whoring for it.

"I came by it honest, mistress," said Martha. "Remember the chocolate you drank?"

"I'm not like to forget it," Kit said, wishing she had a dish to calm herself at that very minute, "but what does Spanish chocolate have to do with earning five pounds, since it is so costly?"

"I be thinking one day and remembering helping Cook bake a spice-and-apple cake at Bournely Hall, and I thought me to make a chocolate cake, and all the customers be going mad for it. The innkeeper gave me three pounds to speak the secret to his wife to write down and give it no other."

Kit was surprised at the idea, and yet there it was, so plain to see. "Chocolate to carry in your hand! Clever Martha, now I know that you will make your way in the colonies. I need not fear for you."

Martha met Kit's eyes, and although one of Martha's was still swollen almost shut, there was pride in them at Kit's recognition.

They threw the irons into a narrow alley and made their way to the Westminster water stairs, two foppish town gallants leading a ragtag trio, drawing some curious glances from people scurrying past.

The Thames was full of boats and lighters removing people's goods from the advancing fire, but one was just emptying as they reached the stairs.

Jeremy spoke to the waterman. "Know of any ship bound for the Virginia Plantations?"

"Aye, the *Merry Friendship,* lying well below the Tower near Deptford, due to sail on the next high tide."

"Take us to her," he ordered, paying twice the usual fare to secure the boat.

They were rowed past the fire, which now extended as far as could be seen. They silently watched the city burning. There were no words to describe it, except for the occasional sharp intake of breath as a familiar landmark was caught by flames, and the words "Oh, dear God!" uttered because no others would do.

The tide was outflowing and they rowed between the pillars of London Bridge, still smoking on its north side but not burning to the Southwark bank, then past the Tower, which had escaped the flames, and, hugging the south bank, came at last to the *Merry Friendship.*

Jeremy stood and hailed the ship. "Have you room for three more passengers to the Virginia Colony?"

They waited until a voice shouted down to them. "I be master here. You want passage?"

"Aye, Captain, for three—a woman who can pay, and a man and boy who will work for their keep."

"I have need for seamen, not useless lubbers."

The cutpurse called up to the bridge, "I have sailed twice to the Jamaica Plantations, Cap'n, and will sleep on deck, and my lad here has shipped as cabin boy."

Jeremy rounded on the man. "Your tongue is as nimble as your fingers."

"Nay, 'tis true, except for the lad here, and I'll teach 'im."

"Come aboard, then," the captain called down, "and hurry, for the tide is fast rising."

Kit and Martha embraced. "I be always keeping you in my heart, mistress," Martha said.

"Try to get word to me that you are safe arrived. Master

Jolly will know where I am, and I will answer with my news."

With her arms still around Kit, Martha whispered, "I be ever sorry. . . . About Master Jeremy and all. I know he . . . I know ye—"

Kit stopped Martha's mouth with a finger, shaking her head. "Regret nothing, for you go with my love and friendship, Martha."

Jeremy helped the cutpurse and the boy up the ship's ladder, then took Martha in his arms and kissed her cheek. But Martha turned her head and kissed his lips heartily, although her face went instantly red with embarrassment and pleasure. "I never be forgettin' ye . . . husband." She said the word as if tasting chocolate on her tongue for the first time, and then having embarrassed herself mightily with her own boldness, she scrambled up the ladder, hung over the railing for a time as the river boatmen pushed off, and then was gone from sight below.

Kit and Jeremy sat in silence, avoiding each other's faces until they reached the water stairs at Whitehall, where a tangle of boats loaded with household goods blocked the river.

They retraced their echoing steps past Covent Garden to Bedford Street and closer to Master Jolly's, coughing as the wind, lighter now, carried smoke to them. Finally, Kit could stand the silence no longer. "I am forever indebted to you," she said softly.

"I forgive any debt you owe me."

Kit could not discern from Jeremy's tone whether blame or sadness was in him. She took a deep breath, forgetting to watch out for her sword, nearly tripping and grabbing Jeremy's arm to steady herself. "I cannot accept your forgiveness. What you did was the most noble of—"

He was angry now, and his voice held some desperation. "Do you think I want you in a debtor's prison . . . even my own? Do you think nobility is what I want you to seek from me?"

What do you want? But the question remained unasked because he walked on faster, forcing her to run, almost tripping over her sword to catch him at Master Jolly's door. A puffy-eyed steward admitted them, saying the master had retired, and returned immediately to his own bed.

"Change out of your breeches and quickly, and then I would speak with you," Jeremy said, "for I doubt this jape has ended. The Fleet warden is a suspicious man." He entered the withdrawing room before she could question his meaning.

Kit raced up the stairs to the costume room and shed her breeches, happy to be rid of the sword that had threatened her every step, declaring under her breath that she would master it if it took her a lifetime. When she entered the withdrawing room, Jeremy had stoked the fire, adding more sea coal, and poured two tankards of sack. He handed one to her, his hand brushing hers deliberately, she thought, and then also thought how little she minded his touch. She admitted for the first time, wondering at her lost will, that the liberties she hated in other men, she secretly celebrated in Jeremy.

They drank silently with a thirst that they hadn't thought to completely quench all the long night of desperate adventure, delaying the coming moment when they would have to speak what was in their minds and hearts.

Jeremy fixed his dark eyes on her and they seemed to have bottomless depth in the firelight, his thoughts unknowable. "I find I like you even better in petticoats than I do in breeches, and I liked you mightily in breeches." It was an attempt at his old careless manner, but she did not believe it, because there was a breaking undertone in his voice, echoes of angry thoughts or hurts unspoken.

She could not read this strange mood, but she knew with a sinking heart that she had failed him when she owed him so much in Martha's name. "Jeremy, please quiet your anger. Do not think that—" She lost her way and tried to begin again. "Jeremy, I—" How could she tell him that she thought him the best man in all England for what he had done? The words caught in her throat. She had no right. He was married.

He laughed bitterly. "You call me noble. Do you think I wed Martha for your sake? Why would any man do such a thing . . . wed one woman for sake of another?"

"I do not know, Jemmy," she said, which was not entirely true and not entirely untrue.

He moved closer then and placed his hands on her bare shoulders before she could step away from the iron in his grip. "You must know, or all will be for naught," he said, leaning toward her until his lips were against her cheek so that she felt as well as heard each aching word.

"I don't know. It is beyond my imagining." Another woman's voice spoke, because Kit certainly didn't recognize it as her own. His hands felt like firebrands on her skin, the heat of them spreading through her. She must stop him; she must want to stop him.

His lips moved down her cheek in a trail of flame to her mouth, which was open to him. "Jemmy. Jemmy, I cannot—"

But she could. Her warm, searching kisses made her words into instant lies.

Kit finally broke away, her hands cupping her breasts in a futile effort to calm her breathing.

He stared at her, but she could not read his face until she heard his words. "I love you, Kit," he choked. "I love the way you stumble upon your rapier. I love that it takes you not one second to bring up your chin at a slight. I love that your eyes grow wide just before you engage your wit. I love you for many things, but not for your gratitude."

She smiled tentatively. "Gratitude comes later, Jemmy, if you are the man I hear you are."

"Alas, gossip gets around," he said, grinning.

Kit had been using the words of a coquette, and she could not believe she'd thought them, let alone spoken them. Oh, wondrous Jemmy. She had been blind to the truth of the bower and the violets on her bed. The rogue she'd tried to hate had never existed. Here was the man of which her poetic dreams were made, the perfectly flawed, loving rakehell of a man. And he wanted her.

She began tugging at the laces on her bodice, her hands following no thought but some part of her woman's nature that now commanded her.

He caught her to him again and they were so together that she could not escape him. He lowered his head to her unfinished bodice, pulling the laces out with his teeth. Kit was shivering and laughing at once until she could not bear it and pulled at the last laces with her own hands until the gown fell over her hips and she stood in her plain linen shift.

Surprised, Jeremy stepped back. In the firelight, he could see the full curving lines of her body as he had first seen them at the abandoned cot, and knew that he would ever remember this moment and his great need for her if he lived into a new century. And if he did not, he would remember this moment with his last breath. He stripped off his blue silk doublet and fine lace-point shirt, flinging them toward Master Jolly's upholstered great chair, where they hung for a moment and then slid to the floor, already forgotten.

Kit could see that his wound was still puckered and red on his shoulder, but he looked quite recovered otherwise. Indeed, more than recovered. His shoulders and arms showed a strength that made her want what she had never wanted willingly from any man. At that moment, all memory of Sir William's vicious attempt to ravish her and of her decision to remain without a master in this life seemed to slip away from her as easily and naturally as rainwater running down eaves.

Slowly, their eyes locked together, they sank as one body onto the brilliantly colored turkey carpet in front of the carved-stone fireplace, whose smiling cupids looked down on them as Kit's hair spread in a glowing, golden circle about her head, vying with the firelight. Praying for control he knew he was about to lose, Jeremy lowered himself gently on top of her, feeling his body fit onto hers as if they were perfectly matched, like a pair of the king's new high-tailed Arabians prancing in St. James Park. "You look like a sun goddess. . . . So beautiful." His hands were on her hips, stroking them through the thin shift, his head buried against her breasts, his tongue seeking her nipples. He could not repress a groan that frightened Kit.

"If your wound is hurting—" she whispered against his dark hair.

He rolled to her side, took her hand and guided it to his swelling cod. "This is where my pain rests, Kit, and only you have a cure for it."

For a brief moment, she remembered Sir William forcing

her hand to his cod, but that feeling of awful loathing was not what she felt now. Her own privy parts were hot and aching. Near breathless, she choked out, "Show me what you want of me, Jemmy."

"All, Kit. I want all," he said, groaning again, but softly this time. As her hand stroked his smooth, hot shaft, his fingers moved from her thigh through her thicket to caress her vibrating womanhood, until she rebelled against her emptiness and began to beat her free hand against his back.

"Dearest heart!" he gasped, and mounted her arching body, beginning to move against her. Her legs opened wide to him as if he had turned the only key. She clutched the carpet to keep from crying out, but she couldn't stop moaning his name again and again. "Jemmy. *Jemmy!*"

He covered her mouth with his, his tongue stroking hers as his cod thrust through her hot, slippery passage, to be stopped by her maidenhead. He thrust again harder and harder again until he broke through. She shivered and screamed into his mouth, and felt her warm blood bathing him as he plunged so deep he reached a place of exquisite burning pain, a place of torture and paradise. One thought raced quickly through her: Sir William had not taken her. Jemmy was the first.

Jeremy felt her gripping his cod in a tight inner embrace, her mounting spasms matching his until he could hold back the tide of his love no longer, and with a deep cry he spent himself. Breathing heavily, he knew he had lost the last natural caution of a man when he heard his own words: "I love you, heart, only you, forever."

The same words were singing in her depths, but she was afraid to speak them, although her feeling for him demanded truth. "Jemmy, I have never known this before."

He rose up on one elbow and ran a hand down the tantalizing curve of her hip. He looked into her eyes, soft with lassitude, and couldn't lie to her, though he knew such information could be dangerous in the wrong woman's hands. "Heart, neither have I. Never."

He lay his head on her bosom and they were at peace together until he felt his cod stir to full life. But a loud banging began on the front door, and shouts—"Open, in the king's name!"—demanded hasty dressing to present a most disheveled appearance.

Soon several gentlemen of the court, with their hands on their swords, crowded into the room, the leader saying, "We have a warrant for the arrest of one Jeremy Hughes and an unknown gentleman."

Throwing Kit a warning look that begged her silence, Jeremy stepped forward. "I am Jeremy Hughes."

"What of the other young gentleman who joined you at the Fleet this night with my lord Rochester, in disturbance of the king's peace?"

"I know of no other gentleman, sir."

"That's what my lord Rochester says—that the warden must have been drunk, for there were only the two of you involved in the jape. Come along, then."

"On what charge?" Jeremy asked, pretending puzzlement.

"Lying to a king's prison warden to gain release of capital prisoners, and forging a royal document. My lord Rochester also faces a count of destroying the king's favorite sundial."

Two men in the king's red livery took hold of Jeremy and marched him to the door, Kit following on weak legs, close enough to hear what was said. "You have the devil's own luck, Master Hughes," one of the guards said as they entered the coach waiting outside. "The warden at the Fleet wanted you for himself, but my lord Rochester asked that you be taken to the Tower to join him, and His Majesty graciously granted his request, although it may be the last one my lord of Rochester receives if he keeps his head, and if you keep yours, Master Hughes."

There was hearty laughter at that as they drove away in the night.

But as Kit stood clutching Jolly's door and staring after the receding coach lanterns, she heard a voice she knew well, raised in song:

> *"I am a lusty, lively lad, arrived at one and twenty,*
> *I'll court and kiss. . . ."*

As a good-bye, it was the sweetest she'd ever heard. As an attempt to reduce her fears, it was a total failure.

Chapter Sixteen

Command Performance

Kit awoke at dawn a week after Jeremy had been taken to the Tower, having slept much against her will from exhaustion and worry, in the third-floor room Master Jolly had given her and Elizabeth to share. With many thousands of Londoners burnt out of their homes, there were few rooms available. Since the city continued to smolder, she'd walked north around the old walls to the Tower several times, but had been denied entry. She'd begged the guards, first with coquetry, then with tears, to take Jeremy a message, but without the necessary bribe, she had been threatened with arrest herself.

Each time, she'd also searched for Alain in the flimsy tent camps raised by many thousands of homeless Londoners at Moorfields, but that, too, had come to naught, raising her anxiety further.

She dressed hastily by candlelight, thinking of Jeremy, doting on the memory of those last hours with him. No matter how she blamed herself for the danger he was in, her mind and body relived those moments in the grand parlor on the turkey carpet, feeling again his skin touching hers, breathing in his man smell, seeing the glazed, haunted look in his eyes as he hung over her and vibrated deep inside her, relishing each sense of him even though she knew her emotions were a cunning trap set by man to master a woman's body. Yet he had said he loved her, and his voice had trembled with sincerity. Dare she believe so practiced a cuckold? Still, he had no need to say he loved her to lure her to his bed. She had submitted with little modest hesitation. . . . In all honesty, with *no* hesitation. But if she believed him truly, then what was her future? Faith, she could ponder no further on it without reaching the idea of marriage, and that was unthinkable. He was married to Martha. But almost as important, marriage gave man complete mastership over woman in the eyes of both church and law, a duo few modern women had been able to resist. Though she must . . . somehow, if it came to that.

Donning her mask and hood to interrupt such rampant, troublesome thought, Kit stepped into the cobbled street and around the corner to the baker's to fetch bread for Master Jolly's table, many loaves, since he was now feeding all the actors forced out of their lodgings by the great fire.

After five days the fire had been stopped at Temple Church, but not before it had consumed much of old London within the ancient walls, including Fleet Prison. As she walked through the pall of gray smoke that still hung over the city, wafting ash on the late summer breezes, Kit exalted in the memory of having saved Martha from such a fate. It pleased her to think that heaps of ash and stones were all that Sir William found when he arrived at the prison to claim his revenge, though she knew he would not long stay his search for one Katherne Lindsay.

The baker's penny loaves were now outrageously priced at two pennies. But the price of bread was not the only change the fire had wrought. The news sheets announced that above thirteen thousand structures had been destroyed, giving employment to masons and carpenters, crowding in from as far away as York in the north while ruining many London shopkeepers. It seemed to Kit that God had taken with one hand and given with the other, for while the ancient city lay in ruins, it had been cleansed of plague.

Retracing her steps, she wondered what such destruction would mean in the future. Would a new and better city rise? Yes, she thought defiantly as she approached Master Jolly's house, and the theaters would open.

"Alain!" she called, and began to run as he looked up from where he was slumped against the door, twisting his cut and horribly swollen mouth into an awkward smile. He held his hands away from his body, and she could see even from a little distance that they were raw red, blisters seeping blood, skin hanging in strips.

"I could not knock, *ma chere,*" he said simply in a voice that quavered with pain.

Kit dropped her five loaves of bread and pounded on the door, calling loudly for Master Jolly, who quickly came. Together they helped Alain into the great parlor and into Jolly's upholstered chair. Kit held a bowl of wine to Alain's lips and he drank thirstily, choking and coughing up black sputum.

He hunched over himself. "It hurts to breathe."

"Alain, tell me quickly where you found the doctor, Wyndham by name, you brought to the Lion's Head for Jeremy?"

He opened his reddened eyes. "Is Jeremy safe?"

"More than safe," Kit said, without lying or giving worrisome detail. "Now, where do I find the doctor?"

"Hard by the apothecary in New King Street . . . near Drury Lane."

She was out the door in an instant, praying to find the doctor at home. She found him breaking his fast with three much-wrinkled old dames waiting in his parlor to buy his Infallible Miracle Salve.

Mistress Wyndham, a sweet-faced, very pregnant woman, opened wide her door, and Kit rushed upon the doctor. "Hurry, good doctor, a man at Master Jolly's is in sore need of your care."

"Sit you down, mistress," he said, sipping more of the China drink from his bowl. "You must calm yourself or you will swoon. May I offer you refreshment? Did you not follow my instructions for the knife wound?"

"I did, and he is much recovered. This is another man, sir, and you must hurry."

The doctor raised his eyebrows and they near reached his towering three-tailed peruke. "Is it the plague? I have heard of no new case."

"His hands are badly burned and he is beaten about the face. I know few doctors will come for the plague."

"I am one who would, mistress . . . though my specialty is burns of the extremities." He stood quickly at this new urgency, picked up his bag of medicines and instruments, which he slung over his shoulder. He kissed his wife, and she blushed. "Kate, my dear, see to the other patients until my salve is gone. I will have to make another trip to the country before I can make more." He took her face in his hands, turning it this way and that. "Ah, your sweet face is my only bill of advertisement, wife."

Kit turned away from the intimate scene, the love between them making her heart ache from memory.

Taking two steps to Kit's every one, the doctor followed her to Covent Garden.

Master Jolly had already arranged for a pallet in a corner of his grand parlor. The doctor knelt beside Alain, who opened his eyes and tried to smile.

"Ah, *mon Dieu*, Josiah Wyndham. You must be the busiest physico in all London," Alain said, but pain wracked him and he clenched his teeth on the words, failing the light-hearted touch of a Frenchman for perhaps the first time.

"Not the busiest, friend, but the best, I vow," the good doctor answered, and Alain smiled again though it hurt him. Wyndham held a dark unstoppered bottle to Alain's lips. "Some poppy, sir, to ease the pain. There is no hurt so great as a burning, and you, sir, have foolishly put your hands in the fire."

"To save a friend."

Doctor Wyndham put his ear to Alain's chest. "And you breathed in much smoke, my brave sir. But how come you by the injuries to your face?"

"Monsieur *le docteur*, some men accused me of being French and a Catholic, which I, of a certainty, could not deny, and more. . . . Of starting the fire, which I did deny. Though they easily believed the first, they thought the second a lie." Alain attempted a look of disdain but gave it up midway, since it required the use of his swollen mouth.

"You have been badly used, sir. Londoners are looking for a cause of their great trouble, first of plague, then of fire, and it is made simple to blame the Dutch or the French." The doctor gently felt Alain's face. "Nothing broken, though you will ache much, and mayhap retain a scar above your lip, though I will use my finest stitches."

Alain's eyes began to close.

"The poppy does its work," the doctor said, "but you both must hold him, because now I will work on his hands."

"Don't hurt him," Kit said, and knew her request was ridiculous. She breathed more easily when the doctor began to carefully cut away loose skin and Alain groaned briefly but did not start up from his pallet.

"There," the doctor said, sitting back on his heels after applying a thick coating of Wyndham's Infallible Miracle Salve. "Although there are many secret ingredients, my salve is of a goose-grease base which never hardens. . . . Best for healing burns. Some swear by a honey poultice, but I have better success with my own salve, which does not surprise me. Now I will need much clean linen to wrap the hands. I must wrap each finger apart."

"Why apart?" asked Jolly.

"So the fingers will not heal together. 'Tis a mistake too often made by my colleagues, who have not the advantage of my training at the University of Padua and Bologna."

"Bologna, too?" Kit asked, looking up, a slow smile starting. "What about Oxford?"

"For a time," the doctor answered, followed by a wink.

Kit returned it, beginning to like the little doctor, and fraud or no, to believe he was indeed taller than his stature would admit.

After putting three small stitches in Alain's lip and applying salve to his face, the doctor mixed a soothing decoction of coltsfoot and honey. "Heat this and have him drink it three times each day to clear the lungs. I will call on him again tomorrow." Handing Kit the small bottle of poppy juice, he ordered, "One swallow as he needs it. You will know."

Kit sat beside Alain for that whole day, and thought she

saw the pain in him diminish. He took some broth from a bowl toward evening, and smiled on her without as much hurt, though she still kept a dozing watch from Master Jolly's upholstered great chair that night.

With the fencing master, Kit was practicing all nine rapier parries in the box, a square outline on the floor, that she could not cross without losing points, when Master Jolly burst into the rehearsal hall, waving a piece of paper.

Distracted, she glanced at Jolly for a moment and felt her sword leave her hand and skip across the floor. "Devil's stick!" she swore. "You take advantage, sir."

The fencing master bowed. "Mistress, that is the true nature of fencing."

George Jolly advanced, beaming. "Enough, mistress. I have here a summons from the king. He has heard that I have finished my *Lord Lovemore and the Lady*, which my lord Rochester praised much . . . before he left for a visit to the Tower. The king wishes us to play for him at Whitehall tomorrow after he dines. His Majesty does love comedy and comic actors above all, and his court is in need of good cheer now that the great fire is contained."

Kit fair screamed her answer. "He has the best comic actor locked in a Tower cell, suffering untold agonies!"

"Ssshh, mistress, one of our other young gentlemen can take the part."

She did not mean her voice to remain so harsh, but it did. "I will not play it without Jeremy Hughes."

For once, George Jolly was amazed. "Mistress Kit, you cannot order the King of England."

"Master Jolly, I would not think of ordering His Majesty. I but order myself."

Jolly raised his eyes to the ceiling as if communing with the white plaster cherubim of the rehearsal hall. "I suspect you are prone to sick headache, mistress, if denied." He sighed mightily. "My days have grown ever more complicated since you came to me. Your every action seems to provoke drama."

"Sir, that should but confirm you in your decision to take me as pupil for the stage."

He narrowed his eyes and pursed his lips, but she could detect a lurking smile. "Prepare yourself then, Mistress Mighty, to meet your king and plead your case. He may respond favorably to youth and beauty, as indeed he has been known to do. . . . Or deny us both any future in the theaters of his realm. I must be mad to do this."

"Sir, you are not mad. You think me right."

Kit called on Elizabeth to help her prepare, and together they dressed her in a creamy satin gown with openwork aplenty and a rose silk undershift that peeked through every opening, a froth of lace at her bosom that did not completely hide her upthrust breasts. Kit surveyed herself in the wardrobe's long mirror and was very pleased. "It is forward without being obvious," she said, "like a mask that does not hide the best feature."

Elizabeth painted her face and bosom, added a moon and circling stars to one cheek, dressed her hair in fashionable hanging curls. Kit was right satisfied as she presented herself to Alain, who had been moved to a small second-floor room.

He was sitting beside a window, watching the street below, his hands resting gingerly on his lap. He held them up to her. "The funny little *docteur* says they are healing well and the fingers will bend in time. They will not be pretty." He bit his lip and winced from pain, since the wound had not completely healed. "I will needs visit my glover anon, *n'est ce pas*? White kid, I think . . . umm, or maybe red and yellow." He brightened, and the old Alain spoke next. "I will wear the most elegant gloves when next I dine at Lockets. All London will follow my fashion." He sat taller at that and motioned for her to turn about for him.

She twirled. "I go to meet the king and beg for Jeremy's release to play Lord Lovemore."

"From the Tower? You take much upon yourself, *ma chere amie,* but you do not surprise me."

"I must try. Jemmy could be tortured, racked, burned with hot, sizzling coals, blinded even." Her voice caught on these fearful words. "At this very moment, he could be screaming my name."

"Ah, I see how it goes, *ma belle*."

Kit was certain that he did.

Alain struggled to his feet without using his hands. "I also see Elizabeth's work on your face, Keet." Awkwardly, he took a handkercher from his shirtsleeve and even more awkwardly began to reduce the paint on her face, removing the moon and circling stars. "Before you use patches, *ma belle,* you must learn their language. One at the corner of the eye says to all that you have a passionate nature, in the center of the cheek that you are very merry, and one on the nose that you are impertinent. All are true in you, *ma petite,* but you do not mean the king to think of your great purpose in any of these ways."

Taking out her pocket mirror, she cried, "Alain, you have made me plain!"

"Never that, Keet. I have made you different. Do not try to best Castlemaine or the court ladies. Now, since I cannot, take your hands and pass them through the curls. Let your hair flow where it will."

"But that is not the mode."

"*Exactment!* One follows the mode until it is seen everywhere and then one changes it, so said *ma mere*, the greatest Parisian *coiffeuse*."

Kit knew Alain was right; he always made her see herself in a new way. "Alain, if you know all, tell me what I should say to His Majesty."

"You will know what is true, and so will he. Truth is refreshment for a monarch . . . for any man, *n'est ce pas*?"

"Alain, sometimes you are very wise, but why—?"

"Why am I not wise for myself?" He laughed quietly, but some of his old surety was back, and back to stay. "That is the hardest wisdom, *ma chere*, as you should well know."

"Did you save your friend?" she asked softly, looking at his bandaged hands.

"Non, ma chere." He turned his face to the window.

She kissed his cheek and left him there, not wanting to awaken further grief. She could feel Alain's gaze on her and Master Jolly as they walked toward Whitehall, and she turned to wave, her heart already broken for Jeremy, breaking a little more for Alain.

After they had made their way through gardens and courtyards, they found the audience room at Whitehall full of petitioners at this hour of the morning. Master Jolly talked with the majordomo and passed him a coin.

Kit waited on a bench for Jolly, reliving her last visit to the palace with Jeremy, and what had followed. It seemed her mind always took the path that ended on the turkey carpet in front of the fire in Jolly's great parlor, though she doubted that was the heat she remembered. She prayed for the words to free Jeremy, and the wit that was said to move the king when naught else would.

"We must wait," said Jolly, sitting down beside her. "The king has retired to his closet on urgent business and may not see petitioners today."

"Then he will not see *Lord Lovemore and the Lady* tomorrow."

"Hush, lest you be o'erheard, Mistress Mighty. Have a care for your head, and mine."

They waited how many hours Kit did not know, since there was no clock in the audience room, for obvious reasons.

At last the huge doors opened, and although petitioners rushed forward, the majordomo pounded his staff twice upon the floor and called the name of Master George Jolly.

Chapter Seventeen

The King's Closet

"Speak only if His Majesty addresses you, and then demurely . . . if you can," Master Jolly whispered as they wound through the magnificent inlaid-marble hall of the sprawling old palace's presence chamber, past two men at arms with pikes, and into the king's privy closet, which contained, most prominently, propped against a far wall, a very large, nearly naked portrait of a reclining Nell Gwyn.

Kit saw that the door to the king's bedroom stood open. The room was dominated by a huge bed with great golden eagles atop. The outer closet was lined with clocks, all ticking and chiming with no regard for the correct hour.

"Your most gracious Majesty," Jolly said, sweeping his hat into a very formal bow.

To one side of him, Kit dropped a curtsy, lifting the side of her skirt, taking a step back on one foot and bending her knees with a little push of her skirt to the rear. Pleased with this performance, she dared to look up as the king spoke.

"Very pretty, very pretty indeed," the king said, staring at her, one of his beribboned spaniels curled in his lap. "Is this the young comic actress we are to see in performance tomorrow, Master Jolly?"

"It is that for which we are come, Your Majesty."

"Then we're vexed to inform you that you are a full day early, sir."

Jolly took a deep breath. "We've come not to perform but with a request for Your Majesty."

The king sighed and half turned away, tapping a long finger against his long nose. "Our chiefest city lies half in ruins, sir, with many of our people hungry, though we did send them all the naval biscuit stores. It is a poor occasion for a request, and you would not make it if you had to govern this isle as we do."

Jolly bowed again, but Kit spoke, forgetting to hold her tongue.

"I would not burden Your Majesty at such a time after your brave personal defense of the city, which is much praised by all your people, if it were not to Your Majesty's good," Kit said, hoping her face showed proper respect and not the impatience behind it.

The king smiled. "To our good, you say, mistress. It is not usually so with our petitioners. We would know the lady who does us such a kindness."

"Mistress Kit, Your Majesty," Jolly answered, "a most promising . . . *most* promising young actress."

"Master Jolly, is it no longer the fashion to have a family name?"

Kit curtsied again. "Though I am gentle born, I am setting a new fashion, Your Majesty."

The king laughed, rearranging the folds of the fine purple velvet sable-trimmed robe he wore, careful not to disturb his little golden dog. "We do see that, but we warn you not to be so bold, mistress, since the ladies of the court think they set all fashion."

Kit lifted her chin, and intrigued, the king bent forward. "Then, Your Majesty, I will not disclose to them that all fashion will soon follow the theater."

"Most bold," the king said, "most bold. Castlemaine will not be pleased. Let us perish, but we envy you your youthful impudence." The king was laughing most heartily now. "Mistress, we are yours to command."

"Your Majesty, I am yours *without* command."

The king's face came alive at the wordplay. "Nay, mistress, we are yours to the ends of our realm."

"I am yours to the ends of the moon and stars." She swept into another curtsy, trying not to laugh at Master Jolly's open mouth.

"Mistress, we would be yours in our bed." The king looked mighty merry, but Kit doubted not that he meant his words.

"Your Majesty, I would serve you in hell, but not in your bed, though it be another heaven."

The king's mouth twisted in wry amusement, and he almost clapped his hands. "Well said, Mistress Kit!" The king stood, clutching his little spaniel, and held out his beringed hand for Kit to kiss, which she did, liking this monarch more than she had thought to do.

"Now, mistress," the king said, amusement still trembling behind his voice, "what is this service you would do us?"

Kit swallowed, thinking she could not go much further. "If I may make so bold again, Your Majesty, I would save you from an inferior entertainment."

"Surely you do not mean yourself, Mistress Kit. We do not take you as the most singularly modest of your sex."

Kit could tell that the king delighted in matching wits with her, but she did not know whether to be grateful for his humor or forewarned. She took a deep breath and continued. "No, Your Majesty, I do not mean myself. I am speaking of Jeremy Hughes, the greatest comic actor of your reign. He not only plays Lord Lovemore, he *is* Lord Lovemore. To see Master Jolly's play without him would do no honor to the reputation of your court theater for fine masques and plays." She stopped and curtsied again, suspecting how much too far she had gone. "Your Gracious Majesty."

The king sat down abruptly and stared at her, smoothing his mustache and raising his dog for his kiss. All distracted, he looked about him and placed a hand on a stack of parchments. "These are some initial plans from our Deputy Surveyor of Works, Mr. Wren, for the rebuilding of our city. Many thousands of our subjects have lost all. Great matters of governance are before us, and you bring us a petty request for one man who has broken our law . . . though doubtless under the sway of that rogue Rochester."

Jolly bowed hastily. "Forgive us, Your Majesty."

Kit feared that all hope was lost. She continued, knowing she should not, but far from being able to stop herself if she could do aught to save Jemmy. "All you say is true, great sir. I have selfishly wanted only the best actor in your realm to play against so that I would look most worthy in your eyes."

"We think that is only half the truth."

"I would not burden Your Majesty with deeper feelings."

"God's fish! We do understand such sentiment from our own verses." He stroked the dog again, and his voice was thick with emotion when he spoke. *"But I live not the day when I see not my love. . . ."*

An unbidden tear came to Kit's eye, and she blinked it back.

"A fine, melancholy feeling, Your Majesty," Jolly said, bowing deeply, his hand covering his heart.

"Mr. Dryden himself has complimented us on our poetry," the king said with satisfaction and a sad smile for Kit, for he was obviously thinking of someone. . . . Someone as lost to him as Jeremy was now lost to her.

Jolly bowed again very formally, and Kit dropped into her best curtsy, the warning in Jolly's eyes telling her to say no more. For once, she heeded him.

The king was still looking at her, his eyes locked upon her bosom, but she could not read his face as they backed out of the privy closet and retraced their steps through Whitehall.

They exited onto the cobbled street, and Kit said despondently, "Did all we say go to no good?"

Master Jolly shrugged. "Kings may do as it please them, but I advise you from affection and on long experience to grant a king his wish rather than withhold his pleasure for your own."

Jeremy looked at his thirteen cards and placed the jack with his last shilling on it on the table, in the almost continuous game of basset he and Lord Rochester had played in their Tower cell. The remains of a roasted fowl sat on another table beside a cheerful fire. Indeed, he had been far less comfortable in a good many inns than he was in the king's Tower prison, thanks to being a boon companion of a peer of the realm.

Outside, lions roared out their hunger in the king's

menagerie, as viewers applauded feeding time from the visitor's gallery.

Rochester drank from his wine bowl, looked at the cards in his hand, chose a seven and placed a shilling on it. "Guard," he called, "we need a dealer."

A guard propped his pike against the open door and stepped in, turning up the bottom card of the deck.

"A seven and I am matched!" crowed Rochester. "I win. Now deal the cards again, and stop pining for that wench Madame Rampant. You would be trapped into vile marriage with a hoyden if I had not given you the country wench to wed. . . . For which I have received no due thanks, no due thanks at all, sir." He flashed a very wicked smile.

Jeremy held tight to the angry words he could have spoken, and said softly, "Then I will try not to long for Kit to close that marriage trap about me, my lord, though I do long for it, and I never thought to say that in this world. Can a man love so much that he goes against his own nature? Is marriage not the only result of such love?"

Rochester looked away quickly, as if he saw something in Jeremy's face that he did not want to believe existed. "Come, no philosophy, but another hand. You will lose less to me than to that lady love. . . . Less, I vow."

"I don't doubt it, my lord, but I have wagered my last shilling," Jeremy said, tired to death of Rochester and of basset, and hoping never to play the game again in this life, since they had played without ceasing for more than a week. Instead, he would have rather lain upon his narrow bed, thinking of Kit, wondering if she thought of him and what it was she thought, trying to keep the details of that last night with her at bay for fear his cod would rise to betray him to Rochester's everlasting amusement.

Rochester drew coins from his purse. "I will make you a loan."

Jeremy held back an anguished groan. "Did anyone ever best you, my lord?"

A trumpet sounded in the yard below.

"What the devil!" Rochester jumped up and went to the window casement. "A messenger, and from his red livery, direct from Whitehall. I knew it. His Majesty is ever forgiving and gracious."

Jeremy slapped the guard on the back. "Go and bring back the message, man." He could not believe that the king had relented so quickly. He had been prepared to spend months into the freezing winter within these stone walls.

The guard returned empty-handed. "The message is for the chief warder, my lord."

Within the hour the chief warder was on the winding stone stairs to their Tower cell. "My lord earl," he said on bowing, "the king has ordered you to your lady mother's home at Ditchley, there to remain until you are summoned once again to court."

"The devil you say! I had rather face the block than my mother and her prating country preachers."

"The king has ordered an escort, your lordship, to ensure your safe arrival into your mother's arms," the chief warder added, smiling slyly.

"And what of me?" Jeremy asked.

"You," the chief warder said, not smiling, "will await the king's further pleasure."

"My God!" Jeremy slumped onto a backstool.

"Come, sir, I but jest," the chief warder said. "You await the king's pleasure, but you do so at Whitehall on the morrow."

He handed Jeremy a bundle of clothes and a smaller bundle of manuscript.

Kit rushed at Jeremy in the small tiring room set up for costume changes behind the court stage in the king's presence chamber, and touched him gingerly, frantic to know that he was as well as he looked. He had no prison pallor and no marks of the whip or hot iron upon his arms. They must be hidden. "Jemmy, my dearest, are you tortured? Are you starved?" She was breathless and near to helpless tears as she touched him gently, her hands renewing her memories of his face and chest and finding them intact. How could a man come from the Tower looking like a rested country gentleman?

Jeremy kissed her and held her close. "Aye, heart. I was tortured. Tortured for want of your kiss. Starved for the taste of you." He kissed her again and moved his tongue gently between her lips.

Confused, she stepped back to look at him again. "But I feared you were . . . racked and broken."

He laughed. "I was racked mightily, having to play basset with my lord of Rochester for days and nights never-ending."

Her voice hardened. "I did not sleep, sir. I could not consume aught but a little wine for my stomach's sake, so worried was—"

Jeremy laughed. "Then it seems I must insist His Majesty rack my bones well to satisfy you."

Fury took over from fear. "You know that is not my meaning. Do not play with my anguished affection, Jeremy Hughes!"

He grabbed her hard to him and whispered into her ear:

"Ah, but, heart, I intend to play with your affection this very night. You may rely upon it."

He was laughing at her and she could no longer delay her own relieved laughter. Why did this man torment her so?

Before she could grope toward an answer, the musicians in the gallery struck up one of Lully's stately overtures and whispers of "The king! The king!" echoed through the presence chamber.

"To your places," Master Jolly called.

Jolly had written a longer version of his earlier scene, and added other scenes so that Lord Lovemore's fantasy turned ever more preposterous, even riotous. They were to dance, sing and fight upon the stage. "It is a burlesque, Kit," Jeremy said, with one last look at the script, "and we actors are to have as much delight in it as the audience."

Although she trembled to play before the king, Kit entered upon the bowered stage, speaking, "What will become of me? I am but a woman, and what am I good for?" She heard muffled giggles at that line.

She pouted then, her chin jutted forward toward the large canopied throne set at a little distance away in which the king, magnificently dressed in court robes, smiled and covered the smile with one emerald-ringed hand. Other courtiers and many actors from the Theater Royal clustered behind him, but she could not see their faces as Jeremy entered in his monstrous foppish clothes, breeches so wide he could scarce walk and a towering wig, declaiming, "Lady, I will teach you what a woman is good for."

Kit was thrilled to play Lady to his Lord Lovemore, and as they settled into the rhythm of the speeches, it was like tossing a ball, first from one and then from the other, never letting the ball drop or the rhythm slacken.

On one of Lord Lovemore's visits to the lady, she was singing in her bower, and he joined her, the king applauding with a "Bravo!" as their voices wound deliciously with hautbois and celli through "She Loves and She Confesses, Too."

And then, near out of breath, Kit came to the final scene. "Let us give it our all, heart," Jeremy whispered, as if she needed to be told, when she was longing for him to fling himself upon her.

Which he did.

More than once, they embraced so vigorously in the bower that the rose-trimmed arch rained petals down upon them. Flushed pink with clothes all awry, they scrambled to take their bows.

The king approached the stage, applauding and smiling broadly. "We think that you do, indeed, know what a woman is good for, sir. And, Mistress Kit, we also believe that you would make a heaven of a bed, though you deny it."

Jeremy bowed and Kit curtsied, sweet-smelling rose petals wafting from her hair to settle on the stage in front of the king.

"Charming, most charming," the king said repeatedly, until Nell Gwyn arrived and placed her hand on his arm. Though the actress was very small, she was quite beautiful, with overflowing bosom, two tiny feet that peeked from under her modish gown, and chestnut hair lustrous with reddish highlights. "Your Majesty, have you forgotten your intent?" Her husky voice belied her size, but not the brazen tilt to her head, commanding the king's attention.

"Of course not, Nellie. Master Hughes and Mistress Kit, we do wish you to be in our company and perform at the Theater Royal. You do make a most delightful mad couple.

Master Jeremy, your . . . ahem . . . former japes are forgotten as long as they are not repeated."

"You are most kind, Your Majesty, and this lady has cured me of all trickery," Jeremy said, his hand tightening in triumph about Kit's shoulder.

But at that moment several familiar actors from the King's Theater approached the stage, one female walking very fast, speaking very loudly, and pointing toward Kit. "Your Majesty, you are the one tricked, for you honor a thief who was dismissed from our players and set upon the open road from whence she came."

Madame Lucy Wylie smiled her Lady Macbeth smile, her malicious gaze fixed on Kit's face.

Chapter Eighteen

In Which a White Glove Is Delivered

The king's privy closet next to the presence chamber was crowded. Every eye was looking at Kit and Lucy Wylie, back and forth, waiting for the clash to begin.

Nell spoke first, her face full of mischief as she flipped open her feather fan and tossed her chestnut curls. "God's lugs, Your Majesty, it is mighty easy to accuse. They call me witch because I do command your . . . uh, private attention."

The king smiled broadly. "Ah, Nellie, we, too, have wondered at your devilish powers."

Nell dropped a coquettish curtsy, not too difficult because she was more porcelain doll than woman, until she opened her bawdy mouth, which, it was said, the king loved to excess.

No one seemed to be the least troubled that Nell Gwyn, the subject of the lascivious nude painting, leaned lasciviously against it. . . . Certainly not the king and, as Kit could well see, not Jeremy Hughes nor Master Jolly nor any of the gathered gentlemen, who were most obviously admiring both painting and subject. Didn't men know that the less seen, the more imagined? She was momentarily distracted from her anger at Lucy Wylie by the suspicion that men knew no such thing.

Lucy's voice was shrill with impatience. "Your Majesty, this Mistress Kit was found hiding monies not her own. All the company did accuse her. A notorious thief would bring disgrace to the Theater Royal."

The king's attention swung to Kit, who stepped forward, standing very straight and tall with her head high. She made her practiced curtsy. "I did not steal the money I collected as gatekeep when I was a strolling player, Your Majesty," she said, her voice shaking with outrage, though she tried mightily for control. "Mrs. Wylie is a most false accuser for her own reasons."

"And we would know what these reasons be," the king said to Lucy, mild curiosity upon his face.

"None, Your Majesty, but the keeping of the king's justice." A slow, satisfied smile spread upon Lucy's lips.

Jeremy cast an angry glance at Lucy and bowed to the king. "I was the master player of the company, Your Majesty, and I can name several reasons. . . . Youth, beauty, talent and my dearest regard for Mistress Kit, with which Mrs. Wylie took great exception." He rubbed his barely healed shoulder and looked a warning at Lucy. Damned if he would not accuse her of a high felony!

"False! She is his lover and the chiefest whore in England," Lucy shouted, her mouth twisted into a most unflattering grimace for an actress in performance before the king.

Before Kit could speak, Nell looked up, indeed did a little jig, her bosom bouncing up to the nipples and down again, acting all amazed. "That cannot be truth, Your Majesty, and I will *not* have it said for the commons to hear." She stamped her very red-heeled green satin shoes, the same satin as her dress. "All England knows that I am first whore, and I will not be thought less."

The king, his dark eyes sparkling, laughed so loud that one of his perfumed and curled spaniel dogs ran to hide behind Nell's portrait. When the king again faced the throng, his face showed the beginnings of a change of interest. He addressed Thomas Betterton, leading actor of the Theater Royal: "We have pressing state business, and would leave this disagreeable task to your judgment, Master Betterton."

Betterton bowed to the king and pronounced in his noted King Lear voice, "Your Majesty, since we bear your name, we needs guard our reputation most carefully. I would take Jeremy Hughes, but not Mistress Kit."

"No, Master Betterton," Jeremy said. "I don't play without her."

Nell Gwyn slid closer to her monarch's side, her fan scarce shielding her lips and providing no cover at all for her amused voice. "Charlie, when your reputation is guarded by the theater, it is truly lost indeed."

Only the ticking of clocks were heard until the king laughed again, and mighty merry the two put their heads together behind Nell's fan.

With bows and curtsies, everyone began to exit backward from the privy closet, lest they witness the royal breeches coming down. Lucy looked as triumphant as a queen.

Kit fought to keep her deep disappointment from showing on her face and giving Lucy even more satisfaction. But, most of all, she did not want Jeremy's pity. It would be intolerable. She would rather face the tooth-drawer ten times over.

Jeremy led Kit firmly and quickly through the adjoining presence chamber, the bower and strewn rose petals still on the stage, mocking her memory of a triumph snatched from her almost at the moment of its creation.

"I will not allow you to sacrifice for me, Jemmy," she said, choking out the words, her heart breaking a little at the thought that now they would never be the mad couple of the London stage. "Tell Betterton that you will take his offer, since I doubt that my lord Rochester will get his theater warrant from the king in this reign. I will not have you lose all for my sake."

"There is no hope for Rochester's theater, Kit. He has gone too far this time. . . . No, not the Fleet Prison jape. In a drunken rage, he attacked and o'erturned the king's favorite sundial in his privy garden. The king may never forgive such spite."

"Then you *must* tell Betterton that you will join the Theater Royal company, and I will be truly glad of it in my heart."

He looked over at her, walking tall beside him, her head up and eyes steady. Aye, courage she had in plenty, and he loved her all the more for it.

They had moved outside the presence chamber and were on a path leading through a small walled garden to one of Whitehall's outer gates when Lucy bore down on them like a ship of the line, an embarrassed Thomas Betterton in reluctant tow. She began shouting from a little distance. "I call you whore and whore you will be to all, Mistress No-Name. You will never play upon London's boards, for I will see to it. I will spread such calumny that you will not be allowed to jig naked in the streets."

As Lucy's anger propelled her too close, Kit felt the spittle from Lucy's mouth upon her face. Feeling defiled and blinded by white rage, Kit raised her open hand and slapped Lucy's cunning face, which showed she now fully believed the insane lies she'd contrived.

Lucy recoiled into Betterton's arms, sputtering, "You will pay dearly for that. . . . With your life!"

Jeremy pulled Kit away. "Enough, Lucy, or I swear I will call a constable and show him the wound you gave me."

Regaining a measure of control, and sickened at heart by the ugly scene, Kit walked quickly with Jeremy out past the Banqueting Hall and did not look back. "I am not sorry," she said, though her hand yet stung from the force of her anger.

Jeremy tightened his arm around her. "Nor should you be, Kit. But she is a dangerous enemy and holds some sway over Betterton."

"I can well imagine one of her holds." Kit stopped on the cobbled street. "God's nails, Jemmy! On my life, you will not refuse Betterton's offer. From the Tower to the Theater Royal in a single day. What could be a greater triumph for you? I could never allow such a sacrifice in my name."

"Hush, we will not speak of it now."

"When we do speak of it, my mind will not be different."

"I am in no doubt of that," Jeremy answered, already marshaling arguments for his plan.

Later, after visiting with Alain, Jeremy and Kit sat with Master Jolly in his great parlor before the fire, the evening being chill for September.

Kit was forced by conscience to confess. "Master Jolly, I owe you much, but I cannot continue in your training since

I have no future in the London theater. I have it in mind to start a dame school so that I may repay you for all your kindness."

Jolly, sitting with his chin on his chest and an ale tankard propped on his belly, looked up, an ironic smile playing upon his lips. "I would have a care for the young scholars of London, and save them from your temper, Mistress Mighty." He sat up and leaned forward, irony replaced by a serious mien. "You are an actress born and would waste yourself on any other endeavors. In faith, I would not have thought you, of all womankind, to give way to threats."

"Not so, Master Jolly. I am a woman and, therefore, completely practical. If I am denied the theaters, then where would I perform except as know-all in the schoolroom or as some lady's maid, pretending gratitude?"

"The Cockpit Theater," Jolly and Jeremy answered together so that the words bounced merrily about the room.

Jeremy leapt up and began pacing in front of the fire, his moving shadow cast high upon the walls. "Aye, many have played there while waiting a call to the King's or Duke's theaters. Lucy herself. I have thought much on this since we left the king's closet. If Master Jolly will allow us the use of his play for the benefit of every third performance, then we can open it in the Cockpit. It is not a licensed theater, but it is popular with the people." He did not bother to keep the excitement from his voice.

"Done!" Master Jolly said. "I doubt John Dryden at the Theater Royal would welcome me as a new play writer in the end. He hates farce, though I would argue that my play is high farce."

Both Kit and Jeremy had the presence to agree heartily,

since new playwrights were particularly sensitive of the slightest absence of accord.

Serious now, Kit stood, holding her chair to steady herself, allowing this new path to open before her. "Jeremy, would you forgo the Theater Royal for a theater within a tavern?"

"What difference a theater within a tavern, or a tavern within a theater, as most are? I could have what I want most . . . you and I together, the maddest couple on any stage."

Master Jolly clapped his hands, sloshing ale upon his breeches. "Huzzah! It is done."

Kit was confused as to the right of it, but she had not long to think.

A commotion sounded in the street outside. Shouting and cheering accompanied a loud knock on Master Jolly's front door.

Jolly heaved himself up and left the great parlor to open his own door, having saved the expense of his late majordomo.

Kit was frightened for Jeremy. Had they come again for him, the king having changed his mind as kings could do on a whim? But the shouting was of her name, and it sounded like the hawking of a penny news sheet.

"God's nails! What now?" she asked, looking at the door as Thomas Betterton entered.

"Be welcome, sir," Jolly said, following him.

"Mistress Kit," Betterton said, bowing with the greatest ill ease, obviously wishing himself in any other place but Jolly's grand parlor. He held out a lady's white kid glove to her.

Jeremy was instantly at Kit's side. "Thomas, have you lost all sense? You cannot challenge a lady."

Betterton shifted his feet. "Dam'me, Hughes, I am only second to Mrs. Wylie. She is the aggrieved party, having been assaulted by Mistress Kit, and insists she must defend her honor with a rapier."

Jeremy took a menacing step toward Betterton. "If this is a jest, Thomas—"

"No jest. The challenge is already in the penny news. Listen."

Kit went to the window and opened the casement. Two boys were hawking their news sheets on the cobbles outside. "Actresses duel at dawn in Hampstead Heath, Thursday next!"

"This is a true case for Bedlam," she said, turning back to Betterton, who was edging toward the door. "What now of the reputation of the Theater Royal, sir?"

Betterton lifted his wig and swiped his handkercher over his perspiring shaved head before replacing it. "Mistress, I have exhausted all my persuasion. Like Shylock, Lucy will have her pound of flesh." He took a stance and quoted Shakespeare: " ' 'Tis mine and I will have it,' she says. I fear she will not be moved from her revenge."

"Nor I from my right of defense, sir," Kit said, wondering even as she said it at the twists her life had taken since she ran from Bournely Hall in the hope of safety.

Jeremy reached her in two steps. "Kit, you cannot play Lucy's insane game."

"Jemmy, I will play it and I will win it!" She plucked the glove from Betterton's hand, took the letter knife from Jolly's writing table and slit the glove open from wrist ribbon to fingertip. "Here, Master Betterton, return this to Mrs.

Wylie as my answer. I will meet her at Hampstead Heath in two days' time."

"Who will second you, mistress?"

Kit answered simply, "Jeremy Hughes."

Betterton paused no longer than a breath and then bowed himself out, something like admiration on his face. "Mistress, I may yet rue the day I turned you from the Theater Royal."

"You will, sir, most assuredly, and soon," Kit said, throwing the words after him.

As the front door closed, Kit and Jeremy stood looking at each other as if alone. George Jolly cleared his throat and said something about sending for the fencing master to train Kit on the morrow. Neither Kit nor Jeremy answered, and Jolly added that though present company was very merry, he was for an early bed and quietly let himself out.

Kit sighed loudly, the full impact of what she had done showing in her face.

Jeremy stepped closer. "Are you determined in your course?"

"Yes," she said, but Jeremy did not hear her usual clear yes, but a yes that could just as easily have been a no, and so he waited.

When he did not argue with her, she put her arms about him and laid her head upon his shoulder. "What else could I do and not have all London call me coward?"

Jeremy, now shaking with anger and fear, pulled away. "Kit, are you crazed? Cowardice is not a woman's concern. A woman's honor is forever tied to a man's."

Anger sparked from Kit's eyes, and she shrugged off Jeremy's hand on her arm. "Who made that rule? Is it only a man's heart that is broke to have all honor lost? I have been called thief and whore to the king."

"The king cares not."

"Do you not care?"

"All actresses are whores to the mob."

"This is one who will not be so thought, nor love a man who would care nothing for it."

"Kit, you but twist my words. I care more for your safety. Let me guide you in this. I am a man and rightfully—"

She flung at him the only words ready on her tongue. "I will have no master!"

"You have need of one!" he said, his voice strained through dread to harshness, but the door to the grand parlor slammed on his hasty answer, and he was left standing alone, his anger mounting to near explosion. He dropped into Jolly's great upholstered chair before the fireplace with a curse on his lips. "Damn all women!" He had been right to avoid their tangles and the breaking heart that followed love as sure as winter followed summer. There was no reason in women, and Kit was the most unreasonable woman of them all.

After some time, faintly from the rehearsal hall, he heard the harplike plucking of harpsichord strings and recognized the song they had sung as Kit's audition for the strolling players and again as Lovemore and the Lady while the king and his court had sat silenced for once and admiring. Without intention, Jeremy began singing softly "She Loves and She Confesses, Too," and as he sang, his anger fell away and he was left with only the cold ashes of their quarrel and a deep emptiness at the great folly that faced them.

He was sleeping off two large tankards of burnt claret in front of a dying fire when, near midnight, Kit, wearing her night shift and a cowled cape, quietly entered the room, carrying a platter of cold sliced mutton, some soft Essex cheese, bread and tart if somewhat wrinkled apples. She placed the platter on a small round table and set it before him. The movement wakened him. "*I* could not sleep," she said, somewhat accusing, and then confessed what she'd come to say. "Jemmy, it was not my intent to have harsh words with you, so newly freed from the Tower."

Jeremy sat up and sniffed the food, aware that he had not eaten since morning. "You were never one to save your harsh words for later, Kit," he said, breathing deeply and reaching for the mutton and bread, not quite ready to let her know that he forgave her that and more besides.

"Please, Jemmy," she said softly, her rich contralto voice not heavy but soft and sensual, her hand reaching for his and closing round his mutton and bread. "I know that our two humors do not seem to fit us together, but . . . if natures can be taught, we can do it."

He leaned across the platter and caught her trembling lips with his own. "I suppose I must forgive you or I will nevermore be allowed to break my fast."

She smiled at his raillery, and realized not for the first time that it set him apart from most men, who were careful of their words to women, careful to speak of nothing important or anything that required more answer than a simpering smile. Jeremy spoke to her as he would speak to one who was equal in ability to play a game of quips and retorts.

Finding his hunger not for food after all, Jeremy pushed the table away and pulled Kit into his lap, her long legs dangling over the chair arm, his mouth very close to hers. "Are you truly intent upon this crazed duel?"

Kit's blue eyes lost their sparkle as she struggled to answer Jeremy's question. "It is not I who is intent on fighting, but Lucy. She will have the duel now or she will have it later, but she will have it, that is plain. She wishes me great harm because she believes that I took her love from her."

"You did, though love was ever in her mind and never in mine."

Kit smiled and snuggled deeper into Jeremy's lap, her hand fumbling with the neck cloth at his throat. "As I recall it, you did follow me and make me love you."

He laughed softly, though heat flashed through his limbs to settle where a man most notices heat. "Mistress Kit, we look at the same act and find two meanings. Why is that?"

She pulled his lips down to hers and softly licked them with her tongue's tip. "Ssshh, Jemmy. The time for talking is past."

"For once you speak excellent good sense," he said.

Chapter Nineteen

Of Love and Rapiers

Jeremy lifted Kit and lay her gently on the turkey carpet before the fireplace, the exact spot where they had lain together on the night they had freed Martha, after which, as he recalled with no effort, he had freed Kit's maidenhead from its prison.

Looking on her face, he said, "We must be careful, heart, lest I get you with child."

Kit flushed. "Elizabeth gave me some beeswax pessaries mixed with bitter herbs. She swears they are a sure prevention and no bar to pleasure."

He knelt next to her, slipping the cape from her shoulders and gently undoing the ribboned bows on her night shift, exposing and kissing one part of her slender, trembling body at a time until all was there for him to see and kiss again, the while taking deep, ragged breaths.

"Jemmy, please," she urged, heat storming through her shivering limbs, her heart beating at a pace not seen since the last race at Newmarket, and now her inexperienced hands were pulling at his shirt and breeches with a desperate desire to feel his skin next to hers. She inhaled deeply to smell again his man essence of spiced wine, leather and something completely Jeremy, his own elixir, a scent she'd recognized from that first moment by the horse trough when he'd captured her and tied her hands, some special scent that had no other name but his and needed none.

He had his shirt and breeches off the faster and lay against her side, his cod ripening as it touched her leg. "I dreamed in the Tower of being here with you like this every night and every day," he whispered, his voice catching on the words and the memory.

"Jemmy, pray forgive me my earlier anger. My mouth runs away with words."

"Heart, I knew when I heard you playing in the rehearsal hall—"

"That I was sorry and almost immediately so."

Jeremy smiled into her face. *"Music so softens and disarms the mind. . . ."* he began.

". . . that not an arrow does resistance find." He knew her favorite poet, Edmund Waller, this perfect man.

She raised her lips for his kiss and he obliged most satisfactorily.

"You have the best kissing lips in all London, heart."

She pushed her full lips into a pout. "Only London?"

"Maybe the surrounding shires, then, but I have kissed no farther yet, or not much farther," he lied softly.

"Nor shall you, sir," she said, determined that the best kissing lips in all London would keep him from the provinces.

The firelight danced across Kit's body, drawing Jeremy's mouth to her shadowed nipples, first one and then the other, where he lightly tugged when he wanted to suck hard. But he knew that she was too late a virgin to want aught but gentleness. "Two of a good thing is twice as good as one," he teased, cupping, then stroking her breasts and licking his lips most wolfishly.

She passed a forefinger along his eager cock, saying slyly, "One of a good thing is also very good, my lord Lovemore."

His laugh was more a shiver with sound, and it was only with the utmost control that he could stop his scalding need to take her at once. His cod was as hard as a marble column, but he forced himself to go slowly. This was a woman who deserved all his skill. As forbidding as she sometimes was, there was something that drew him fiercely, a secret hunger for her that he scarce could name with ordinary words, and nay, not even with poesy.

To slow his cod, which was about to ignore any but its own need, he whispered his love in her ear, thrusting his tongue inside to lick little circles along the ridges, coming out to lap at the lobe. His hand trailed upon the soft, flushed skin between her breasts and down in a straight line to the beginnings of her light-colored thicket.

Kit moaned, the sound vibrating with need. "Jemmy, please, I beg you, for sweet pity's sake. I have thought of nothing if not of you dwelling inside me. If I should die on the heath Thursday morn, give me this last memory."

"You will not die, heart," he said, the dire word burning his throat.

His hand did not stop at the thicket, but his finger entered, searching back and forth along the narrow corridor for her sweet nub of pleasure.

"Do not stop," she begged, and pressed his finger deeper. "Oh, my love."

Kit's body arched, her hand finding his cod again, her mouth and her hand begging urgently: "Jemmy, now, for the love of—"

She stopped, deciding not to bring God into it, but there was no need.

Jeremy moved quickly atop her, holding himself on his hands, looking down into her face and seeing all that he had hoped to find there. "Guide me, heart," he choked. She clutched his buttocks and pulled him to her aching well, and without further requests for help he found entry and thrust deep, then deeper, possessing the entire hot pathway to her very center. And thrust. And thrust again, evoking sharp moans from each in unison until the fire ignited an explosion that melted them both into a heap of limbs and hot flesh.

Her mouth was open against his and he tasted her cry of ecstasy, collapsing against her but not removing his cod.

"A narrow compass," he quoted, once his chest stopped heaving, *"and yet there dwelt all that's good, and all that's fair . . ."*

"Ah, Jemmy, I'd love you for that if I did not love you for all else."

"Surely not *all,* my love." He smiled and saw himself reflected in her searching blue gaze. "Careful, heart, I have a good memory for ladies who profess to love me." He gently removed from her with a kiss; then reached to the table and took some cheese and bread, placed the food upon her stomach, and fed her tiny bits between his own bites. "A workman must be fed, mistress," he said in all seriousness. When he reached the last crumbs of cheese and bread, he licked them from her sweetly rounded belly while she laughed, delighted in her turn.

Every hunger satisfied, they fell into an exhausted sleep

where they lay. When Master Jolly opened his grand parlor door the next morning, he saw their pale bodies still entwined in front of his hearth and quietly retreated, a sigh of memory upon his lips.

The fencing master kept Kit in the rehearsal room practice box all day with nine parry drills repeated over and over. *"Prime, seconde, tierce . . ."* he shouted until Kit's head was buzzing with the words.

"These parries will protect every quadrant of the body," he said, "making your sword a shield."

They practiced and practiced with Jeremy watching. "Footwork!" he would shout. "Lucy is very quick with her feet."

"She is a cow!" Kit puffed, but gave more attention to first leading with her left foot and then her right.

The fencing master lowered his steel. "Hughes, stand in for me so that Mistress Kit can face a different style."

Jeremy took up a blunted practice rapier and moved swiftly to the box. "Watch yourself, Kit. I won't hold back."

"Nor would I want you to, sir, as you well know," she said with a smile that held another meaning. Then she attacked with cuts, thrusts and swipes, which Jeremy parried, delivering counter-cuts.

He caught her sword low and held it to the floor, stealing a quick kiss.

Kit was amused. "Truly, you hold back nothing, sir."

"As you well know," he taunted before resuming with a round of thrusts for her to parry.

Finally, Kit cried out for a respite. "Enough! The duel is tomorrow, not today."

The fencing master racked the foils, drew on his cloak

and wished Kit good fortune. "Remember, mistress, attack the sword, not the person. The sword is your enemy. Be bold but not stupid."

"I thank you, sir. This duel is stupid and not of my doing, but I will not disgrace your careful instruction."

He nodded, bowing to her and Jeremy before leaving. Kit heard him talking to George Jolly on the stairs. "Try to stop this duel, Master Jolly, before your beautiful actress is scarred and useless for the stage or much beside."

Jeremy whirled to face Kit, his hands clutching her arms as she tried to pull away from him. "He is right. I will have nothing to do with it!"

"You have chosen, then," she said bitterly, turning away.

"Dam'me, Kit, you mistake my meaning. I have dueled and killed the man who came against me. I have no liking for the game."

"Nor I."

"Again . . . your woman's honor," he said, turning the strange words over in his mouth.

"Always the honor of a Lindsay," she said, her color very high.

In the darkest time of night with only a sliver of new moon lighting his way, Jeremy, finding he could not allow Kit to meet Lucy Wylie without him, hired a carriage. Kit, dressed as the young gallant of the Fleet Prison rescue, hooded and masked, stepped from Master Jolly's front door into Jeremy's arms.

"I prayed you'd change your mind," she said, her nerves calming at the sight of him.

"Think you I'd allow you to show your legs in those tight

breeches about London without me?" He allowed his pride in her, but not his fear, to show on his face.

A halloo from a second-floor window stopped them, and they waited until Alain joined them in the coach for the ride to Hampstead Heath.

With a crack of the whip, they rattled toward the northwest.

"*Ma chere,* I could not let you do this thing without me to cheer you on." Alain pulled a pair of bright red leather gauntlets from beneath his cloak. "These will protect your lovely hands, *n'est ce pas*? Lucy will not be near so well gloved." He looked pleased with that.

Kit scarce squeezed a laugh from her tight throat. "Is there a mode now for dueling ladies, Alain?"

With a sniff, he flicked his cloak across his shoulder, where it landed in a perfect fold, and answered in his haughtiest Frenchman's tone. "*Ma belle*, there is a mode for everything."

The coachman for hire had not much experience in driving a lady to a duel on Hampstead Heath at dawn, but he had not expected his carriage to rock with laughter. "The quality be crazed aright," he muttered to his horses, who picked up their pace.

Chapter Twenty

Duel!

The sky had brightened to the east though ground fog swirled under the oak trees as the coach reached Hampstead Heath. The coachman called down: "Sirs, be we stopping with the other coaches?"

Jeremy opened the door and leaned out. "My life! Half of London is here."

Kit pressed her head against the tattered upholstery of the hired hackney. She was a spectacle. The same people who crowded the road to Tyburn to see a hanging had come to see a woman skewered, probably her, since Lucy was a popular actress. They would take it ill to be deprived of their sport, but deprived they would be. She clasped her gauntleted hands together so that Jeremy and Alain would not see them shaking and turn the coach back for London.

"Coachman," Jeremy said, "stop well away from the crowd." He picked up the mask she'd discarded during the ride, having cut the eye holes bigger for better vision. "Mask yourself again, Kit. You are still wanted for murder."

When the coach stopped, Jeremy handed Kit down after

Alain had seen to it that her hat was cocked at the right angle. Before her, she saw a small meadow ringed with gnarled oak trees and many public and private coaches. People afoot were settling on a low knoll to eat from round loaves of bread and bags of fruit. A farmer was selling provender and small-beer from his wagon. Did the scent of blood not stay the appetites of the mob? She bowed low in her breeches, sweeping her hat to the crowd and then to the carriages, and a series of huzzahs rang out from everywhere, not for her, she knew, but merely an homage to style and to hasten the duel.

Jeremy took her arm. "You take your bows first like any cautious actor," he said, though he was not laughing, his dark eyes darting from her face to the crowd. "You can change your mind, Kit, and stop this," he said, his hand very warm on her shoulder. "I like not the mood. They would as soon leave bait a bear as have you and Lucy for sport. They could lose their good temper and want mayhem, and I will see they do not have it."

He gripped his own sword hilt with such determination that Kit would not have been surprised if he'd swept her up and carried her back to London. That he did not forced her to admit that he respected her choice.

One of the opposite coaches started up and drove to within a short distance of them, the horses snorting and stamping, still lathered from a fast drive from London. A very handsome young man leaned from the coach.

" 'Tis the Duke of Monmouth," Jeremy whispered.

All England knew the name, for the duke was the king's oldest bastard son, and, being a witness here, he was breaking his father's law against dueling.

"Your Grace," Jeremy said, bowing. Kit bowed even

more formally, sweeping her hand to the ground in a good imitation of Jeremy at his best, a dozen questions racing through her mind.

"So this is the second actress who has enchanted my father within the year," the duke said, his boyish face, the dark image of his father in youth, surveying Kit.

"God's lugs," an amused voice spoke. From behind the duke appeared chestnut curls with a hint of added henna, a softly rounded face with a sweet pointed chin, albeit with a brazen pout. " 'Enchanted' is too strong a word, James. 'Entertained' is perhaps the better choice if you would escape my foot up your half-royal arse." Nell Gwyn smiled sweetly. "Good morrow, Master Hughes . . . Mistress Kit."

Kit returned the smile, thinking one of her questions now answered. The duke was here because Nell Gwyn was intrigued, and according to court gossip, could work her bawdy charm on anyone. "My thanks to Your Grace, and to you, Mistress Nell, for this honor."

"Call me Nellie hereafter, and I confess it that I honor none but mine own curiosity. This is the best play in London today and I would never miss it. I perform breeches roles aplenty and would study your rapier technique. Do you follow the French *duelle* or the Italian *duello* school?"

"Neither, Nellie. My aim is not to play a role, but to prove Mrs. Wylie the liar."

Nellie laughed until she almost choked. "Then you come to your work too late. She is known for a liar one hundred times over."

"This will be one hundred and one, and finally proved to the mob's content," Kit said, half to impress Nellie and half to bolster her own courage.

Nellie grinned. "I do not doubt it, my dear. I wish you

very well indeed, for I do like your audacity, as I like your choice of escorts."

Kit saw Jeremy bow again, a wide smile on his face. What man doubted a pretty woman's compliment?

"This is most unusual, mistress," the duke added, motioning to the line of carriages, "but half the court is here incognito."

"Most kind, Mistress Nellie . . . Your Grace," Kit said, bowing her head in modesty and to cover the truth of the fright that must have shone from her eyes no matter how she willed against it.

Kit and Jeremy took their leave and walked back to their carriage, hearing the cheers of the crowd, who were shouting for the duel to begin, despite the tumbler and juggler seeking their pennies.

"Are you ready, heart?" He looked into her eyes past her light-colored eyelashes that would have disappeared in the sunlight had they not been so thick. He had to plead once more because his own fear was growing. "Don't you want to think further on it? There would be no shame if you were taken with a sudden ague," Jeremy said, having little hope that Kit would give up this adventure, and doubting the crowd would agree to it.

Kit looked at him and spoke gently to calm his fears and her own. "I am ready."

She looked up to see the little doctor with his tall wig riding up on a very large horse. "Doctor Wyndham, be welcome," she addressed him with pleasure.

The doctor took his feet from the high stirrups and slid down the belly of his horse. "Mistress, your servant," he said, a little short of breath. "I read the penny news and thought to be here if you had need of physic or stitching, for

I would trust your beauty to no canting quack. During my student days at the University of Padua"—he paused and smiled broadly—"et cetera and et cetera, I attended on many duels."

"I hope not to have need of your office," Kit said, the little doctor making her smile with his exaggerated sense of himself, "but I have need of your friendship."

"Mistress, my friendship has been yours since our first meeting."

Wyndham bowed, jumped up to unhook his physic bag from the pommel, and went to sit under a tree, taking a small breakfast from amongst his vials and pilasters. He looked very important even while eating a cold meat pie. Bless him, Kit thought, somehow comforted by his presence.

Alain was pacing, plainly agitated as the mist began to disappear under the rising sun. "They are not come. *Pourquoi?* Lucy has played us for fools, never intending to do more than challenge you, *ma chere*."

As if answering a call, a carriage turned from the road into the meadow, Lucy hanging from a window, waving her handkercher to the cheering crowd, the coach making a complete turn about the field before coming to a stop a proper distance from Kit's coach. Thomas Betterton stepped out and handed Lucy Wylie to the ground, she doing a little caper in her breeches for the crowd and then turning a leg for them to get a better look, which pleased them mightily, judging from the laughter.

"No one can say she doesn't play to the gallery," Jeremy murmured, the remark giving him some small relief.

Lucy already had rapier in hand and was taking practice thrusts and swipes, to the delight of her audience, who yelled a chorus of "Thrust! Thrust!"

Jeremy laid a cloth upon the ground and unwrapped several rapiers for Kit to choose from. She grasped the rapier she'd used in training, minus its blunting device.

Jeremy watched as she made a series of passes and parries. "Good. Remember, though you have advantage of height and reach, she will use any stratagem and come at you with surprise." He rubbed his shoulder. "I well know that she is a trickster who will follow no rules. As your second, I will be there with my sword ready to knock hers away if she tries any unlawful thrust. And her second will do the same to you."

"No need," Kit said, her stomach churning, and glad that she had not broken her fast or it would have emptied on the spot, disgracing her before this crowd. "The woman who stands before you will defeat Lucy Wylie within the rules of the art. If she is reckless, I will be steady."

"You are too brave and that could make you foolish," Jeremy said, unable to hide either his admiration or the care that weighed upon him. "Take no chances, heart. There is more to lose than your life. . . . There is mine, as well."

"Jemmy, I—" She pressed the palm of her hand against his chest and felt his beating heart, unable to speak more and finding his words unbearably, wonderfully sad.

Betterton approached and Jeremy went to meet him. The crowd quieted to a murmur, straining forward to hear what was said.

Jeremy bowed, as did Betterton.

"A melancholy event," Betterton said, looking no happier than when he delivered Lucy's challenge.

Jeremy took a deep breath and made one last attempt to settle the matter peaceably. "If Mrs. Wylie will apologize, Mistress Kit will do likewise."

Betterton shook his head. "Lucy is determined on this course to prove she is the better woman. I know nothing in the world that offends me more than this affair, but I must do my duty."

Jeremy bowed, his back rigid as he walked away.

"And look to yourself, Hughes," Betterton called after him in a low voice. "She is full of hate."

Jeremy drew his rapier and exercised with Kit, instructing her constantly. "Keep your back to the trees and your form will not be in outline. Don't face the sun. Watch her blade, but also watch her eyes. Her thoughts are in them."

"Enough!" Kit said. "Jemmy, my head is swimming."

He lowered his sword and tied her mask tighter to keep her hair from clouding her vision. He chalked her gloves to prevent her hands from slipping on the hilt. And then he could delay no longer.

Kit walked by his side through the meadow's grassy clumps to the center of the sward where Lucy and Thomas Betterton waited. The weakness in her stomach was gone and the hard earth was solid under her. She felt the sun on her face and smelled the warming dewy grass along with a breeze bringing the smoky scent of London to her from the east. Someone in a carriage, playing a lute and singing, broke off his song. Jeremy took shortened strides close beside her, his shoulder touching hers for comfort. All her senses were attuned to this place and this moment and her living in it. She admitted her fear, taking a firmer grasp on her rapier. God's nails! She had faced danger before—rape, hanging, the great fire—and she would come through this day.

Her mind was whirling with memories when she reached the slight rise upon which Lucy was standing. The crowd, now well into its third tankard of morning beer, roared its excitement.

Kit said nothing in greeting, but took a stance and saluted Lucy with her rapier.

Lucy returned a sneer. "Does she fear to face an audience that she comes masked?"

Kit's eyes narrowed, accepting the challenge. "I fear nothing, Mrs. Wylie, but I mask myself because I am not as proud to be here as you are. There are better stages for an actress."

"You call yourself an actress!"

Betterton stepped forward, his hand up in warning, and cleared his throat as if preparing to speak a prologue upon the forestage of the Theater Royal. "As seconds, Master Hughes and I will watch for any irregularities. If either combatant may, perchance, slip, be disarmed or be wounded, we will knock away your swords. At the first blood drawn, the duel will be stopped, and the matter considered settled. Is it agreed?"

"Agreed," Kit replied, and Lucy echoed her swiftly, shifting eagerly from one foot to another, her rapier circling in menace.

"*En garde!*" Betterton called.

Kit took the *prime* position and began to move sideways, keeping the sun from her eyes, which was difficult because the sun was still low in the morning sky, though hazy from the smoke of debris still burning in ten thousand London cellars.

Lucy, waving her sword like a windmill, began to swipe at her from high and low, seeming determined to finish Kit quickly. "Stand still and feel the bite of my blade, you long-legged strumpet," she yelled.

Kit bit her tongue, determined not to spend any energy in retort. She parried and caught Lucy's blade on her own and slid down to the hilt, pushing her back.

"Ah, you are afraid to engage," Lucy said, their faces so close that Kit could again feel spittle below her mask and see Lucy's cruelly curving mouth.

With sudden strength, Lucy tried to twist her rapier and dislodge Kit's blade from her hand, but Kit stepped back quickly, allowing Lucy to come to her. Lucy was older, fleshier and she must tire sooner, although she gave no appearance of it as yet, pursuing Kit with vigorous steps and strokes.

Kit took Lucy's measure very quickly. She had little style and was impetuous and therefore dangerous. Kit talked to herself: parry, pass and retire . . . keep her moving, exhaust her.

Both Jeremy and Thomas Betterton moved with them, one on either side, their swords ready to knock away a killing thrust.

Though he followed the duelers with an exact eye, Jeremy's mind was full of self-recrimination. How had he allowed this great farce to happen? He should have tried harder to control Kit, and most certain would in the future. Though she rejected any will but her own, she obviously needed a man's less-impetuous management. She would have to accept it! He would seduce her to it! And yet . . . and yet as he looked on her now, a polished ivory beauty, her golden hair glinting on the turn of every parry and pass, her lithe figure showing each lovely curve, curves that his own hands had cupped but hours earlier, she was more goddess to be worshiped than mischievous child to be disciplined.

Kit tried to slow her breathing and make it deeper so that

she would not become light in her head. Her arm and legs were still strong as she circled away from Lucy.

"Ah, you fear me," Lucy yelled, as Kit backed away from her thrusts, blocking the older woman's sword with parries.

"You will see," Kit said, smiling to see Lucy growing angrier, her face contorted and red.

Faint in her ears, Kit heard the calls from the crowd, which seemed to be yelling Lucy's name far more often than her own.

Lucy fought Kit toward one oak tree that had grown apart from the others, until her back was touching the rough bark. Lucy crowded in upon her, the menacing blade aiming for Kit's face.

"Whore, Jemmy will not like your face when I finish painting it with your blood!" She sidestepped, turned her sword and hit Kit on the head with the hilt.

"Foul," cried Jeremy and knocked up Lucy's sword with his own. "Lucy, you forfeit the match."

"Never!" screamed Lucy, but Betterton had a strong hold on her.

Jeremy had his arms around Kit, holding her up against the tree. "Your honor is satisfied. Come away, love."

Kit's head ached and she felt a bump on her head, but dizziness quickly left her. She looked to Betterton, who was glaring at Lucy's ugly, flushed face and wild eyes. Kit saw the crowd, their mouths open, yelling words she could not hear, and hoped that the blow to her head had not caused a deafness.

"We must leave with all speed," Jeremy said, and to her relief, she heard him plainly. He took her rapier from her hand, pulled her away and began walking her toward their carriage.

"Watch out!" Betterton shouted behind them.

Kit and Jeremy turned as one to see Lucy charging with her sword held shoulder high, obviously determined to attack and kill. Jeremy pushed Kit to her knees and tripped Lucy, who fell flat, her breath escaping in a loud whoosh.

The crowd had left its knoll, some dancing a jig of excitement. Cheering began again as Lucy clambered to her feet, her blade in hand, and faced Kit.

"Jemmy, quickly, my sword!" Kit yelled.

He tossed it across to her and she caught it on the blade, which sliced through her glove. She felt her hand burning from the cut.

Taking the *prime* position again, she stared at her enemy. She had been cautious: *Take no chances, heart,* Jeremy had ordered. But cautious combat could mean her death with this untamed woman. Bold was what she should be, and bold was what she would be.

She ran at Lucy, striking furiously from every quadrant, pushing her back and back toward the crowd. Attack! And attack! This was Kit's debut before a London audience, and she would allow no other actress to upstage her nor fault her performance.

Back and forth and around the meadow they fought as the sun mounted in the cloudless sky, Lucy obviously tiring, her reactions slower, her legs and arms appearing heavy though still dangerous, and kicking out with her foot more than once.

Kit knew she was losing strength and wind, as well, and her glove was filling with blood, but she refused to show the wound and lose the fight as long as she could grip her sword.

Gradually, Kit became aware that the crowd now shouted her name, and saw that it maddened Lucy.

Finally, after another furious round, Lucy sank down on the sward, gasping, trying to stop herself with her sword, snapping the blade in two.

"Yield!" Kit ordered.

Lucy began to scramble and crawl away as the crowd booed her cowardice. She fell on her side with a groan, one hand kneading her knotted leg muscles.

Kit stopped and raised her sword in salute to Lucy and to the crowd. They roared their huzzahs, shouting Kit's name.

Betterton bent over Lucy and tried to dislodge the broken sword from her hand, but she clung to it ferociously, gasping a final insult. "I have not lost to that ill-favored doxy!"

"Madame," Betterton said in a low voice, "save what little is left of your reputation, for this affair is finished. You may yet regain some of the common's regard if you are gracious in defeat. Allow me to take your sword and escort you to your lodgings."

"May Hades take you all!" Lucy said, unable to rise to more than ill words.

Doctor Wyndham approached, bowing. "May I be of service, sir? I have some skill in these matters."

"Thomas," Jeremy said, "this is our doctor, Josiah Wyndham."

"A doctor of physic and chiurgery and member of the Royal College," the doctor added, "with a specialty in spasms of the limbs and natural female weakness."

The doctor knelt in front of Lucy and looked into her eyes, listened at her heaving chest and raised her legs one by one, while she screamed with pain.

At last he stood. "I fear, gentlemen—"

At that moment, Monmouth and Nellie alit their carriage, Monmouth shouting orders to the scarlet-coated royal guards acting as his footmen. "Disperse the rabble," he said, waving a gloved hand at the crowd now approaching from the knoll. "I am all *amazed . . . amazed* that a duel is being fought against the king, my father's, law," he said, in a very loud, carrying voice.

Nellie pulled a droll mouth. "Jamey, you owe me a gold guinea, since my lady won."

James Stuart, Duke of Monmouth, slapped a coin into Nellie's outstretched hand, and continued issuing orders to his footmen now advancing on the crowd, who were growing restive at the end of their sport.

Monmouth mounted the stair to his carriage and addressed the people. "Even in this enlightened age, it is not in the right that the weaker sex should fight like animals in a jungle for the sake of a man. Women who do so but add to their sad reputations and degrade the man over whose affections they quarreled."

Nellie winked at Kit. "Come, Jamey, you have done your duty by your father's law."

"Doctor," Kit asked, coming closer but still keeping a safe distance from Lucy Wylie, "what ails her? Is there aught to do?"

"She is suffering exhaustion, mistress. Even my Infallible Miracle Salve will not avail. She needs rest and"—he pulled a bottle from his bag—"Tincture Solaris, which thins the blood and induces healing sleep. I have rarely seen it fail—"

"The waters," Nellie said. "I have been to Tunbridge Wells and all do say that the waters are a curative for female complaints of every kind."

"Then all do say wrongly, madame," the doctor replied, looking Nellie in the eyes, since both were of a height.

"Water that tastes foul is not an automatic cure for anything but the love of water."

Betterton, who had been standing aside in all puzzlement, asked, "Then what are we to do?"

The doctor sniffed. "As I have prescribed, sir. Take her to her bed and give her rest and the tincture, three times daily. I guess her at near two score years, mayhap even older, and fear her age far too advanced for such activity as dueling, for it does heat the blood most excessively."

Kit stared down at Lucy, whose face paint had melted, taking youth with it, and although her enemy did not deserve of much pity, she felt it.

Betterton picked up Lucy and returned her to his carriage as she protested weakly to the crowd that she had been cheated. The crowd began to throw fruit at her and advance menacingly. Betterton ducked inside the carriage, and it pulled away quickly, before the doors could be closed.

The duke, obviously thinking it better to return to London, hastened Nellie into his own carriage, which was away at once with her tiny beringed hand fluttering from the window in farewell.

Kit pressed against Jeremy, needing his strength, her hand throbbing as she passed Jeremy the bloody hilt.

"Doctor, you have a new patient," Jeremy said, anxiety clouding his dark eyes. "Can you physic her on the road?" At the doctor's assent, Jeremy added, "Tie your horse behind and let us leave this cursed heath."

"Not a deep cut, my dear," Dr. Wyndham said in the carriage, after he'd scissored the glove from Kit's hand. "But you will need stitches when you return to your lodgings. I will not ask you if you are brave enough to suffer them, since I have already seen that you are brave enough for any trial. You remind me greatly of Lady Anne Gilbert, a one to match e'en your courage." He regaled them with tales of the lady's adventures with the famous highwayman John Gilbert, until they reached London.

A lone carriage remained on the heath, a hand beckoning an outrider to come closer. "Follow that last carriage, man. Bring me news of where the lady lodges and of her comings and goings, and you will have several gold guineas in your pocket for it. Fail me, and you will have my whip on your back."

"Aye, Sir Pursevant, I will not fail ye."

Chapter Twenty-one

The Cockpit Theater

Kit was wonder-struck and a little frightened as she and Jeremy turned the corner. Drury Lane was choked with elegant coaches, hired hackneys and throngs of people all moving toward the Cockpit. "All these people are come to see us play?" she asked, not believing her own eyes.

Jeremy's arm tightened about her. "They've come to see you, Kit. You are the most fascinating and talked of woman in all London for a week past."

"The most notorious, you mean, and don't think you have escaped the gossip's tongues, m'lad."

"True," he said, laughing, "but tongues always wag about me. In this instance, surely I was the most innocent and unwilling cause of a duel."

She arched a brow, her eyes mocking in fake annoyance. "I have yet to see you either innocent or unwilling, Jeremy Hughes."

He gripped her tighter to his side, a deep throb in his laugh that told her he was thinking of the love they'd made when he'd caught her alone early that morn at the harpsichord in the rehearsal hall. "And you never will see me innocent, my sweeting, nor incapable, though modesty should keep me from saying so."

For that bit of arrogance, he received a sharp pinch.

"Ouch!"

"I pray pardon, sir. I did not mean to trod upon thee." The gentleman who spoke wore Puritan garb, indeed was one of many men in the severe black suits, white collars and large dark hats of the Puritans lining both sides of Drury Lane to the very door of the Cockpit.

Although a cool autumn rain had fallen earlier, clearing the running gutter of stinking refuse, there was a tension in the air and a rumble of distant thunder that warned of an approaching storm to match the cries of "Filthy! Heathenism! Sinful!" that rang from both sides of the lane, as they approached the theater's entrance.

"Lady, do not enter this ungodly place of base corruption to the minds and souls of men!" someone shouted almost in her face.

John Rhodes appeared at the door. "Away! Away, you canting preachers. I am owner here, and if you halt my business I will call the beadles, who take not tender care of dissenters from the true and only Church of England."

With some muttering and not a few prayers to heaven for hell-damned souls, especially of a lady dressed in Satan's satin, the Puritans began to move reluctantly on down Drury Lane, turning their attention to the brothels that displayed their prettiest wares from upper windows and balconies.

"Come," Rhodes said, "I have set up a retiring room for you where I keep my ale kegs. You must costume yourselves and begin the play on time or my patrons will riot, low-born and quality alike." He produced a very satisfied smile. "Wine sales are brisk. The pit is full. All London wants to see the mad couple."

Kit blushed at the title, although it was one that she had sought. "I see that I am notorious in truth, Jemmy," she said as they made their way behind the curtained stage to the retiring room, furnished with a cloudy mirror, a three-legged table, two overturned kegs for stools and several candles in open-faced lanterns for applying their face paint.

She removed her mask and began to set a number of velvet patches beside her eyes and her mouth, applying cochineal to her lips and finally trying mightily to tame her hair, which the damp air had sent flying.

Jeremy bent to kiss her, his own lips coming away much redder, his hand sliding down inside her shift to cup a silky breast that fit his hand as if created for it.

Jeremy leaned in for another kiss, and Kit could not resist twirling a finger in the dark, springy curls on his chest, watching all in the mirror, which seemed to magnify the kiss and the touch and heat her body to an extraordinary temperature. The fire was always slow-burning beneath her belly when she was near Jeremy.

Jeremy clasped her hand to his chest, and she flinched. "Forgive me, heart," he said, "I forgot that your wound has not completed its healing."

The sounds of a restive audience . . . tankards pounding on tables, feet stomping, and orange girls crying their wares . . . reached them before John Rhodes knocked upon the partition. "Begin the play, sir and madame, I pray you, and at once!"

"Anon, Master Rhodes," Jeremy called, pulling on a very handsome embroidered suit of matching breeches and doublet trimmed with gold ribbons, while Kit donned a lovely silver-lace-trimmed violet hood and short cape over her blue satin gown. Pulling Lord Lovemore's towering peruke from its linen bag, they stepped to the back of the stage and Kit entered, saying her opening line and then saying it again, since the audience had not stopped its clamor. A boy was floating mutton-fat candles in troughs of water at the foot of the small stage, a haze of smoke rising to set the people on the front-row benches to coughing loudly.

Kit declaimed her opening speech over the noise with a fluttering fan and quivering voice, again not in control of either. Would she never stop the nervous beating of her heart and the weakness in her legs at the beginning of a play? With a deep breath, she did as Master Jolly had taught and thought herself not in the Cockpit Theater but in a true rose-covered bower, waiting for the man she intended for a husband, no matter what he intended. She readied her next line, then settled under the arch, now more than a bit shabby from being brought by cart through the rain from Whitehall.

A moment before Lord Lovemore's entrance, she caught Nellie's winking eye and smiled her gratitude. Sitting near the center of the pit, lighted by the chandelier hoist to the rafters, the actress had obviously brought half the players from the Theater Royal to see her and Jeremy. There beside Betterton were Charles Hart and Moll Davis, who had visited Master Jolly's school on occasion. What kindness. How could she ever thank Nellie for her generous interest?

As Jemmy blustered upon the stage in his comic peruke, Kit felt her confidence return as it always did with him nearby, and the play began to move all the faster for her.

"What are you, a man or a devil?" the Lady asked Lord Lovemore, as he strutted about.

Not surprisingly, the audience roared, "Devil!" Especially obliging were the ladies, Kit couldn't help but notice, calling his name and brazenly beckoning him from the pit. The bolder ones even approached the stage, throwing lacy handkerchers at his feet. Jeremy did not seem to mind, retrieving one, wafting its perfume before his nose and throwing it back to screams of delight.

"Control yourself, Jemmy," Kit whispered, striving to sound more amused than she was, and probably failing.

"Of what am I guilty?" Jemmy asked innocently, with that grin that infuriated her.

Kit repeated the line that had been drowned in female squeals. *"Tell me, sir, man or devil?"*

"Lady, I am no devil," responded Lord Lovemore. *"I am a man."*

"But, my lord, they say devil."

"Then I will prove it," he said, and the audience hooted mightily, one masked lady clutching her heart as if in a swoon.

"My lord, do you intend an impudence . . . to disrobe?"

"Why, yes, lady, else how is my manhood proved?"

"I'm ruined, ruined!" the Lady shrieked as Lovemore advanced toward the bower, to the pit's intense delight.

The dialogue, now well rehearsed, passed swiftly between them. It was their best performance.

They were singing their duet when Kit saw a man, dressed darkly and caped, wearing his flopping great hat low on his head, standing beside the entrance. She lost a note. Although the dark figure immediately left the pit, she had recognized him. All the terror of an early morning in an attic room at Bournely Hall this past summer rushed in upon her once again.

"Are you certain sure?" Jeremy asked her later in the retiring room. "Candlelight can throw such shadows as to misrepresent a face and form."

"I am certain," she said, worry marking her face. "He was one of Sir William's grooms and looked as I saw him many times, but perhaps—" The more she thought, the more she wanted to deny the fear, a fear that had dogged her, nonetheless, all these last months, a fear that even in Jeremy's arms lay like a sinister shadow between them.

Jeremy sighed and lightly stroked her cheek. "There, you see, you are not certain sure after all. You needed more rest after the duel. I should not have agreed to this opening date."

"No, no, Jemmy, I am perfectly rested." She smiled in the mirror at him. "Except when you do keep me wakeful."

"Do I hear complaint?"

"None," she said into his reflected face. "I was mistaken in the man after all."

Yet the groom's murky face stayed in her mind and troubled her dreams so that she woke in the middle of the night and could not sleep again until dawn.

The second night, she searched every face in the pit, but saw none she knew except for Nellie Gwyn, who had brought half the court along, including that great rake the handsome Duke of Buckingham to see them perform.

"I was all mistaken, Jemmy," she told him later as they removed their face paint with the good Doctor Wyndham's Infallible Miracle Salve. Then they walked upon the street to Lockets, having been invited for an early supper with Nellie and her friends, of which there seemed to be an endless supply.

Jeremy kept a sharp eye upon all who passed them by or loitered in shop doors, and more than once looked behind them. To save Kit from worry, he had pretended to believe she had been mistaken in the man she recognized. Perhaps and perhaps not. He would take no chances with her and would not allow her in public places without him. "No doubt the man was a groom, but not the man you remembered. All grooms dress alike. Still, you must promise me that you will not go upon the streets without me or Alain."

Kit, still in performance mode, played the coquette. "Am I to be more your prisoner than I already am, my lord?"

Serious suddenly, he said, "Aye, and always will be, just as I am prisoner to you, heart." He pulled her into a shuttered shop doorway, and as he confined her in his arms, felt her trembling like a captured animal. He cleared his throat because he knew his voice would waver at the next words he must speak. "We cannot marry, Kit, which is my dearest wish. . . . You know that I would if—"

Startled, her old fears returning, Kit's body grew rigid. "It is best, Jemmy, for you know I rightly fear any master, having suffered one." But the words rang hollow in her ears, more so each time she repeated them.

"A loving master," Jeremy persisted. "A master who uses his power to protect you. A master who is loyal to you above all women. Kit, that is the way of the world. You cannot deny it."

"Next you will quote St. Paul and tell me women were created second, but sinned first, therefore men are meant to rule over them."

Jeremy frowned, but even his dark look conveyed more intrigue than gloom. "I will not preach that sermon, Kit, but it might not be a bad idea. You are stubborn enough to try a saint's patience."

They walked farther, almost to Lockets, troubled because

so much between them remained unresolved. They were stiff as two sticks until Kit stopped and faced him in a temper born of regret, while passersby stared in curiosity. "God's nails, Jemmy, what is this contest about? You are married to Martha. How can you be angered because I will not marry you when I cannot?"

"Because, heart, my love is not rational. I want to know you would if you could. I am near crazed with that want most times." He grinned at her, but it was rueful.

Quietly, quietly, she told herself, stay from saying more. In her deepest part she knew he was the one man in all the world who had the power to make her happy or miserable, and he must *never* know it. She must hold the knowledge tight within her, for there was no greater mastery a woman could give to a man than all her self.

She smiled tremulously and took his arm, making Jeremy regret any unreasonable words. Still, he'd done no wrong but give his heart, and that thought fueled his silence as they walked on without further hurtful discourse but with no true reconciliation.

They joined a merry gang at Lockets, Nellie as lively seated at table as when jigging before an audience at the Theater Royal. Jeremy was soon in better humor. Only Betterton continued to look glum.

"And how does Lucy Wylie?" Nellie asked, raising her syllabub cup after a hearty beef pudding and sallet of fresh young leaves of lettuce and dandelion sprinkled with rosemary, a skewer of various ripe fruits erect in the center.

"Mrs. Wylie is not well," Betterton replied, looking remorseful. "She accuses me of betrayal and has taken herself off to the Duke's company, where she is not welcome and not offered lead roles."

Kit felt weighted with some regret. "It was a sorry affair, but none of my doing, Master Betterton, as you know well."

Nellie snorted. "Not to worry, Kit. Lucy lives to make trouble." She pursed her lips in a way that suggested her wicked wit was engaged. "I think me nothing will satisfy Mrs. Wylie, not even getting what she wants. Leave her alone and yet you won't be rid of her. She is like a tuneless beggar who sings loud for a ha'-penny, but must have twice that amount to stop." Nellie arched an eyebrow and laughed heartily for one so slight, her amusement infecting the other diners, who knew not why they smiled until the sly jest at last came round the room.

Jeremy watched Kit through troubled eyes. An extraordinary good gingerbread was served, and he observed that she took no more than one bite and that difficult to swallow. He could not remember now how their silly argument began or what it was truly about.

Strolling back to Jolly's in the dusk, seeking to distract the pensive Kit, Jeremy rattled coins in his pocket. "Fifteen shillings, heart, enough to begin paying your debt to George Jolly and perhaps to finding new rooms. Would you like to be mistress of your own lodgings? Would that please you?"

"Yes, Jemmy, it would," she said, looking at him, her useless and now silly pique flowing away in a flood of relief to be fully with him again. She could not bear even the thought of contention between them, and an actual quarrel would have been worse than the Puritan's hell. He smiled at her, and she knew all was forgotten. The smile lines at his eyes and the way his waving black hair lay upon his shoulders caused the familiar hot pulsing to begin, an almost unbearable pleasure, but one she hoped she would have to bear as best she could over and over again.

She could not help but notice how the women passing them in the street looked at Jeremy, how their eyelids fluttered and they quickly bit their lips to make them plump and red. She clasped him tighter and closer, which seemed to please him mightily.

Betterton summoned Jeremy to the Theater Royal the next morning, and Nellie came to call on Kit soon after. She was bubbling with gossip. "Thomas has seen the patronage you have at the Cockpit and would like it for his own theater, as would any good manager," she said. "That's why I insisted upon his attendance at your play. He has you both in mind for Dryden's new play, *Feign'd Innocence*. I am to play Lady Wealthy in *The English Monsieur*."

"You are a most generous friend to us," Kit said, and meant it as more than a thank-you.

"And you, Mistress Kit, are a most intriguing personage. Together, we command all the gossip in London." Nellie smiled slyly. "If I must be outshone, I would bask in your reflected light."

Kit curtsied. "You do me too much honor."

"God's lugs!" Nellie said, shy of Kit's honest admiration. "We are much alike, we two, though we have led much different lives, I vow. Does that offend you?"

Without waiting for answer, Nellie bounced about the entrance hall, looking at everything. "Although Charles Hart and I play the lead comedy roles at the Theater Royal now, there will soon be a place for another mad couple," she said, looking closely at a wall hanging that depicted cupids shooting arrows at voluptuous ladies floating in a lake full of swans. "I have higher, much higher ambitions." Her saucy mouth was alive with meaning. "But that is not why I am come. I want your company for the morning."

Nell Gwyn's coach rattled over London Bridge to the Clink prison on the Bankside. "You are all generosity, Nellie," Kit said, looking across to the seat, where the other woman, sitting next to a large basket of ripe oranges, dismissed the compliment with a wave of her feather fan. Jeremy had made her promise not to go on the streets alone, but he'd said nothing about carriages, especially one that carried the king's crest. No one would dare accost her, traveling under the king's protection.

Nellie closed her fan with a decided snap. "I was unkind last night at Lockets to jibe at Lucy Wylie, especially now that she has gone over to the Duke's Theater, lesser than the Theater Royal in all degrees. Lucy was spiteful and quite a bit more than difficult when at her best, but now she is half-broken and pitiable. There is no way I can make amends to her, since she would not allow it. . . . So I make amends another way."

"At the Clink?" Kit said, astounded.

"Yes, I'll buy some poor woman's arse out of her debt." Nellie withdrew a small leather pouch that rattled with heavy coins, guineas, no doubt.

Kit was overwhelmed. "Why do you do this?"

"Because I was once starving and friendless, and once I was imprisoned here."

The look on Nellie's face told Kit that there were horrors her friend would never reveal. "I'll go with you, gladly," Kit said. She meant every word.

From their first meeting, Kit had liked the young actress immensely, as if they had always been unmet friends, though Kit knew that was impossible. Gossip said that Nellie was born in her mother's brothel and mayhap had prostituted herself as a young girl before becoming an orange seller at the Theater Royal. She smelled of orange blossoms by design, having remarked that it would be a lie to deny her life. Rising to the stage, she was quickly London's most popular actress and soon with talent and wit had achieved the affection of the king. All the poor and commons of London loved her because she was one of their own raised high, and one who had not forgotten them.

The crumbling stone prison called the Clink squatted alongside the south bank of the Thames as it had for centuries, reeking from generations of unwashed and diseased bodies, whole families swallowed and forgotten because they couldn't pay their debts.

After Nellie bribed the captain of the guard, they carried the basket of oranges down dark stone stairs to a level Kit thought probably lower than the Thames. The stairs opened into a chill room barely lit with a few guttering candles, filled with gaunt women and even thinner children sitting on matted straw. The stench of urine and vomitus made her queasy, but she did not cover her nose or shield her eyes from such misery. She saw Nellie smiling, holding out an orange to a small boy with enormous, starving eyes.

"How long have you been here?" Kit asked the mother standing behind the boy, trying to smooth her tattered apron.

"Forever and more, lady," the woman said, a tear cleaning a path down her dirty cheek.

Nellie took her hand. "Today you and your boy leave this place."

The woman was too stunned to do other than bob her head.

"Take this to the carriage, Kit, if it please you," Nellie said, handing her the empty basket, "while I arrange their release with the warden."

Kit hastened to the carriage, only too happy to escape so much sadness, though she vowed that she would follow Nellie's charity when she could. On the street, thunder rumbled about her and the darkened sky hid any ray of sunlight.

Closing her eyes and drinking in the cleaner air, she paid no attention to the sound of another carriage slowing on the street beside her until rough hands lifted her bodily though an open door and dropped her on the floor at Sir William's feet. For a moment, she thought she heard Nellie's voice calling, and she opened her mouth to scream her answer. Then all was black as she was blinded with a dark cloth, gagged with another, and her wrists and ankles tightly tied.

Jeremy! She screamed his name into the rag though no sound emerged from her mouth.

The carriage horses moved at a gallop down the Bankside as the storm broke over them. She bounced in the bottom of the conveyance, each jolt a shock to her body, but she heard Sir William's jubilant laugh and felt his feet settle upon her back, pinning her beneath him.

Chapter Twenty-two

Self-Mastery Goes Unrewarded

Kit, straining to hear every sound through the tight bandage over her eyes and ears, heard the small door in the roof of the carriage opening above the creak of straining wood and the pounding of horses' hooves.

"Is that stage whore's carriage behind us still?" Sir William shouted.

"Nay, Sir William, I lost 'er sure," the driver shouted, his denial echoed by the footman.

Kit felt Sir William's boots shift from her body, but she was so bruised from jouncing hard up and down and from side to side as the carriage careened through London and onto rutted country roads, that the absence of his boots provided only a small relief to her. Although William would not know what she said, she spat every foul name she'd heard on the streets of London into the filthy gag, gaining a measure of courage from the doing.

Strong, soft hands, which she remembered too well, hauled her from the floor and sat her upright in a seat. The blinding cloth was whipped from her face, but she almost longed to have it back. Sir William sat grinning across from her with his groom, who looked angry even though fingering a gold coin.

As Kit's eyes became more accustomed to the darkness of the vehicle's interior, she was amazed at the change in her captor. Sir William was thinner by several stone, the jowls on his face empty of flesh and even more pronounced than his sharp, cruel features, his hair noticeably grayer so that he looked much older than he was, although the changes more reflected the state of his soul than his age.

"Ah, you find me changed, cousin," he said, attempting amusement and failing. "No doubt you can guess the reason. I was out of my head for days from your loving ministrations to that part of me, and then faced with the death of my dear wife, your cousin Lady Joan." He bowed his head in mock prayer, the sight of which reduced Kit's sorrow at her cousin's death to a prayer of thanks for her deliverance.

Kit's contempt broke through in a muffled curse, and Sir William leaned across to within a few inches of Kit's face. "If you give me your oath that you will not scream and frighten the horses, I will loose the gag."

She nodded slightly, and he pulled out the gagging cloth. She licked her dry lips and swallowed. "I did not strike you," she said as her palate moistened. "I swooned as you attempted rape upon me."

"Attempted, my lady?" he asked, smirking and knowing, which was now his almost perpetual cruel visage, as if painted on his face.

Kit smiled, and she let him read her eyes, which told him he'd failed even that and also told him, with their reflected passion, how she knew it. She watched as his sneering smile was replaced with a rage that had festered these last months.

He continued softly, and Kit was swamped with the hatred in his voice. "Our babe was stillborn, and my lady wife grieved so that she died of the milk fever." His eyes narrowed. "You owe me two lives . . . a wife and a son, cousin, though I doubt not I owe my broken head to that kitchen slut Martha, who will suffer hell's torments when I catch her."

"She is well beyond your grasp forever," Kit said with some small satisfaction, little enough considering she was tied in a northbound carriage, kidnapped by a man who wished her the gravest ill and would no doubt visit it upon her at his first opportunity.

He flicked an imaginary speck from a waistcoat that was much too large for him and all out of fashion. "Some even thought such misfortune meant that witchcraft was at work. Could that be?" He smiled widely, showing wine-stained, uneven teeth. "You do not practice the devil's arts, do you? I would ache to see you burn."

"We live in a new and better age, sir," she said with contempt for his threat.

"New, perhaps, but I doubt the better for it. A better age is one in which wards do not defy a master's will and fleshly needs."

Kit swallowed her answer. It would only content him. She listened hard for the sound of following horses and heard nothing except for the occasional *clop clop* of a lone rider. Her heart sank to her stomach. William had made good his kidnap, and she was his prisoner. She dared not imagine what might lie ahead.

She tried to see between the canvas window curtains as they slowed on the rain-bogged road, but she could see nothing except Sir William's satisfaction at her failed effort. She longed for the touch of Jeremy's strong, warm hand, the surety of his voice. The thought that she might never be with him again, feel his loving flesh mingling with her own, increased her body's dull pain far more than had Sir William's heavy boots. Though she knew she would deny it if ever she was safe again and had the chance, there was one fact far worse than being in Sir William's grasp: the fact that it was her own fault for not heeding Jeremy's warning, for rejecting any mastership but her own. This torment, then, was her reward for stubbornly going her own way. A small part of her mind clung to the idea of self-rule, an idea that still felt right to her, but she had to admit that these sorry results had not matched the inspiration. . . . No, not at all.

The groom had two primed pistols in his waistband, which he put hands on when he felt her eyes on him.

She bent her head in prayer: God, of blessed name, do not allow Jeremy to come after me only to die for my folly. But, Lord, please, I must see him again. She must try to force herself not to think of him. . . . To forget him for long minutes, if she could.

"Ah, a prayerful whore," Sir William said, lacing all the evil in his heart through that word. "There, you see, dear cousin, if you beg God's pardon and mine, though you have disgraced yourself as a common London harlot and cost me mightily in time and fortune, I will honor you as the daughter of Sir Robert Lindsay."

"I have memories of how you honored me, Sir William," Kit said, her tone mockingly polite, her mouth still dry and her body steeled against a blow that did not come, although she saw his fingers curl white against his palm.

"You had ever a sharp and disrespectful tongue, cousin, and I see you did not lose it on the London stage. I vow a time in the country will be most instructive as to the proper deference a maid owes a master." His smile now was a grimace, and Kit could tell that he was racked with a need to smash a fist into her face. For the next few miles, she wondered why he did not do so, and could not arrive at an answer that satisfied. It was not like the Sir William she knew to hold himself away from what he wanted.

On and on they drove through the cloud-dark day, the driver's whip cracking incessantly, rain pelting the carriage roof, Sir William cursing the roads, the groom in his corner looking warily at his master.

At last the groom spoke, after leaning far out the window and looking ahead. "The horses be much in need of rest and watering, Sir William. There be an inn, the Swan by name, not a mile on, and I know the innkeep as a man who can hold his tongue for a shilling."

Was this her mode of escape? She looked at Sir William. He smiled as he read her mind. She must guard her thoughts carefully, if they were so plainly writ upon her face.

When the carriage finally slowed to a creaking stop, she heard the sounds of an inn yard plainly, chickens clucking, other horses neighing welcome and an innkeep's greeting as he opened the coach door, lowered the step, bowing and wiping his hands upon a bloodied leathern apron.

"Your worships be most welcome to the Swan. We have a warm fire and a fine calf's head pie with my own good wife's ale to break your fast. This way, sir, if your worship pleases."

Sir William had quickly pulled Kit's hood to shadow her face and her cloak to cover her bound hands and feet. "My lady is unwell, innkeep. She will be staying in the coach, as will my groom."

Kit leaned back, watching the groom's face grow angrier.

A fire and a meat pie were quite obviously something he very much desired, along with a chance to stretch his cramped legs. "Master groom, I don't know your name," she said politely when it was safe to do so.

"Jack, mistress."

"I apologize to you, Jack, for your having to guard me in this cold carriage when you deserve a hot meal and a warm fire. You were so clever to find me. It was you at the Cockpit, was it not?"

"Aye," came the sullen answer, "though some good it be to me now. The master does complain that I spent too many days at it, and cut my reward by several guineas."

Kit watched his dark eyes and saw that he was not a happy servant. "Some masters are exceeding hard to please, Jack." She smiled what she hoped was a sweet smile and not one of desperate calculation. "I would most certain hire you if I had someone to find."

"Thank 'e, mistress," he said, his face relaxing its anger lines a little. "And I would pay my shilling to see you on the stage . . . or on Hampstead Heath."

"You were there?"

"Aye, with Sir William."

"How very clever you are, Jack."

"Thank 'e again, mistress."

Kit allowed several minutes to pass in silence as the groom's face relaxed into something akin to satisfaction. In a small, weak voice, she said, "Jack, I have need of a closet of ease."

"I cannot allow you from the coach," he answered, sitting up straighter.

"For shame. Would you force me to soil myself?"

"Nay, don't do that, lady!"

He opened the door, to find Sir William with his foot upon the step. "Leaving, Jack? Did you allow the doxy to cozen you?"

"Nay, Sir William. Not so."

They drove on, Sir William picking his calf's head pie from his teeth with a gold pick he carried in a carved ivory box, oblivious of the hunger in his groom. For her part, Kit doubted she could eat, even if he didn't intend to starve her.

When the coach became unbearably hot, Sir William ordered the curtains rolled up, and Kit looked out to see the countryside passing while her mind was racing faster than the horses. Would Jeremy be so angered by her disobedience that he would allow her to suffer the consequences of her behavior? She could not believe it; she did not want to believe it, and knew that this was as much a trap for him as for her.

Miles passed under their wheels in silence, and Kit was glad of it. Soon enough she would know what William planned for her. Toward the last of the evening hours, they turned onto a familiar road. Startled, she looked at her cousin, who gave no sign. "This is not the road to Bournely Hall," Kit said.

"No, cousin, you should know it well."

"I do," Kit answered, her heart sinking as the gentle forested hills flashed by. "It is the road that leads past Rosevere."

Sir William bent toward Jack. "You were leaving the coach against my orders. It grieves me, but I can't have a man in my service who . . ."

As the groom half stood, crouching as far from Sir William as possible, his master opened the door latch of the swiftly moving coach and pushed Jack out.

His scream as the rear coach wheels rode over his legs,

leaving him crippled in the road, rang in Kit's ears and sickened her to tears of rage at such cruelty.

"Now, my lady Katherne, you owe me a groom as well as a wife and son."

"Surely God will punish you, William."

One side of his mouth curled down. "God may do as he likes in his heaven. On earth, I will do as I like . . . as you will learn very soon."

She shut her mind to what that could be.

Chapter Twenty-three

Pursuit and Prison

Kit!" Jeremy called, racing up Jolly's stairs, taking two at a time to the rehearsal hall. All the students were practicing the country dance cuckolds-all-in-a-row, which was the rage at court this season, and, Jeremy thought, nowhere more true. In the past he would have seen it as a great jest, since he had put a cuckold's horns on more than a few husbands at that court. He was struck still for a moment by the change in him and wondered how it had happened almost without his knowing. Then the warmth of the true reason came upon him. Kit. His heart. When he had become a wish in her eyes, and maybe before, he had ceased to have any real desire for another woman. He shrugged slightly. Though, 'twas true, he could not say he had ceased to occasionally have a man's regard for female beauty.

Still, he stood with one hand on the rehearsal hall door, shaking his head in not a little consternation. Jeremy Hughes had been the first to laugh mightily at the idea of faithfully loving one woman to the exclusion of all others. Indeed, he had advised other young swains against it as mightily unnatural. Grinning at the memory, he knew that now he was laughing at himself.

Jeremy did not see Kit among the dancers and hurried on to Alain's room, knocking, then entering.

Alain was reading, his hands now free of bandages though not completely healed and quite scarred. "*Mon ami*, why must you English make such noise to—"

"Kit!" Jeremy interrupted. "Have you seen her? I have great news. We are to join the Theater Royal, and there is a place for you, if you want it. . . . Only minor parts at first, but you're to be master of the wardrobe."

Alain leapt to his feet and laughed aloud in delight. "*Mon Dieu*, master of the wardrobe," he said, blowing a kiss into the air, smoothing his doublet before frowning. "Keet left with Nellie two hours gone."

"What! Where did they go? How?" It was all Jeremy could do to stay himself from grabbing Alain's now perfect doublet and shaking knowledge out of him.

Alain leaned away from Jeremy's furor. "By Nellie's carriage, *cher ami*, I know not where. She said nothing to me."

"God save her!" Jeremy flung himself from the room, with Alain scrambling after him. At the bottom of the stairs, Jeremy opened the door and o'erleaped the entry stoop, running a few steps in each direction as if his will alone could make Nellie's carriage appear.

And it did.

Two lathered horses pulling a mud-spattered coach entered the street from the direction of the Strand, circling, scattering carters carrying bricks for the rebuilding of the old city, and fruit sellers with the last of their wares, before pulling up to stop where Jeremy stood in front of George Jolly's house. Jeremy could scarce wait to berate Kit. How dare she cause so much worry with her thoughtless, willful ways.

Nellie leapt from the coach before he had a chance to lower the step or help her. "Kit is taken," she said in an amazing carrying voice for one so small, though she seemed to be struggling for breath.

"Taken?" Jeremy asked, his face reflecting all the fears that suddenly threatened to overwhelm him.

Alain supported Nellie with his arm, throwing a warning look at Jeremy. "*La petite* is in distress. She has need of a warm posset and rest or she will swoon."

Although Jeremy wanted to shout against it, he could see that Alain was in the right. Nellie needed to collect herself before she could tell her tale.

They half carried her into Jolly's grand parlor. He was there at his writing table with his manuscripts. "Madame Gwyn," he said, rising to bow.

Jeremy carried her to the large chair and set her gently in it. "Jolly, some brandywine for Nellie."

It was produced and she gulped it, ample chest heaving, resting her head against the chair's upholstered back. "I asked Kit to accompany me to the Clink."

"The Clink?" Jeremy all but shouted.

"For charity's sake," Nellie said, still breathing rapidly. She stopped and held out her bowl for more. Jolly poured it full.

Jeremy stood before her, clasping his hands behind him. He did not dare loose them for fear he would throttle Nellie. Though he knew it unfair to blame her for taking Kit abroad, he was in no mood to be fair.

"Continue," he said in a strange, strangled voice.

"She was standing by my coach in front of the prison

when my driver says a private coach came alongside, pulled her up and in and carried her off." Nellie took another large gulp of the brandywine. "We followed within minutes and came close, but lost them at a turning. Now, Jeremy Hughes, will you say what is happening? For there is much I don't know about this affair."

"There is no time. I'm off as soon as I can find a horse for hire."

"Two horses, *mon ami*," Alain said, pulling his breeches lace tighter.

Nellie stood, weaving a little. "Two strong horses, sirs, four the better, because they're pulling my coach. If you are going after Kit, I must be a party to it, since I was an unwitting party to her kidnap. Do not think for a moment to leave me behind."

Jeremy shook his head. "Much too dangerous for a woman," he said, ending the matter.

"God's fish!" she said, using the king's favorite curse and drawing up to her full height, which reached to Jeremy's doublet's second horn button. "I earned my way in my mother's . . . er, establishment when I was but seven. Say you the same?"

Alain laughed. "Do they breed all Englishwomen with strong spines?" he asked of no one. "*Et maintenant*, we must be off, and Nellie could not ride so far. A coach *would* be more comfortable in this plaguey English weather."

Four fresh horses were soon brought, and they were off into the countryside, the roads so muddy that they made a slower passage than Jeremy would have liked. Although he recounted all he knew of Kit's original escape from Sir William, his voice sounded strange in his ears. He held himself in an iron grasp, his anger at Kit's disobedience burning away in the hot fires of his fear for her and then returning again, his mind swaying with the carriage, vacillating between anger and fear. Damn her! She had but to do as bidden to be safe. And now she was in danger of . . . He swallowed hard at the thought of that lout of a country knight lying atop her, caressing her and . . . Devil take her!

His pounding heart felt like a young boy's again. Memories of his dead mother and lost sister rose from the dark places where he'd hidden them for so many years, the all-too-familiar anger at his abandonment and loneliness filling him, reminding him that now he'd lost Kit, too. That old pain returned in strength, only this time there was no place to hide it. If he could not save her, he would be lost himself. Did she know he would turn God's earth upside and down to rescue her, or was she frightened near to death? His breath caught in his throat and he was strangled by it. He did not dare to think what was happening to her at this moment, a weak woman in a monster's grasp.

As Sir William's carriage stopped at the gate to the long yew-lined drive to Rosevere, Kit saw her captor lean through the carriage window, and with little hope of success and a great effort, she raised her bound feet and caught him a blow against his side, knocking him back into the opposite seat. She had some desperate, crazed idea that she might find friends to help her at Rosevere.

With a strangled curse, William swung a fist that caught her above the ear and sent her spinning onto the floor again. He bent so that his mouth was close to her ear, his hand clutching at her throat. "Do not try my patience further, my lady, else you will regret it mightily and soon."

Kit believed him.

The last flashes of the low, setting sun slanted through the swinging window curtains, again closed. The rays shone on her as if to light her misery. She heard old Thomas greeting his master and opening the gate, but Kit dared not cry out lest Thomas now pay a price for hearing her. She was only too aware that Sir William was ruthless to the point of murder.

They drove into the stables behind the ancient fortified manor, built more than three hundred years earlier by an ancestor who, returned from crusade with fortune repaired, had quickly replaced an earlier timber-and-thatch home. Her father's father had widened the arrow slits to make diamond-paned glass windows, and her father had planted leisure gardens of rare beauty. She did not need to see them to remember.

The driver opened the carriage door and lowered the step.

"Welcome home, Lady Katherne," Sir William said, a sneer in every word. "I trust you will find your accommodations adequate." She wondered why he laughed at that as he walked toward a horse saddled and ready beside the mounting block, held by a footman. "I must see how Bournely fared during my absence. Bring the carriage to me when you are finished here," he ordered

Two pairs of hands seized her and lifted her from the carriage. One man bent and untied her bound feet, though she did not know how she would walk since she had no feeling in her legs, and her head was still spinning from William's blow. When she tried to take a step, she pitched forward and would have fallen facedown in the stable midden had not the two men caught her, one on each side. She looked in their faces and did not recognize them. They were not her father's men. She'd known all their tenants from childhood.

They did not speak to her, but led her with iron grips on her arms toward a rear entrance to Rosevere through the crushed knot garden. With each step, she gained more feeling in her feet so that she had little trouble climbing the few wide stone steps into the winter kitchen. All was dark and no fire flamed under the turnspit in the huge fireplace, no scent of roasting meat where once whole pigs had basted, nor bread baking in the wall ovens, reached her nostrils. Thick dust and spiderwebs covered all.

One guard lit two candles to light their way into the great hall.

"Where are you taking me?" she asked, but received no answer.

Across the raftered hall, the candlelight scarce reaching into corners, Kit's gaze moved quickly from one familiar scene to another. Gone was the great turkey-carpeted table under which she and her brothers had played games of castles under siege. The still-brilliant Arras wall tapestry of St. Catherine tending lepers was gone, no doubt sold for its glinting silver and gold threads. She would grieve for a lifetime for what had been taken from her unless, somehow, she could outwit William and win all back . . . Rosevere, cottagers, Arras tapestry and great table. All of it, just as it had been.

The guards opened a low iron-bound door and they started a long, winding descent, the smell of moldering stone and the sound of dripping water reaching up to meet her. Kit knew exactly where she was being taken, damn William's soul to hell. She and her brothers had played there as children, despite having been forbidden to do so.

The ancient cellar had once contained wine casks, and before that a cell for holding prisoners for the lord's court, although it hadn't been used since the old queen's time, when priests of the old faith had also hidden there in a priest hole that had once sheltered them from Protestant searchers.

One of her guards led her to the cell door, which was rusting on its hinges, but was still capable of being locked with a huge key that hung on the opposite wall.

She clutched the cell bars, iron rust transferring to her hands. "Surely you do not intend to keep me in this lowly prison without food or drink or a blanket. Even the prisoners in the Clink fare better."

"We do as we be told," said one, as they both prepared to mount the stairs again. "I think 'twould be best for you, my lady, to do the same. There be none in the country would go against Sir William, as ye have, and live to tell of it."

"For God's sweet pity, at least leave a candle to light the dark."

"Nay, Sir William said no comforts of any kind."

She watched until the light disappeared around a bend in the staircase and soon heard the sound of the door to the great hall closing heavily again.

Kit looked high in the tower to the one window she knew was there, but she could see no moonlight. She was hidden where Jeremy would not find her, hungry, cold and alone.

When she heard the skittering of rat claws on the stone floor, she tucked her skirts between her legs and under her waist ties and began to pace the length of the cell, forward until her shoe hit a wall and then back to the cell door, back and forth, to keep the rats away from her.

At least she was alone no more.

Chapter Twenty-four

The Tower Room

Jeremy watched the gated entrance into Bournely from behind a stand of trees and underbrush. He'd had little sleep in the rocking carriage, but his eyes were clear and sharply focused on the comings and goings of the manor, which so far this morning had produced nothing unusual. If Kit were behind those walls, she had created no disturbance in the usual work of a busy country estate, preparing animals and soil for the fallow season of the coming winter.

But she must be here. Mayhap hurt, or worse, raped for certain this time. He near had to swallow his heart when it leapt into his throat as the ugly image filled his mind. That bastard Pursevant!

Jeremy smashed his fist against the trunk of the ancient elm that hid him, immediately regretting it. He was still sucking scraped knuckles when a coach appeared with two armed footmen up behind, heading west. He caught his first glimpse of the squire, and his hands itched for Pursevant's throat. Though he strained to see, Kit was not in the carriage. How had the rogue knight dared to leave her behind in a familiar house with people she knew, knowing how resourceful she was? Or had he? With a murmured prayer that he was right, he raced to where Nellie's coach was hidden in woods off the Bournely road.

"Nellie! Alain!"

They answered sleepily.

"Pursevant just drove away. I think we should follow, but not closely. Best not to be seen."

"A strange carriage with the king's arms would attract unwanted attention," Nellie offered drolly. She sneezed. "Oh, la, this country air is so thick and full of perfumy scents that I can scarce breathe. My lungs long for the smoke and sewers of London. What say you, Frenchman?" she said, coughing for emphasis, and Alain joined her, thus amusing themselves while they drove slowly on.

Jeremy stayed his jaw-clenching anger at their levity. He knew they were mightily worried for Kit, but even their worry could not halt their appetite for fun and, in a way, he envied them. Thus he had been, not so long ago when his heart was free, but the knowledge of Kit in danger had stripped him of everything but his need to find her . . . unharmed. Yet his mind was roiled with overwhelming thoughts of violence against her lovely body, the body she had freely shared with him. What if she had suffered rape and the worst degradation, even now carrying the seed of that miserable bastard? What if . . . oh, God, of blessed name . . . she was dead, murdered, her broken body lying untended in some byway that he had passed without seeing? Jeremy's muscles were rigid with purpose. If Kit were dead or hurt, he would kill Pursevant and sweep away his acts with blood. . . . And hang happily.

As they drove, keeping just out of sight, he wondered,

too, if he was being led away from Kit. Still something urged him on, a prickling on the back of his neck, a nagging idea. Could it be that Pursevant had taken Kit to her childhood home since that would be the blackguard's idea of exquisite torture . . . to strip away even her last place of safety? From all she'd told him, this wagon track was the true direction to Rosevere, the one she had walked with Martha as they made good their escape that summer's evening.

Pale dawn glimmered from the high tower window, the rats retreated, and Kit slumped down against the damp stone walls of her cell, crossing her arms on her knees and cradling her head. Her mind was exhausted with useless railing against Sir William, her own complicity in her kidnap and her fear that her stubborn will had put Jeremy in danger. Her belly was rumbling with hunger and she had a raging thirst, which she had thought more than once to satisfy with the moldy drippings down the walls of her cell, but as yet had resisted.

She must have slept, dazedly dreaming of Jeremy as Lord Lovemore standing before her in the rose bower, one side of his mouth lifted lazily. The dream was so real that she felt torn from his arms as she woke slowly and raised her head to her one light source. It was full day, the window now lighting the ceiling of the old dungeon and the swaths of spiderwebs swaying above all. Keep hold, she told herself, there will be a way out, even if it is to bloody death.

A key grating in the iron lock at the top of the stairs brought her to her feet. Pride made her smooth her gown and try to tame her hair. Pity would not move William's heart; a confident captive might at least give him pause.

Her two jailers appeared first with a lantern each, and one

with a hamper. Kit was not the only inhabitant to smell the food. She heard the rats squealing somewhere in the walls. A small table was produced from a corner and laid with a haunch of venison, bread, soft cheese and ale. It was all she could do as an actress not to allow her hunger to show in her face as Sir William came into view around the stair's last turning.

"Leave us now, but stand guard in the great hall above," William ordered, and the two retreated back up the stairs.

He took the key from the wall and placed it in the lock, turning it several times before it clicked in the rusty keyhole and swung the creaking cell door open. Bowing, he held out his hand, which she ignored, though her senses were so acute that she smelled he was clean shaven, washed and his doublet sprinkled with rosewater and nutmeg like a lad come a-courting. Her empty stomach heaved at the thought of what that would mean. . . . The touch of his hand, his brutal mouth on hers.

Two small wine casks were set to serve as stools. He bowed her to one and took the other.

Kit didn't think for a moment to refuse the ale, but poured a tankard and downed it, setting her head to spinning, which forced her to eat as best she could with her fingers, Sir William having thoughtfully not provided her with a knife to plunge into his heart. He cut generous pieces from haunch and loaf and, though she tried mightily to eat in a mannerly way as her nurse had taught her, she was too hungry, and provided sufficient entertainment to bring a satisfied smile to her cousin's face.

After she had eaten all that was on her plate, she could refuse more, and did.

"My lady," Sir William said in what he obviously thought

was a courtly manner, but was, indeed, more menacing for his effort. "It grieves me to see you thus. If you but say the word, you will be mistress of both Bournely and Rosevere. Although you have lost your virtue—"

She raised her head, presenting him with her chin. "I have not *lost* my virtue, cousin, but freely given it."

He frowned, his fingers closing upon his silver-handled knife, but he did not frighten her.

"And would give it again for love of Jeremy Hughes and, on my life, only to him." She straightened her shoulders, feeling every bruise from the carriage ride as if fresh. "Virtue given lasts forever, cousin. You will never know that, and I pity you for the loss."

She steeled herself for a blow. It was obvious that she had stung him in a way he did not comprehend but knew he should. Still, he was a master at concealing his hurts, e'en from himself.

"Tut, Mistress Saucebox, you are in no position to taunt me. Pox take your virtue. It is your dowry I want."

At once she saw that he would withdraw those last words if he could. He cleared his throat, obviously trying to think of some recall, but failing. Kit's mind raced around what he had said and what the words revealed. Without meaning to, she spoke her thoughts aloud. "You have my dower rights with my wardship, so what need do you have to protect them with marriage when you could find a widow with a fresh fortune? You can leave me here to molder or kill me, and I wonder why you do not."

She saw him shift on his cask, a fleeting fear cross his face, and suddenly she knew. "Ah, Sir William, you fear my new friends at court may know about this business. Mayhap the king himself—"

He leapt to his feet, menacing her with his fist, but he could not bully her because she saw his weakness. "And you dare not try to force me into a public marriage," Kit said slowly, her voice calm and knowing as she looked into his eyes, unafraid. "Not a divine in England would marry a woman to her guardian against her will. That I did not want you would be exposed to all, and make mockery of your manhood. Even your meanest cottagers would laugh behind your back." She smiled when she saw him redden at the truth she spoke, and smiled again at an even more delicious truth he would never know. Poor William, all his scheming was for naught.

She felt an immense satisfaction to know what he did not. Sir William had no real problem; he could continue for his life to gain the rents and use of Rosevere because she would never claim her dowry by taking a man to marry. Unfortunately for William, he did not know her mind. How could he? She had not known it herself until he had taught her to hate the mastership of men like him, and to shield herself from a law that said man and wife were one flesh, and that the man's.

Kit almost laughed at the way his behavior had turned on him, and would have laughed had she not seen that William was desperate in his desire to smash his cocked fist into her body to show her his man's strength and her woman's weakness. She steeled herself for the certain blow.

Instead, he grabbed her arm in a hurtful grasp and slung her along to the other side of the stairway that led to the great hall above. "Cousin, I hold the high card in this game."

To her surprise, another stairs lay hidden inside the old priest hole. They climbed the opposite side of the hollow turret. "These were not here when I played as a child."

He did not answer, but pulled her tripping on her skirts up the stone steps, until they reached the top and a locked door.

She knew that she would fight him with all her strength, for she had no doubt what he intended. He would finish what he had started months ago. She pretended to stumble and quickly palmed a loose stone, lying against the curving wall, which she prayed she would have time to use to good effect though it might mean her death.

William pulled a ribboned key from under his doublet and opened the door, forcing Kit across the threshold. Once inside, he locked the door behind him.

She grasped her stone tighter, but she did not use it.

A window high in the circular room beamed light into the small, crowded chamber. But it wasn't the long table she remembered from the hall or her father's great bed and chair, or a shelf lined with her father's dozen precious books that filled her with wonder. It was the white-bearded man who sat in the shaft of sunlight, looking at her with eyes as deeply blue as her own.

William bowed in his mocking fashion. "Sir Robert Lindsay, may I present Lady Katherne, who so disliked being orphaned I am truly surprised she has no daughter's loving greeting for you."

Jeremy halted Nellie's coach when Rosevere's stone towers came into view beyond the fields where men were busy scything and stacking hay for the following hay wains to take to the barn for winter feed. He recognized the gray towers instantly from Kit's description. He could see in the distance Pursevant's carriage stopped at the head of the tree-lined lane to the manor, and a man walk back to close the gate, then enter the nearby cottage. This must be the

Thomas of which Kit had spoken. He had no choice but to discover if his guess was correct.

"Wait off the road," he ordered Nellie and Alain. "Pretend you are repairing a wheel. And drape over the king's arms, lest you have every cottager crowding around."

"*Mon ami*, don't fight them alone," Alain begged, his hand on his sword.

Though she was seated, Nellie stamped her foot. "And I have not endured this chilly night and noxious air to be left behind!"

Jeremy walked away without hearing. It was intolerable to be so close to Kit without being free to storm the walls of the old manor. He held himself together, determined to do nothing foolish. If he were caught or silenced, Kit would pay for his recklessness, and Nellie and Alain, as well. When the plowmen were at the far turn, he slipped into the gatekeep's cottage.

The startled old man reached in alarm above the mantel for his fowling piece, but Jeremy put up both hands to show he had no weapon in them. "Thomas?"

"Aye, I be Thomas of Rosevere."

"Good Thomas, hear me. I am Mistress Kit's friend, and she is in need of your help."

"If you be true friend, what do ye here? I be not seeing my mistress for many months, though I remember her to God every night when I bend my knee."

Jeremy looked about the small room, but the man was alone and, judging from his tattered breeches, had no women to care for him. "My name is Jeremy Hughes, and Kit spoke of you in gratitude for your help when she was escaping the hangman's rope." Jeremy gave him details of that help, convincing Thomas he was indeed Kit's friend.

"Then she be safe, praise the Lord of blessed name."

"No, Thomas, not safe. I believe her to be kidnapped by Sir William and brought here."

Thomas was so startled, he abruptly sat on the one stool by the fireplace. "I be never seeing her these many months, Master Jeremy," he said, and lines of worry deeply etched his brow as he spoke.

"Did Sir William come here yesterday eve?"

"Aye, and came he again this morning, which be most strange, since he comes not to Rosevere so often, though his men be always at the manor house."

"Thomas, think of yesterday eve. Was he alone in the carriage?"

Thomas's eyes opened wider. "I be never seeing inside, for the curtains be drawn tight. Do ye think . . ."

Jeremy was certain now. If Pursevant had taken Kit to Bournely yesterday night, why would he come here to Rosevere that same night and come again this morning? "Yes, Thomas, Kit is prisoner here in her own home."

"Have ye come to free her? There be many cottagers on Lindsay land who be loyal and longing for the old master's time."

"I have need of fighting men this day," Jeremy said, smiling at Thomas's shining face, "or those who can certain act the part. I left two of Kit's friends in a carriage not a furlong down the road to Bournely."

"Ye stay here lest ye be seen, and be pleased to break yer fast," Thomas said, pulling on an old felt hat. "I'll fetch them to ye."

"You are a brave Englishman, Thomas."

"Nay, sir, I but loved the old master and his daughter, who be the prettiest sweet child I e'er saw in my born days."

Jeremy clapped him on the back, too full of instant affection for the gatekeep to say more.

He ate some bread and drank some new and bitter ale, keeping watch up the avenue to the manor house, thinking of that pretty, sweet child, blond hair flying as she ran about Rosevere, asking questions, perhaps a dog leaping after. These new pictures in his mind actually displaced the far worse ones that had been there, but surprisingly hurt near as much.

He was pacing the packed dirt floor when Nellie and Alain slipped into the cottage, their color high, ready for adventure.

Chapter Twenty-five

Reunited, or Love Preserv'd

"Father," Kit whispered, kneeling before the old man, tears streaming from her eyes, tears unshed for years and now loosed in a torrent. He seemed not to recognize her, so she gently turned his face to hers as she had often done as a child to command his attention. "Is it truly you?" She blinked back more tears, gathering in her racing thoughts. "But you were given up to Cromwell and hung."

Sir Robert reached for his neck and she saw the wide red scar of the rope. "Sir William has been hiding me from Cromwell's men. Who are you, lady?"

"I am Katherne, Father. Cromwell is dead; the king has returned and sits on his throne."

Sir Robert shook his head, disbelieving all. "Nay, lady, Cromwell still rules and my daughter is a young one scarce to here," he said, touching his shoulder. His voice was thin and rasping, his eyes with only memory of the young girl on the verge of womanhood he'd left behind to serve his king. All the years since seemed lost to him.

Kit swiveled on her knees to look at William, her hatred

now deeper than she had thought it could be. "You were the one who brought the news of my father's death by hanging and took me to Bournely when I was a child." It was not a statement; it was an accusation of cruelty beyond human understanding.

"Aye, and all was true," he said, obviously stung by her tone. "True, that is, until two years later. He wandered into the village, out of his head. Fortunately, two whores befriended and hid him, then brought me word. They have lived well since."

She ignored the taunting tone he'd reclaimed. "But that was five, six years gone. All this time, I was your servant and my father your prisoner. You allowed me to think that I was alone and friendless in the world and you did not tell him that—"

Sir William's raised hand silenced her. There was no remorse, only victory in his face. "And now, cousin, you are both my prisoners, unless you agree willingly and openly to marriage, binding Rosevere and all your dower lands to me forever. So long as you do my bidding, your father will live comfortably as you see. If not . . ." He smiled the smile that said he was well pleased with himself. "I am a generous man and I will even allow parental visits from time to time, though it is useless, as you see. He will never know you for his daughter."

Kit turned back to her father, clutching his shirt, shaking him gently, her voice raised in an agonized whisper. "Father, I'm Kit, your youngest child. Know me!" She was pleading, but as she spoke she could see that the recognition she longed for was beyond his power to give.

Her father's eyes, puzzled, stared back at her, and he struggled to do as she asked. Whatever he'd suffered had left him alive, but with memories that stopped as he'd been cut down from the scaffold. He reached to pick up a book open on the table beside him, placed it in his lap and looked at it. She knew that he was not reading because she saw no comprehension. He was going through the motions of being himself, like an actor who remembered the stage moves but had forgotten the lines and their meaning. Kit stroked his hand, unmoving on the page, the skin white and drawn tight over thin blue veins. She stood to face Sir William.

Although her heart felt empty of all feeling, it was still beating and she knew what she must do if she had the courage. She must give up every dream of Jemmy and their love and of being with him, part of a famous mad couple on the London stage. She clenched her fists and drew in a great breath. Courage, even forced courage, gave her strength, just as surely as despair would sap her energy.

The words she must say were in her throat but choking her.

William obviously thought she hesitated still. "Come, Lady Katherne, you will have what you want, and I will have what I want. I will be the largest landholder in Essex. There could be an earldom in it, and you could be my countess. What say you to that?" There was just the smallest echo of pleading in his tone. Though he hoped she would do anything to keep her father alive, he did not understand sacrifice and, therefore, did not trust it.

Her answer to him was as emotionless as she could make it. "I care nothing for your lands or your title, and I care less than nothing for you, and ever shall. But I will marry you."

He stepped closer, and there was a cold hardness in his gaze. "You will care, my lady. You will do a great deal more than care. I will keep you breeding until you die of it." He was so delighted with himself that he was almost dancing in his high boots, but something in her eyes stopped him short of mocking laughter. She could see that he was still a little unsure of her, and she planned to keep it that way. It would be the only power she retained.

With a prayer for endurance, she stepped forward, refusing William's hand, and they retraced their steps to the small door. Once, she looked back and saw her father framed in the shaft of light, the sun shining through his hair, wisping about his head like a halo. "I'll be back, Father," she said, her voice breaking as William shoved her through the door.

Down the circular steps and then up the other steps to the great hall they went, his hand firmly on her arm. She felt for the stone in her hand and found it stuck to her skin, so tightly had she held it. She quietly dropped it, knowing that now it would serve her no good purpose. Her future was sealed.

William knocked on the door at the top of the stairs, and it was opened by one of the guards.

"All quiet?" William asked.

"Aye, Sir William," said one guard. "The cottagers know better than be coming near to the manor house."

But the guard spoke too soon, for from the entrance to the hall leading to the winter kitchen stepped Jeremy, Alain and Nellie, the latter wearing a pair of tattered breeches, all with resolute expressions and swords drawn.

"Jemmy!" Kit's warning scream bounced to the corners of the great hall as she was thrown hard to the parquet floor.

Jeremy saw Kit hit the floor and would have rushed the three men had not Alain put out a hand to stay him. "Careful, *mon ami*. They are three to our two."

"Careful yourself, Frenchman, if you don't count me," Nellie said. "I have weapons that are more powerful than their swords." She undid the ribbons to Thomas's old linen shirt, exposing two very alert breasts.

Alain saluted her with his rapier and kissed the hilt, then they both moved rapidly after Jeremy, who had heeded no warning and bounded across the hall in great leaps, reaching the three men advancing down the center of the hall.

Heedless of danger, Jeremy engaged two swords at once, frustrated that Sir William dropped back behind his guards.

"Sir William is mine," Jeremy shouted to Alain, and then with one hasty look saw that Kit was sitting up, shaking her head as if to clear it. "Stay quiet, heart," he called to her, hoping she heard him and even more that she would obey.

Jeremy fought two swords alone until Alain engaged. Jeremy had faced his share of ruffians in the streets and fought more than once for his honor with gentlemen, and even more in the theater. Breathing, footwork, smooth transitions were the same on- or offstage, and this fight was for Kit's freedom, not the crowd's applause.

He met the first guard, who ran at him, his sword raised in attack. With a quarter pivot clockwise, he made a right-to-left swipe at his belly, pushing him back, and then faced the second man. But Alain and Nellie rushed in to engage both guards, Nellie cutting to one guard's right shoulder while his eyes were fastened on her breasts.

"Ha, *ma belle*," Alain called, "you are right, *oui*. . . . You have the best weapons of all!" Alain cut to the other guard's left hip to disable, and Jeremy slipped behind them to face Sir William's sword.

Jeremy circled his blade above his head in a hanging parry, taunting as he advanced. "Have you a taste to fight a man, Sir William?" Jeremy easily parried a wild swipe at his head, batting it away impatiently as if it were an insect. "Or do you limit your battles to rapine on women? As you see, you have chosen the wrong woman in Lady Katherne. She has more courage than most men. It is one of the chiefest reasons I love her madly." Jeremy deliberately slit Sir William's doublet at the heart. "Though courage is not the only reason, there being many more to recommend her to a man, reasons which you will never know, Sir Dog!"

But instead of Jeremy's taunts making William rash and reckless, William sidled toward Kit, who was now standing a bit unsteadily against the wall. Jeremy ran around to block him, but was too late.

William's sword point rested on Kit's throat, drawing a tiny bead of bright red blood that ran in a straight line to disappear into her shift. "Drop your weapons, you scabby villain, or your proud bitch dies before you!"

"Do not disarm, Jemmy, or he will kill you!" Kit said in a low, steady voice that carried. She expected the words to be her last as William deliberately moved his rapier against her throat, drawing fresh blood. She felt nothing because she knew what she must do. She would step into William's sword and end this danger to Jeremy and her dear friends. She was not afraid to die for love. Rather death than to live without it as William's wife for all her days.

Kit said a quick prayer for her soul and gathered herself for her final step into eternity. She looked at Jeremy one last time, an image to journey with her to paradise, when Nellie stepped forward, leaving Alain to watch the guards, who were both nursing slight wounds. "Sir, my pardon," she said in her most witty stage voice, "but I cannot drop *all* my weapons."

William was furious at her interference. "Quiet, whore! You may charm our Frenchified king, but not—"

Nellie stamped her foot not once but twice. "You speak treason, sir, for which Charlie will have your tongue, I vow."

"And if the king does not, *imbécile*, this Frenchman will," Alain shouted.

Jeremy saw new blood trickling down to disappear into Kit's shift, but that did not alarm him as much as what he saw in her eyes. He had seen it before in battle when all hope was gone and only letting go of breath remained. "No, heart. *No!* If you leave me, I swear to you that I will follow."

She stared at him and saw instantly that he meant his words.

Jeremy spoke aside to Nellie and Alain. "Do as Sir William asks," he said, sucking in a quick breath like a man come up from deep water. He dropped his rapier. "I cannot see Kit die for my revenge."

Reluctantly, Alain and Nellie complied, and the guards, quickly retrieving their own weapons, menaced them.

"Take all but the Lady Katherne below to the cell," William ordered. "She will be my wife this day, on her word."

"That's a lie!" Jeremy cried.

"Ask her," Sir William said, rolling the words like sweet sops off his tongue.

But Jeremy did not need to ask. The answer was writ large on Kit's face. What had William done to her to make her agree? His fingers flexed, longing for the man's throat.

Kit's mouth opened to speak farewell, then snapped shut, her wounded gaze sliding away from Jeremy's toward the rear of the great hall.

From the winter kitchen the sound of voices and many

heavy wooden shoes scraping on stone grew louder and louder until the men and women of Rosevere, led by Thomas, burst into the great hall, carrying harvest scythes and wooden pitchforks, pruning knives and mallets.

At least two dozen cottagers advanced in a straight line stretching across the hall, their eyes never leaving Sir William and Kit, the sound of their clogs making measured thunder through the room.

"Mistress Kit, we be coming for ye!" Thomas called, carrying his old fowling piece at the ready.

Fury mounted in William's face. "What is the meaning of this, Thomas? Back to the fields, all of you, if you don't wish to lose your holdings. I'll enclose all into sheep runs, if you . . . back! Back, I say!"

The men and women of Rosevere continued their slow advance, their eyes on Kit, showing no fear because she didn't.

William's face was red with rage. "Are you crazed to defy your lord? 'Tis a hanging offense you do here."

Thomas spoke as the advance continued like an inexorable storm. "Sir William, we be only concerned for Mistress Kit and her safety."

A dozen ripostes swept across William's face, but he was unable to sputter any of them.

Kit, though she had a rapier point at her throat and could feel the warm blood trickling between her breasts, spoke in a loud, clear voice. "Good people of Rosevere, Sir Robert Lindsay, your true lord, is alive and hidden in a secret tower above the dungeon, thinking Cromwell still rules. Sir William has kept him prisoner these many years while you toiled for him." William's hand began to shake.

From the cottagers an angry roar rose and swelled until it

filled the great hall to its rafters. And from every throat came words long suppressed. "Kill him! Kill him!"

As Rosevere's people continued their advance, pointing their weapons at him, hatred and murder upon their faces, William's hand became so palsied that his sword fell to the floor.

Chapter Twenty-six

All Restored... Almost

As a cowering Sir William was surrounded by menacing cottagers, who were only too happy to poke him with their rake handles and menace him with scythe blades, Jeremy scooped a sagging Kit from against the wall. It was unbearably sweet to hold her close again in his arms. "Heart, heart," he whispered over and over.

"I had to promise him marriage, Jemmy, for my father's life," she said, her lips moving against his forehead as he kissed the throat that still trickled blood. He tore the lace from his shirt cuff and pressed it gently against her wound.

Nellie, ripping the hem of her shirt as she came to Kit, tied the linen around to form a loose bandage. "Friend, this would not play on the stage of the Theater Royal. No, not even as high drama could it be believed." Little Nellie's eyes blazed with excitement as she looked about for more mischief to subdue.

Kit gave Nellie's arm a quick squeeze of thanks, and called a greeting in French to Alain, who had Sir William's guards at sword point once again. He saluted in response, while eyeing his gold-braided sleeves now hanging in shreds.

"Jemmy," Kit said, just managing to catch her breath, "get the key to my father's prison from around William's neck." She watched him rip the ribbon from the humbled Pursevant.

As Jeremy and Kit passed through the door onto the dungeon's steps, he yelled two quick orders: "Alain, ask Thomas to calm the Rosevere people. Nellie, you come with us. You can bear witness for the king. I fear a great crime has been committed."

Kit, surprised to have the strength, raced down and then up the stairs, hand in hand with Jeremy. As they passed her cell of the previous night, he tightened his grip. "I could skewer him for that alone."

"I was not afraid, Jemmy. You were with me."

He swallowed hard at that and hoped it would ever be so.

They continued up the hidden stairs in back of the tower and opened the small door. Kit's father was sitting as she'd left him, dozing in the sun shining through his window. But as she went forward, he awoke and beckoned her to him.

"Thank you, lady, for coming again."

Kit was overcome, her throat full, her chest tight, unbidden tears flowing, and she blessed Jeremy for speaking, since she could not. "Sir Robert, the rightful king sits on his throne. You are free to come out of hiding and have a care for your lands and people. They are below, waiting to greet you."

Her father hesitated, and Nellie came into view, decently covered again. "Good Sir Robert, I am come from the king in Whitehall, and he wishes for all his faithful subjects to return from exile."

Jeremy bowed. "They do speak truth, sir. I am your escort."

Kit's father looked at Jeremy. "But Sir William will not give me leave to—"

"Sir William is completely engaged at this moment," Jeremy said, and bowed again courteously.

Sir Robert allowed Jeremy to help him from his chair. He slowly donned a doublet and hat. "I cannot leave my books, my bed. . . ."

"They will be returned to their proper place within your house, sir, this very day," Jeremy said gently, putting his arm around Sir Robert's shoulder to steady him. He was frail enough for Jeremy to feel through flesh and sinew to bones, but as the knight and king's cavalier pulled back his shoulders, there was yet strength in him. Jeremy sensed that he had endowed his daughter with what she had needed these last days, for there was no fright or fainting in her. Old Will Shakespeare had said that love goes toward love, and, in truth, courage goes toward courage.

Slowly, then more quickly, they made their way back to the great hall, hearing angry shouts that grew louder with each step. As they moved through the open door into the great hall, Sir Robert shrugged off Jeremy's arm, standing straight and blinking hard at the sight that met them.

Jeremy moved swiftly, drawing his sword and shouldering through the crowd to cut down from the rafters a still-kicking Sir William Pursevant. He lay on the floor, gasping for breath, his legs jerking, a glimpse of hell in his eyes.

Jeremy straddled his body and faced the bloodlust of the cottagers. Some men moved forward menacingly. They were angered by years of oppression, but also distracted by the sight of Sir Robert Lindsay, the kind knight who had been lost to them and had now reappeared, as if by magic or witchcraft. Some of them thrust their thumbs between their first two fingers, making the sign of the cross to ward off evil.

"Go, greet your true lord," Jeremy commanded in a voice that had to be obeyed, his sword point pressing against William's breast and a boot resting on his privates. "Some free advice, Sir William . . . lie still and be silent if you would save what is left of your miserable life. My hand aches so to spit you through for what you did to Kit that I would gladly go to the gibbet for one thrust. Beware, sir, you are an inch from the devil."

William gargled on his own spittle but said not a word. He would wear the red necklace of the hangman's rope for the rest of his life.

Kit and her father were instantly surrounded by cottagers. "Speak to them, Father," Kit said gently.

Sir Robert looked about him, his face showing some anguish and bewilderment but a growing understanding. "Good people of Rosevere, I know your faces and your loyalty to my family. I have been long ill, but I do believe"—he smiled into Kit's face—"that with the lady Katherne's help, I will be well ere long, and all will be as it once was with our good King Charles on his rightful throne."

"Huzzah!" called Thomas, a shout echoed by all the cottagers, and as they shouted, much anger and revenge fell away from the people of Rosevere. They filed past Sir Robert, bending a knee and asking for his blessing, which he freely gave, becoming stronger as each familiar face passed by.

Thomas was last, and he knelt on both his rheumy, rickety

knees. "Sir Robert, I be now ready to die in peace, knowing ye be alive and my sweet lady Kit by yer side."

Sir Robert bent to lay his hand on Thomas's shoulder. "There has been enough of dying, good Thomas. I will need your advice and help to put things to right again in our Rosevere."

Thomas's weathered face grew eager. "Yer knot garden, Sir Robert. I be helping ye with that right gladly."

Sir Robert nodded and took Kit's hand. "Now, daughter, we have much to talk about."

Kit trembled with joy and relief. "You do know me, Father."

He kissed her temple, frowning at the bright red spot on the bandage around her throat. "I am beginning to understand what the years have added to you, and see that you bear a great resemblance to your mother. I have not lost my memory. I just ceased to use it. They say that if you can see nothing, hear nothing, you can grow blind and deaf. When they cut me down from the scaffold and tossed my body onto a pile of corpses, I was more dead than alive. Later, in the dark of night, I crawled away and wandered, a beggar, truly out of my mind. . . . I know not how long until I came to the village. Sir William then told me—" Remembering William, Kit's father walked, steadier now, to where William lay on the floor, his gaze darting fearfully from face to face.

"You were my *kin*." The word carried an accusation of great wrong.

William coughed, and when he spoke his voice was thin and piping like a lad's, as if his faltering manhood had been squeezed out of him by the rope. "Uncle, at first I truly hid you, but then . . ." He moved his gaze from one stern face to another until he came to Kit with Jeremy's arm about her, and her expression showed him no mercy.

Years of scheming had gone for naught. He had sought what was not his, and in the seeking lost himself and whatever he might have come to. But her voice showed no pity. "Your greed would not allow you to return me to my father, nor return Rosevere, and when first Cromwell and then the king confirmed you in your holding, you thought it yours in truth."

William's words begged understanding. "But he was ailing. It was enough I kept him alive. I could have killed him and no one would have been the wiser."

Kit frowned. William was a man who wanted to believe his own lies. "Your men would have known. Your whores would have known. You could not risk it, and there was always the possibility that you could use my father to bring me to heel if needs be."

The look on William's face as he struggled to sit up told her that she had come very close to the truth, and that even William had to acknowledge it. "What will you do with me?" he asked Sir Robert in a whining voice. "I treated you well."

"Well?" Sir Robert asked. "You took years from my life, and would have taken all of it, had not my daughter and her loyal friends—"

William scrambled to his feet now, recovering his anger if not his voice. "Your daughter and her loyal friends are nothing but actors and whores upon the London stage, unfit for your regard."

"Hell and furies!" Kit yelled, grabbing Jeremy's sword from his hand and thrusting it at William's heart, where it parted the already slashed cloth on the front of his fancy perfumed doublet. She needed only one more forward motion to part the cloth on the back of his doublet and finish him.

He immediately fell upon his knees before her, his hands in prayerful attitude, surely his first prayer in years and now most blasphemous.

Jeremy smiled grimly down at him. "You are truly a brave man, Sir William, to put God and Mistress Kit out of humor at once."

Alain moved beside Kit, his sword circling inches from Sir William's lungs. "And I won't be addressed as a common actor, a *mot injuste, monsieur*."

Nellie joined them and rested her blade against the tip of Sir William's nose, a broad smile on her face. "An uncommon actor then, Frenchman."

Alain grinned. "Much the better."

Sir William, completely undone by three swords, with his guards having quietly slipped out of the hall, lost the last of his small store of courage. "Cry mercy!" he sobbed.

Sir Robert was unsteady with fatigue and Jeremy produced a leather chair for him, from which he sat as judge over his now prostrate nephew. "Sir William, you must return all that you have taken from Rosevere since the king regained his throne."

"But that would be six years of rents and—" The horror mounting on William's face showed that he was making quick mental calculations. "I cannot return all those monies or I would be beggared. Sir Robert, think of my five children—"

"I am thinking of those innocent ones or I would take this matter entire to the king at once. I doubt not that he would see you to the Tower, sir."

"More like the scaffold!" Nellie said with some glee, as William cringed.

Sir Robert continued: "If you do this, William, I will only ask the king to recognize my right to Rosevere. Otherwise at any default . . ." The threat hung in the air, but not for long.

Sir William rose again, bowing shakily, and nodded. With one last menacing look at Kit, Jeremy, Alain and Nellie in turn, he limped from the great hall.

"Father," Kit said, watching until William had passed out of her sight, "you cannot trust him. He is more evil than you know."

Sir Robert stood. "I do not trust him and he will no doubt plan to cheat me, but I will demand his records, and that will add more to my coffers. He does not know it yet, but he is a broken man. All of Essex will soon be whispering his disgrace and make of him a pariah, which for an ambitious man like William is worse than death." He looked around him at the near-empty hall. "And now I would put my house in good order."

All the rest of the day former servants drifted back to Rosevere Manor, and soon the kitchen was emitting the odors of roast piglet, baking bread and minced apple tarts. The refectory table was brought down from the turret room, and even the old Arras tapestry was found rolled and hidden in the barn loft, to be rehung in the place that had held it for more than a century.

Before the sun went down, and in the warm glow of an autumn afternoon, Jeremy and Kit walked the orchards ripe with unpicked fruit, looked into the teeming fish ponds and strolled the neglected gardens hand in hand. Kit saw that even the untended roses were still blooming. "I am all amaze," she said, stooping to smell one, "that such beauty can thrive through neglect."

Jeremy bent and plucked the rose, scattering the petals about her shoulders. "One day, heart, this will all be yours," Jeremy said, seeing around him more of wealth and quality than he would ever own. Observing Kit in her natural place had made him painfully aware that poor boys from the Welsh border could hardly hope to aim so high.

Kit held his arm tighter, half reading the thoughts that caused the muscles on his arm to tense and his mouth to draw into a straight line. She was aware that she could not share his struggle, and since his face did not invite inquiry, she talked of her childhood, drawing close to him, touching his leg with hers as they walked. She was near sick with her need for him and schemed of a time to find love's physic.

That evening, Sir Robert Lindsay sat at the head of his table near a roaring fire, Kit on his right and Jeremy on his left. Thomas was seated between Nellie and Alain, near overwhelmed at the honor of breaking bread with his master.

Nellie speared a slice of roast piglet basted with pear juice, having eaten nothing since early morn. "Sir Robert, I must leave at first light for London, where I have missed two rehearsals for *The English Monsieur* and will be fined for it. I doubt Master Betterton will believe my true story. Who would?"

"I am sorry for your trouble on my behalf, Mistress Gwyn," Sir Robert said, and Kit saw him perplexed at the very idea of a woman on the stage.

"Nay, sir, I would not have missed it for a dozen better roles. If you prepare your petition tonight, I will see that the king has it in hand by late tomorrow, although he will think it fantastical when I relate this adventure."

Sir Robert looked at Jeremy. "And you, sir, what are your plans?"

Jeremy avoided Kit's gaze. "I will return to London and the Theater Royal, Sir Robert, with Mistress Gwyn and Alain."

Kit started where she sat and would have spoken, but for her father's hand that covered hers.

"We must speak alone, daughter."

Jeremy stood at once, bowed, and said, "I will see that Nellie's driver has prepared the carriage and horses for the journey." He walked from the great hall, his back very straight.

With Godspeed until the morrow, Thomas bowed and left for his cottage, while Nell and Alain, with elaborate yawns, retired to the rooms that had been prepared for them.

Kit spoke first. "Father—"

"Hush, daughter. My mind has been asleep, but I have not lost my ability to see what passes between a man and a woman, what is in their eyes and on their faces. This Jeremy Hughes has courage to match your own, and the demeanor of a great lord. It is a father's duty to provide a husband for his daughter, therefore I would be proud to call this man son." He paused at her silence, squinting a little, trying to read her face, and finally asking, "But is there something I should know?"

Kit bowed her head. "Jeremy is already married, Father."

Sir Robert's face showed astonishment and anger. "How then, daughter, could you . . . could you bed him?"

She told him, then, a part of her story. The hoax played at

the Fleet Prison and Lord Rochester's cruel trick, demanding marriage between Jeremy and Martha.

Sir Robert frowned. "This Jeremy Hughes is a more honorable man than I suspected. If this marriage was fraudulent and unconsummated, daughter, then perhaps an annulment could be obtained."

Kit's shoulders dropped into dejection. "Perhaps, in years and years through the ecclesiastical courts, though that is not the only impediment."

Sir Robert's shrug was now full of exasperation. "What then, daughter?"

Kit took a deep breath. "I have made a great vow never to marry and submit my independence to a master."

"A foolish vow, Kit, one that God would not hold a woman to, nor I, and one that you most surely will regret."

She could not tell him that regret was already a great part of her; she could not admit it to herself. The idea of being her own master was so deeply set in her mind that to remove it would leave a hollow that she doubted she could fill with anything, mayhap not even love.

Her father poured her another bowl of Thomas's new ale, since William had long ago removed Rosevere's wine stores. Her tongue loosened, Kit related all that had happened since Sir William had taken her to Bournely; how she had escaped his ravishment, how Jeremy had helped her, taught her, and how she had discovered her true way as an actress, and hoped soon to have an honored place in the London theater. "It is wondrous, this acting, Father. I can be myself but more myself than I ever knew. I love to be on the stage with Jeremy, to sing with Jeremy and—"

Sir Robert raised his hand to stop her, a slight smile on

his lips. "There are things a father can guess but does not need to hear the particulars of, daughter."

She helped him to his room, which contained his bed and chair and beloved books, his Bible and the poets Ovid and Homer, with the folio of Shakespeare's plays that she had once read and reread. She tucked the coverlet about his shoulders against the chill night air and kissed his bearded cheek, just as he had once put her to bed with a kiss as a child.

When Kit opened the door to her old room, Nellie was sleeping soundly. Quietly, Kit closed the door, and lifting a shielded candle from a side table, lit her way to the stables, taking less time to reach her destination than ever before.

The horses, carriages and cattle belonging to Rosevere were housed in an ancient tithe barn built in the fourteenth century before the first great plague, to hold half of all crops peasants owed to their lord. In modern times it held the stables under its soaring Gothic rafters, arching high over the stalls like a cathedral for animals.

Kit called softly, "Jemmy."

When he didn't answer, she called again, but had no reply.

She found him wrapped in his cloak, lying next to his sword on the clean hay that would be forked to the horses in the morning. A lantern hung on a nearby post and cast a flickering, dim light on his face. His lips were moving in his dream. She leaned close, but she could not understand the words.

Carefully, she lay down beside him, the chill night air fleeing the warmth he radiated through his thin cloak. "Why, Jemmy?" she whispered, but she was unsure of just what question she was asking or what answer she awaited. She wanted him always just as he was, and hated what a woman had to give up to obtain *always* from a man. But did she really hate the thought of having a master, or was the hate only a habit, as she suspected? Sometimes she admitted in the quieter reaches of her mind that Jeremy might make a fine master. She clenched her fists. She could have screamed out her fury at the doubt he raised in her, had she not known it would be unfair. It wasn't Jemmy she was furious with, but Kit Lindsay, who seemed to be ruled by her body and not by her head when Jeremy Hughes was near.

His lips were parted in sleep, and already the dark shadow of a beard was growing along his raised cheekbones and strong jaw, his waving black hair tangled through with straw. She bent closer to watch his lips, tracing their outline with a finger, remembering the pleasures of his flame-fueled kisses, and felt her resolve to maintain her freedom melting away completely, overwhelmed by the longing to be truly part of him again. The recollection of their nights together was taking control of her, and she ached with the concentration of those heated memories in the place they always seemed to settle. Before she could stop her hands, she had opened her gown and shift and shrugged out of them.

She reached down to stroke his cheek gently, watching the thick sweep of dark lashes against his cheek, certain she had never felt more alive than when next to him. "I love you, Jemmy," she said, so softly she could have denied it.

"Spare me not," he whispered back, something of the old mockery in his voice. "I am at your mercy, my lady of Rosevere." He pulled her deeper into the hay mound and covered her with his cloak.

Though she continued to shiver, it wasn't from the chill evening air. "Let me explain, Jem—"

He covered her mouth with his, murmuring against her lips, "Don't explain. Don't examine and reexamine your words or mine. Don't do anything but love me."

She took him at his word, sliding her leg over him and rising until she sat atop his hard, muscled belly and felt him shuddering beneath her.

"Heart, do you know what to do next? I can tell you, but if you would be the master, I would rather see you play the role without direction." His voice was raspy in his throat, though she knew there was a challenge behind his crinkled eyes.

"I accept, most gracious sir." Her voice was teasing, though she, too, had trouble with her breathing, since she felt his cod rigid as rock against her left buttock. When had he shed his breeches, or had he been anticipating her visit? The villain!

He grinned up at her, moving his cod slightly against her skin, seeming to command its movement at will, his teeth flashing in the lantern light. "Sorry, heart, it seems a man's nature to lend a hand . . . or in this case, a—"

"Be serious," she said sharply, to hide her own amusement and not a little arousal. She began to undo the horn buttons on his doublet and then the ribbons on his Holland linen shirt, exposing his powerful shoulders and the tightly curled dark hair on his broad chest, the divided, sculpted muscle of breast, each centered with a dark nipple. She allowed her gaze to take in all of his flesh, her body burning

"Is this the end of scene one?" Jeremy asked, an eyebrow raised in amused question.

She saw herself return his smile in the lantern-lit surface of his dark eyes.

For answer, Kit bent to kiss first one of his nipples and

then the other, sucking and licking until they were both erect and the dark hairs surrounding them were plastered wet against his chest.

Jeremy, far beyond amusement now, reached for her breasts, but she stopped him. "No," she said, though it was more gasp than word, "that's for scene two."

Jeremy shifted her as if she were no weight at all and she felt his hard cock slip along her cleft, sending molten flames spinning through her and definitely shortening the time she had planned to spend at this sport.

"That's not in this part of the play," she said, though she scarce had breath to say it.

"It should be. This scene needs more action or the audience becomes restless." She noticed the muscle in his cheek pulsing rhythmically as he fought for control.

Kit put her blazing cheek against his and lay still for a moment to master her desire, which was urging her to hurry on to the final scene.

Jeremy turned his head and put his lips against Kit's. She parted her mouth, and he thrust his hot tongue inside, seeking to conquer at least this part of her. She was vibrating under his eager hands, which were following the curves of her body to where they were arching against him.

With a great groan that caused the nearest stallion to whinny and kick the side of his stall, Jeremy broke off and rolled Kit over, atop her now.

Kit was in a frenzy of need, but he held himself above her, drinking in the cloud of her golden hair mixing with the hay, gold on gold.

"Jemmy, please. Now! Don't wait."

He bent to tease her lips with his tongue. "Are you even now the master on your back, sweet Kit?"

But before anger could rise or time elapse to cool their passion, Jeremy gripped her unresisting legs and placed first one then the other around his back, and as she opened wide to him, he pushed his way into that throbbing warm glory, the one place that erased his memory of all the women who had gone before and melted all desire for any other woman to follow.

He moved slowly, and though she begged him to hurry, he would not. Ha! Who was master now? And then as his own need rose to a higher and higher degree, he realized that he was not master, either. They both had the same need for each other. Love was a balance. He knew that now and somehow he must teach this truth to Kit and make her accept it.

Since he was moving too slowly, teasingly, Kit, her longing about to explode, began to move faster, forcing him to drive deeper with each rise of her body, each clenching of her hands, opening and closing against his broad back, trying to grasp the elusive need that might take her a lifetime to capture and hold. She heard mewling sounds coming from deep inside her chest . . . or was it his?

When it came in a rush, the soaring frenzy of their passion and the final cascading of melting ecstasy, the harsh sound of their breathing and moaning sent the animals into frantic activity, and Jeremy collapsed, smothering Kit's mouth with his, though they were both repeating each other's name.

"Jemmy!"

"Heart!"

Then they quivered into quiet.

They lay exhausted for some time, his cod still encased in her deepest womanhood, neither wanting to write "Exuent" to the last scene. Finally, Jeremy gently slid away and rolled to her side, throwing his arm across her, his eyes searching her eyes. *"When I first saw you I fell in love,"* he said, calming his breathing to recite words deeply felt, *"and you smiled because you knew."*

She shivered with delight. "I don't remember smiling. I thought I hated you."

"Oh no, heart, you were smiling then, but it just now breaks through."

And it did.

Chapter Twenty-seven

A Jest Exposed

At dawn the next day, after Kit had hugged both Alain and Nell, Jeremy handed them into the king's coach.

Kit called up to Nell, "Tell Betterton that we follow to rehearse for *Feign'd Innocence* as soon as my father is stronger. Within a week, no more."

They waved as Alain and Nell, hanging merrily out the windows, drove down the long, overarching avenue of trees and out Rosevere's gate for their journey to London.

As they turned toward the manor house, Jeremy spoke without looking at Kit. "Your father has asked me to join him in his bedroom as he breaks his fast."

"Alone?"

He straightened his dark eyebrows. "Yes, I do suspect he has a father's duty to perform now that I am staying here with you."

She took his hand. "I will be with you."

"No, heart. He has the right to question me as he protects his daughter."

Kit was disturbed in her mind and just a little angry because the tone of his voice introduced a strange new seriousness between them. Jeremy Hughes, strolling player, the bawdy tittle-tattle of London's ladies in their private closets, now knew and considered a father's duty. This was a great change in so few months. Time to put a halt to this and at once! "No one will decide my way but me," she said, and stomped off, feeling a little ridiculous, and, she had no doubt, looking it.

Infuriating wench! She set him to burning one minute, then laughter, then fury and finally back to burning. And damn Rochester for his tricks! If he were free to marry Kit, he would find a way to free her from her fears of the right order of men and women, and himself from this circle of madness, free them both.

Jeremy knocked on Sir Robert's door and heard his voice ask him to enter.

Sir Robert sat at a table before his fire, looking stronger than he had just the day before, his freedom seeming to be an empowering elixir. He motioned for Jeremy to take a seat on the settle opposite. "You love my daughter," he began, spreading his hands toward the bread, soft cheese and hot buttered ale in invitation, "though you are married to another." As Jeremy started to speak, Sir Robert put a hand up to stop him. "I know the circumstances, but I must have an answer. Do you love my daughter?"

"Yes." It was a single word, and no matter what his tumbling thoughts had been just a moment gone, the word carried with it more than quiet acknowledgment because he put his whole heart into it. Even a concerned father could sense what was deeply felt.

Sir Robert leaned back in his chair, toying with his knife and the loaf of bread. "If you get her with child, she will be disgraced, and I will be forced to challenge you." He handed a thick slice of the wheaten bread to Jeremy.

"I would want neither such result, sir," Jeremy said, accepting the offering. "I will petition the king to allow his bishops to grant annulment. But, pray do not discount, sir, that your daughter is uncommonly firm in her desire to rule herself."

Sir Robert cleared his throat and resumed a tone of reasonable man to man. "Although Kit seems to have the mind of a male and I confess I did allow her to be educated with her brothers, she is yet a weak woman and subject to Eve's womb frenzy." He cleared his throat. "However, as is well known from Greek times, a woman cannot conceive unless she *enjoys* copulation. You have guarded against that, Hughes." It was a question wrapped around a statement.

"Absolutely, sir." Jeremy fought to keep his face serious. It was a commonly held belief that a lack of ultimate pleasure in women protected them from pregnancy, although some modern physicians disputed it and his personal experience belied it completely. Yet how could a man tell a father that his daughter was a most sensual woman and enjoyed the sweets of love better, even, than the most storied of her sex?

"Well, then . . ." Obviously relieved, his fatherly duty discharged, Sir Robert poured more ale for Jeremy, whose mouth was now quite dry, and they talked of the workweek ahead.

Leaving Sir Robert, Jeremy was in a thoughtful mood. He must not get Kit with child. He had now made a promise that involved his honor as well as hers.

The following days were busy ones, with harvests to store or take to market, animals to butcher and salt and monies to extract from a reluctant Sir William, who pleaded poverty more extreme by the day. At last Kit's father, growing stronger and more in charge every hour, was satisfied with Rosevere's progress and with his rapidly filling treasure chest.

Only one thing troubled Kit. Although she left her door off the latch each night, Jeremy had not come to her. Not once. When she reproached him, he said, "I cannot take you in your father's house when I have no right to your bed, nor you to mine. We cannot risk it without further protection." He hurried off to some work or other, leaving her perplexed and angry and wondering why the stables would not do as well again. Yet she held tight to her heart. Was he tired of her so soon? Men were so changeable and capricious, though they saw more of these faults in women than in themselves. Yet how would they recognize weaknesses, Kit wondered, if they did not have them in plenty? She determined to discover what he was up to and put a stop to it. And she would not wait long for a better answer.

A week after Nell and Alain's departure, bowing her head for her father's blessing, Kit said good-bye, promising to return when the roads were again passable in late spring. Jeremy loaded and primed two pistols and holstered them near at hand in the coach. "Highwaymen," he explained.

"But the high roads are safer now that Gentleman Johnny Gilbert is retired, indeed knighted and, I understand, a doting father. Those remaining pirates of the road are less courageous rogues, I hear, looking for lone riders or timid clergy."

"I'll take no more chances with you, heart, and in this my will rules," he said. His face and his voice, though stern, enveloped her in a sense of great comfort and safety.

They had scarce driven from Rosevere, with a final good-bye to Thomas at the gate and onto the London road, when Kit jammed her fan in the handle of the trapdoor in the ceiling to prevent the driver from raising it. Lifting her skirts, she fell onto Jeremy's lap, face near to his face. "And now, sir, on the high road it is my will that rules." Though the words were a reprimand, her face held a soft yearning.

"It's true, then, as your father did warn me," Jeremy said, pretending astonishment. "Each woman has the temptress Eve within her."

Kit coyly tapped a finger on his mouth and bent to put her lips against his new-shaven cheek. "I spent many hours at the apple harvest, if that's an aid to your imagination."

The carriage lurched and threw her hard against him, so close that there was scarce a finger's width between them. His hands slid down her thighs and, as they rode, caressed her curving hips. "Lady Katherne, you are wearing no drawers."

"You disapprove?"

"Heartily," he answered, though his face said otherwise.

She thought to tap him with her fan and then remembered it was performing another useful function. Instead she spoke huskily, her throat aching. "Sir, you have already agreed with my forsaking of the wooden corset, and now of drawers. Are there any clothes you would have me wear?" She flushed at her own bold manner, not yet wholly used to daring talk. "Do you think me shameless?" she whispered.

"Yes." The word was accompanied by a formidable curse from the driver, the crack of his whip and the creak of straining harness.

"Are you always this honest with women?"

"No."

"Then why with me?"

It was shadowed inside the coach that her father had lent them for their journey, metal grill windows shutting out the gray autumn sky, threatening rain, but Jeremy could see Kit well enough to know that the minx was leading him to folly. Reluctantly, he removed his hands from her naked hips and took her firmly by the arms, pushing her away, but only a little, since he was just in control of his promise to her father, not of his desire.

"Heart, listen to me. We cannot risk your getting with child. I would not have my love bring disgrace and hurt upon you. Your father did nudge my conscience most thoroughly."

She opened her mouth to dispute him, but he shook his head. "Listen well. Beeswax may not protect you forever. When we arrive in London, I will call upon our good Doctor Wyndham, who has—"

Kit reached to one side and opened the large brocaded pouch that contained a money bag, some prettily embroidered night shifts, thus far unused, a few books and a black lacquered box, which she handed to Jeremy, a look of triumph on her face.

"Is this more of Wyndham's salve?" he asked, but he pulled aside the tiny latch and lifted the top. "Where did you get these, hoyden?" he asked, a smile curving his lips. Despite an attempt to stop it, it spread wide.

"After the sheep butchering, I heard the men talking that they used the intestines for sheaths if their wives wanted no more babes, so I took some. . . . For large sausages, I said."

He laughed heartily, the laughter bouncing Kit up and down so that she had to hang on to his doublet even tighter. "Kit," he said after some trouble controlling his mirth, "this is just a rustic's belief. They may protect against the French pox, but not against the planting of seed. The French call it a shield against pleasure and a cobweb against pregnancy." Now it was Kit's turn to laugh, but he commanded her attention. "As I said, I will call upon our good Doctor Wyndham, who has, I've heard him say, the thinnest of kid-leather sheaths imported from Italy, that when used with his Infallible Miracle Salve are—"

"Two more days I must wait. God's nails!" The words were more shattered hope than oath.

He laughed again raucously, throwing his head back against the leather high seat of the coach, lifting her a little above him in his delight. "You are a ravenous minx! Do you think, my love, that since Eden, lads and lasses have not found safer ways to pleasure?"

"Put me down!" She could not bear to be even inches from him. "Do you know them, these safer ways?" she asked in a challenging voice that told him to make a more-than-careful answer.

"I have heard tales of them."

She grinned at him, her face full of mischief. "Sir, you may instruct me, for I would know all that you know about the art of pleasing."

"Ah, my queen, these are powerful ways of loving," he said, nipping her earlobe. "You might faint, and I have no feathers to burn under your nose for cure."

She tightened her hold of him, pressing against him, filling every inward curve of him. "Jemmy . . . Jemmy, love is my sickness and you are my only physician and teacher." She sighed, and her hot, sweet breath swept along his cheek.

Jeremy seemed to study the matter gravely. "Well, mistress, I have heard that you can use . . ." He held up a hand before her eyes.

She considered the matter. "I see that possibility clearly, but is that all?" she asked, biting her tongue like a student about to guess at an answer. "I have heard jests that mentioned, using . . . well . . ."

In his stage voice, Jeremy said softly, his voice husky: *"O! then, dear saint, let lips do what hands do."*

"Uh . . . ah," she stammered, " 'tis a thing only whispered, really almost unmentionable . . . a dreadful sin."

"Then give me more sin, heart."

"Jemmy, this is not what Shakespeare meant," she said, scarce breathing as he lay her gently on the opposite seat, kneeling to show her his full meaning. She gasped. "I didn't know. . . . I didn't know. . . . How wonderful . . ."

"I hear that often," he said, and she knew that he would never give over his teasing.

Thus in loving and delightful discomfort they jounced in the coach along the rutted roads toward London, arriving at dusk, exhausted, sleepy and hungry but happy withal. Flares lit on all four corners of their coach announced their arrival, though it wasn't their heat that warmed the coach.

They were met by Alain at Master Jolly's door. *"Bon soir, ma belle, mon ami,* I have waited the entire day for your coming. What delayed you?"

Kit blushed as he kissed her hand.

"Ah, I see," Alain said, and Kit reddened further, suspecting that he did only too well.

She clasped his hand. "You must tell us everything, Alain. How does it go at the Theater Royal?"

Alain bowed, his gloved hand on his heart. *"Bien,"* he said with his impish smile. *"Tres bien.* Everyone is dressed better, even Betterton. Ha!"

Kit linked one arm through his and the other through Jeremy's, and they climbed the stairs to the open door. "Alain, do you never leave off fashion?" she asked, laughing.

"Alas, my fashion sense is the larger part of me." He waved a handsomely perfumed lace-point handkercher under her nose. "I'll die a martyr to it."

Kit and Jeremy laughed at Alain, and Kit hugged his arm. "Then I must give you immediate absolution," she said, tapping his head with her now somewhat bent fan. "And I'll start with new gowns for me and suits for Jeremy and every other thing we need." She clapped her hands at a new thought. "And a handsome velvet suit for you, to repay your kindness."

Alain bowed, taking the challenge to his talents with obvious interest. "*Ma chere,* we will begin early on the morrow. A semptress, a glover, a hosier, a booter and I will oversee all, for I know the next mode. . . . Since I will establish it."

They were very merry when they jostled through the door into Master Jolly's great parlor. He greeted them with bowls of brandywine and would have the story of their adventures at once.

"Thanks be to God of blessed name that you are safe, Mistress Kit, or should I call you Lady Lindsay?"

Kit smiled. "I hope you will call me friend and pupil still, and one who pays her just debts." She counted out several gold guineas and placed them in his hand.

"Ah, you are a great heiress now," Jolly said, "thus you will want grander rooms elsewhere, although my third floor *is* vacant and at a very good rent, convenient to theater, dining and the palace." He looked from Kit to Jeremy, smiling, and added, "With bread and warm ale of a morning and a bowl of chocolate drink . . . a large bowl . . . on Lord's Day."

Kit thought it a perfect solution, but she looked to Jeremy and was relieved when he smiled in agreement.

"A minor heiress, perhaps," she said, rattling her purse, "but I hope you will help me to be a major actress."

Jolly bowed solemnly. It was obvious to all that Kit was never in jest about acting.

After some discussion, they agreed on six shillings a week, which Jeremy thought very fair since they would be earning twenty-eight shillings together in the weeks they played, he fifteen, she thirteen, though he thought not to explain that just yet.

After a cold supper of mutton pie, Jeremy carried a very sleepy Kit up the stairs to their rooms above the rehearsal hall, helping her remove her gown and don a clean night shift, her body glowing in the firelight. He wondered if she would be in want of a maid to dress and undress her now that she was Lady Lindsay, and hoped not, since he rather liked the work. He kissed her cheek and drew up the covers, arranged her golden hair on the pillow as he liked to see it, and sat for some time near the fire, staring hard into it as if some truth lay hidden between the coals and ashes. Somehow, this trouble that underlay everything between them must be better resolved. How? Divorce required an act of Parliament and was only granted after years of disputation, and then only to lords who must have heirs. Bigamy was a capital crime, though he had no doubt, it was practiced by the desperate. He might petition the king at a favorable time. He held his sorely aching head in his hands. *There had to be a way!*

Finally, Jeremy succumbed to his own fatigue and, stripping to his shirt, joined Kit, holding her warm, scented body close to his. She said his name, though her eyes were yet closed. He said her name and closed his own.

The next morning, promptly at ten of the clock, after a flurry of earlier appointments for fittings, Kit and Jeremy walked into the King's Theater on Bridges Street and reported to Thomas Betterton for rehearsal.

"Welcome!" he shouted from center stage, costumed in a long, dark robe trimmed in gold braid. "Come up, come up, and let me greet you. Alain arrived but minutes ago and can show you to your tiring rooms and introduce you to the dressers."

The curtain was open and some sweepers were clearing away the orange peels from the pit floor, setting green baize-covered benches upright, other maids cleaning the double row of boxes and the galleries above the pit, sprinkling rose-water in the royal box. Thick waxen candles were being mounted in their holders, the huge chandelier lowered on pulley ropes for that purpose.

Looking about the grand theater, Kit felt a wonderful sense of peace, as much at home as in Rosevere's great hall. "At last," Kit whispered, and Jeremy quickly took her hand and they smiled into each other's eyes.

"Aye, heart," he said, "where we belong and where I do believe we will make our life and fortune together."

They climbed the few steps to the forestage and Betterton advanced, kissing her hand and exchanging bows with Jeremy. "You have much to learn in two weeks, and your parts are in the tiring rooms. Tomorrow morning we will rehearse the first act on stage, so you must learn many lines in a short time. My pardon, but I am rehearsing for Hamlet, and the gatekeep opens the doors in two hours—" He stopped and called abruptly: "Alain! Frenchman! Come show the new members of our company—"

Before he finished, Alain was there, ushering them about backstage to the tiring rooms, the wardrobe, the closet of ease, the stairs to the upper walkway where a series of pulleys could produce clouds or angels or take actors to heaven if the play demanded. A trapdoor in the stage took them in the other direction.

Alain was bubbling with excitement in the wardrobe. "Already, *mes amis*, the King's company has surpassed the Duke's company in costume. The Duke's actors are in absolute tatters! They use old costumes higletty-pigletty with no sense of—"

Nellie interrupted, rushing to them on her tiny feet from a side entrance, looking, as usual, a delightful imp. "God's lugs! I am all happiness to see that the two of you are not yet buried among the rustics." With a satisfied little smile, she added, "The king signed a charter returning Rosevere to your father, and has yet to determine Pursevant's fate. His Majesty wishes to see you in his private closet later. I am to take you to him . . . since I know the way well."

"We are honored," Jeremy said, bowing.

"Come, I would speak with you," Nellie said, taking the much taller Kit by the hand and pulling her quickly to the women's tiring room.

When they were safe inside, Nellie handed Kit the script for *The English Monsieur*. "Would you please read out my lines for me? Alain has helped, but I'm not yet certain of act two, especially the second scene."

For a moment Kit hesitated, confused by the request, and then nodded. "Of course, Nellie."

Nellie sat across from her, her lips slightly aquiver, though she held her head high. "I cannot read or write."

"I didn't know."

Nellie flushed. "I hate a liar, worse than all things, but I was embarrassed to tell you before. You seem to know much, and you are a lady."

Kit laughed and then quickly sobered, lest Nell think the laughter directed at her. "Nellie, my dear friend, it is your courage and confidence I admire above all. I doubt any other woman could have risen so high."

Nellie frowned, though her chin came up even higher. "I am a whore."

"You have made the king happy."

"I am a very good whore," Nellie admitted with a wry smile, and then softly added, "and I love him most dearly and will be true to him until death."

Tears welled in Kit's eyes, though she would not allow them loose. "You have achieved much more than I have, Nellie. Jeremy wants to marry me, and I cannot even grant him the knowledge that I would if he were free. What you don't know is that I am ensnared in my pride, trapped in a web of my own weaving."

Nellie kissed her sweetly, and they worked on the trouble-some scene until it was time to watch Betterton as Hamlet, his most famous role.

The King's Theater was ablaze with candlelight, and excited milling crowds hallooing to arriving friends, and orange girls crying "Will you have any oranges?" over the dancers and musicians entertaining people who had come early to gain a good seat. Promptly at three of the clock the scenery of a castle parapet was pushed along grooves in the back of the stage, and the play began.

"Would you like to play Ophelia?" Jeremy whispered, taking a seat beside Kit in the box.

"Why not Hamlet?" she said seriously. "Someday, I will play everything."

Jeremy joined his hand to hers and they sat thus for near three hours, communicating by touch every emotion Shakespeare had given his Prince of Denmark. She was still caught in this trance when they arrived at the palace of Whitehall.

Nellie stopped the carriage at the stairs that led to a secret rear entrance to the king's closet. When one of the red-coated palace guards offered to usher them up the dark stairwell, Nellie declined, wearing her wicked girl smile.

The king was playing basset with the Lord of Rochester, and winning, judging from the coins piled near his hand. Nellie whispered, "I forgot to mention that he'd been recalled. The king does love him like a prodigal son."

"Ah, it's Master Hughes and my lady Lindsay returned from high adventures," the king said in greeting, his narrow mustache twitching with interest as Kit curtsied deeply and Jeremy bowed, sweeping his hat before him. "You are acquainted with my lord Rochester, I believe, now returned from . . . ahem, a country sojourn."

"Yes, Your Majesty," Kit and Jeremy said in near unison, offering Rochester a slight bow and curtsy, not as grand as his station demanded, a slight that brought higher color to his face.

He bowed in return, his handsome face looking thinner and browner from his exile. "Master Hughes, Mistress Kit, I am most delighted to see you again and in such great humor. I look forward to your appearance at the Theater Royal.

Feign'd Innocence, is it? Dam'me, but a fine title for the pair of you."

Jeremy's hand twitched toward his sword, but Kit held tight to him. Drawing a blade in the king's presence was a hanging offense.

The king tapped his beringed hand on the table. "Enough, my lord of Rochester. We do think you prod these young people too much." The king frowned. "We remember a great jest you were telling us and believe you have something of interest to relate to these king's players. We would have you speak it or risk our great displeasure."

Rochester bowed his agreement, having had all of country life with his religious mother that he wanted. "Good friend Jeremy, it was a jape only, and I ne'er thought you would believe it, knowing me as you do, and then I left for the country and—"

Jeremy stood a step toward the lord. "Believe what, my lord?"

"The Fleet marriage."

Chapter Twenty-eight

All to Some Purpose

For the second time in less than a fortnight Jeremy Hughes wanted to kill a man. He had spared Sir William because he wasn't worth hanging for, but Rochester just might be.

"Come, Jeremy," Rochester said, reading Jeremy's face and backing up a long step, "where is your humor, man? The *reverend* was a lawyer imprisoned for debt, acting the divine, and rather well, Your Majesty. If you could have seen Jeremy's face—" He broke off and motioned toward Jeremy, laughing until it trailed off for lack of appreciation.

This time Kit was advancing on him. "You have caused great harm, my lord, and lost a loyal friend in the doing. Have you so many to lose?" She curtsied as court etiquette demanded, but slowly, which served to underline the furious irony of her question.

Sobering far too rapidly, Rochester picked up his wine bowl and emptied it, his face handsomely regretful, although Kit could not discern whether from remorse or a jest spoiled.

"So be it." He bowed to the king. "Your Majesty, have I your leave to withdraw until a happier occasion presents?"

The king, laying a hand on the coins he'd won and without looking at the earl, said, "My lord of Rochester, you have our *command* to withdraw."

With another deep bow, Rochester backed out of the closet in some haste.

Jeremy was shaking with rage. The man whose ale-aching head he'd held through many a long morning after a night's debauch, the man who'd relied on Jeremy's sword at his back when yet another cuckolded husband and his family had set upon him, had repaid his loyalty with the most hurtful of japes, one that could have been easily revealed and yet one that he chose not to make known to prolong a secret pleasure. There was something deeply wrong, even evil, in such a man. His lordship was ever of two handsome faces: his libertine's merriment oft a hurt to others, and yet a poet of exquisite wit and sentiment, who would be in those good things most probably quoted down the ages. Jeremy shrugged, physically throwing off his old friend as too heavy a burden. Perhaps only the king could rule the earl, and that barely.

His Majesty stood, and Kit and Jeremy curtsied and bowed again. "And now to that rogue Pursevant," the king said, his mood troubled by Rochester and endless unpleasant duties. "We have it in mind to punish the dog!"

At the word "dog," several of the king's perfumed spaniels jumped from his silken bed, where they had been happily shredding a scarlet-and-gilt tassel, tumbling toward him for a sugar fop, which he obligingly gave each from a nearby tray, his mood changing at once as their leaping, twirling, yelping, ear-flopping antics made him laugh most heartily. "Quiet, children!" he said, though they didn't obey, and that seemed to amuse him all the more. They were the only subjects who never had to obey their king, unless it was Nellie. She came forward as the king sat once again, and with a rustle of satin, took the chair opposite him, her lovely little face radiant. "Charlie," she mouthed, in a pout even a king could not resist.

Kit curtsied deeply, knowing their time now was limited. "Your Majesty, may I speak for my father, Sir Robert Lindsay, who was hanged near to death after the battle at Winchester in your service."

The king waved his hand in agreement though his gaze was on Nellie, who was bent forward, her swelling breasts near to straying from her gown and out onto the basset table.

"My father asks that Sir William Pursevant be spared prison," Kit continued. "He is a ruined man, shunned by his former friends and admirers, his money box empty, his daughters without dowries. This is a terrible punishment for a proud and ambitious man, and one that will last his life through." Kit tried and failed to keep all the satisfaction out of her voice.

"Yet, my lady, we think you also have cause to see him greatly punished."

So Nellie told the king everything. "Yes, Your Majesty, but I would spare him for his children's sake, since he failed in both his rapine and kidnap. I have my father returned from the dead. . . ." Here Kit paused and looked at Jeremy, who moved closer to her side. "And all my days to spend in joy and work in your theater. I require nothing more."

The king, pensive, stared at her. "Most unusual. Are you a silent Quaker, perchance, my lady, one of that pernicious group that deals in forgiveness?"

Kit flushed. "No, Your Majesty, I claim no such goodness."

"What do you claim?"

It was a royal challenge, and Kit was surprised to have an answer to it. "I hope, Your Majesty, to claim an ability to live my future days without dwelling on past injustice. I would not so poison my heart, since I have better uses for it."

"Ah," His Majesty breathed, slightly amused and perhaps not a little startled, "you aspire to a philosopher's life. God in his mercy aid you, Hughes. Beauty and philosophy is an uncommon strange jumble in a woman."

Jeremy bowed, relaxing a little.

"And now, Master Hughes," the king said, "your lady has had quite enough of duels and high adventure." He lifted one side of his perfectly barbered mustache to indicate that he knew of the affair at Hampstead. "And you will be free to marry Lady Lindsay and tame her."

Jeremy bowed again, his face a perfection of composure. "Your Majesty, we have decided not to marry."

"God's fish!" The king seemed amused and shocked at once as he turned his gaze to Kit. "You are a most surprising and very mad couple."

Nellie was shuffling the cards for basset.

"But we remember now an important affair of state."

Nell shuffled again, although it was clear from His Majesty's face that basset was not in the cards.

Completely distracted, Charles II handed Kit the warrant with his state seal imprinted on red wax hanging by ribbons from the heavy rolled parchment, returning Rosemere to Sir Robert Lindsay and his heirs. Kit and Jeremy backed from the closet with due haste. Nellie's teasing laughter, then shrieks and the unmistakable sounds of chairs overturned in a merry monarchial romp followed them down the dimly lit stairs leading to the secret entrance.

They walked together out of Whitehall in polite silence, Jeremy holding up his arm gallantly for Kit's hand to rest on.

Kit spoke fiercely after one backward look. "I will never allow anyone to call Nellie whore in my hearing. She is a true love to him."

Jeremy didn't look at her. "The king will never marry her or Castlemaine or any of his mistresses, for he will not set aside the queen, though she has not given him an heir and his ministers would have it so. There is something strangely loyal in him withal."

Kit drew in a deep breath. "It is obvious, Jemmy, there need not be marriage for true and lasting love, but I was so . . . so pleased to hear you say it." She peeked round at his face to gauge his reaction. She had been anything but pleased; she had been completely taken with amazement. Why did he no longer want marriage? *Just like a man!* He wanted it when he could not have it. Now that he could, the idea had lost its glitter. Kit walked on a little faster, wondering why her mind was not more at ease now that all had been settled to her liking.

Jeremy could guess her thoughts from the tight grip of her hand. Her glorious dark blue eyes darted everywhere but to the cobbled path ahead, telling him the tale of her mind. He flicked a fallen ash from a nearby chimney off his tabby-cloth doublet, his own mind firm. He would not ask her to marry him. A man had his pride. But he would see to it that she asked *him* for marriage. Begged him on her knees, she would! A plan was half-formed and needed only opportunity to take full shape, and if needs be, he would make the opportunity ere too many days had passed.

"Why are you smiling, Jemmy?"

"It is a bright day, heart." He began to hum the tune "I Am a Lusty Lively Lad"

Kit stared at him. It was overcast and threatening rain. Did she really know him at all?

They walked on to Doctor Wyndham's and stopped in astonishment at the line of men outside his entry. The good doctor saw them, waving them forward and into his private quarters while his wife, now obviously delivered of her babe, served up wooden box after box of Wyndham's Infallible Miracle Salve to his patients.

Kit smiled down at the short man, who was wearing a new wig and satin suit, obviously prosperous. "Doctor, I thought you specialized in women's complaints and complexions. Now I see naught but men at your door."

The doctor bowed to Kit and to Jeremy. "Sit you down, mistress and sir, and I will tell you a true tale your ears will not believe." He called for his wife, Kate, to make the China tea drink and closed his door, telling the waiting men to return on the morrow morn at ten of the clock.

When they were sipping their tea and Kate was nursing her babe, a healthy boy named John (the proud father could hardly take his eyes from him), the doctor began in his deep, rumbling voice so at odds with his size, "You recall, mistress, that I told you of my friends Sir John Gilbert and Lady Anne."

Kit nodded. "Yes, and I, for one, travel with far less fear now that he is reformed of his former life."

The doctor frowned. "Mistress, many a crime was laid to him that he did not deserve. I found him to be a wise, courageous and honorable man, who served his king near to death, and his lady the same."

"My pardon, good doctor. Of all people, I should not believe common gossip."

The doctor bent a little forward as if in confidence. "Well, it was said that Sir John had been . . . your pardon for the indelicacy, er, unmanned by Lady Anne's most wicked husband, the late Earl of Waverby, who showed a . . . er, removed male tool of pleasure about London town, claiming it as Sir John's. Even the king believed him to be . . . er—"

Kit nodded that she understood, so that he would not have to search for another word to describe a cock for her delicate ears. She had to take strict control of her desire to laugh.

The doctor leaned back at ease, smiling at his wife and nursing babe. "John Gilbert had tricked the earl, but this was not known. Still, Sir John and Lady Anne produced a daughter this past spring, and now—"

"Josiah, thee speaks of God's miracle," Kate said softly.

Josiah coughed and beamed at her and then continued in scarce controlled good humor, "But, my sweet, Kate, all who know me to be their physician do think I can cause a manhood to grow in truth." His eyebrows rose nigh off his forehead at the thought. "Though I deny it and have spoken before the College of Physicians thusly, many the man in London who has . . . er, lost his pleasure plunger . . ."

"Josiah!" Kate said, blushing mightily.

"Ah, or . . . dear lady, I mean by that his nature, come to me demanding my Infallible Miracle Salve, and many do attest to its agency in the streets . . . *in the streets,* dear Mistress Kit, that they have the manhood of a man half their age, and their wives do confirm it in full voice."

He sat back, smiling in great delight to have told the story with such delicacy. "It is a great puzzlement to me that the more I deny that my salve has any such specific properties, although I admit it has most others, the greater the commons do clamor for it, and many gentlemen of high quality, as well. It is in my mind to prepare a paper on this phenomenon of human belief, which I have observed on many other occasions." He shook his head happily, tilting his new wig until it looked much like the old one.

Jeremy grinned. "It is a comfort for a man to believe that which makes him a man is always capable of being replaced."

"Just so, sir, just so!"

They finished their tea very merry, and were about to depart after Jeremy pulled the doctor aside and made his purchase of kid-leather sheaths, which the ladies pretended not to notice.

Kit stopped at the doctor's door. "Good Dr. Wyndham, I have a favor to ask of you."

"Anything in my power, dear lady."

"You know the Clink prison?"

The doctor nodded, stepping closer, as if for a confidence.

"I would deem it a great service if you would undertake to visit the women and children prisoners on occasion, and see if you could provide curative medicines. Many are ailing."

The doctor frowned in thought. "My experience, Mistress Kit, has been that there is little or no hope for the poor in prison. Noxious vapors and rotten food are most to blame for their ill health."

Kit pressed two guineas into his hand. "Would you do

what you can, Doctor? I will pay what is required for your good office."

He bowed and when he rose, his eyes were shining suspiciously. "You are not as you seem, mistress, but an actress with a great heart."

Jeremy took Kit's arm. "I will confirm that, Doctor, but I pray you, tell no one. A *dueling actress* will fill more benches in the pit."

The doctor kissed Kit's fingers, shook Jeremy's hand and stood on his stoop to watch as they walked away rapidly in a gathering storm to study their lines for rehearsal the next morning. Betterton was not known for being tolerant of unprepared actors.

The next few days were filled with morning rehearsals, afternoons spent watching Betterton's Hamlet alternating with Nellie's romp as Lady Wealthy in *The English Monsieur,* and evenings of suppers before the fire in their small withdrawing room, where they refined their lines and practiced their gestures. Alain and Master Jolly often came to read other parts so that at times their room became a stage and Jolly's students would gather at the open door to listen and applaud.

As the hour grew late, Jeremy firmly ushered them out and closed the door. Lifting Kit so that her satin shoes rested on his boots, he danced her backward, his lips on hers, into their bedroom.

He laid her upon their bed and sat down, loosing the ribbons from her gown. *"Give me but what this ribband bound."*

"Jemmy, if you quote Waller to me, you may *take all the*

rest the sun goes round," she said, finishing the couplet, her face alight with her love for him.

Kit pulled him down atop her, taking his mouth with hers, teasing his eager lips open with her tongue.

"My lady," he said, breathing as if he had won a footrace during a country fair, "hold tight to this idea of yours while I undress me."

"Quickly, Jemmy!"

He dropped his clothes beside the bed and stood a scarce moment in the flickering firelight, the muscles on his shoulders flowing into his arms so that all looked most right and beautiful in her sight. She was trembling when he came to her, her teeth chattering.

"Are you ill, heart?"

"Yea, but nothing you cannot medicine." Kit was a little frightened. The more they made love, the more she wanted him. Was she bewitched or truly a bad woman destined for hell's brothel?

He held her hard against him, and she tilted her hips upward, softly moaning as her need gathered in strength. "Now, Jemmy, please now. I've waited all the long day. You do not know how much—"

"I know, heart," he said, rising a little so that she could see his face. "But we must have a care." He grimaced. "I must go for a sheath."

She groaned and quivered, and he could feel the sweet moisture flowing when she opened and pushed against him.

"Kiss me, Jemmy," she begged, and in spite of all good intentions, he fell on her, planting rows of hot, hard kisses on her face, neck and breasts.

With a cry filled with delicious pain, she shuddered

violently, her body arching against him while he simply held to her.

When, after a lingering quiver, she was still, she turned her face away, tears in rivulets on her cheeks.

"It's all right, heart."

"Oh, Jemmy, I am so sorry. I did not know there could be such high pleasure without—"

"Without the cock crowing?" He rolled to her side but refused to ask her to content him. It must be her idea.

She reached for him and took his erect . . . er, tool of male pleasure into her hand, giggling a little like a naughty maid.

"Why so merry?" he asked, more question than complaint.

"I was just thinking of the little doctor and all his efforts not to say the common word for this." She slid her hand along his smoothly velvet shaft, lightly but firmly up and down, up and down, her forefinger caressing the little slit at the rounded tip. He swelled until he was so hard she feared he must burst, and her own passion began to rise again, when he did erupt.

They lay close to each other, touching their heated bodies together, gathering the last of their love tremors into the smallest personal space.

"Jemmy, I like most to have you filling me."

"I know, heart, but remember, we may not marry and I will not give you a bastard. I did promise your father and my honor would not survive it, let alone yours."

"But—" Kit paused, unsure of how to proceed, and as she thought of first this way and then another, all soon discarded, her mind whirled with doubts that self-mastery for a woman was worth such a price. Immediately she retreated from such thoughts only to approach again from another direction. Without conclusion, she thought to say something further, but before she could think of aught, she heard the deep breathing that told her he was sleeping. It was some time before she joined him in slumber.

The next day Jeremy and Kit finished rehearsals. Betterton pronounced himself well pleased with act III, and Alain demanded they come backstage for a final costume fitting.

Alain was happier than Kit had ever seen him. He was surrounded by great swaths of silk, satin and velvet, had access to the best French wigs and the most excellent Spanish cochineal so that his cheeks became rosier and rosier.

Kit donned the gown she would wear for *Feign'd Innocence*, staring wide-eyed in the candlelit, cloudy mirror above her dressing table.

Alain fussed about, adjusting a fold here or there. "*Ma belle*, I have made it true to your part. Very high at the throat and then it plunges to—"

She saw very well where it plunged to. "Alain, this is shameless!"

"But, Keet, it is the very essence of your role, all false modesty. The audience will gasp."

"Aye, but perhaps I should not!" She laughed as she clutched the two sides of her gown together. "Perhaps a little bone stiffening here"—she ran her hands down the sides of the open cleavage—"would make it less likely that I lose my . . . humility."

Reluctantly, Alain agreed, though he mumbled that the loss of such might mean a richer gate.

Jeremy raised a brow. "Kit, Alain is master of the wardrobe. You should listen to him."

Angered that Jeremy would disagree with her, she turned her back. "I listen to my own self in all things."

"Ah, for one moment only I did forget."

Without another word, he climbed up to the top floor to get his wine-colored satin suit from the semptress, who was just finishing attaching the most extravagant braided gold bows that Alain could imagine.

Kit, who had been berating her tongue, looked up as Jeremy waved the suit above his dark head and started down. How he tripped she would never know, but he came down hard, tumbling without a cry, until the railing broke and he fell from the last few steps to land with a heavy thump, sprawling crookedly at Kit's feet.

Kit heard herself screaming and fell to her knees by his side. Red welts were already rising on his face and a bump swelling on his forehead. "Jemmy," she sobbed, afraid to touch him because Alain was yelling at her not to move him for fear of a broken head.

She was yet kneeling by him, sobbing, holding his hand with both of hers when Dr. Wyndham rushed in. Was ever good fortune so well served? He had been in the theater treating Betterton with juice of licorice to cure a rheum and cough that London's foggy and moist air all too frequently gave the actor during cooler weather.

"Doctor, you must save him!"

Surprisingly strong for a man so small, he lifted Kit. "Mistress, please you to sit"—he pointed sternly to a shawl-draped settee against the wall—"while I examine my patient." The doctor bent to listen at Jeremy's chest, and opened one eyelid, staring in, then proceeded to feel Jeremy's limbs for broken bones, straightening each limb as he went.

"Doctor, will he speak? Will he live?"

"Most puzzling," Wyndham said, probing the bump on Jeremy's head.

Kit was almost certain she saw Jemmy wince. "There, Doctor, he moves. Does that mean—?"

"It is too soon to know whether there is rupture in the spleen, mistress, but I think it is safe to remove him from the floor." He motioned to Alain to help him lift Jeremy and place him upon the sofa that Kit had just vacated.

"I will bleed him to relieve any internal swelling. As I recall, Mistress Kit, you are not of the squeamish sort, so I will have you to hold the bowl."

Though she had never been the squeamish sort, Kit was now not so sure. It was one thing to watch a man be bled, as she had watched Jeremy Hughes at the Lion's Head in Milk Lane so many months gone, a man that she was merely intrigued by. It was quite another to watch the bright red lifeblood flow from the Jemmy she adored and had deeply wronged.

Aye, she had wronged him, and could not escape the knowledge that her stubborn will and refusal to allow him his rightful place in her heart had distracted him, maybe even *caused* his fall. If he were badly hurt, she would spend the rest of her life ministering to his needs. While dramatic scenes of sacrifice raced through her mind, Dr. Wyndham was clearing the room.

"Before I proceed, I must be alone with my patient. There are probes I must attempt too delicate for a lady's eyes."

Before Kit could protest that she had seen all places he was most likely to probe, she was ushered outside and leaning against the wall, her hands covering her face. Alain tried to comfort her, but he soon left off and began to pace, wringing his gloved hands, which caused him obvious pain.

Inside, Doctor Wyndham drew up a stool and sat down beside the sofa that held his patient. "You may open your eyes, Master Hughes."

Jeremy did so and smiled. "My thanks, good doctor, for not announcing my fraud at once."

"I have not agreed to be a party to fraud yet, but I am most curious why you would risk serious injuries to play a part *behind the stage*. What if I had not been attending Master Betterton?"

Jeremy smiled slyly. "Betterton mentioned you would be dosing him at this time, and I did not court an injury. I have taken many a worse tumble on the stage as a roving player in the provinces and thought to do so again, but I fear I am not as practiced as I once was." He gingerly touched the swelling on his forehead, making an appropriate grimace.

Dr. Wyndham squinted at him. "You are attempting to bring Mistress Kit to—"

"Her senses."

Wyndham laughed softly. "That is not done easily with such a woman."

Jeremy winced again. "As I continually learn, good doctor, to my regret. Say nothing, I beg you, and all will soon be made right. Now bind up my head, if it please you. It is pounding like all the carpenters in hell."

Wyndham looked skeptical but nodded. "Binding will reduce the swelling."

Five minutes later, the doctor opened the door to Kit. "You may enter now. He will . . . live. I have left hartshorn drops for fits or faintness, his or yours, a cure recommended highly during my extensive studies at"—he grinned—"well, almost everywhere."

Forgetting every good courtesy, even of simple thanks, Kit rushed past him to the sofa, knelt and took Jeremy's hand in hers, bathing it with tears. "Jemmy! Jemmy!" The door closed quietly behind her.

Jeremy struggled to sit and she helped him, but she stayed at his feet in all supplication, her face streaming with tears. "Come up beside me, heart."

Kit did as she was bid without a thought of it. "Marry me, Jemmy. I did not know how much I wanted to be yours until I thought you might be lost to me."

He smiled, more widely inside than out, but he did not feel the triumph that he had thought to experience. Perhaps he had rattled his head after all.

"And you will acknowledge me as your master. . . . Lord and master?"

Without hesitation, she caught at her breath in a little hiccup. "Yes, oh yes, my dearest Jemmy."

Jeremy straightened his shoulders. "Well, mistress, I will not have you."

"What!" The word exploded from Kit, her body going rigid, as she angrily brushed her tears away. "Say you this after I knelt at your feet like a peasant, surrendering all that ever you asked."

He bent toward her, looking extremely fine with a white bandage binding his dark hair. "Nay, mistress, I mean to say that I will not have you as you are not, without your saucy looks, your sureties of self, your delicious tempers and witty arrogance that first drew me to your side. Indeed, I would not have you a minute if you were simpering and sweet. God spare me such a woman now that I have known a better one."

Kit's shoulders crumpled in relief, although a small smile crept to her lips. "Is there no pleasing you, sir?"

"Aye, and you know how, as I remember," he said, pulling her closer, his hand wandering upon her breast, which was not difficult since her new gown had come completely undone.

Shortly, but not too shortly, he raised his head and spoke again most soberly. "Lady Lindsay, before we take our final marriage vows, we must be very certain that we have complete understanding as to our expectations of each other's good behavior as wife or husband. We can make a prior nuptial compact that if—"

"Unbroken in all regards in but one month—"

"Anyone may keep a bargain for a month, and I would have you very sure. But say for a year—" He was grinning at her.

"A year, then. A decade. Whatever you want."

He nodded solemnly, but he must know that she had no reservations. There was a bright light glinting deep in his dark eyes. "Hold, wench! I would bind us in a marriage with certain conditions—"

"What conditions?"

"I am not a lawyer that I have the right words already writ. We must spend some hours in thought and agree on what will give our two equal minds and hearts the most pleasure."

"Jemmy, I agree now."

"Wait, heart, until you hear all my proposal."

Chapter Twenty-nine

The Contract

Applause exploded on the opening night of *Feign'd Innocence* as Jeremy and Kit walked to the jutting apron. She had not allowed herself to look at the audience until that moment, afraid that who was there or who was not there would break her concentration and the comic rhythm that flowed between them, their hasty entrances and exits, her swoonings, his roarings and all the hiding behind skirts and doors to overhear the other's plans.

The curtain was drawn, and Kit's gaze swept from royal box to gallery to pit while the chandelier was lowered to light the audience. Many were standing and crying huzzahs. The ladies were shouting and waving handkerchers at Jeremy. . . . Did they never tire? But the men were calling Kit's name. She was surprised and somewhat embarrassed to realize that tears were gathering at the realization that she was now a true part of the theater world she had so hungered to join.

"Look," Jeremy said in her ear, "in the second row of the pit."

Kit saw Dr. Wyndham and his wife, Kate, and to one side of the bench George Jolly and all the nursery, even Elizabeth, who was now the mistress of Lord Tensington, and wearing a heart-shaped ruby in proof, which could be seen from the top gallery seat. Kit smiled a special greeting to each in turn. Then as custom demanded, both actors turned together toward the royal box and the king, who sat forward, waving his beringed hand and nodding. Behind him Nellie was calling "Bravo" and Alain "Brava," his latest suit vying with the king's for ornamentations.

Jeremy raised Kit's hand high as she curtsied low to the crowd already seating themselves again for the epilogue, and then spoke in his carrying resonant baritone: "My lords, ladies, sirs and madames, silence, if you will. We have some words to share with you beyond our lines in this happy play, which we hope you will praise to your friends to the benefit of our purse." He bowed at the laughter. "I announce to all gathered here that I am intent upon marrying this lady. . . ."

As Jeremy paused for effect, most of the crowd grew still, but some others derisive, one wag shouting, "You will sorry be, sir!"

Jeremy smiled and repeated in the rhyming couplet of an epilogue, "I am intent upon it, sir, though you may frown. I would not trade her for a crown." He bowed low again to the king.

Kit felt a hot blush rise to her face. She had not expected so public a discourse of their private talk.

"Yet," Jeremy continued, his voice carrying over all, especially the disappointed cries of some ladies, "before we are churched, this woman would have certain assurances that her deepest wishes will be respected by her husband, and I that my wife will do the same for me. This contract as to our marital desires and pleasures we present to you so publicly that neither of us may hereafter deny a one."

Kit curtsied to king and audience again, not so certain that this was the prior marriage agreement she had contemplated to ensure that she would not be subject to an all-powerful male master. *But so be it. She would not allow Jeremy Hughes to upstage her.* She faced toward him, taking her hand from his and placing it upon her hip in a saucy manner that was not at all unlike her normal stance. "Sir, my will is that henceforth all our secret business will be private and not shared with others in alehouses, private salons or theaters."

Jeremy bowed. "Agreed, and lady, my will is that you do not interrupt or correct my telling of a tale upon some minor point."

"In public?" she asked, a finger pressed against her cheek in contemplation.

"In all places, lady."

Sighing as if deciding at that moment upon it, she replied: "Agreed, sir, if there is not endless talk of trivial matters . . . minute descriptions of horse races, card and tennis games or a tale of triumph that has been told many times before in my hearing."

"To which end, my lady, my will is that you do not ignore my pleasure in the retelling or turn glassy eyes in the midst of it."

The audience was laughing, husband looking at wife and wife at husband with all knowing. An orange girl put down her basket and shouted: "And write it in stone that if he snore like a bear, he sleep outside the marriage bed!"

A man's voice shouted from a bench in back of the pit.

"And that her head does ache like the pounding of demons only during the day!"

Jeremy raised his hand for silence and looked with solemn gaze into Kit's face, the candles at the foot of the stage reflected in his dark eyes. "And my will is that when you shall be breeding you will stay abed as long as you like."

"And my wish is that you stay there with me." Her voice had grown softer, and the audience was leaning forward to hear her words. "And my further wish," she added, in a louder tone, her mouth clenched with unspent laughter, "is that you do not teach our children to pass wind noisily."

This was too much for someone, who did so to the general amusement of those not seated nearby.

"Agreed," Jeremy said, nodding vigorously, "if I may come and go as I wish and sit at your tea table for no longer than that part of an hour that amuses me."

"Aye, so long as I may go and come with any she-friend of my liking and have chocolate at my table upon a whim."

He grinned. "Your demands are so far reasonable and womanly. All is agreed so long as I need not be perfect to succeed in your eyes."

"Aye, sir, so long as I may err from time to time and yet be loved e'en with my faults."

"My word upon it, mistress, and with these reasonable provisos I will prove a loving and giving husband, willing to listen without scorn to gossip and change my way more than a little if I should disturb your peace of mind."

"And I, sir, if I have your compliance for a year hence, as is our bargain, will be your loving wife and e'en guard my willful tongue and ways. . . . As oft I can." She glanced at the audience, then winked at Nellie, though the king winked back to her embarrassment, thinking it meant for him. Sighing, she said in an aside to the pit as if in private thought, "I think I must have Jeremy Hughes above all men, or live and die a sad and lonely maid. . . . For no man equals him in my mind." A chorus of feminine sighs and tremulous sobs rose from the audience.

Jeremy had drawn her closer and closer, and as he spoke the pins fell from her hair, which descended like a sunlit cloud about her shoulders. "And with these good people and our sovereign king as witness, I seal our contract with this kiss."

Kit felt the applause and stomping feet shake the stage beneath her feet, but she saw or heard none of it. All her senses were channeled into the thrilling promise of Jeremy's kiss, which she returned with all her heart. Her head whirled with the knowledge that each had given way and yet they had come together at the same place.

Though all London talked of this pact to make marriage as pleasant and true for wives as for husbands, with many a bedroom door slamming and men complaining in their wine bowls at Lockets and Longs, and the walks of pleasure gardens filled with disputing couples, Kit and Jeremy were aware of none of it.

They lay near together, naked but not touching, each looking into the other's face as if it had not long ago been completely memorized. They were softly singing "She Loves and She Confesses, Too," and perhaps because only she could hear him and he could hear her, it was the sweetest, truest song they had ever sung, a gift instead of a performance.

Jeremy began to kiss her warm, lovely skin, to lap at its creamy softness, a shaft of moonlight joining the firelight to illumine each part of her body, showing him where his lips should touch, where they should tarry and where they should move next. Ah, perhaps to the inside of that lovely knee, where his lips had not gone before.

Kit twisted toward him as he slowly proceeded to nibble and kiss the most unlikely parts of her, from toes to nose, his hand splayed upon her privy part, buried deep in golden curls. She tried to reach him to bring his mouth to hers, but he dodged and stayed away, even his longish dark hair causing her hot miseries as it swept back and forth across her body, teasing and unmerciful.

She gasped his name. "Is it your intent to drive me insane!"

Jeremy stopped above her, his shoulders and arms quivering with his need for her. "Heart, we have this day as good as published the first banns. We must find, within the year, a parish church for the other two to be heard."

She moved her hips under him. She couldn't help herself though she knew it was wanton. "Don't you think it wicked, sir, to talk of Providence in this position?"

"Not at all," he said, his lips closing on her lips, his tongue slipping through to toast hers.

Breathing rapidly, she broke away. "You are a most complete rogue, Jemmy," she said, moving her hips against his hardness, which she knew would tempt him to provoke her all the more.

"Would you have me otherwise?"

"Nay, my will is that you never change."

"Heart, that is one condition I cannot agree to. My will is to be a better man for my future wife and all my sons." He grinned down at her.

"You would have no daughters!"

His eyes were burning into her, but he flashed his white smile. "Hold, wench! Think you I could deal with more like you?"

She pummeled him about the shoulders, and in sweet combat he grabbed her arms to save them both an injury as they rolled from the bed to the floor. He lay with his weight pressing her until, shaking with laughter mixed greatly with desire, she lay still.

"Make all haste, sir," she said, her eyes shining up at him, a freed hand stroking his thick hair now falling about his face and hers.

"Would you tell me my work, strumpet?"

"Aye, if I can assist you, since you do seem to dawdle in the part."

"Say you so," he answered with pretend anger. "And how would you play it, lady?"

"Faster, Jemmy. Much faster."

"Heart, I am all obedience in this regard." If not all others.

In late August of the following year, 1667, the seventh of King Charles the Second's restoration, a carriage bearing the king's crest drew up to the old parish church of St. Martin-in-the-Fields, Nellie and Alain being the first to alight. Jeremy came next and held up his arms for Kit, whose fine sky blue velvet gown was bulging suspiciously in front and freshly watermarked in the rear for all who took notice of such things. It seemed this babe was in a hurry to be born.

"Quickly now," Jeremy said unnecessarily, as nervous as any bridegroom and father-to-be.

Kit grit her teeth as she stepped cautiously down. "If you want quickness in me, sir, you should not have been so quick yourself these nine months past."

Alain and Nellie rolled their eyes at each other and made soothing gestures to both their friends, who were in such a fret as to be difficult.

"Just a few steps, *ma chère* Keet, and soon all will be done."

"In right order, I hope, first marriage, then a babe," Kit said, attempting a smile, and clinging now to Jeremy, who looked as if he had not slept this fortnight past.

Although Jeremy said nothing, he was free to think that the right order of things would not have been in question if Kit had not held stubbornly to their contract until the last possible minute. He blamed himself. He had at first insisted on a year to test their contract, but it was half in jest to teach her a lesson and show his will. The jest had come back to bite him.

Although the weather did not warrant one, Nellie wrapped her cloak about Kit to hide the stained gown. "Are the contractions closer?"

"The same, Nellie, but I know not how long that will be, for they are sharp." A sudden quick intake of her breath told all what "sharp" meant.

Nellie, who had surprised everyone with a parish church she regularly attended and where Jeremy and Kit's banns had been announced, murmured reassuringly, "I have asked the curate for as short a service as can be holy and legitimate."

The church, built in King Harry's time, was dark and cool after the humid summer heat of the city, and the aisle to the side alter where the priest waited was not long. Kit grit her teeth, and leaned heavily on Jeremy as another pain rolled through her.

"My brave heart," he said, and felt his own stomach

churn with fear for her. "Just a few more minutes and we'll have you back in our rooms, where the midwife waits and Dr. Wyndham will give you some poppy syrup."

Nellie rushed ahead to the curate, and Kit heard the clink of guineas. "This lady is not well, sir, so speed the service, if you please."

Adjusting his robes and opening his Book of Common Prayer, he positioned Jeremy on his right and Kit on his left and began to intone the Solemnization of Matrimony.

"Dearly beloved, we are gathered together here in the sight of God and in the face of this congregation. . . ." He paused, since there was no congregation, and moved on quickly to give the three reasons that the honorable estate of marriage was instituted. "First, it was ordained for the procreation of children. Secondly, as a remedy to avoid fornication, and thirdly, for mutual society, help and comfort, that the one ought to have of the other—"

Jeremy, holding tight to Kit, hardly heard the curate's words or saw the consternation in his face as he spoke them hurriedly.

Kit thought the pressure just short of more than she could bear and had a great urge to lie down upon the cool stones. She would have done so had she not had the strength of Jeremy's arm about her. She could sense rather than feel Alain longing to redrape her gown.

"Who giveth this woman to be married to this man?"

Alain stepped forward and placed Kit's hand in Jeremy's.

"I, Jeremy, take thee, Katherne, to my wedded wife, to have and to hold and with my body I thee worship . . . and thereto plight thee my troth." The bride's rapid breathing allowed him to skip several phrases.

Kit, in a small and halting voice, repeated her vows and

received the gold circlet on her fourth finger, after which she sagged into Jeremy's arms.

"We will omit kneeling," the priest concluded sensibly and then said with a certain speed, "Those whom God hath joined together let no man put asunder. I pronounce that Jeremy and Katherne be man and wife together."

Jeremy scooped Kit up as the priest blessed them: "I require and charge ye both, as ye will answer at the dreadful day of judgment—" He carried her quickly toward the hot August light of the open sanctuary door and the carriage.

Kit looked up at him with pain in her eyes but a one-sided smile on her lips. "Though you have rightly fulfilled our compact, my husband, it was for somewhat less than a year."

He bent his head to kiss her cheek. "Now it is for life, heart, so let us not quibble." As Jeremy lifted Kit into the carriage, she bit into her lower lip and cried out, a long, quavering, shrill cry that descended into a groan that tore at his heart.

"The babe comes," Kit said, trying no longer to control a force that, once started, could not be stopped.

Nellie stepped forward. "I came prepared for this," she said, pointing to a bundle and large flask. "Put her in the carriage. Jeremy and you, too, Alain, hold the horses."

Jeremy frowned. "But the midwife—"

"There's no time. I will help her. I acted midwife first when I was but seven years in my mother's broth—er, establishment. Now, go and hold the horses fast, lest they move."

"I must be with her."

"You are a strange man, indeed, Jeremy Hughes, to want to mix in women's work, but as you must see, there is no room."

Jeremy reluctantly nodded and walked to the horse's heads with Alain, but within minutes at the sound of Kit crying his name, he ran back and opened the carriage door. He bent inside, took her hand and put his cheek next to hers, singing softly in her ear because he could think of nothing else to help her. He did not know if she heard the words, but he was certain she felt his touch. She gripped him with astonishing strength. Opening her eyes, she attempted a small jest. "A strange place for a lying-in," she said, but could not finish the smile before another pain tore at her.

Jeremy had closed his eyes, unable to bear her hurt when the babe came, catching at its first breath, and crying out in a full voice. Nellie laid it upon Kit's breast and grinned at Jeremy. "A fine boy," she said.

"Jesu bless us," Jeremy said. "It's over, heart," he added, bending to Kit, who was trying to see the babe's face and grope for his little hand.

Nellie laughed. "Nay, not over. You be twice a father this day." And a few minutes later, after a last exhausting push by Kit, Nellie laid another babe upon Kit's breast, who yelled lustily and waved her arms like a windmill. "A girl babe just as big as the boy, and from the sound of her, just as ready to win your heart."

Kit, pale with exhaustion, looked up at Jeremy, smiling into his dark eyes. "You do nothing by halves, sir, though I'll thank you to try harder in the future." She slept then, but when Nellie tried to take the babes, Kit's arms tightened about them. Only Jeremy was able to remove them.

No one, not Jeremy, not even the dire warnings of Dr. Wyndham, could keep Kit abed for the required month. She was up and rehearsing by mid-September when the new season started at the Theater Royal. Refusing to send either of her babes to a country wet nurse, little Charles, named for his godfather the king, and little Nellie, named for London's newly famous midwife, slept and supped entr'acte under Alain's watchful eye in the wardrobe room.

At the end of September a new play, *The Mad Couple*, opened on a pastoral scene, Kit entering stage left dressed as a great lady, and Jeremy shambling in stage right, dressed in a cottagers' clothes, carrying a shepherd's crook. Aside to the audience, Jeremy said, "I am no shepherd, but I'll deceive her to see if I should take or leave her."

Kit glared at him haughtily but said aside, most slyly, "This country wit acts the false part, but I would rule his playful heart."

"And so you do," the shepherd whispered, so only the lady could hear.

But all in the audience knew.

A Few Notes from the Author on the Characters in This Book Who Really Lived, Though All Dialogue and Situations Are Fictional

Historical novelists generally follow two paths. One group believes every fact must be accurate. The second group will bend a fact or a date if it works for the story or characters. I probably fall somewhere in between these two groups. I will bend a historical fact, but only for a good purpose. For example, although John Wilmot, Lord Rochester, did open a doctor's practice under the name Doctor Alexander Bendo and specialize in treating infertile women (with some *success,* as I wrote), he did so a few years later than the setting of this book. My apologies to all historical purists, but this was just too delicious a fact to omit when defining an age and a character for a reader.

Lord Rochester is one of the most intriguing personalities of the reign (1660–1685) of King Charles II, generally called the Restoration Period. A renowned and sensuous poet and playwright, he was also a determined and busy libertine, who died in his early thirties from drink and disease, his handsome body a wrecked shell. It was said he converted to Christianity on his deathbed, his mother finally having her way. His final confession of sin circulated for decades as a warning to the ungodly. None of his friends believed it.

George Jolly, a retired actor, really did have a "nursery" for beginning actors in London, although I was unable to discover exactly where it was located. I placed it near the theaters of the day, as that seemed a likely place.

Nell Gwyn was a popular early actress who rose up from the gutter to lie down in the king's bed. Although she acted in Restoration plays for only a few years, hers is the name most remembered. Other actresses, more famous in their time and longer-lasting on the stage, have been forgotten by all but theater historians. Nell was noted for her wit, her charity and her common touch. Once, when abroad in the king's carriage, she was booed by Londoners who thought her one of the king's foreign Catholic mistresses, and began to pelt the carriage with refuse. Nell stuck her head out the window and yelled, "Leave off! I am the Protestant whore!" I hope, one day, to write again about the fascinating Nell.

To me King Charles II is a more intriguing monarch than Henry VIII. Just as highly sexed as Henry (whose prowess was honored by becoming a popular oath—*by the great Harry!*), Charles didn't behead his cast-off mistresses, but made them rich duchesses, refusing to divorce his childless queen. He is remembered as the Merry Monarch, and he probably did love his little golden dogs best of all those in his lascivious court.

Both Jeremy Hughes and Katherne Lindsay are characters wholly from my imagination, although I hope they are true to the theater people of their day. If they didn't really live in history, they lived for me . . . and now I hope they live for you.

If you would like to read more about this fascinating period of English history, I recommend: Samuel Pepys's *Diary,* Graham Green's *Lord Rochester's Monkey,* Antonia Fraser's *Royal Charles,* Liza Picard's *Restoration London,* and *The Cambridge Companion to English Restoration Theatre.*

Read on for a sneak peek at
the next Restoration-set historical romance from
Jeane Westin

Coming in August 2007

In the following pages, orphaned Meriel St. Thomas, servant to Sir Edward Cheatham, has recently arrived in London with Sir Edward's family and been mistaken by the king's spymaster for Lady Felice, the Countess of Warborough, with whom Meriel shares an uncanny physical resemblance. That Lady Felice is married to the man Meriel secretly honors above all others sets the stage for adventure and romance. . . .

That night Sir Edward found his wife somewhat improved and praising a court physician to the heavens. Sir Edward was so pleased that he allowed Meriel to take young Edward and Elizabeth to walk about the palace.

"Remember to give way and to bow and curtsy if the king or other high lord should pass," he instructed his children, and then they were off.

The halls, with all sconces alit, were filled with people: lords, ladies, mere gentlemen and common servants, hurrying in one direction toward the sound of music.

Meriel stopped a boy wearing the king's red livery. "Where is the revel?"

"In His Majesty's presence chamber, girl, but such as you cannot attend."

Meriel shrugged. Someday . . .

The lad smiled, giving her cheek a pinch just before hurrying away. "Go up the stairs at the end of this hall to the gallery opposite the musicians, and you can watch the quality until the majordomo sees you and gives you his boot."

"Yes, please, please, Meriel," cried young Elizabeth. Edward tried to hide his eagerness under a lordly pose, which he could not quite, as yet, maintain.

"If you promise to be quiet and obedient." But Meriel was off and leading them down the hall and up the stairs to the gallery, the sounds of strings, hautboy, and bassoon, and many feet tapping a pattern upon marble floors coming closer and closer.

Meriel crept along the wooden gallery, bent near double, the children holding to her gown, and came to a wide place that afforded a view while hiding them well. She looked down through the carved railing onto a mass of lords and ladies, moving in the stately pattern of a French sarabande, the colors and rich cloth of their gowns and doublets, many inlaid with jewels, glowing in the light of a dozen glittering candelabra. Immense gilded mirrors at each end of the presence chamber magnified the color and light until Meriel had to squeeze her eyes tight after focusing on the splendor below.

She put a finger to her lips to shush the children, and realized that it had been herself who had said, "Ahh!" Best she keep her finger where it was, since she could not trust her mouth.

Meriel's gaze was drawn to the throne dais, where the king sat laughing with a chestnut-haired young woman standing before him, whose lithe body seemed to be dancing, though she did not move a step. Meriel realized at once that this must be Nell Gwyn, the king's favorite actress, notorious for her high wit and japes about London, the delicious gossip carrying her fame as far as Canterbury. It was said that the king was besotted with her entertainment, while not neglecting the queen or his other mistresses, and—some nights, it was rumored—seeking further sport with the Duke of Buckingham and Earl Rochester at Madam Ross's establishment. No wonder commoners called the king "Old Rowley," after his amorous stallion. Meriel flushed hot at her thoughts and the images they evoked, which were ones that no decent maid should entertain, although she suspected many did because they came unbidden and refused to leave.

Her attention was next drawn to a couple dancing near to the throne, the lady, wearing a dazzling gown of lilac velvet trimmed with large pearls, just turning into Meriel's view.

She sat suddenly and hard down upon the wooden gallery floor in as much amazement as she had ever felt. Was she looking in a mirror? It was her face she saw, her black hair, her olive complexion, and though she could not see the eyes, she knew somehow that they matched her own gray color.

Meriel removed her pressing finger from her lips, for she no longer feared that she would make a revealing sound. She was incapable of words, but her mind was swiftly dealing with the amazing resemblance. This must truly be the Countess of Warborough. Felice, the spymaster had called her. Meriel had no more wonder at his mistake. It was perfectly natural, and no doubt would happen many times, until Sir Edward was forced to send her away. Back to Cheatham House or into the London streets. On her oath, she knew that a countess and a common maid could not share the same face in the same place.

Meriel gathered herself to leave. She must speak with Sir Edward at once before some high personage came to him with complaint. Quickly, she looked one last time through the gallery railings to assure herself that she had not suffered some sudden malady of the eyes. Seen what was not there. The countess and her partner—judging from the gold braid on his doublet, the glittering medals, the blue ribboned star of the garter order, he must be the Earl of Warborough. Meriel was looking upon the form of Lord Giles Matthew Harringdon, her beloved hero.

She could not see his face in shadow, since they had danced away from the nearest chandelier, but she did not need to see, since she knew it from tracing her fingers across his marble features countless times. But now his form caused a quick intake of breath that made her dizzy enough to grasp at the railing. Though she knew she should take the children and leave rather than be discovered and draw all eyes, she could not move from staring at her hero made flesh.

He was a man of more powerful manly stature than she had ever seen, taller even than the king, but with greater shoulders and a more elegant turn of leg, although few would probably say as much aloud. And who had not heard of Lord Giles's courage during the Battle of the Four Days against the Dutch? He had been splattered by the blood of his slain younger brother and yet had stayed on the deck of the burning ship, spars and sails raining down upon him, fighting against a dozen Dutch sabers, astride the boy's body. Every Englishwoman had sighed with pride to think of such a courageous lord, who was said to be the handsomest man in all the court, a court swarming with handsome men.

Meriel's cheeks blazed as a sweet and fiery elixir coursed through her, heating her blood with a need she had scarce acknowledged before. Still, she recognized what that need meant. It was what kitchen maids whispered about and then hid behind nervous laughter as one of the footmen passed by. Even the kitchen spit boy came in for his share of glances and sighs from the younger maids.

Against her will, which she realized at that moment was not as strong as she had thought, Meriel looked again. His lordship held himself rigid and apart from his wife, as if her body's touch would turn him to ice. Could it be that Lord Giles disliked Lady Felice? His own wife! Meriel fought a wild desire to smile, admitting the crazed feeling. What did it matter to her? That it did—there was no denying—frightened her because it made no sense. And she had a sensible mind. Or so she had always prided herself.

Grasping the children, she crept along the gallery to the stairs where they had entered, casting glances behind as if Beelzebub himself were flying after her with all his imps of hell. She must get to Sir Edward before she was exposed to Lady Felice or her husband. And how would his lordship react to another face he so obviously disliked? Or worse, she could be taken to the king. Though this was a modern age and she did not have to worry that she would be burned for a witch, still she would have better treatment from her master than offended quality. *How dare a low-born maid have such high, mocking features?*

Another thought propelled her to the door leading to the stairs. Was she bewitched? How else could she account for such close likeness as Lady Felice to her? Although she had rejected witchcraft as lacking reproducible proofs, as had many scholars of this modern age, there seemed to be no other explanation but wizardry for such a thing.

Shushing Elizabeth and young Edward, who did not want to leave the king's ball, though their eyelids were drooping, she hurried them down the stairs.

William Chiffinch, the king's spymaster, stood at the bottom.

He bowed to her, very low and mocking, his hand upon his heart, as if she were truly the aristocratic Lady Felice, throwing his shadow high up on the marble walls until it seemed to hang, with dark menace, over her.

"Sir," she acknowledged with a hasty curtsy, but did not breathe again until she turned the corner and was out of his sight.

All your favorite romance writers are
coming together.

SEE WHAT'S NEW FROM SIGNET ECLIPSE!

Lady Anne's Dangerous Man

by Jeane Westin

0-451-21736-5

Lady Anne was eager to marry until her fiance conspired to have her virtue stolen. Now she must trust a notorious rake with her life—and her heart.

The Music of the Night

by Lydia Joyce

0-451-21706-3

Sarah Connolly leaves a past of desperation in London to help an old friend in Venice. There, she discovers a world of dark secrets—and a mysterious stranger lurking in the shadows.

penguin.com